LOW SEASON in ST TROPEZ

By Kiki Astor

Printed in Great Britain
by Amazon

61628535R00178

Low Season in Saint Tropez by Kiki Astor

TABLE OF CONTENTS

Table of Contents

Chapter 1

Constance shivered and wrapped her teal silk peacock-print dressing gown around herself tightly. The marine layer had rolled in overnight, and the morning was chilly. Still, not too bad for November. She could see the sun starting to peek through the clouds, its rays zinging between the masts of the ships around her. Constance had been happy enough to spend these past couple months on Carlos White's yacht in Marina del Rey. The neighborhood was a great place to visit, with easy access to everything Los Angeles had to offer. Exploring the city with Carlos had been a real treat. After all, billionaires had a different way of doing things. They had snagged the best tables at the trendiest West Hollywood restaurants and had done a spot of shopping on Abbot Kinney; not too much-she hadn't wanted to take advantage. There had been parties in the Bird Streets, brunch at Little Beach House in Malibu, and weekend jaunts to Santa Barbara and Catalina Island. It was all so easy. But it certainly made it even harder than usual to focus on work.

Constance selected a porcelain coffee cup, one in the Bernardaud pattern that happened to bear her name, from the open teak shelves above the coffee station, and made herself a triple espresso. Nature's Adderall. Constance's eyes ran around the main saloon, taking in the exquisite surfaces she had chosen: teak, leather, enamel, and linen, in soothing shades of cream, sand, and blue. This space embodied tasteful nautical decor at its best. It was pretty close to perfect. That last guest cabin, however...

Constance forced herself to banish the intrusive thought, at least for now. She was in a good mood this morning. A great mood, in fact. But she had to admit; she was getting antsy.

Feeling generous, or guilty, she made a second cup of espresso, this one with some frothed milk on top, and took it down into the stateroom.

Carlos was just waking up. Her billionaire client was significantly older than Constance, but still youthful, with short-cropped blonde hair and an athletic build. He sat up in bed and took the coffee, a grateful expression on his tanned face, and patted the empty spot next to him, gesturing for Constance to come back to bed. She hesitated. She had work to do. But a little pleasant distraction couldn't hurt.

Suddenly, her iPhone, which was charging on the lacquered built-in nightstand, rang shrilly, ruining the peacefulness of this almost relaxing morning on the yacht. Constance swore under her breath and hurried to pick it up, if only to silence the annoying device. But she knew she'd left it on Do Not Disturb, which meant that the caller could only be one person. Hazel eyes narrowed, Constance glared at the screen, glanced apologetically at Carlos, and started to hustle out of the room. Carlos shrugged and gestured for her to stay, obviously still hoping for a morning romp.

Constance sighed, moved to the end to the bed, and answered at last, feeling herself make a funny face that was at the intersection of a smile and a wince.

"Why are you still there?"

The nasal voice belonging to Harold, her boss at the design company, blasted through her speaker. Harold was not just her boss. He was her uncle. Her godfather. Her de facto guardian since she was a teen.

"You're supposed to be back," Harold chided. "And I'm fielding complaints. Mrs. White looked over the orders and claims that the mattresses that were installed are not the ones she requested."

Constance rolled her eyes.

"I can assure you that these are more than adequate," she said.

In fact, Constance had been sleeping on one of those mattresses for the past few weeks and had tested it quite thoroughly. Constance wasn't a homewrecker. Mrs. White was Mrs. White in name only. As Carlos had explained, his ex-wife had negotiated the right to use the yacht for a quarter of the year, and she was milking it. It was a pain, but still better than the alternative, which was selling the boat that Carlos loved. And then, there was Carlos' adult daughter, Sophie, a spoiled troublemaker, who was always angling to get involved.

"Constance, if I find out that you are doing anything I wouldn't do…" Harold warned.

"Uncle Harold, how am I supposed to know what you would or wouldn't do? Especially back in your Studio 54 days…" she teased.

But she knew damn well that Harold would not approve of her actions. She looked guiltily over at Carlos. He was pretending not to listen to the conversation.

"I've heard rumors," said Harold, "that you're up to your old tricks."

"I don't know what you're talking about," said Constance.

"How close are you to completion? I need you back here in Miami. You know I can't handle Thanksgiving alone. Oh, and you work for me, remember? I need you for a few new projects."

"I'm almost done," said Constance. "I'll book a ticket home for Tuesday…well…maybe Wednesday."

Now, Carlos gave her a pointed look. She ignored it. Wednesday was less than a week away. She was going to have to pull that cabin decor out of a magic hat, but now that her brain had latched onto the tantalizing prospect of new projects, she would do whatever it took to wrap it all up, and her mental gears were already spinning at top speed.

"I'm looking forward to coming home," she said.

And it was true. The dalliance with Carlos was growing old. And Art Basel Miami was coming up very soon. Which meant lots of great parties. Miami in the winter was the place to be. All glamour and chic people and fabulous weather. But something about what Harold had just said was bothering her.

"Wait. What do you mean, 'a few' projects? I thought you were assigning me to…"

She didn't even have time to complete the sentence. Harold knew exactly what she meant.

"No, Constance, I'm giving that to Penelope."

Constance scowled. Harold was giving the most high-profile project of the year to Penelope. Penelope was her nemesis, her main competitor. She had apparently supplanted Constance as the golden child of their design bureau. It felt like Harold had been handing Penelope far too many of the big jobs of late. Which was ridiculous, because sure, Penelope might be skinny and stylish, hyper organized, with a degree from Parsons, while Constance was a little scattered, to be sure, and had skipped out of Princeton a semester shy of getting her Master of Architecture to go bum around Europe, but Constance was confident that she had a much better design eye. It was innate.

"Penelope? Why?" Constance asked, her tone indignant.

"You know damn well why," said Harold. "Goldfarb is a very important project. I need someone who will be dependable and who can be counted on not to consort inappropriately with the client."

"Consort? I can't believe you would insinuate that," said Constance.

"And I can't believe I have to say it to you. If you weren't my niece, I would have fired you long ago. This needs to end. It's going to hurt your career."

"Sorry," Constance muttered, the wind gone out of her sails. Harold had spoken the sad truth. Her attention to detail was not what it should be. The only reason she was successful at all was because of her taste, and because she was able to charm billionaires into signing off on her designs even when they were not quite finished, or not quite right. Yes, she was generally good at what she did, had great ideas, but sometimes she grew distracted, and her muse had the decidedly inconvenient habit of leaving her high and dry just when she needed her most. Constance had to admit that she did tend to run away from her problems and, well, some would refer to her as flighty, and flaky.

She hated that word, flaky. It sounded brittle. Fragile. She wasn't fragile. She just knew when to cut and run. That was the advantage of working in the yacht world. Projects rarely took more than a few months, and then, she could literally sail off into the sunset or, more accurately, jump ship. She could drop anchor whenever she pleased, wherever she pleased. Well, within reason. She loved the entire imagery of yachting. She'd grown up around boats; her parents had had a classic 1960's Italian DeFever yacht that she still regretted them selling. After all, it was the only real home she'd ever had. But it had been necessary, to keep taking care of her mother during her devastating illness.

In any case, Constance had been destined for this sort of career. She did have wonderful ideas, she reminded herself, and it wasn't her fault if sometimes, when the Muse decided quit on the early side, she utilized a harmless way to compensate. Mostly harmless. She had principles. She didn't mess with married men, for example. In fact, once, she had been discovered in a rather compromising position in a stateroom with a very handsome tech billionaire who had apparently been engaged, a fact he had conveniently not shared with her, and she had been livid, and had refused to finish the job. Which had been rather convenient. But in general, Harold was being hard on her. Most of her liaisons were mere flirtation. They never went anywhere. Operating this way protected Constance's delicate heart. Harold may have thought her a female Casanova, but she was only this way because the one time she'd attempted a serious relationship, with Lorenzo, an Italian photographer, it had almost destroyed her.

"Well, don't worry, I'm almost done here," said Constance, all business now. Now that the unwelcome thought of Lorenzo had entered her brain, she instinctively stepped away from the bed, evading Carlos' hand as it sought to reach her.

Her mind raced. She had overheard a designer she recognized from Instagram at the marina gym talking about some stateroom furnishings a client had rejected and that she was trying to unload. As long as they fit, Constance could have them installed by the handyman she had chatted with at the bar at Scopa a few weeks earlier and charm some designer friends in town into selling her a few bolts of extra fabric and lending her a seamstress. She'd seen a lamp at West Marine that she could buy in multiples and fashion into a ceiling light. She would buy a few decorative knickknacks in that overpriced antique mall in Venice that was near that coffee shop she liked. And she would buy Harold a little souvenir in the cafe's gift shop to improve his mood.

"From your sudden and uncharacteristic silence, I'm guessing you're preparing another one of your magic tricks. Good. Just get yourself back home," said Harold.

Home. That word snagged on the whirring gears of Constance's brain. She didn't have a home. But Harold was still talking, and she forced herself to pay attention. "… Thanksgiving. And then we're going to need to have a team meeting on Monday."

"Sounds good," said Constance, hoping she'd kept the panic out her voice.

Chapter 2

Constance noticed Carlos getting up and wrapping himself in his flannel bathrobe, the one Constance had bought him at the beginning of the project, after he'd mentioned that it was unfair that she had her own elegant dressing gown, while he hung out in sweats. She had chosen a vintage tartan, green and navy, that suited his light coloring. But she was starting to chafe at the feel of faux domesticity that this his-and-hers sleepwear conferred on their relationship. To be honest, she had been getting a bit sick of him, and sick of the project. She had been hitting her head against some creative stumbling blocks. Her damn muse had left her, again, and she was going to need to chase her. She knew she owed it to Carlos to finish what she started, but it was almost impossible for her. Her brain was already far too busy strategizing about future projects and opportunities. Maybe taking a break for Thanksgiving would be exactly what she needed, even though the idea of returning to Marina del Rey after seeing Harold in Miami felt nothing short of impossible.

"Was that your uncle?" Asked Carlos.

"Yes. He needs me back in Miami."

"I thought we were having Thanksgiving together," said Carlos. "I was going to fly us to Aspen. The snow is already building up."

"No, you know how it is. My uncle and I have always had Thanksgiving together. I've never missed a single one."

"But you're not done here," Carlos protested.

"I'll come right back," Constance lied. "I know it may look like a lot, but in reality, there are only a few little things to be done."

"You'd better," Carlos grumbled. "You need to supervise the install; last time they messed it up because you weren't there."

"I was there!"

"Well, then, you weren't paying attention."

Constance tried to switch her demeanor back into flirtation mode, but it was growing impossible to do.

"Don't worry, baby. It'll get done." Her throat constricted, making it hard to get the words out.

"Why do I get the feeling you're not coming back?" Said Carlos.

"I don't know," said Constance. "Maybe you're the one who doesn't really want me to come back. I feel like maybe you're getting tired of me."

Men like Carlos liked to be the instigator of an idea, to be the alpha who decided things, so maybe this little reverse psychology would prompt him to send her off. She held her breath. Would it work? Carlos could be unpredictable, but he was still a man.

"Well, yeah, this project has been going on for a while, Constance. I do need to move on with my life- I wasn't planning on staying in Marina del Rey this whole time. I have things to do in Saint Barts."

"I know, I'm so sorry I've been keeping you here," said Constance, trying her hardest to look contrite.

"It's OK. As long as you supervise from afar..."

"Exactly," said Constance, relieved. "OK. Well, let me get cracking on this," she said.

Now that her mind had focused and latched onto returning to Miami, she found it hard to wait a single minute more. Also, now that she had put the seed of the idea of her leaving into Carlos' mind, she could almost see his thoughts turning to the possibility of finding another willing bed partner in Saint Barts. Damn, that did hurt her pride a little. But it was better than the alternative, which was having to ghost him against his will and garnering a bad review of her work.

"You haven't told Harold that I've been staying here with you, have you?" asked Constance.

She felt guilty that Harold was shelling out a hundred dollar per night charge at a local hotel, but it wasn't exactly breaking the bank. He'd gotten a special rate, and the hotel was pretty depressing compared to the yacht.

"Of course not," said Carlos.

And that was the end of the conversation. He ambled over to the bathroom to take his shower, and Constance's mind turned to booking her plane tickets back home. Once that was done, she created a checklist of what still needed to be done for cabin #2, which was more than she had let on, but she couldn't stop fantasizing about which new projects Harold would send her way. She hadn't really missed it, but it would be good to be back in Miami, she decided. Art Basel was around the corner. Her friend Chiara had been tempting her with all of the cocktails and fun times they would have together once she was back. The prospect of finally decorating her apartment was a pleasant one, too, wasn't it?

Ugh. It was harder to lie to herself than it was to lie to a client. She dreaded the idea of her sterile apartment. The cocktails were just a means to power through her boring life, and she'd gone to Art Basel so many times that they all ran together.

And then there was the other problem. Penelope. Harold's new favorite golden child of the decorating firm. How had that happened? Oh, yeah. It had happened because Constance had dropped the ball a few too many times. You would think that Harold would have a little bit more family loyalty, but clearly, Penelope had managed to worm her way in. One of Penelope's projects had made it into Miami Living, and Constance was beside herself with jealousy. She needed to have one of her projects published, and fast.

Chapter 3

The moment the plane touched down at Miami Airport, Constance breathed a sigh of relief. Not that she was so thrilled that she was back in Florida. But she was away from Carlos's demands, questions, and ever-increasing neediness. She'd finished that project to the best of her ability, under the circumstances. Mrs. White was still bitching about the mattresses, but her ex-husband had signed off on them, so there. The cabin was unfortunately missing a few details, OK, all the details, but it wasn't her fault that everyone had gotten out of town early for Thanksgiving, and she could handle all of that later, virtually, couldn't she?

Constance should have been looking forward to getting back into her own space, a two-bedroom apartment in an older building in South Beach. She liked the quirky aesthetic of this part of town, and decided she missed, without really having experienced it, the time when it used to be far more authentically Cuban. The authentic Art Deco buildings were now few and far between, but her apartment complex was a throwback to a more glamorous time. It was a small grouping of twelve apartments, low slung one- and two-bedroom casitas in an old Florida-meets-Mediterranean style, grouped around two courtyards, one with a small plunge pool surrounded by green metal chaise lounges, the other one containing a seating area that no one ever used, arranged around a fountain that hadn't worked since just after she'd bought the place. Maybe they turned it on for realtor tours. When she'd first visited it, Constance's apartment had been significantly darker than she would have liked, but she had known it would still be a good purchase. And after she had bought it, the landlord had finally trimmed up the giant Bird of Paradise outside her windows and all of a sudden, it was a whole new place. People would gasp at what a great deal she had gotten, even though the apartment itself was singularly unfurnished, surprising for an interior designer with Constance's sophisticated aesthetic. Was she worried about people judging her for making an interior design misstep? No, it really was her own fear of commitment. She decided this year would be the year that she would finally get it done. Unless she decided to do something crazy, like just sell the place and move to Europe. She'd been having these thoughts more and more, and it was ridiculous. She didn't have a life in Europe. She didn't have anyone in Europe, but then again, she didn't really have anyone here either, except for Harold, and Chiara, and both of them were rarely available. She needed to figure out what she was going to do with the next chapter of her life. She wasn't getting younger. She needed to settle down. But every time she got 'home' after an absence and saw the place with fresh eyes, she felt depressed. She always described the style of the apartment as minimalistic. But the place wasn't minimalist. It was downright impersonal. Undecorated. As much as she had once fantasized about making the place her own, she was never in one spot long enough to actually implement any of her numerous ideas. And committing to a single one? Terrifying. Last year, she'd thought Caribbean chic may gain a toehold at last, but she had changed her mind and had put the driftwood coffee table and the woven straw baskets she'd once thought so perfect up for sale. Ditto the Kenyan beaded chair from another bout of design inspiration. The oversized mother-of-pearl framed mirror from her brief beachside glam period had made a quick exit, as had the lot of Indian block print pillows she had purchased on a whim, not to mention the large black and white photographs she quickly tired of, the regrettable midcentury sputnik chandelier that felt played out before she'd even had a chance to install it, and the overpriced custom bouclé sofa she'd waited for patiently, only to decide a week after it had arrived that she was kind of sick of it. The sofa was too heavy to move, at least, so it remained. The owner of the consignment store down the street had more than once joked that Constance should open her own shop. Maybe Harold and others had a point. Maybe Constance was flighty. Maybe she was flaky. But that was not the way she liked to see herself. Was it so bad to hold out for the perfect design idea, the one that would make her apartment into a place she could finally call home? Because as much as she told herself she would enjoy being in Miami, after a couple of months, she would start getting itchy again, desperate to see what was happening on other shores.

As she waited for her luggage to come off the conveyor belt, Constance text messaged her one college friend Chiara, who was always good for a laugh, a drink, and the crucial gossip Constance needed to catch up on after having been away for any amount of time.

Back! Meet me at the Faena tonight?

Chiara wrote back almost instantly

Yay! 7:00 PM?

Fantastic. That meant that Constance had a few hours to settle in. Stock her refrigerator. Deal with paperwork. Get bored. These everyday pedestrian tasks were far from enjoyable for her. In fact, she'd been dreading them ever since she'd known she was coming back, but she had found out long ago that procrastinating would not help.

Chapter 4

At 7:15 PM, Constance found herself at the Saxony bar at the Faena, perched on a barstool near a taxidermy albino peacock, scanning the room, looking for Chiara.

Long, lean, and golden of limb and hair, Chiara, who had been a nerdy art major in school, was now a well-known art blogger and art influencer, a perfectly modern muse whose appearance and style were diametrically opposed to Constance's old-fashioned look, which skewed more Botticelli than Instagram model. Though she had learned to appreciate her thick red hair, ever since puberty, Constance had despised her body, which was all overly ample curves and milky skin. All of her paramours called her figure classic and seemed to revel in her lushness, but she had a hard time believing that she was any match for a skinny supermodel type like Chiara, or like the supermodel that Lorenzo had unceremoniously dumped her for.

No matter what she did, no matter how much she starved herself, Constance's figure remained resolutely curvy, so of late, she'd decided to try to just start enjoying her life and stop worrying about it. Which didn't mean she was happy. It just meant she had decided that to do otherwise would be boring. And besides, pleasures of the flesh were that much more intense when there was more flesh to please, weren't they? Some of the men she had met in the past had put that in less elegant terms involving cushions and pushing, but she'd had to agree with them. Her style of dress also went well with more feminine forms, and now, it was mostly only when she tried on something trendy that she started to judge herself again.

"Hey," said Chiara, tapping her on the shoulder. Constance jumped. She'd been distracted again, she realized. She hopped off the barstool and enveloped her friend in a huge hug.

"Hey, silly, I was over there, waving at you." Chiara gestured across the bar. "You seem distracted…I mean even more than usual. But you also look beautiful," said Chiara, leading her to the opposite side of the bar. "Your hair has gotten so long; I can't believe you were away for a whole 3 months."

Constance frowned briefly. Three months. That was nothing. "Yeah, it's good to be back," she semi-lied. "Are you looking forward to us prowling Art Basel? It's going to be a blast."

"About that," said Chiara. "I'm going to need to be out of town."

"But I thought you're an art influencer. Aren't you supposed to be there? Isn't this the epicenter, at least for that week?"

"It is," said Chiara, "But I have work stuff."

"What's that supposed to mean?"

"My biggest clients are sending me to their storage unit in Switzerland. They're wanting to reevaluate their collection and I need to be there to do inventory. And photograph things."

"Well, that sounds anti-fun," said Constance, dejected.

"No joke," said Chiara. "Here. I ordered you your fave."

"My fave?" Constance looked at the russet-colored cocktail Chiara help up blankly.

"A Negroni, silly."

"Oh," said Constance, "I actually have a new favorite ... "Her voice instantly faded out. She was being rude. "But don't worry-I'll drink the Negroni."

"Did your mother know how you would be when she named you?" Chiara smiled. "If the bartender hasn't made my drink yet, I'll drink yours."

Chiara held up her hand for the bartender, a lanky, tattooed man with floppy chestnut hair and striking almond-shaped eyes, whom Constance knew to be a secret entrepreneur who had sold his startup at twenty-five and had been bartending and making art ever since.

"Did you make my drink yet?" Chiara asked.

The bartender shook his head. Constance saw him discreetly dump a finished drink into the sink.

"Oh good," said Chiara blithely. "My friend will have..." she looked towards Constance.

"Old-fashioned. With Whistle Pig 10 Year."

Constance smiled at the bartender. He gave her a not-discreet-enough flirtatious wink. They'd had a brief fling a little while back, but it had not gone anywhere. There had been no hard feelings, and he treated her to a free glass here and there whenever she was in town, in hopes that they might reignite things. Not that Constance had any intention of that happening.

"So, what's next? In terms of work, I mean?" Asked Chiara.

"Harold is calling a full team meeting on Monday morning. He'll be assigning new projects."

Constance didn't mention that she had the distinct feeling that Harold was going to throw her scraps and not give her the big project she'd been counting on. Not a good sign for her career. She'd once assumed that if she worked for her uncle, she would end up taking over the company one day, but so far, it seemed like he was in no mood to give up the reins. She didn't want him to retire, anyway. He loved the design firm he had built. In any case, the way things looked now, when he finally did cede control, he might give it to that bitch Penelope.

As if reading her mind, Chiara asked, "How's your nemesis?"

"Apparently working double time ingratiating herself to Harold," said Constance bitterly.

The image of Penelope, with her Chanel jackets, her sheets of dark, straight, perfect, glossy hair, and, most infuriatingly, her bird-like frame, filled her mind. Just like Chiara, Penelope could not be more different than Constance. It was like they'd been genetically engineered to be absolute opposites, both physically, and in their work styles. Penelope might not have been the most creative, but Constance supposed she needed to hand it to her. The girl was thorough, she was professional, and well, you could count on her not to flirt with clients. If that was the sort of thing you were looking for. How boring.

"When do you leave?" Constance asked Chiara.

"Early next week."

"What? But there's a new restaurant I wanna check out."

"We'll go when I'm back."

"When's that?"

"Not sure yet," said Chiara. "Oh, stop making that face. I'm sure you'll find someone willing to accompany you to Art Basel and any other parties. You always do."

"I suppose," said Constance, taking a sip of her drink.

She was sick of being single, she realized. Chiara was happily engaged to an elegant Norwegian businessman. They had met him at the same time, at an art gallery a few years before, and Constance had flirted with him first, but he'd been immune to her charms. But of course he was, because Chiara had shown up then, and she was absolutely stunning and brilliant, and skinny. Who wouldn't want that, if they had the choice?

The bartender came by and deposited a second drink in front of Constance, with a wolfish smile that did not go unnoticed by Chiara, who had finished her cocktail, too.

"Someone still has the hots for you. And I might as well be invisible."

Constance shrugged.

"Anyway, what else are you planning on doing while you're here? Other than breaking hearts all over town, are you planning on finally getting your apartment done?"

Constance shrugged again.

"Oh, come on. How hard can it be? This isn't marriage. Just do it up enough so you can enjoy it when you're here, silly. And if that doesn't motivate you, so you can Air BnB it next time you're out of town."

"Yeah, maybe I'll do that. I'll go to the design center, and I'll decide," said Constance.

"Perfect. I can't wait to see it when I'm back. So what else are you up to?"

"I'm not sure," Constance admitted.

Now that she thought of it, without Art Basel, without outings with her friend to look forward to, and without knowing which projects she was going to be assigned to, the expanse of the rest of her winter in Miami lay in front of her without very much dimension or detail. It was a bit disturbing, in fact. And now she realized: how often did she have plans that went far into the future? The truth was, she truly lived in the day-to-day. And in the past, sadly. Much as all of those productivity coaches and yogis said to live in the moment, she wasn't sure that this was what they meant. You had to have some idea of the future, didn't you? Did Constance even know what she wanted for herself in the future? Many of her friends had married in the past few years. She'd gone to her share of weddings, cursing the brides who chose bridesmaids' dresses that clashed with her red hair. She'd had to plan a million bachelorette parties and wedding showers and wedding brunches. She had politely evaded catching the bouquet on multiple occasions. She had selected a handful of dates, when she was allowed a plus one, some of which had been a good memory, though a fleeting one, some of which had barely left a mark on her psyche. She was one of just a handful of old maids she knew. Not that she kept in touch with that many of the girls who had gone to college or even boarding school with her, but she knew from Facebook and Instagram that most had found an advantageous match and were now starting to pop out adorable babies clad in matching seersucker outfits.

Was that even what Constance wanted for herself? She wasn't sure, but once in a while, she would look at a child and think that might be nice to have a family, and then half the time she would look and think, I think I may be allergic. Did other people really know what they wanted, though? Surely, she wasn't the only one? Or was she singularly rudderless? There she went with the nautical references again. That was what happened when you lived in the yacht world, she supposed. She was similarly unmoored where family was concerned, having lost her mother at a cruelly young age. Her father was now happily ensconced with his second, much younger, wife, living in Hawaii, in a pristine home where Constance certainly did not feel welcome.

Lorenzo had been the one exception in her love life, the one person that she thought she could have seen herself with. But what a terrible choice that had been.

How could she even plan or settle on anything, when she knew that she made the wrong decisions when it counted, and that maybe her ideas weren't that smart after all? Good thing that she could still rely on flirtation and on her unique personal skills, but what about when her looks faded? She couldn't very well depend on that for the rest of her life, could she? Even now, if it wasn't for Harold, she would probably be screwed. Jobless, alone and miserable.

Stop it, Constance, she thought. She was turning into a sad drunk.

"How many of these have I had?" she asked Chiara, pointing to her glass.

"Enough that I'm cutting you off. Come on, let's go eat something."

Chiara dragged her out of the Faena, and they hopped into an Uber, heading to the Arts District, where they sat down at a small Cuban place that wasn't particularly authentic, and was a front for the speakeasy-style nightclub in the back, which one entered through the walk-in freezer. No one actually ate at the restaurant. Except for Chiara and Constance, and it made them giggle every time.

"I just want to see you happy," Chiara said. "You know, sometimes I feel like you're always looking for the next best thing because you're not confident that what you really want is good enough."

"I don't know what I want," said Constance.

"I think you do, but you're afraid to admit it."

"I don't. But I'll figure something out. Don't worry."

But Chiara did look worried.

"Have you ever thought that maybe you can't fix me?" asked Constance.

"Maybe. But maybe I'll keep trying," said Chiara. "That's my tragic trait, isn't it?"

Chapter 5

Constance was in Harold's kitchen on Thanksgiving Day, dicing some onions to create the stuffing for the Cornish hens. Harold was far too sophisticated for Turkey. They had experimented, in the past, with pheasant (too gamey), quail (too dry), goose (not super appealing), and grouse (glorified pheasant and nearly impossible to source). A couple years ago, they had thought they had settled on duck, but a couple of Harold's social X-ray friends had complained that duck was far too heavy. As if those socialites ate anything at all, but in any case, they had eventually settled on Cornish hens.

Uncle and niece had discussed at length how to set the table, settling on an incongruous mix of brown Spode and Portuguese Bordallo Pinheiro cabbage leaf, which did come off as appropriately autumnal, without clashing too much with the view outside of Harold's window, which was of the wide expanse of Atlantic Ocean and bright blue sky.

Harold's Thanksgiving parties were legendary. They attracted the old guard of Miami and Palm Beach and Key Biscayne, who would all jockey for position at his twenty-person table.

"Like Caroline Astor's ballroom, but far more exclusive," Harold liked to say, which always made Constance smile. Harold would choose his outfit months in advance. A smoking jacket, some cheeky Stubbs and Wooten slippers, and an Ascot. Harold could out- Howell Thurston Howell himself. There was a fixed cast of characters, the inner circle, and then, ten people brought in for novelty and entertainment. Still, the feel was usually the same. It felt comforting. When she'd been a child, Constance remembered Christmases around the Japanese fisherman's fireplace on the DeFever yacht. It was always just their nuclear family; no space for anyone else. She realized, now, that her father had isolated them. These cocktail party Thanksgivings, so festive and full of dazzling chitchat, were definitely her preference. The best part of Thanksgiving was that it signaled the beginning of the holiday season. There was nothing better than the sweet, intimate Christmases she spent with her uncle, always in a different, magical setting. Well, there was one thing better, but she couldn't think about that right now. But then, of course, the thought came barging back in: the one Christmas she'd spent with Lorenzo and his mother, at their country house in Italy. There had been a cocktail party on Christmas Eve with all of the local landowners, followed by midnight mass. And then they'd enjoyed a sumptuous dinner of oysters, champagne, and truffled foie gras. The next morning, they'd gotten rid of their hangovers with a bracing walk through the woods. Later, they'd opened gifts under a spindly European Christmas tree, decorated with antique mercury glass and Murano ornaments collected by Lorenzo's mother.

But since the breakup, which coincided with the untimely death of Harold's partner Stefan, Constance had been happy enough to spend every Christmas with her uncle. After all, they were all each other had. Even though Constance's father was alive and well, they were not on speaking terms. At first, Constance had blamed her stepmother, but little by little, she had taken to blaming her father more. He was the one who had let this woman decide whether he would see his own flesh and blood. And Constance considered this a more egregious failing than simply being the bitchy stepmother. Her stepmother was, after all fulfilling her role, in a stereotypical way. But still, Constance wondered what her father was doing now, what he would be doing for Christmas. She wondered where she and Harold would go for Christmas this year. The two of them were orphans, free to explore the world. They usually didn't go too far afield, Bermuda, once. Harbor island. One memorable year, they had gone to Paris. They hadn't discussed it yet, but she thought she might suggest Austria this year. As she aged, Constance was feeling more and more at home in Europe. Not that she would ever admit that to Harold, who counted on her to be closer to him. He was not getting any younger. She could see that a time was coming when he would be much more dependent on her. Hence the purchase of the apartment in Miami. Soul crushing as she might find it, it was a necessary evil. She really did love her uncle Harold, more than anything.

Harold emerged from his bedroom at last and walked into the galley kitchen. The apartment, though in a newer building, had been laid out like something more traditional. The kitchen was less grandiose, designed for staff. And the entertainment rooms were large, with ornate details and classical proportions.

"How do I look?" Asked Harold.

He twirled around. He was wearing a forest green smoking jacket this year, to complement the table setting, of course. His Stubbs and Wooton shoes by Scalamandré featured jumping zebras on a green background. A brown checked shirt and an Ascot in purple, green, and mustard completed the look.

"Uncle Harold, you've outdone yourself," said Constance. "I don't know if I have anything in my closet that will give me even a chance of holding a candle to you.

"Obviously, you're wearing that green velvet dress with the embroidered butterflies that I bought you in Paris," said Harold. "That was the one I was thinking," Constance smiled.

The dress set off her eyes, making them look greener than hazel, and highlighted her curves, while skimming over any problem spots. She hoped it still fit. She'd been eating up a storm with Carlos. She shook her head to try to banish the negative thoughts. She'd tried to appreciate her curves, just as all of the men she'd been with had obviously appreciated them, worshipped them even. But then, when Lorenzo had left her, for a skinny supermodel, her confidence had come crashing down. Well, that wasn't completely true. Her confidence had been taking a hit even before that. She didn't know whether it was social media, or paying too much attention to magazines, or hanging out with the skinny fashionista types in the design center, but little by little, her confidence had eroded, and the negative self-talk had grown louder. She would, more often than she cared to admit, find herself wishing that she were just twenty pounds lighter. Well, maybe 30. She wished she looked cuter in skinny jeans. Dreamed of being the kind of girl who could throw on an oversized sweater and look gamine. It was a challenge, in this time in history, to look stylish with her figure. Chiara always told her that she was being ridiculous, that she was classic and gorgeous, and looked like a goddess. But in Constance's mind, Goddess was a synonym for fat. After all, look at the Venus of Willendorf.

"How are you on timing?" Asked Harold, interrupting her negative thought spiral. Constance checked the checklist she always created when she was cooking.

"Good. I just need to get these birds stuffed, and most of my sides are under control, so I think that I'll be able to go home and change in maybe half an hour or so, and I'll be back in time to help you light the candles and start up the cocktails. What do you think?"

"Fantastic," said Harold. "If I get too drunk to say goodbye to you, or if you sneak out, remember, we have our brunch at noon tomorrow."

He coughed and turned away, dabbing at his lips with a handkerchief he pulled out from his pocket.

"And don't worry, I'm giving you permission ahead of time to not clean up after the meal. I know how it pains you," he said. "Thanks, Uncle Harold, but someday, I'm going to need to learn to clean up my messes," said Constance, though it was true; doing the dishes was torture for her. She didn't know why, but she had an absolute mental block against it, even though she knew she should help Harold more. She really owed him everything. After growing up sailing all over, followed by her parent's divorce, her mother's death, and years spent in boarding school, he had tried to give her some of the stability she'd so been lacking. He'd started giving her traditions, things to look forward to. The least she could do was a few dishes. Besides, this year, Harold had not extended an invitation to random socialites- it was just going to be the core group, and considering how tired he seemed, and how frazzled she was, Constance had to admit she was relieved.

She finished stuffing the last of the Cornish game hens and covered the tray with a sheet of aluminum foil.

"OK, I'm going to go beautify myself," she said. "I should have just brought my dress to your apartment. But I was so scattered this morning."

"You? Scattered?" asked Harold.

He was one of the rare ones who really understood how her brain worked. But even so, he would sometimes tease her. She needed to let him know how much it bothered her, not that she didn't deserve it. She could be difficult to live with, to work with.

"Why don't you set your alarm, once you're home, so you don't get distracted," Harold suggested.

Once she got home, she dutifully set the alarm. This annoyed her a little, but Harold had been correct. If she didn't do that, she couldn't be sure of leaving on time, instead starting to focus on something completely peripheral, and losing track of time. She couldn't afford to let Harold down, not with his friends. Not at this party, which was his most important party of the year, for him, especially since he had lost Stefan. She prided herself on making sure she was always at her most charming. This was, after all, where she shone- not so much with the follow through, but with first impressions. She was a champion conversationalist. Great at inspiring people and throwing out ideas.

She decided on just a quick rinse, and then emerged from the bathroom, pulling her green velvet dress from the closet. She went into a drawer in her dresser and pulled out her trusty pair of Spanx. Hopefully, they would give her the confidence to flaunt the dress. Not that it was tight by any stretch of the imagination, at least not last time she'd put it on. Unfortunately, Carlos had loved taking her to all the restaurants. She berated herself for not having more self-control. She pulled on the dress and let out a sigh of relief. It still fit. She gave herself an appraising look in the mirror, selected a pair of high heeled rust-colored shoes and set about carefully doing her makeup. Carlos had been complimentary about her looks, but he was older, and she therefore didn't value his opinion that much. She had an old-fashioned aesthetic, as Chiara mentioned regularly. Was that a veiled insult or an actual compliment? She didn't know- she'd have to lean into the positive side of it. But having Harold's friends ooh and aah over her and rave about how pretty she was would certainly at least help her to feel a little bit better about herself, and about her life choices up until this point. She was debating on which lipstick to put on when the timer went off. Damn it. She couldn't spend any more time. This time thing had to be a hard and fast rule, or she would start ignoring it. She swiped on a hastily chosen lipstick, grabbed a handbag from the closet, and turned off the timer. Time to go impress some old people.

She locked up and trotted over to the street, where she had scored some primo parking for once. There was a young couple admiring her Mini Cooper as she walked up to it. Her car, more than her apartment, was her pride and joy. It was the first thing she had bought herself after working for Harold for a few months. The Mini Cooper, in a custom shade of Kelly green, had been someone else's custom order, which they had decided that they didn't like, after all. Constance loved it. She had liked the price, too. She had added cheeky needlepoint pillows with inappropriate sayings on them to each of the seats. Constance collected those whenever she could find a good one, and people tended to gift them to her. She had quite a few repeats, but she didn't mind. Notably, 'not my circus, not my monkeys' and 'Please leave by 9' and 'My other house is in France'.

After answering a bunch of questions about the car, she zipped over to Harold's. He did not live too far from her, but his building was in the more recently fashionable northern part of town, while she was in the old South Beach. She again caught herself wondering whether she would stay in Miami for the duration, or whether she would decide to start living her real life, the one she secretly dreamed of, before it was too late. Stop thinking about things that you can't do anything about right now, Constance chided herself.

Chapter 6

Constance let herself into Harold's apartment. She was expecting to see her uncle in the dramatic, navy-lacquered dining room, zhushing up the table and rearranging the flowers, which he always claimed Constance never did properly, being entirely too impatient to respect the principles of ikebana. But he was nowhere to be found.

Then she heard it. Coughing coming from the bedroom suite. She froze for a moment, listening. That cough. Last winter, he had blamed it on a winter cold. But it had never really abated. He'd had it all through the spring, explaining that it was allergies, and it had lingered all through summer- post-nasal drip from a sinus infection, and at one point he'd gone so far as to keep her at arm's length, in case it was contagious. She would have been more worried, but she knew he'd had it checked out at the doctor's. Harold was always fastidious when it came to his own health and appearance, and he was constantly going to get his levels checked. He and his friends swore by some hormone therapy that kept them young, and Constance was pretty sure he'd gotten a little nip and tuck along the way as well. Harold did look fabulous for his age, though a little tired these days, which of course could be attributed to the excess of work his company had taken on. Constance felt guilty again. She could have done better in helping Harold to shoulder the burden of the numerous design jobs he oversaw.

Everyone thought that interior design was a light, creative, superficial pursuit, but in few other realms were the jobs so unpredictable, the level of skill required so lofty, and the clients quite so difficult. Interior design was not for the weak. And Harold had ruled his company with an iron fist in a velvet glove. But these days, Constance had felt a change, and as Harold's niece and heir apparent, it should have been up to her to pick up the slack. She'd been a slacker, instead. She would have to apologize to Harold and find a way to turn this around. It was not fair to any of them. He had taken care of her from the time she was a teenager, and she wasn't holding up her end of the deal. Not that Harold had any real expectations of her. But still.

Finally, Harold emerged from his room, just as Constance was setting a few appetizers onto his prized cabbage leaf platters.

"Looks beautiful, smells great." He smiled weakly.

"Are you OK, Uncle Harold?"

"Of course. Why do you ask?"

Just as Constance was about to point out the obvious, the doorbell rang.

"Ooo goodie," said Harold, color coming back into his cheeks. "Let the games begin."

Constance had been looking forward to Thanksgiving for a while, she realized. The social ballet of witty repartee, pronouncements about the state of design and modern society, riffs on pop culture and Ancient Greece, which vacation spots were hopelessly passé... And of course, the guests were as diverse and colorful as the conversation.

Almost more than Thanksgiving itself, Constance looked forward to brunch the next day, which meant a recap and postmortem of the proceedings, along with copious quantities of gossip and conjecture, with a side of Rombauer Chardonnay. It was harmless, but evil, fun.

Harold opened the door, waving in his old friends, Boris and Natasha Ivanov, a couple of Russians who split their time between Saint Barts, Healdsburg, and Miami. Natasha, a statuesque beauty, was dressed in vintage Missoni, the colors of which perfectly set off her platinum bob. Boris, shorter, darker, mustachioed, sporting artsy red eyeglasses, had on a velvet smoking jacket similar to Harold's; they must have called each other to discuss their wardrobes. Constance often joked that Boris was gayer than a gay man, and Natasha took it in stride. She loved having a decorative husband. "It's like having a pet peacock," she liked to say, "without the annoying cries." Natasha had brought a platter of her signature lox, which she marinated in vodka, salt, sugar and capers for three days before the event. Boris also had a special treat for them. An illicit tin of Sevruga caviar.

"Maybe we should start on this before the others arrive," Boris laughed. "I would hate for Sean to get any of it."

Sean and Boris were good-natured frenemies. Sean was a big restauranteur in Miami. His spectacular new concept in Key Biscayne, a tropical chic space reminiscent of a vintage Florida supper club, but higher end, was the latest trendy destination for the ladies who lunch and the local gay mafia. And Boris was jealous, because he claimed he had thought of it first. Also, Sean had refused to allow him to invest, so Boris in turn wanted to refuse to patronize the spot, but of course Natasha had decreed that their Pata Negra Cuban sandwich was the best in town, so they were forced to begrudgingly go at least once a week. At least, each visit presented the opportunity for Boris to unleash another dose of vitriol.

"I wonder what Sean will wear today," Boris sniffed. "Remember last year? That hot pink get-up? It was like Liberace died and threw up all over him."

"Boris, you're starting to worry me," said Natasha.

Boris smiled and gave her a tap on the ass.

"Drinks," he boomed.

Harold didn't need to ask what they wanted. He fetched the bottle of vodka from the freezer and poured them both a neat shot, adding pomegranate seeds to Natasha's.

"It's officially a fruit salad now," said Natasha.

The doorbell rang again. Before Harold could even make it to the door, in swept Carla, a self-proclaimed Countess, though Constance had never been able to ascertain which country or region she was supposed to be a Countess from or of. Carla had a pet Vietnamese potbellied pig that featured prominently on her Instagram account, and she was wont to wearing over the top caftans. In fact, she had on a rather spectacular one today, in tones of mustard, burnt umber, and chartreuse. She also had on a silk turban and a large pair of bejeweled earrings that were no doubt the real thing.

"Constance. You look beautiful," Carla breathed.

Carla had decided long ago that Constance was her de facto goddaughter, and far be it from Constance to turn her down. Carla was fabulous, and always good for a decadent lunch or cocktail once in a while. She was rumored to be quite wealthy, but Constance didn't know whether this was true. She lived in a tiny cottage, which was outfitted in the most incredible fashion, all Fortuny pillows and Zuber wall coverings and display cases full of Venetian glass, but she seemed never to travel anywhere other than in her prodigious imagination. No matter: Constance thought Carla was the most fascinating creature she'd ever seen.

"Well, I guess Sean is late, as always," said Boris.

"You're all right on time, if not early," Harold smiled. "And we're still expecting Liam. And Valentino, Liam's new boyfriend."

"Where is Valentino from? Who are his people? Do we know any of them?" Asked Carla.

"You're such a snob," said Natasha, good-naturedly. "But yes, what do we know of this character? And is he good enough for our Liam? Also, I always thought Sean and Liam would end up together."

"He's been singularly mum on the subject," Harold admitted. "I guess we'll have to quiz him when he arrives."

As if on cue, a brief rap rung out on the front door. Harold opened it to reveal Liam, handsome as always, wearing his uniform of white linen shirt, tan linen trousers, and a casually rumpled navy blazer. Next to him, a bird of paradise. Valentino, presumably.

"Hello, everyone," said Liam, in his charming Irish brogue. "Happy Thanksgiving. May I present Valentino." He uttered this as if introducing a particularly dangerous circus act, which probably summed up what Valentino most resembled. Valentino had on a feather headdress that made him look rather like an exotic turkey, but there was something about him that Constance found immediately likable. Other than the headdress, he wore an ascot, a colorful Madras jacket, embroidered trousers, and velvet slippers.

"Wow," whispered Carla, almost miffed to be outdone, by a man, no less.

"I've seated you next to each other," Harold responded in a stage whisper. "You'll be able to fight it out. See who comes out on top in the pecking order," he smiled.

"Touché," said Carla, readjusting her turban. "Speaking of, have you seen that new wallpaper with Hummingbird feathers? Thousands of dollars a square yard? I wonder who would pay for that?"

"More importantly, who can we make pay for that? I want to see it and pet it in real life," said Boris. I have an idea; I'll tell Sean that I might use if I open a restaurant."

Now the doorbell rang, and without pause, in swept Sean, presumably too familiar to the house to wait for permission or for Harold to open the door for him.

"You're all here already" asked Sean. "My God, how American of you. Have you never heard of fashionably late?"

"We just wanted to finish the caviar before you got here," said Boris.

"I see the assassins have failed again," Sean retorted, giving Boris a half smile, "but if you dared to eat the Sevruga before I could steal your portion, I'll kill you myself."

Constance suppressed a giggle. Everyone needed a good frenemy. It really improved one's quality of life, she decided.

"Excuse me, but what kind of creature is Liam's new pet?" Sean whispered to Constance. "And do you think he brought it along specifically to provoke me?"

"Provoke you?" Asked Constance, but she was needed, to fill glasses, to be charming, to giggle, to listen to the conversation and to give her opinion when there was a dispute. And disputes did arise. Good-natured, but still intense. Standing in a corner, Constance smiled, almost content for the first time in a long time. These people were wonderful. This was an international crowd, travelers, hailing from all over the world. You just had to find the right flock and attach yourself to it.

As her Apple Watch displayed the hour of midnight, Constance discreetly let herself out the door, giving one last wink to Harold. Once back in her empty apartment, she quickly went to sleep, looking forward to brunch the next day at Joe's Stone Crab.

Chapter 7

Constance woke up to a text message from Harold.
See you at 12:30.
I thought we had said noon. Not that it matters,
Constance wrote back.
I have an appointment, Harold wrote back.
Laconic, but OK.

Constance made herself a much-needed triple espresso and
turned her attention to her closet. What would she wear for their
yearly gossip post-Thanksgiving brunch? Stone crab was truly one
of her favorite foods. She found a pleated skirt with an elastic
waist in an intriguing shade of Nile green and paired it with a
light rose silk camisole and a lightweight caramel leather jacket.
She was happy to have her Miami wardrobe back, after living out
of a suitcase in California.

When she arrived at Joe's Stone Crab, the Maître d', greeted her
warmly. She and Harold had been regulars for years- it was
always their restaurant of choice for a celebration.

"Is my uncle here?" She asked.

"You're the first. But I got you your favorite table," he said,
leading her to a spot in the corner.

It was the perfect vantage point from which to watch the other
diners, and to gossip without fear of being overheard. Constance
sat down and checked her phone. No messages. She'd already
heard from Chiara and had gotten Thanksgiving wishes from a
few friends the day before, but she would have thought that
Carlos might send her a text. She checked her calendar. It had
already been populated with a frightening number of
appointments for Monday and Tuesday. Nothing beyond that.
Weird. Probably a glitch. She checked her email. There were a
few announcements from vendors teasing new color ways and
holiday specials, but nothing interesting. She was scrolling
through social media when Harold finally made his appearance.

"Wow, you look hung over," she said, rising to greet him and
give him a kiss on both cheeks. "You really overdid it, didn't you?
she asked.

"I must have," said Harold. "I'm sorry I'm late. My appointment was delayed."

Constance would have asked him what kind of appointment he had, but she felt it was maybe a bit indiscreet and focused instead on the sommelier, who had come up to the table and was inquiring as to whether they wanted their usual Rombauer Chardonnay.

"Of course," said Constance. "Hair of the dog, right, Uncle Harold?"

"Yes, yes, of course," he said, though he lacked enthusiasm.

Once they had put in their order for their crab legs and their wine and had clinked their glasses together, Constance said, "Time to start gossiping. I really need to know what's happening between Liam and Sean."

"Oh, it's a doozy," said Harold. "But first, we need to have a serious chat."

Alarm bells sounded in Constance's head, but she decided to downplay it. Instead, she groaned.

"Today is sacred. Can't we save that for tomorrow, or even better, Monday morning?"

"No time," said Harold, gravely. He took out his phone and pulled up some photos.

"Look at this yacht."

Oh, good. Better than a thousand other things he could have brought up.

"Yeah. It's another vintage yacht," Constance sighed.

"Not just any vintage yacht. This was the yacht that Princess Grace and Prince Rainier spent their honeymoon on…"

Constance cut him off.

"It's still a vintage yacht. If you're thinking of offering me this as a consolation prize, know that I'm sick of vintage. If I have to design one more 1920s themed stateroom, I'll either get indigestion or fall asleep at my desk. I want to be challenged! I want to do a more modern boat that's going to have some press and some attention by my contemporaries. I want to start attracting a more global clientele for us, Harold. I thought you wanted me to do that!"

Harold closed his eyes, as if his patience was already wearing thin.

"The way you do that, Constance, is through attention to detail. It's an honor to have the opportunity to redo this classic yacht. I almost gave it to Penelope instead of to you, so if you don't want it..."

"No, it's fine," said Constance hurriedly. "I'll take it." Shit. She knew she was skating on thin ice, but this felt like one of those last-chance situations. "Where do I have to travel for this?" She hoped she didn't have to go too far afield.

"That's the thing. We're still at the bid stage, and time is of the essence. Vision boards, sketches, scope of work, proposed budget...It all needs to be in by Sunday night so I can look over it. But I want it to be perfect, do you understand?"

"So, if I do a great job, I can still get the big project here?"

"We'll see," said Harold. He tapped at his phone. "I just sent you all the information. Good luck. Now, shall we talk about Sean's latest transgressions?"

"Yes." Constance hoped that she had managed to fake the required enthusiasm. Her weekend was shot. And worse than that, so was her career, unless a miracle happened. That damn Muse had better not think she was getting any time off.

Chapter 8

It was already midday on Saturday. She'd been holed up since Friday afternoon, with not much to show for it. Constance needed to leave her apartment. She had a thumping headache. A strong Cuban coffee might be the only thing that could give her some fresh inspiration for the Grace Kelly yacht, and stepping outside into the daylight wouldn't hurt, either. She slipped on a pair of sunglasses, picked up her computer bag and her purse, and drove herself to Wynwood, the bustling arts zone of Miami. She loved this newer neighborhood. It was always so inspiring and made her feel like she was part of something bigger, part of a community of artists and other creatives shaping the world around them.

Constance parked on the street, stepped into her favorite coffee shop, and smiled at the barista, a young man with multiple piercings and a warm smile.

"Hey Jorge," she said. "Your tattoo. I love it. Is it new?"

Jorge smiled shyly, peering at her through thick eyelashes.

So unfair, thought Constance. Her own eyelashes were thick, but pale. Actually, almost transparent. Other than her signature red lipstick, Constance's other concession to vanity was that she regularly went to have her lashes dyed, so that she didn't look like a naked mole rat when she woke up.

"What does it mean?" asked Constance.

"Oh, it's to center me," said Jorge. "See, it's supposed to be a compass. My brother and I drew it when we were little. He said the needle points to our true north."

"Oh. And what's your true north?"

"I'm still searching a little bit, but this reminds me that I need to spend some time each day trying to figure it out."

"That's beautiful," said Constance. "Maybe I need a tattoo like that, too."

"No. You don't put a bumper sticker on a Bentley," Jorge said, giving her a wink. "Oh, you flirt," said Constance. Jorge was much too sweet for her to ever be interested in. But she enjoyed the attention and the compliment.

"Your usual?" Asked Jorge.

"Make it a triple. I need to concentrate," she said.

Jorge nodded sagely. They both had a touch of the old ADHD. Once she had her coffee in hand, Constance plopped herself down at a table on the beautiful, shaded terrace in front of the coffee shop. She opened her iPad and called up the photos Howard had sent her of the Princess Grace yacht. It was indeed a classic, a beautiful one, even as it was, all polished wood and elegant forms. A floating piece of history. Built in England in 1928 and eventually conscripted by the British for the war effort, where it was instrumental in evacuating forces from the beaches in Dunkirk, it was eventually acquired by Aristotle Onassis, who entertained icons such as Winston Churchill and Elizabeth Taylor onboard. When Grace Kelly married Prince Rainier in 1956, Onassis presented the royal couple with the yacht as a wedding present. They honeymooned on the 147-foot vessel along the coasts of Corsica and Sardinia, before parting with it in 1958. The ship had been recently renovated and was currently being used as a charter ship in the Galapagos Islands, but there was a billionaire who was a huge Grace Kelly fan and had decided that money was no object. He just had to have the yacht and make it his own. Constance examined photos of the existing decor, by award-winning designer Ariana Joyas. Constance could only hope to have a career like this one, and she needed to be sensitive to everyone's ego, while taking the yacht from charter to personal plaything, while reflecting the illustrious history which had, over time, been remodeled out of it.

Constance happily spent the next hour looking up images of Princess Grace. Her jewelry. Her gowns. Her appearances at various charity events, alone or on the arm of her prince. The cars driven by Rainier and Grace. She managed to condense all of this into a digital vision board. A distinct impression of the sorts of colors and materials she might use began to emerge. A bit of shine here. Some diamond-like elements, but nothing too flashy, balancing an over-abundance of wood. She would tie everything together with a few art pieces and new lighting that would modernize the overall design while retaining the historical angle. Lighting is the jewelry of the room, Constance always liked to say. She looked at the floor plan now. It didn't flow, having been broken up into too-small spaces. A yacht needed to flow. It also needed larger closets. Any lady guests would insist on that. She eliminated a few of the extraneous cabins in favor of larger walk-in closets with vanities, and luxurious bathrooms. It was a risky choice, as some clients counted in terms of number of cabins, but for most men she knew, it was the size of the boat that counted. And if the rumors she had heard were true, the man who was thinking of purchasing this particular floating palace very much wanted to impress his lady guests. She absent-mindedly wondered whether she was his type, but then blocked out that thought. From now on, she was going to give the work her full attention, instead of counting on workarounds.

"You're still here?"

Constance looked up. Jorge stood above her table, his motorcycle helmet under his arm.

"Yeah, I guess I am. Feeling inspired. But I still have loads more to do. You closing?"

"No, it's just the end of my shift. You can stay."

"Oh good. See you soon."

Constance got back to work. She looked back over everything. In just a couple hours, she had actually done something she was quite proud of. The colors were original and sophisticated. It worked with the old design, while bringing in a new element, and it expressed a cohesive vision for something that would give the whole yacht an updated feel. In fact, it was probably her best work to date. The fear Harold had put into her heart had for once gotten her Muse's ass in gear. Smiling to herself, she carefully saved everything. Normally, she would have been sending Harold her ideas in real time, forcing him to be the one to keep up with her disjointed thoughts. But she decided to wait. She was exhausted but had another 24 hours in which to get everything not only done, but perfect. She was going to blow him away. He would see.

As if her uncle could read her mind, she received a text message from him at that very moment.

How's it going? You aren't procrastinating, are you?

Constance scowled. Fair, but come on. Not nice.

As a matter of fact, I am nearly done.

She could picture Harold's expression right now, as if he were right in front of her. How many times had she seen him like that, doubt writ large on his face?

Rushing never resulted in anything of quality, he wrote back.

Wrong. She knew one man, for example, who had always been able to deliver a mind-blowing quickie, but she needed to stop thinking about him.

Why don't you wait until you see it before you insult me? You'll have it by Sunday afternoon.

She had to talk herself out of being mad at her uncle. After all, she had more than earned her reputation.

You're right, Harold wrote back. I'm an old man. It takes me longer to do things now. I'm looking forward to seeing it.

Well, that was better than nothing, Constance supposed. She packed up her things and headed back to the apartment. She needed a change of location.

It was unfortunate that Chiara was out of town for Thanksgiving weekend, because getting back to her uninspired space almost sent Constance into a tailspin. Had Chiara been home, she would have met her out somewhere, and drowned her sorrows in copious cocktails. But instead, she went through her old photo albums. Photos of her with her mother. The family on the DeFever yacht on Christmas Day, back when they were all happy. Harold dropping her off at Princeton on her first day of Architecture school, neither of them realizing that, just a couple years later, she would ditch her studies to run after Lorenzo, which had proven to be the wrong decision. She needed to get her own life under control, she decided, and picked up her iPad again, working through the night to finish the proposal.

When she sent her files to Harold, mid-morning, she spent the next couple hours expecting an ecstatic phone call, or at the very least a text letting her know she was a genius, a wizard, or a magician.

But nothing ever came.

She tried to console herself by using that burst of creativity to work on her own place, but it was gone. She spent the rest of the day on mindless TV shows and ignoring calls from Carlos, who never left a message, and went to bed early, exhausted, and dreading the next day's meeting.

Chapter 9

On Monday morning, Constance found herself taking in a deep breath as she approached the glass building on Ocean Avenue that housed the offices of Harold Morgan Design. She had put on her armor, an elegant pantsuit suit in a lively shade of Peridot green that she knew clashed strikingly with her hair. She had piled on vintage enamel bracelets and felt like she could hold her own, at least stylistically, vis-a-vis the ever-classically dressed Penelope. Constance walked through the glass doors and into their offices, waving at Hilary, the receptionist, and communicating to her via signs that she was late, and that they would catch up over a boozy lunch, but ignoring her when the receptionist mouthed what Constance was reasonably sure was something like "How was Carlos White?" Hilary reveled in living vicariously through Constance's adventures. She wasn't a whole lot older than Constance but had been already married for a good ten years and had three school aged children at home. It made Constance shudder to even think about it. Hilary's husband was a yacht captain who would be gone for months at a time, which Constance wasn't sure made matters better, or worse.

She headed to the coffee room, so that she could fortify herself with a good espresso before getting the negative feedback she was sure Harold would give her that morning. She couldn't believe she had been so hung ho about her design. Maybe this was what Harold in fact considered to be the bare minimum, and here she had been thinking it would garner her kudos. His silence had spoken volumes.

Dread in her heart, Constance headed to the conference room. Harold was already seated at the head of the table, wearing a cobalt blue jacket and a colorful bow tie. Constance had always loved Harold's sense of style. It was hard to believe that he had grown up in the same household as her dad, had gone to the same boarding school, no less. She often felt like she had more in common with Harold than she did with her own father, and ever since her father had decamped to Hawaii, Constance and Harold had been so incredibly close that many people assumed that she was in fact his daughter, fathered during a brief hetero phase. They'd even had similar coloring, once upon a time, before Harold's hair had turned white, and he'd somehow acquired a Miami perma-tan. But all of that did not mean that Harold went any easier on her. On the contrary.

Penelope was seated closest to Harold at the conference table, and unfortunately, David, one of the design assistants, was seated on Harold's other side, which meant that Constance did not have a seat of honor at the table. Well, didn't she feel like the redheaded stepchild? Or the redheaded niece-goddaughter, as the case may be. She took a sip of her espresso while she waited for Harold to get down to business, hoping he would keep what was probably a scathing review of her work on the Grace Kelly yacht for a private meeting.

Constance sat forward, smoothing down her trousers, as Harold cleared his throat and began to pull up images of their upcoming projects onto the smart screen presentation board. Constance held her breath as she saw the familiar shape of the Xerces 2, one of the finest mega yachts to have been constructed in the past decade. She knew all about this boat. It was currently docked in Miami. Working on it would be a sure promotion for her. Having her name attached to such a project would mean recognition from the industry, paving the way to maybe one day having her own design firm. She loved working with Harold and had long dared to dream that she might launch the European arm of his company, but this weekend, and what was probably going to transpire this morning, had proven that maybe she should be in charge of her own destiny, and not competing with people like Penelope for jobs. She also happened to know that the owner of the Xerces 2 was a very handsome tech founder, who was also quite the player. Constance viewed this as a fitting challenge for her. She mentally kicked herself, though, that her thoughts went straight to a potential affair with the client. Perhaps Harold was right. This was her default. But there was nothing wrong with a little bit of harmless flirting and even a brief liaison, as long as no one got hurt, was there? And unlike Carlos White, she knew that the owner of the Xerces 2 had no ex-wife. He was very single, a heartbreaker, in fact, one who could get a taste of his own medicine if Constance were to dump him first.

Surely this job was going to go to Constance. Maybe Harold's silence the day before had been to build up the surprise. She was already starting to get ready to thank him for his trust and start presenting some of her preliminary ideas when Harold said, in a tone that invited no contradiction or discussion, "Penelope will be the lead designer on this project."

Constance sat bolt upright.

"What?" she blurted out. "I have more experience than Penelope with this sort of yacht. I've done two similar boats in the last year alone!"

"Yes," said Harold. "And you dialed it in, and you ran off before you finished the last details. This needs to be a top to toe job and it needs to be perfect. Penelope has the eye to detail that you, sadly, my dear, do not."

Constance blushed furiously. He wasn't wrong. But chastising her like this, in front of her colleagues? It was beyond the pale. She started gathering up her things and stood up. She couldn't stay here any longer. This was the final straw.

"Constance, stay," said Harold. "I have an announcement to make to everyone, and it involves you."

Constance froze, her blush turning to pallor as the blood drained from her face. Was Harold going to fire her? Like this?

"I had Constance do a proposal for the Grace Kelly yacht this weekend. She did such a good job that I sent it in immediately. And I found out this morning that, if the client decides to go along with his purchase of the yacht, we will have the contract. He wants it done exactly as designed, no changes. A high visibility project like this one will take our firm to new heights. So brava, and thank you, Constance. In light of this, I have decided to give you another high-profile project, one I was originally going to do myself."

"Oh yeah, what is it?"

Constance was still in shock. Still in disbelief. If she'd done such a great job, why didn't she get the Xerces 2?

"It's the Lombard 4. I want to talk to you about it in more detail. Let me assign the others their jobs and we'll revisit one on one."

As Harold wrapped up the meeting with the others, Constance's brain whirred, calling up her encyclopedic knowledge of yachts and their owners. The Lombard 4 was originally a beautiful boat, but it had been renovated five years back, with what some would call a revolutionary design, and what Constance and Harold would both call absolutely botched, by a design firm based in The Hague. The hull of the boat was still an interesting shade of forest green, but the interiors were now positively icy. The new owner of the yacht, a reasonably handsome, relatively elusive playboy by the name of Peter Holmes, had made his money in mysterious ways. Constance had had Peter on her list for a while, but he was rarely seen out and about. Boris and Natasha had been invited to lunch on his old boat once, on St Barth, but they didn't know much about him. It didn't seem that he went to most of the yacht parties that many of their clients frequented, which was probably a good thing. Their liaison, if there was one, would not impact Constance's reputation much. To be fair, she had probably ruined her reputation pretty thoroughly already, and she kicked herself that she was thinking in these terms again. Where was the new Constance? The one who didn't take shortcuts?

Chapter 10

Once the other designers had left the conference room, Penelope giving Constance a murderous look, Constance turned to her uncle.

"OK, where is the Lombard 4 parked right now?" Hopefully, it was in Palm Beach or somewhere near there, and she'd be able to commute. If so, this was indeed a better gig than the Xerces 2.

"It's in Saint Tropez for the winter," said Harold.

Constance's heart dropped. Saint Tropez? In December? That sounded like an absolute nightmare. The whole town shut down after October. Any of her friends who spent the summer there would be long gone by the time she arrived. And she would be stuck alone, with maybe a few wine makers and a few interior designers who were busy transforming villas before the start of the high season, for company. But she was being silly. She could go see the boat, and then go wherever she wanted while she worked on it from a distance, couldn't she?

"So, do I even need to go over there to measure and take photos, or can we find someone on the ground to do that? Should I communicate with the owner via Zoom?" She didn't want to let on that she knew exactly who the owner was.

"No. You would be the supervisor on the work, my dear. The owner wants everything done by spring. He's planning on throwing a huge party for charity during the big opening regatta, so there's no time to waste."

That was it. Her apartment in Miami would never get decorated at all. None of her social plans would come to fruition. And she would be stuck in a town that was wonderful in the summer but bleak in the winter, with no support system. Could it get any worse?

"So, what's my per diem for my stay in Saint Tropez?" asked Constance. "It's expensive there- even in the winter."

"€50," said Harold.

"A day?" She couldn't find a hotel room and pay for food with that.

"You'll be fine. You have a car at your disposal, and you can stay on the yacht the whole time, thanks to Mr. Holmes' generosity."

Generosity, my ass, thought Constance. Her reputation probably preceded her. Speaking of, she hadn't seen any recent photos of Peter Holmes. Yes, he'd been rather handsome the last time he'd been photographed, but considering how elusive he was, she had no way of knowing if that had changed. And she did, after all, have standards.

Harold grew more serious.

"Constance, I want you to listen to me. You need to be really careful with this one."

"What? Holmes is some kind of sociopath?"

"No. He's fired his last two designers. We want to be the firm to turn it around. And he is intent on having this job covered in at least one magazine by spring."

"So, he is insane, after all," said Constance. "You know as well as I do that it's gotten harder and harder to get press. Unless you have connections I didn't know about."

This was a bit cruel. Harold Morgan Design did great work, But ever since Harold had broken away from his mentor's company, Wilkinson Yacht Works, which was now their greatest competitor, they'd been blocked ever step of the way when it came to publications and awards. Harold had tried to express on many occasions that his departure had been a necessary business decision, but Bob Wilkinson had apparently taken it personally, and could be singularly vindictive.

"I've promised the owner that we would be able to get it done, so whatever it takes. Wilkinson has beaten us out on some of the big jobs, and if we don't win this one, the very existence of this company might be in danger."

Constance blanched.

"I had no idea. Why didn't you tell me?"

"Well, I might be being just a little dramatic. And we can hopefully turn it around," said Harold. "But I'm getting to an age where I could retire. I worry about what will happen to you."

Constance held her breath. There it was. She had operated for years under the assumption that Harold would pass the company on to her. And then, more recently, she'd started to feel that intention change. Her opportunities evaporate.

"You have moments of brilliance," said Harold. "But you're not consistent, Constance."

Constance glared at him. If he made the joke about her not being constant one more time, just like her so-called friends did, she was going to scream. What a sick sense of humor the universe had.

Harold's voice dropped down a bit. He looked at her kindly. "Constance, you know I adore you. And for all that I worry about your reputation, you know I don't judge you. I want to see you succeed. I want you to break this pattern that you've established for no good reason. You're only punishing yourself."

"Punishing myself?"

"Your dad is married to that twat and sipping Mai Tais in second-rate bars and calling that a life. He'll never notice what you do, whether it's good or bad. You might think you're rebelling to make him react. But instead, you're only giving her ammunition to prove to your father that what she says about you is true."

Constance gritted her teeth, on the defensive.

"And what about you, Uncle Harold? What do you really think of me? You might as well tell me the truth. After all, you're sending me to the equivalent of Siberia."

"Oh really? I'll see if there are any projects we can bid on in Vladivostok and you'll see how you feel about the opportunity I'm handing you on a silver platter then. You want to know how I actually feel? I've believed in you, and I've given you chances, and you've shat on them, to be honest. It's getting tiresome having to defend you. Against our competitors, against our clients, and especially against their wives."

Constance looked at him and sighed. His disappointment was warranted and had almost taken the fight out of her.

"The wives thing is not fair. You know Carlos White is divorced and his ex-wife is way out of bounds. I'm not as much of a slut as some people say."

"I know. You're a flirt, my darling. And you command attention."

"Ha," said Constance, weakly. Sure, her gay uncle thought she was a ravishing creature, but that wasn't her desired demographic. "But sometimes," Harold continued, "they have a point. I'm not judging you. I'm not shaming you, but I just want you to look at what you're doing."

Constance didn't have a comeback for that. She leaned in and gave Harold a hug. "Remember, best behavior… follow through," he whispered into her ear. "I love you, kid."

"Why do I feel like this is goodbye? When do I leave?"

"I have your tickets already. You leave tomorrow. 4:25 flight."

"What? What about Christmas?"

What she was really thinking was, what about Art Basel? What about catching her breath? But then, she realized. She had no real reason to be in Miami, and now she needed to turn it all around and be positive. After all, Harold was trusting her with a very high-profile job. Difficult as she knew it would be, annoying as the conditions would be, challenging as it would be to make sure it ended up in a magazine, the payoff could be huge. It would help her business prospects, and it could help Uncle Harold's company in the future. Even if he didn't want to leave it to her, she would hate to see him retire on a sour note.

"I'll fly in, and we can stay at Le Martinez in Cannes."

Constance nodded. A flashback of a memorable winter weekend spent there with Lorenzo entered her mind. Blue skies. A tryst on their private balcony, halfway wrapped in their hotel bathrobes. Tangled sheets, and breakfast in bed.

"Why don't you take the rest of the day off to pack," said Harold. "Don't worry, I got you the extra baggage allowance."

Constance smiled. He knew her well. Packing could send her into a tailspin. She checked her Apple watch, which she hated, but which was a necessary evil, as it pinged and vibrated to alert her as to the appointments, she ran the risk of forgetting without it. It was almost time for lunch.

"Is it OK if I kidnap Hilary for a quick catch-up at LBH?"

"Sure," Harold smiled indulgently.

A membership to one international club of their choice- anything that offered discounted stays around the world for their members- was one of the perks of being a designer at Harold's firm. Constance had convinced Harold that Soho House fit the bill, and when Harold had reluctantly agreed, several of the designers had applied. So far, only Constance had managed to become a member of Every House, including the Little Beach House Malibu add-on, which she had used quite frequently of late. Penelope hadn't managed to get into SoHo House at all. They had probably sensed through her application that she was not cool enough.

Constance stopped by the reception desk.

"Harold says you can come out to play."

"Great, let me just wrap this up and we are out of here."

Constance stood by, sending a group text to Chiara, and their other friend Pam, to see if they could meet for one last sendoff meal.

I can't believe you're leaving us right before Art Basel, Pam responded.

Don't remind me, Constance wrote back.

I'm going to be gone too, Chiara added.

Et tu, Brute? Pam responded. You guys suck. What am I going to do without a partner in crime?

Pick up a new one. That's what I do, Constance typed, with a winking emoji.

We know about that, Pam wrote back. And Chiara added a haha to it. Traitors. She wouldn't miss them.

So, tonight? Constance wrote.

I have a work thing, Pam wrote back. Constance bit her lip. She and Chiara had met Pam out at a gallery a few years back, and she was lots of fun, but they still weren't clear on how her work as a hostess in the private jet terminal of the Miami Dade International Airport could possibly involve so many evening work things, which always remained suitably vague. Chiara had been the one to suggest that she was supplementing her income the old-fashioned way. Well, Constance didn't want to be judgmental, but the least Pam could do is return the favor.

Sven is in town for once, Chiara wrote. Before Constance had time to feel sorry for herself, Chiara followed up with, Come over for dinner.

You sure Sven won't mind? Constance responded.
Not if he knows what's good for him.

Chapter 11

"Little Beach House, please," Constance said to the Uber driver, once she and Hilary had managed to leave the building and snag a car. Knowing lunch would be boozy, Constance had left the Mini at home.

"Oh, that place is cool," said the driver. "You're members? You look like some of those fancy artsy girls, especially you, Red."

Constance rolled her eyes at Hilary, who winked at her.

"Well, what goes on over that place?" Asked the driver.

"Nothing special," said Constance. "Just eating, drinking and socializing, you know, same as anywhere else, I guess."

"I hear there's a lot of coke there. And cockroaches."

"Hmm. I haven't noticed," said Constance.

"What do you do for a career?" asked the driver. He was relentless. "Or are you one of those sugar babies?"

"Do I look like a sugar baby?" asked Constance, not sure whether to be offended or flattered first.

"Well, not exactly, but there's something about you. I mean, you're pretty enough to be one," said the driver.

"Thanks. I guess," said Constance. "I'm an interior designer for yachts," she said. Not that she owed him any response, but she didn't want him to remain on his sugar baby assumption.

"Wow, aren't you the glamour puss?" Said the driver, with a whistle. She could tell he was about to start directing his inquiry to Hilary, so to spare her, Constance asked, "How about you? What do you do when you're not driving an Uber and asking too many questions?"

"I'm a musician," said the driver. "I played a gig a couple nights ago in the Arts district and I had a couple celebrities show up- Jay-Z, I think, and someone who looked like Katy Perry. So, I probably won't be a driver for long."

"Nice," said Constance. "I'll follow you on Instagram," she lied.

"Cool," said the driver.

He dropped them off at Little Beach house. This lunch was a bit bittersweet because, though she was looking forward to Hilary's gossip, this was also a goodbye. Goodbyes were weird for Constance, not just because of the indeterminate time that she would be gone, but because of the way that she felt she would have changed by the time she got back. Did that happen to other people? For her, there was always a disconnect when she returned, and she felt like the girl who came back was never quite the same one who had left. And it was disconcerting. It was almost like she missed herself.

"I am so ready for a drink," she said to Hilary, as they sat down. "Me too- and unlike you, I need to go back to work this afternoon, so we'd better front-load them."

"And I don't want to pack drunk. Or actually, maybe it would be easier."

"Dammit. They sat us near the family with the kids. I'm gonna have to keep my F bombs down, and my gossip G-rated," said Hilary.

Constance glanced over to the next table, where two stylish women sat, each one flanked by two adorable children. They were beaming beatifically and sharing dishes family style. Maybe a few years ago, Constance would have looked at this and thought it was pathetic, but right now it actually looked a little bit aspirational, especially as one of the little girls demanded her lion's share of clams from a bowl of linguine vongole. Cue the flashback to Lorenzo feeding her pasta, making stupid seafood double entendres that nevertheless made her laugh.

"I don't know why they let kids into Soho House," said Hilary, breaking the spell. "They must be European, though," she said. "They look pretty well behaved. Speaking of Europe, I'm so jealous- Saint Tropez?"

"In the winter," Constance corrected. "It's called low season for a reason. 'Cause it's bleak."

"Still. You'll be within a stone's throw of Italy."

Constance considered her friend. Had she told Hilary about Lorenzo? No, it was just a harmless observation. Where in the world was Lorenzo these days, anyway?

"So, I heard that Harold wants this job you're doing in a magazine. That seems like an unfair ask."

"Not Harold," said Constance. "The client."

"Isn't that weird?" Asked Hilary. "I thought most of these yacht owners were pretty secretive about their yachts."

"I know. Maybe he's planning on selling it or chartering it. Or maybe he's got a huge ego."

"Well, whatever it is, I'm sure you'll figure something out. Which is why he gave this job to you."

"Instead of to his golden child?"

"Penelope? Come on… sure, she'd dependable, reliable…professional, but she hardly has the moments of genius, like.you do."

Constance shrugged. She was deluding herself if she thought that occasional moments of brilliance compensated for well, let's just call it what it was: flaking out. Why was she even like this? Was it true what she'd told herself? That the reason she was so flighty was that she'd been so hurt by Lorenzo? Could one messy breakup really form a whole behavior pattern that would ruin her life for years to come? No. She'd been flighty before Lorenzo. And that had been a whole five years ago. She had changed. Maybe he had changed. Except he was probably still surrounded by models. He had blocked her on social media, but every once in a while, she would leaf through a magazine and notice his name in the byline and shudder. Same old Lorenzo. Talented. Seductive. And not the man for her. And it was a shame, because there was no one she'd come across since then who attracted her quite as much as Lorenzo. As much as he infuriated her, he intrigued her. Something about him had always made her happy to come home to. Except when she'd started getting serious and getting scared. Justified, since he'd left her for a supermodel. And she hadn't had any option but to run away again, this time to New York. To another job. Other relationships. He'd tried to contact her at first, but she wasn't having any of it. She had blocked him on all her socials, even though once in a while she still tried to stalk him on Instagram or on Google, and then, he had blocked her back. Why was she still thinking about him? It only hurt. When would it stop hurting? Maybe Harold was right. She was only hurting herself. She wasn't proving anything. Of course, Harold thought her behavior was because of her father, and maybe it had been, at first, but now it was all about Lorenzo, who had probably forgotten she existed by now.

"You OK?" Asked Hilary.

"Yeah. Just dreading packing."

They ordered a pizza and a pasta and a bottle of wine. And after thoroughly catching up on everything that was going on (not much) and that would be going on in the next few months (even less), they bade each other goodbye. Constance felt sad, preemptively, like she was closing another door, ending another chapter.

Chapter 12

Constance got busy with her packing. Since she would be gone for so long, she allowed herself her two largest suitcases. It would be great if she could rent out this apartment during her absence; it would supplement the paltry per diem that Harold was condescending to give her. Yes, she had her salary, but the apartment was expensive, and her living expenses were, too. She had standards, after all. She liked designer cocktails and nice restaurants, and €50 was not going to take her very far. Even in offseason Saint Tropez. She threw absolutely everything she could even think she might want to wear in France, in the winter, onto her bed, and then started picking through that to eliminate some things, because at this point, she had the equivalent of four suitcases' worth. How could she reduce that into a capsule wardrobe that should take her from work meetings to boring solo evenings out, to, well, nothing else? Maybe the gym. She threw in a couple of yoga outfits. Were the yoga studios even open in the winter? She did not know. A bathing suit. Maybe the yacht had a sauna. She certainly hoped so. It got very chilly in any harbor in the winter. A silk dressing gown, her second favorite, a mustard yellow one with coral colored trim and a flying crane on it, because she was sick of the one, she'd worn on Carlos' yacht. A few colorful dresses that highlighted her curvy hourglass frame, a leather jacket, and a few extra cashmere sweaters. She had thin blood after spending so much time in warmer climates. She'd rather be going to Saint Barts than to Saint Tropez right now. A friend of a friend had an amazing villa rental there, and a hot boyfriend who might have some cute single friends. But then she remembered: Carlos' daughter, who by all accounts was a piece of work, lived there for at least part of the year.

There. She was almost done with packing. It was a miracle.

Chapter 13

Constance's phone pinged, and she retrieved it from under the pile of clothes strewn haphazardly on top of the bed. She'd been deluding herself earlier, when she'd thought she was done packing. She'd gone back to the drawing board at least ten times since.

It was a message from Chiara.

How's it going?

Constance rolled her eyes and looked around the room.

Chiara knew her well and was probably quite certain that Constance was currently overwhelmed and underproductive, having reached a complete impasse.

Why don't you just pack a simple capsule wardrobe? Chiara wrote back, adding insult to injury.

Most of what Constance owned was colorful and quirky and not at all suited for winter in a depressing port town- not that Saint Tropez was depressing in general, but she had a feeling that winter was hardly the time to be there.

Do you have anything in neutral colors? Chiara wrote back.

Meanwhile, Constance still hadn't responded to the first message.

I've got some of the black stuff I bought the last time I thought I'd be moving to New York, Constance wrote back.

Is it on your bed? Chiara fired back, sending a winking emoji to soften the blow.

I didn't get there yet, Constance wrote back.

OK, take it out of your closet. And put it on the bed.

Chiara was giving her simple step-by-step instructions, because it was all she could handle right now.

Those sexy black leather trousers you have. Take those. Your black ankle boots, ONE pair of blue jeans.

Constance did as she was told. But added an extra pair of jeans.

A cashmere sweater. A couple shirts. You're good.

Good? That was almost nothing, thought Constance. But she was at least heartened by the fact that Chiara didn't know she had two suitcases. She had a whole other suitcase to add her "just in case" items to.

I'm willing to bet you added a bunch of extra items, Chiara wrote back.

Just let me suffer in peace. Constance wrote.

No way. I want you to get to my place for dinner as early as possible. I'm not gonna see my best friend for months.

I hope you're making your famous spaghetti and meatballs, Constance smiled.

This was a private joke. Chiara was in the habit of making her Italian ancestors roll in their graves, because her signature dish was a very Americanized spaghetti and meatballs, the meatballs sourced straight from Trader Joe's, and combined with a jar of Ragu pasta sauce from the dollar store. Not that Chiara couldn't afford better, but the Ragu somehow held mysterious sway over her. It was a harmless way of being a rebel. At least the pasta was always perfectly al dente.

Thank you, Constance wrote back, more serious, now.

Without Chiara, she would have been spiraling with this packing situation deep into the night. She didn't know what she would do without her, but at the same time, she realized that she'd been resenting Chiara a little bit of late. Her friend was so happily ensconced in her relationship, she had a beautiful place that she loved, and a job she was passionate about. Constance was passionate about design, sure, but she never felt like she could commit to it fully. Couldn't make herself commit to living in one place or doing or being one thing. She and Chiara had had a conversation about it once, and Constance had referred to it as being a multi passionate creative, and Chiara had scoffed at her, before growing serious and taking her hand across the table.

"Constance," she had said. "That's fine, but there's a difference between being scattered and being multi-passionate, and you need to be realistic about the fact that if you're going to do everything and be all things, it's going to take you longer to get anywhere."

"That's fine," Constance had said. "I don't know where I'm going anyway."

"That's what I'm afraid of," Chiara had said.

Another text from Chiara shook Constance out of her reverie.

It's 4:26. Set your alarm for an hour and a half from now and call your Uber when it goes off.

Constance rolled her eyes.

Yes, mom.

But she was thankful to Chiara for helping her to manage her tendency to get caught up in pottering around. And, after all, she didn't have a mom anymore. She set her alarm and wandered around the apartment, trying to see if there was anything she'd forgotten to do. Laptop, keys, cosmetics, passport…Her eyes swept the nearly empty bookcase in the living room and fell on the damn photo album. She really shouldn't, but she picked it up; opened it. Started flipping through the same pictures she had looked at just a few days before, trying to stem the flow of memories that surged forth. There was her mom. Glamorous, in a large straw hat. The whole family on the boat. Constance, doing her homework while sitting in the captain's chair. Various family meals, in different ports of call. A series of photos of a young Constance on beaches around the world, in a series of unfortunate bathing suits. Looking at them, Constance could only too clearly see the progression from happy, confident, carefree, to sullen, shy, self-conscious. From turning cartwheels in an ill-fitting bikini to slouching in a sarong tied tightly over a perfectly lovely one-piece. If only she could get that childish confidence back. If only she could go back to a time when she didn't compare herself- to others, or to an unrealistic standard that she had pretty much set herself. As she flipped through the photo album further, she came to her semester of study abroad in Paris. Harold had visited and had documented every stage of Constance falling in love with Europe. The ham sandwich on a perfect baguette from that surprise place near the train station. Breakfast at Café de Flore. Strolling in the Tuileries. The trip they'd taken to Florence, and Rome. Florentine landscapes, complete with proud cypress trees and hazy sunsets. Dal Bolognese, the best pasta ever. Graduate School. Spending more time in New York with Chiara than in Princeton. The year with Lorenzo. New York. Then Italy. Photos inside his mother's charming country house kitchen. A shot of them enjoying a picnic. She remembered Lorenzo's mother, Carlotta, taking that one. After taking the picture, Carlotta had set back off for the house, picnic basket in tow, leaving them to savor the rest of the afternoon. A photo of her and Lorenzo, this one taken by Chiara, kissing over 2 glasses of red wine. She could still feel the taste of that wine in her mouth, and the feeling of his lips on hers. That last trip to Hawaii, to see her dad, at Lorenzo's insistence. They'd been far from welcome, and then Lorenzo had told her about his big break, a shoot in the Bahamas. She shook her head. These memories, while delicious, hurt too much. After this, only very few photos, most of them taken by Harold at Thanksgiving. The rest of the memories were in her phone, but they were still a blur. It had been almost five years. Los Angeles, for a snip. A return to New York. Pretty miserable, without Lorenzo and Chiara. Then Miami. Trying to buckle down and work for Harold, trying to settle into various apartments. Buying her place. Working for clients who all ran together in her mind. Saint Barth. Marina Del Rey. Monaco. Victoria. Fort Lauderdale. Capri. Ibiza. Abu Dhabi. Yes, she travelled, to wherever the clients' yachts were, but none of it had left a lasting impression. Yes, she'd had some professional wins, had been nominated for small local awards, but she knew that she didn't deserve them. Harold, or a design assistant, or even the client, had always stepped in to smooth over the things that she had left undone.

Five years. She had made friends and lost friends, and overall had found herself much more alone. More untethered than ever. She'd lost her mother years earlier, but it hit even harder now, for some reason. Maybe because she had finally admitted to herself that she'd essentially lost her father, too. Harold was holding her at arm's length. Chiara had gotten engaged, and was excitedly looking towards the future, a future that didn't have much to do with Constance. Sure, it would be nice to be an auntie. But that was hardly a consolation prize. Everything hurt. She hurt.

When she'd been with Lorenzo, she'd thought she knew what she wanted. A simple life in Europe, a bed and breakfast. The opportunity to run a small design company on her own terms. Feeling attached to something bigger than herself. But it was like she'd been self-sabotaging the whole time. One piece had fallen out of the puzzle, and then she'd stomped on the rest of it, just out of spite. She'd punished herself, and herself only. As far as she knew, Lorenzo was living a fabulous life. Hell, he was maybe married, with a couple of children. Children that she had thought she would have with him. When they'd been together, they had discussed names. Margarita for a girl. And Ercole for a boy.

But they had agreed that they wouldn't have children right away. They wanted to enjoy each other, travel, for at least a few more years. And now, those years had gone by without any of those things. To Constance, it felt like she'd lost a whole potential part of her life, one that she had seen glimmering on the horizon, only to have it retreat, like a ship disappearing from her perspective. She'd broken it, and she didn't know how to fix it, or get any of it back. And now, she was being sent on yet another job. Another short-term thing that would lead nowhere. She almost resented Harold for it, but that wasn't fair. She had said herself that she wanted to travel. She had herself acted in such a way that he knew better than to give her the administrative tasks that would keep her in the office. That had been her decision. Her prerogative. And now, it had gone on for so long that there was no way to change it.

Her phone alarm beeped, and she slammed the photo album shut. Of all the things in this apartment she had gotten rid of, this was the one that she wished she had the strength to throw away. But then, what would she have? Less than nothing.

She checked her outfit in the mirror. What had felt like a fun, colorful work ensemble, now felt frumpy and wilted. She changed into a pair of jeans and a black V-neck tunic. A little boring, but it would have to do.

She fished a bottle of champagne out of her refrigerator, which now made the appliance officially completely empty, and called an Uber.

Chapter 14

She was led into the apartment by a very glamorous looking Chiara, dressed in a silk jumpsuit and dangling earrings. Constance looked down at her own uncharacteristically casual ensemble. Packing really had taken everything out of her.

"I didn't know we were dressing up. You didn't invite anyone else over, did you?"

She couldn't possibly handle it.

"No, don't worry. I just got back from a work meeting. I can change into my jeans or jammies if it makes you feel better."

"Silly, you look beautiful," said Constance. "You and your home are a pleasure for the eyes."

Chiara's apartment was just like her: shiny, modern, elegant, trendy. Constance had helped her to infuse it with a few personal touches, a few unexpected moments that took it from soulless to interesting. Why couldn't she do that for herself? Out the window, lights twinkled across the water, on Key Biscayne, echoing the lights cast by the chandelier Constance had carefully chosen for her friend. Luxurious throw blankets were carefully folded on the rungs of a custom-made decorative ladder- a Home Depot one a local artist had gold-leafed by hand.

"Sven is on his way," said Chiara. "We have time to catch up and then he'll join us for dinner."

"Do you ever get tired of him being such a workaholic?" Asked Constance as Chiara poured her a glass of bubbly.

"Not really. I mean. I'm the same way. I guess that once we have kids, something will have to change. But for now? It works."

Looking around the apartment, sipping her Champagne, Constance couldn't help but feel a little pang of envy. Chiara really had her life together, a beautiful apartment, perfect wardrobe, perfect body, a fiancé who loved her, and a job she was passionate about. If it didn't mean that she would have exactly zero friends left, Constance might have let her envy get the better of her.

"Did you get all your packing done?"

"I did. You're a lifesaver. You saved me hours of agony."

As she took a second sip of Champagne, Constance decided that she would not admit to Chiara that she'd spent those magically gained hours that afternoon looking through her old pictures. Snapshots of her time spent in Europe. Flitting around Italy, fantasizing about being lady of the house at Lorenzo's mom's place. Living the good life, day by day, not worrying about what tomorrow would hold- until it had all ended. She had discussed the end of her relationship with Lorenzo with Chiara ad nauseam. But if she was honest with herself, she had held some things back. She hadn't been completely honest to her friend, or to herself. But what was the use, anyway? What was over was over.

"Are you OK?" Asked Chiara. "You look pensive."

"I'm fine. Just thinking," said Constance.

"You don't look too excited to be going to France."

Constance ignored the question and changed the subject.

"Can I help you with something?"

"Nope, spaghetti's done. I have a salad for us. And cookies."

"Tell me you didn't buy cannolis at Trader Joe's. I heard they had them in stock again."

"My Nonna's ghost would come pull out the hairs from my head one by one!"

A racket at the door, and in swept Sven, just as tall, blond, and glossy as Chiara, and dressed in a perfectly fitting suit, his white shirt crisp, despite the Miami humidity.

"Constance, I'm so pleased we get to see you before you go." He gave her a kiss on both cheeks.

"It's been too long," said Constance. She liked Sven, but she most often saw Chiara alone, not just because Sven traveled so much, but also, and this was embarrassing, but because it hurt a little to see two people close to her in such a happy relationship, when she had messed up the best one she'd been in. It felt petty and pathetic to admit that to herself, but if she couldn't admit it to herself, then to who?

"I'm going to go wash my hands. Be right back," said Sven.

"He's going to pee, isn't he? He's so formal," Constance said to Sven's retreating back, so he could hear her. "But he's looking great," she observed, once he was out of earshot.

"Yeah, he's been working out. He wants to look good for our wedding."

"Normally it's the bride who starves herself for her wedding dress," observed Constance. "But in your case, you don't have an ounce to lose."

"It's just genetics," Chiara shrugged.

Just genetics. Leave it to naturally skinny people to be so casual about the fact that they had won the DNA lottery. To act like it was no big deal that sample-sized clothes just happened to fit them right off the rack. Chiara should try dressing Constance's body for once. What would someone like Chiara do with a few extra inches of thigh to stuff into her fashionably slim legged jeans? How would her little camisoles look with less collarbone to hang off of? It wouldn't feel like just genetics then, would it? Constance blushed. What was wrong with her? She wasn't like this, normally. Normally she was able to keep the dark undercurrent of her thoughts at bay. It was something about leaving for Europe. Something about returning to the location that embodied her broken dreams that really had her on edge. At least she wasn't going to Italy, where she might bump into Lorenzo. Again, it irked her that she didn't know where Lorenzo was living these days. Stalking him on Instagram had hurt. Seeing him on trips around the world, in gorgeous locations, both for work and for pleasure, apparently. Bali. Vietnam. Cambodia. Portugal. Iceland. Dubai, the Maldives. All places that she would have loved to go to. If only things had turned out differently.

"Wait. When's the wedding?" Asked Constance, finally regaining control of her emotions. "Have you guys finally picked a date?"

"Summer, I think."

"This coming summer? So soon?"

Not that it was that soon, really- they'd been engaged for a couple of years now, but she'd almost been hoping that Chiara or Sven or both were dragging their feet, that they were unable to commit to something just like Constance was. Stop it, Constance.

"Well, the date's not been decided yet, but it's going to be a small wedding, so it's not like we need too much advance notice. But don't worry, you'll be the first to know."

"Where will it be, do you think?"

Constance closed her eyes. She feared the response.

"The family house, of course," said Chiara.

The family house. Of course. And that meant that something else was a matter of course, too. It meant that Lorenzo would be there. Lorenzo's family home was just a few miles away from Chiara's. Their families were friends, and in fact, that was how Constance had first met him. Well, how she'd first been supposed to meet him. Chiara was going to set them up on a blind date, an "accidental" meeting at a gallery opening. But upon entering the gallery, Constance had decided that she was no longer interested. Forget a stupid blind date. She had literally just clapped eyes on the most beautiful man she'd ever seen, standing in a corner. Dark haired, dark eyed, definitely European. And hopefully, if the electric current that had gone through her body when they'd locked eyes was any indication, maybe she was lucky enough that she was his type, too. She'd felt herself irresistibly drawn to him and was just starting to head his way when Chiara had grabbed her arm.

"Come. I'm going to introduce you to Lorenzo."

"No. I've changed my mind."

Chiara gave Constance that look. The perplexed and a little annoyed but still indulgent one she seemed to keep in heavy rotation with her.

"Why?"

"Because there is no way your Lorenzo has anything on that guy right over there. And in fact, I need to go talk to him. Now."

Chiara had laughed delightedly.

"That's Lorenzo, silly!"

For months after that, Chiara had never failed to mention what a fabulous matchmaker she was. And at first, Constance had been nothing but thankful to her. But then when things had fallen apart with Lorenzo, it had become a sore subject between them. Anytime Chiara mentioned an eligible male friend, Constance would roll her eyes.

"You don't have the best track record," she would say, which was unfair.

In any case, the wedding would be an awkward moment. She wondered how she would be able to turn down the invitation without her best friend hating her. She already knew she was maid of honor. But Chiara also had a lovely sister and a fabulous gay brother, either one of whom, or even both of whom could fulfill that role. Chiara would forgive her eventually, wouldn't she?

"Constance," warned Chiara. "I can see it in your eyes. You're not going to make some excuse not to come. You can't avoid Lorenzo for the rest of your life!"

"What are you talking about?" Said Constance. "I can quite easily avoid Lorenzo for the rest of my life. I haven't bumped into him in five years. Seeing him at your wedding would ruin the streak. Why would I put myself in that position?"

"Well, first of all, because I would kick your ass. And secondly, because maybe you need closure. Maybe seeing him will finally let you move on."

Constance was silent. Chiara was wrong. Seeing Lorenzo would only reignite the feelings she'd had. She hadn't just been in love with Lorenzo. She'd been addicted to Lorenzo. She had found him irresistible. Even when he'd driven her crazy. Even when they'd fought, and boy, did they fight. Even when she'd been jealous. Seeing him might make her sorry they'd broken up. Not that she'd had a choice in the matter. He had left her, and for a supermodel, no less.

Chapter 15

She woke up the next morning, made herself her usual triple espresso, and dressed in a festive orchid-colored silk dress. This was a vintage piece that she'd had tailored to make it look more modern. She would not have the opportunity to wear something like this for the next three months, at least. Who cared that she was just going to the salon to get her lashes colored? She wanted to enjoy every last moment of sunshine.

It felt weird not being in the office on a weekday. She wondered what Penelope was up to. She was probably wearing another one of her impeccable Chanel suits and gloating over her uninspired designs for the Xerces 2. Penelope didn't know what it was like to be worried about keeping her job. Penelope had rich parents. Constance knew they lived in Hong Kong somewhere, and she also knew that Penelope lived in a penthouse apartment in Key Biscayne. Not that she'd ever had Constance over. Or anyone else from the office, for that matter, other than Harold. Just like Penelope, to think that her peers were somehow below her.

Forget Penelope.

But she couldn't.

And, not for the first time, Constance wondered why Harold had really given her the Lombard 4 job- was it really an opportunity, or was he trying to get her out of the way?

Chapter 16

By the time her plane landed in the Nice Airport. Constance was absolutely shattered with exhaustion. She checked her watch- she'd swapped out her usual Apple watch for her maternal grandfather's 1960's Rolex Submariner, which she hadn't wanted to leave behind, but now, she realized that she had no idea what time it was, so pulled out her phone and confirmed that it actually didn't matter what time it was. She focused on what she had to do- Harold had arranged for her to effectively purchase a French car. It was a tax ploy, where you could buy the car and then return it after a few months, and it was a more advantageous rate than renting. The other advantage was that you could return the car with as much damage as you pleased. Constance had some bad memories of getting her rental car keyed in a flea market parking lot near Paris, and did not want to repeat the experience, or at least worry about it. The car she was getting was something she never would have chosen for herself, in a hideous shade of rust that clashed with her hair. She had already gone through customs in Paris, so after picking up her heavy suitcases, she dragged them through the airport, following the instructions the car agency had given her. Of course, their lot was far as possible away from the terminal, and, as luck would have it, it started raining at the very moment she left the shelter of the airport. Upon arriving at the rental office, she realized there was no one inside the prefab building. She searched desperately through her emails, eating up her data, until she found a contact number. A mere thirty minutes later, soaked to the bone, sweaty yet freezing, and profoundly frustrated, she finally got behind the wheel. She plugged the directions to the hotel in Saint Tropez where she was staying the first night into her phone. She was glad that she had elected to meet up with the yacht owner the next day, when she would hopefully be a little bit fresher. Most of the hotels were closed for the season, and she'd been lucky to find this one. This was exactly what she hated about Saint Tropez in the off season. This hotel did not look ultra-promising, and she hoped that they at least had a valet service, because she certainly did not want to imagine herself lugging her suitcases through the cobblestone streets in the rain. And, they had better have room service.

After getting lost multiple times, she finally found herself in front of the hotel. There was no one in sight and the car was double parked, but at this point Constance did not care. Finally, a bellhop came out and retrieved her suitcases. "You have room service, right?" She asked, as she followed him in.

"No, mademoiselle, not in the offseason," said the concierge. "There is an Italian restaurant that's open down the street." Fantastic, thought Constance. My first meal in France will be Italian.

She went to her room, took a quick shower to warm up, and threw on her most comfortable, least exciting outfit. There was no one she needed to show off for.

Finally, checking to see that the rain had stopped, she took herself down the street to the Italian restaurant that the concierge had suggested. There were quite a few people inside, probably because it was one of the only choices in town. After having ordered a glass of local wine and a plate of pasta, Constance decided that things were looking up. Staying glued to her phone was too American, so she glanced around the room to entertain herself. There were a few couples who looked like they lived there full time. A few people who might have been businesspeople, maybe realtors or yacht brokers. An artist type. And someone who looked strangely familiar. No. It couldn't be. Constance narrowed her eyes, waiting for the man to turn his head. Surely it wasn't who she thought it was. The man did look singularly like Lorenzo, but that was just her imagination talking. Lorenzo had long hair that he sometimes wore in a ponytail. This man had shorter hair. Lorenzo had been clean shaven. This man had a bit of scruff. Totally not Lorenzo. But still…definitely her type. Maybe her time in Saint Tropez wouldn't be so bad, after all.

Then, the man turned his head. Crap. It was Lorenzo. He made eye contact, and of course, their eyes locked, like they had the very first time they had met. He at least had the decency to look a little shocked, but then got up and casually walked over to her table, taking his time, as if she wasn't freaking out right now. There was still a tiny chance that this was a stranger who happened to look just like the guy she hadn't been able to get completely out of her mind for the past five years.

"Constance?"

"What the hell are you doing here?"

Not the friendliest greeting, but she felt justified.

"Having dinner."

His typical way of not answering a question.

"Ha. So funny."

"Thanks. What are you doing here?"

She wasn't going to be petty and use his own response on him. Besides, she wanted him to know that she still had a job, the same job, in fact. She wasn't that flighty.

"I'm working. On a yacht project."

"Oh? Which one?"

"The Lombard 4," said Constance, a bit of pride sneaking into her voice.

"Oh. Well, that's a bit of a shit show, isn't it?"

Constance narrowed her eyes.

"What's that supposed to mean?"

"You're not the first designer to work on that project. It seems that the client doesn't know what he wants."

Well, that makes two of us, thought Constance. Harold had mentioned something about the client firing other designers, but she hadn't thought much of it. That sort of thing happened all the time. But if it was common knowledge around town, well, that meant something more serious. So, Harold was trying to get her out of the way. She wasn't going to give Lorenzo the pleasure of seeing that he'd gotten to her.

"It'll be fine."

Lorenzo was staring at her now, a bemused expression on his face. Don't look into his eyes…don't do it.

"God, how long has it been, Constance? Five years?"

"That long? Really?"

It had been four years and ten months, and no, she wasn't pathetic enough to count the days.

"Well," she said, as her food arrived, "It was nice to see you. I would say see you around, but I bet you'll be leaving soon, I suppose you were here for one of your photo shoots?"

"No, not really," said Lorenzo.

That was odd. Constance was waiting for an explanation, not that she cared, really, when Lorenzo's phone went off.

"Sorry," he said. "I have to take this. I'll see you around."

And just like that, Constance was left at the table, her pasta growing cold, her heart aching, as she watched him walking away, his phone to his ear. He was still as handsome as ever. His black hair and his dark gray eyes were a striking combination, to be sure. Which supermodel was Lorenzo having a dalliance with these days? Dammit, she hadn't checked for a ring. It didn't matter, anyway. He would probably be gone soon enough, despite what he had said. And if she did run into him again, well, she wasn't forced to speak to him or spend any time with him, was she? She would be busy with her project. She tucked into her pasta, which, though tepid, was delicious, and took notes in her phone, reminding herself to track down the designers who had been fired from the project. But of course, she couldn't focus, even less so than usual.

Lorenzo, here? What were the odds?

Chapter 17

Constance awoke ravenous. She threw on a cashmere sweater, a pair of sensible trousers that she would never wear in Miami, her ankle boots, which she had realized yesterday were no match for wet cobblestones, and the overpriced- but pretty-parka Harold had bought her in Vail a few years ago and that she had never worn since. She ran a hand through her russet waves and deemed her appearance good enough. Now, she would definitely not run into anyone she knew. That Lorenzo spotting the night before was enough of a coincidence for the rest of the decade. She ran through her morning plan in her mind. Coffee and a croissant. Then back to the hotel for a shower, a change, and to collect her belongings before her meeting with the yacht owner, Peter Holmes. She'd decided to leave her things at the front desk of the hotel until after her meeting. Not that she was planning on flirting with him, but she didn't want Holmes' first impression of her to be of a sweaty, frazzled woman lugging two suitcases and a carry-on onto his boat, like, Hi, you might fire me, but I'm moving in! Again, she cursed Harold for putting her in this situation. Did he really resent her that much?

But she was up for a challenge. That's how her brain worked. No challenge, no interest.

She decided to take an indirect route to the café. She had been pleased to learn that Le Senequier, her favorite local institution, was open all winter. She'd tried to look up which other places were traditionally open during the winter, and not only were they few and far between, but she was sure that Covid had done a number on those, too. She realized with zero satisfaction that she would probably be leaving town just when things started opening up again. She should romanticize her life. It might make her feel better. Saint Tropez in the winter did have a quiet charm, didn't it? She had to admit that the facades of the building were just as pastel and picturesque in the cold December light. And the cobblestone streets, devoid of tourists, felt like they were all her own, which could be cool until she slipped on one and broke her ankle. When she rounded the corner and saw the sparkling water in the harbor, she finally did break into a sincere smile. The rain had cleared for just long enough to create an illusion of summer. Several people were sitting under the red awning of the legendary café, where countless celebrities and politicians had whiled away hours enjoying coffee and pastries over the years. Constance started salivating already as she thought of the croissant she was going to treat herself to. She deserved it. And croissants in France magically had less calories than American ones, right? She chose a seat with an optimal vantage point on the harbor, and on anyone walking by. There was very little people watching to be had, so she wanted to make sure not to miss a single passerby. Most of the people she did spot were dressed quite casually, and were walking dogs, most of them designer dogs. Maybe Constance would make some friends here. Maybe she would find a crew, to go out to dinner with or play card games, or to do whatever they did for fun here when nothing else was going on. Constance put in her order for a coffee and a pastry with the server and then sat back and relaxed. Almost immediately, the items were deposited on her table. She sipped the scalding hot liquid, which was not quite a Cuban coffee, but which held its own, and enjoyed the feeling of her body and nervous system waking up. She was horrifically jet lagged, which gave everything a disconcerting fuzziness and she knew from experience that the worst was yet to come. She turned her head a fraction of an inch to the left, to discreetly check out some of the other patrons in the cafe. One thing she loved to do was to invent people's life stories. She would often use this to inform her designs. After all, what was better than a story? She always told her clients that she was helping to tell their story, or to make their story more interesting, as the case may be. Again, she thought back to the yacht she had grown up on, and how its straightforward, noble, sturdy design was what really called to her, if she had to be completely honest with herself. All of these new money yacht owners who wanted the most modern, the most technologically advanced, the glossiest, and the most luxurious- she had to admit that she felt a little bit of condescension towards them. She was good at her job, and versed in a number of design styles, but she knew what was right. Then, she turned her head ever so slightly to the right and groaned. She was afraid to turn her head much more, but she had taken in a man's aquiline profile, the dark hair cut so that it was just skimming the collar of his shirt. She couldn't see his eyes, because he was wearing a pair of dark sunglasses. Dammit. She couldn't believe that she had forgotten hers in the hotel room. Sunglasses were essential, not just to protect her eyes from the winter sun, but also to be able to people watch more discreetly, and to provide some level of camouflage, not that her traitorous hair didn't give her away instantly.

With a little luck, Lorenzo hadn't spotted her. He seemed deep in thought, anyway. To try to calm down her hammering heart, she turned her own thoughts, almost successfully, to the upcoming meeting with Peter, the owner of the yacht. Would he be nice? Would he be there the whole time? Would he expect her to be there the whole time? She knew that Harold had said she needed to be on site to supervise, but surely, he wouldn't mind if she stepped away for a weekend or two. Not that she had anywhere specific to go, but she was in Europe, for God's sake! And Lorenzo being here meant that Italy was safe for a visit.

On that subject, what was she going to do about Lorenzo? Nothing, she decided. She had grown up in these five years. Lorenzo was not her person. He had hurt her in a way that she had never been hurt before or since. She would never let someone like him in ever again, that much she had promised to herself. From now on, it was all strategy, with everything she did. She and Chiara had developed a test: Will this make me richer, hotter or happier? If it did not, it should not happen. Unfortunately, some things were a challenge, like croissants, because they made her happier, but definitely not hotter. And then, there were the things that she initially thought would make her happy, that she eventually noticed weren't making her as happy as she'd thought they would, and that's when she would cut and run. It wasn't being flaky, it was just a refusal to waste time, she reasoned with herself. Speaking of wasting time, it was time to go.

She ventured a peek to see if Lorenzo was still there. If so, she would escape to the left, hoping that he wouldn't notice her. Just as she turned her head, he turned his, as well, and she found herself staring straight into his sunglasses. He gave her that crooked smile of his, and Constance's breath hitched in her throat. She started to sweat, trying to stop the memories that came flooding into her mind. The happy times. The hot times. Like once, when he had driven her home, and they hadn't been able to wait. She still blushed when she thought about the eyeful that her neighbors had potentially gotten as Lorenzo took her against the door to the apartment complex. There was their one-year anniversary, when he had woken her up with a breakfast in bed, which had been completely wasted, because he'd looked at her in that way. But then of course, there was the memory of when he had left her. It still hurt.

Before she knew what was going on, Lorenzo was getting up from his chair, and coming towards her. Please no, she thought. But she couldn't help noticing that his body was more muscular than it had been before. But he dressed as he always had, in vintage jeans that hinted at what was beneath. A casual shirt tucked into a waistband highlighted by the belt of the day. Lorenzo collected belts and belt buckles, just as he collected watches, and hats, and boots, and today she noticed he wore an Argentine polo belt, probably gifted to him by his friend Diego, an Argentine polo player who was now making wine in Napa with his wife.

Constance wanted to look away. Really, she did, but instead she just kept staring, as Lorenzo came closer and closer, weaving his way between the tightly packed tables and chairs. It was too late to run away now, wasn't it? Too late to fake a fainting spell or to disappear under her chair. Before she knew it, she was looking up at him.

"You again. What are you doing here?"

"Coffee and croissant. Same as you, my darling."

"I'm not your darling anymore," said Constance. "And you know I don't mean what are you doing at Le Senequier, I mean more like, what the hell are you doing here in Saint Tropez?"

"I live here," said Lorenzo.

Constance almost choked on the last sip of cold coffee she'd been pretending to take just to act more casual.

"What do you mean, you live here? That seems like career suicide."

"It would be," said Lorenzo, "except that, unlike you, I have changed careers since the last time we saw each other."

Great. They'd had fights over their respective careers, how they weren't conducive to a serious relationship, and now he had decided to change after they had broken up? Great timing. He was definitely married. She went to check for a ring, but his hand was in his coat pocket.

"Well, what are you doing now?"

"That," said Lorenzo, "is a conversation that we should have over dinner. Are you busy this evening?"

Constance shook her head. She wasn't going to play so easy to get. After what Lorenzo had done to her, it was absolutely not an option. Sure, if she got bored enough, maybe she could toy with him…no, that was impossible. Too dangerous.

"I don't know if I'm busy or not," said Constance. "I'm here for my client- I'm probably going to be at his beck and call."

"Well, that has always been the case with you and your clients, hasn't it?" Said Lorenzo, a bit bitterly, Constance thought. As if he was one to judge.

"I'm sure we can see each other sometime," Constance offered, kicking herself for giving in.

"Well, yes, I imagine so. Saint Tropez is a small town, especially in the offseason. I think it would be impossible to avoid each other completely," said Lorenzo.

Funny, now he was acting like she had wronged him.

"Well, I need to go," said Constance. "It was great seeing you. I'm sure I'll see you around."

"Well, if you're not as busy with your client tonight as you thought you might be, and if you're interested, there's an event I'll be at. You should come."

"Sure. Maybe. What is it?"

"A magazine pre-launch."

A magazine pre-launch? Now this was fortuitous. When Harold had first said that the yacht owner absolutely insisted on having his yacht photographed and featured in a magazine, she had scoffed at the absolute impossibility of it. But the owner hadn't specified how big or established said magazine needed to be. Regional magazines were a dime a dozen, but one based in Saint Tropez would have a certain status attached to it. Sure, maybe the magazine Lorenzo was referring to was an art magazine or for some other niche that would be of no use to her, but it couldn't hurt for her to check out the event. In fact, maybe she would even bring her client. If he was still handsome, maybe it might make Lorenzo a bit jealous, retroactively.

"Can I bring my client if he's interested?"

"Sure," said Lorenzo, his mouth briefly forming into a straight line that showed his displeasure. Good. Constance liked that about him. He didn't have much of a poker face.

"Here, give me your phone number," he said, "and I'll text you the details."

"It's still the same one," said Constance. "Or did you delete it?"

"I have it," said Lorenzo.

She tried to tamp down the little flutter that snuck its way into her heart. She wished he wasn't wearing sunglasses, so she could see the look in his eye. She hadn't deleted his number, either, but if he had moved to another country, he'd probably changed his.

"Got to go- I'll see you around," Constance said, standing up. Being face to face with him almost took her breath away. He's bad for you, stupid. Remember, you closed that door. You're not going there again. He showed you what he's made of.

As she walked away, heart beating hard, feeling nauseous, she wondered how she could possibly take her power back. Maybe Lorenzo would be good for an affair, something with no strings attached. After all, she knew that they fit together quite neatly. He did know what made her tick. What made her moan. And she knew all his secret spots, the ones that made him growl like some kind of wild animal. Stop it, Constance. It was impossible to have no strings attached with that one. There was something about him that drew her in. She was as if addicted to him. For her, he was like cigarettes. Some people could do it, but she had found that she couldn't smoke just one. Fall into bed with Lorenzo just for fun, and she would find herself wanting more, and more. And life was hard enough without that. Still, she found herself thinking of how he had changed, physically. Had she changed, in his eyes? Did he still find her attractive? Why does it matter? You don't care, remember? She reminded herself.

Chapter 18

Showered, changed, packed, she checked her watch one last time, checked out, and speed-walked back to the harbor. Thankfully, the Lombard 4 was parked by the harbor parking, and not right in front of the Senequier, because if that was a place that Lorenzo frequented often, she would hate to think that she would be within his line of sight as she woke up in the morning and as she went to bed at night. As she approached the end of the waterfront walk, she saw it. The Lombard 4 was a large, wide, yet streamlined yacht of recent manufacture. She didn't quite know why it was being redecorated so quickly. She'd confirmed that Peter had been the one to commission the previous boring design, so why was he so intent on changing it again, so soon? Maybe he had better taste than she thought. Or maybe the yacht held some bad memories for him. In that case, better just to sell it. Constance knew that bad vibes would magnify on the water, or at least she believed that. It certainly had held true for what had happened in her family. Her parents' arguments, on their DeFever, had escalated so quickly that it had almost been dizzying, and before she had known it, her father was out and happily ensconced on a motor catamaran with his mistress. In that case, the water had precipitated their marriage, and the mistress had quickly become stepmother #1. And then, her mom had gotten sick, they'd had to sell the boat and move to a rental apartment in a dismal second-rate marina, and after her mom had died, she'd had to move in with her dad. Stepmother number one was an absolute angel compared to Stepmother #2, who came along within six months, but neither one had been very keen on having Constance be a big part of their lives. She supposed that was understandable. She had made it rather a hobby as a teenager to be as difficult as possible and to test the limits of anyone's affection. Some might say she was still doing that.

As she examined the boat more closely, she took in its unique green hull. Funny, Peter's previous boat had been red. So, he was a guy who liked unique colored boats. The yacht had many gleaming wood details remaining in the outside spaces. This was a pleasant surprise, as the interior was all carbon and poly fibers. It opened them up to more design options, should they choose to keep the wood, which she hoped they would. As she approached the gangplank, Constance had a gnawing feeling in the pit of her stomach, the anxiety that always formed there when she met a new client. But this time, there was a lot more riding on this. She needed to try to do this job without any crutches. No design assistants. No getting Harold to smooth things over. And no flirtation. She'd been furious when Harold had pointed out her foibles, but he did have a point. Besides, none of the so-called relationships with her clients had ever yielded anything worthwhile. All that time, all that effort, and she had nothing to show for it, save a few handbags that soon went out of style, or a few pieces of jewelry that she felt guilty wearing in the first place. She wasn't any closer to her dream of settling down, having a family, and living a meaningful life.

She would finish this job, she swore to herself, and then she would decorate her damn apartment in Miami, and then she would try to see how to stop being flaky and flighty and inconstant.

The gangplank of the yacht was down. Oddly enough, there were no staff members that she could see, but she supposed that this was a function of it being off season and of the yacht not being operational or currently being used for entertainment. She stepped up, calling out, "knock, knock." The sliding doors opened, and there stood Peter Holmes, in an awkward sort of antechamber to the main saloon.

Peter Holmes was definitely still a good-looking man. He had bit of a dad bod, but he carried it well. His light chestnut hair curled over his ears, cut in a relaxed style that whispered that he did not need to work in a conventional office. She knew from her research that Peter Holmes was at the head of several multinational conglomerates. She wondered how people like that got it all done. Was that the solution for her? Head up several companies, so she could jump from spot to spot without anyone judging her for being flighty? How was that different from what she did? Oh yeah, the billionaire part.

She shook his hand. No sparks whatsoever. Good.

"Harold tells me that you're going to be able to carry out my vision," said Peter, "and though I respect his optimism and his faith in you, that remains to be seen."

"I relish a challenge," said Constance, which was true enough. But she was growing worried.

"Good. I've already lost two designers. They couldn't hack it."

Ohh no, thought Constance. Peter Holmes was attractive enough on the outside, but she was starting to suspect that on the inside it was a whole different story.

"Yes, let's talk about that," said Constance. "Tell me about what you wanted, and about what went wrong?"

"Isn't it your job to figure out what I want? And I'd rather not talk about mistakes in the past," said Peter.

Great, thought Constance.

"I think the first step is for us to get to know each other a bit. That way, hopefully, we'll start to narrow down an aesthetic and a concept that will suit you."

Constance smiled reassuringly at Peter, more to calm her own nerves than to make him feel good.

"Why don't you show me around?" She suggested. "I have to tell you, my first impression is, it's a gorgeous boat."

Peter shrugged.

"Yeah, it's fine."

Oh great. So, he was one of those. People who took the fact that their belongings were top-notch as a matter of course. They were definitely not off to a good start.

"You've seen this space," Peter said, gesturing around them to the small, bookcase-lined antechamber. "Let's go look at the main living room first."

He led her into a large saloon, complete with a striking but slightly gimmicky central fireplace. Large windows opened out onto expansive views of the Golfe de Saint Tropez. Constance knew that this was one of the big challenges with boat design: making spaces feel homey and comfortable, while working with space restraints and taking advantage of the views; trying to create something that felt decorated, without taking away from what was outside. Which brought her to her first question.

"Peter, do you tend to stay in the Mediterranean, or do you plan on taking this yacht across the ocean?" She did not admit that she knew that Peter's previous craft had been mostly parked in St Barts.

"I would like to have the option to do both the Mediterranean and the Caribbean," said Peter. "My staff would take it over."

"Do you plan on renting it out or having it chartered?" Asked Constance.

"I'd like to have the option," said Peter.

Great. Another noncommittal answer. But Peter continued.

"But it's not something I would prefer to do. Right now, I can afford not to, and I'd rather keep my space to myself, if I can." That made sense. Even though most owners did not spend too much time on their yacht overall, if they could afford to, they kept them for their personal use. Yachts tended to take quite a beating from the elements to begin with, and if you factored in irresponsible charter clients, it could be a disaster inside and out.

"Do you have a dedicated captain who's been working with you for a while?"

This was an important question. A long-term captain might have some asks when it came to the design, which an owner would be sensitive to.

A thundercloud crossed Peter's face. Oh oh… had she asked the wrong question?

"I'm interviewing new candidates," said Peter.

Oh, so that was why the boat was in a harbor traditionally not used for renovations. He didn't have anyone he trusted to move it. And this was clearly a sensitive subject. She wondered what that was about. At the very least, she was starting to understand that this whole project was emotionally fraught.

"How about the style? Is this something that you like, or are you trying to depart from this?"

"Well, I think it's a little boring," said Peter.

"Got it. And you might want to open out the space, eliminate the foyer we entered through?"

"No!"

Constance snapped to attention. Now she was getting somewhere.

"That's a place I've been using to read and get away from it all. When people aren't visiting, of course. I know it's awkward, but I like it."

"Ah, got it," said Constance. "So, I could create a library for you."

She was pleased to see a strong opinion, and a new side to Peter's personality. That he liked to read made him rise in her esteem just a little bit. Also, she had always felt that the spot just inside of the sliding doors was a prime space- both public, and private. Yet in many boats, it was wasted, frequently taken up by stairs, and a weird dining room, or simply opening directly onto the main saloon, without transition. She could definitely create a fun library. It would have to function as a pass-through yet remain intimate.

"That'll be a fun challenge," she told him, her enthusiasm temporarily making her throw caution to the wind.

"What do you mean, challenge? Have you not done a library before?"

Ugh. She'd said the wrong thing.

"I have done libraries before," said Constance, "but I like to push myself to do something new each time, hence the challenge. What most decorators like is to always be reaching for something new."

"Oh. That's not what I got from the other two," said Peter.

"We're not talking about them, remember?" Constance said. She hoped that by agreeing with his refusal to talk about the past, she would win some sympathy points. But this was hard work. She and Peter Holmes did not exactly have what you might call instant chemistry. Of course, she thought about Lorenzo again. That party he had mentioned. She could tell that Peter was probably dying to get away from her. Her thinking she might take her new client to a party now seemed delusional, even if it had been her M.O. in the past. Would she go to the party? She forced herself to focus on the job at hand.

"So, in terms of seating, and in terms of capacity, are you planning on entertaining a lot on this yacht, or not so much?"

"I'm entertaining less and less these days," said Peter. "When I was in Saint Barts, I had another boat that I ended up selling. I got a little sick of the nonstop lunches with the same old, same old people…so personally, I think I see this yacht as a getaway for myself. I just need to eradicate any bad vibes."

Right. Bad vibes. Yikes. Did he think there were bad vibes on this boat?

"I know they have a thing called Feng shui. I don't know if that's what I need?"

"Yeah, I'm familiar with that," said Constance. "OK, let's move to the next space, shall we?"

Peter guided her to the front of the boat, where there was a thin hallway opening to two staterooms, each of them with spectacular views to the front of the boat. It was a little odd, Constance thought, to not capture the front views with an owner's suite.

"How many bedrooms do you need on this boat? How many are here now?" She asked.

"The main stateroom is downstairs. And there are two more cabins, and bunk rooms for the staff."

"Is that sufficient, or do you want more? I'm wondering if you would be amenable to reorganizing the space so that it flowed better?"

"That might be a good idea," Peter allowed. Constance examined both staterooms. They were pleasant, they were lovely, but nothing that special. Pretty run-of-the-mill high-end yacht design. She could certainly do better than this, but she wondered what the key mistake was that had gotten the previous two decorators fired.

"All right, shall we look below deck? she asked.

Peter showed her around- first, the galley, which was surprisingly large, pleasantly so.

"This is large- unless you cook yourself. Do you?"

"Actually, I do," said Peter. "No one's ever asked me that before. Everyone always assumes that I have a chef, which of course I do. But I do like to piddle around in the kitchen."

Constance made a note of that.

"How often would you say that you cook?"

"Pretty often, now that you ask," said Peter. "Ideally, my idea of entertaining would be just cooking for two or three people and enjoying some great food and great views together. I don't need to have massive yacht parties or even a catered lunch, and terms of the everyday, I don't need a crew to be cooking every meal for me. I can make my own breakfast."

This was different than most clients, thought Constance. She knew that the charter set liked having a dedicated chef because it was different from what they had at home. But somebody like Peter Holmes probably had a full-time chef wherever he went, so cooking would be a novel and pleasant experience. Still, she would need a full crew kitchen, for caterers or for anyone who would charter the boat, or for resale value. But maybe there was something that could be done to personalize the experience of cooking here. Also, the staff quarters were cramped. No reason for the crew to live like animals. After all, this was a very large boat. She mentioned this to Peter, cautiously, and was pleased when he agreed.

"By the way, you can choose any of the bedrooms down here for yourself. I'm upstairs," said Peter.

Ah. So, he had taken one of the above deck staterooms. This reinforced her thinking.

"OK, so what's on the top deck? Can we go look at that?"

They made their way up to a gym and a bar and a small indoor-outdoor saloon that took up almost the whole upstairs indoor space of the boat, other than the control room. Large decks surrounded the space, including a front deck with a hot tub and deck chairs. There might be room for another dining area up here because honestly, Constance had always disliked the traditional location of the main dining area, on the back of the main level, which meant that it would be closest to the harbor. there was nothing wrong with using this space when one was moored further out, or in a home marina where one could socialize with friends from there, but in a harbor like Saint Tropez, Constance thought it was a bit pathetic and try-hard to eat looking back at all the people who were staring at you, wondering who you were, and how you made your money. She made the calculated risk of mentioning this to Peter.

"Ha. I've always thought that, too."

She almost earned herself a full-fledged smile for that one. Not quite, but it was a start.

"All right, I can start getting some vision boards together," Constance said. "I guess I'll go get my things from the hotel…"

It was a bit awkward to be staying on the same boat as the owner, especially as there had not been any kind of a romantic vibe from him, and she intended to keep it that way. She thought back to Carlos White. She'd known from the first five minutes that their relationship would get personal. Within two hours, they'd been going at it in one of the cabins, and within a week, she had essentially moved in with him for the duration of the job. Carlos had been charming. She really had liked him, but she didn't have feelings beyond that. It had felt good to play at being a housewife on a yacht. If you were going to be the housewife, that was the best kind of housewife to be. And it had been lovely, fantasizing about these things, but frankly, it had been a relief when Harold had called her back, and now, she felt nothing more than guilt at the fact that she had not finished the job. Nothing strong enough that she might feel like picking up the phone to send Carlos a text to see how he was, and to organize how to order some of the last elements the yacht needed. Better to let him simmer down, maybe. He had been pretty pissed off when she'd left so quickly, after all. Why had he been surprised? Most times, relationships around yachts were just as fickle and as changing as the weather out on the ocean. And frankly, that suited Constance.

"Alright, I'll go pick up my car and my luggage, and I'll get cracking at this," she said. "I know that you're in a bit of a hurry." Peter didn't react one way or the other, so she soldiered on. "In terms of the manufacturers for things, we do have access to a shop over in Grimaud. I'll go chat with them once we start to nail down a concept."

"Sounds good," said Peter.

He seemed a bit distracted. Was he already thinking of firing her? Hard to tell. She headed back to the hotel, thinking about the project, but unfortunately her brain's gears were spinning, but not producing anything beyond static. She ran through her mental rolodex of fabrics, of textures, of shapes. The ideas kept slipping away, ever elusive. Come on, Muse, show yourself, bitch, she thought. This was ridiculous. How could it be that she could sometimes come up with a genius design and finish something in a few hours that would take most people weeks to do, but now, she was drawing a complete blank? She would grab some more inspiration as she went, but time was of the essence. It took a long time to fabricate elements for yachts. There were long waiting lists. The artisans were busy. She didn't want to end up with a last-minute type of situation that would stress everyone out.

Chapter 19

Later that afternoon, Constance sat in her bedroom on the yacht, almost catatonic. Her interaction with Peter had left her disconcerted. His demands seemed vague, his communication skills non-existent, and she wondered how she was going to hold it together to keep working on this project, to carry it through to fruition. But right now, she deserved a break, after having dug into the furthest recesses of her mind to try to come up with some kind of a unique plan to decorate this God-forsaken yacht. Seeing something different and new, and perhaps even meeting some new people, people who might help her to get this yacht in a magazine, would do her a world of good. Seeing Lorenzo was a necessary evil. She opened her suitcase on the bed in the large but poorly designed space, determining that future bedrooms would need a suitcase rack. She felt briefly guilty about dirtying the silky bed covers, but decided that those would be changed as well, so it ultimately did not matter. Completely redesigning a yacht was a big waste of money, because since so many of the elements were custom, they would need to scrap almost everything. Resale was not expected, but she might try. Maybe it would give her an extra influx of money on top of what Harold was offering her. 50 Euros a day. Ridiculous, she scoffed. How dare he? Still, it was 50 Euros that she would not be getting if she was in Miami. She went through her suitcases, glad she hadn't listened to Chiara, or she would have packed none of the unique pieces that would be appropriate for social events. Ultimately, she found her trusty pair of black leather trousers, a printed silk blouse, and a blue cashmere cardigan, which she would top with her black coat. She added a pair of vintage earrings and a swipe of red lipstick. She gazed at her reflection and noted that the mirrors in the new design should have better lighting. This cabin was ridiculous. It was obviously designed by a man who didn't need to check his makeup. She ran a brush through her hair, and then added some of the oil she had discovered in Saint Barts. This product was perfect for smoothing down her waves and giving her hair the scent of a tropical vacation. How she wished she was back in Saint Barts.

She looked at her reflection again. She looked OK. Well, it was now or never. She went upstairs and was pleased to note that Peter was not in any of the public spaces. Stepping off the yacht and into the harbor, she felt strangely exposed, as if on stage. What must it be like in the middle of the summer, when everyone was staring from the cafes across the way? She hoped her outfit would be appropriate for the event. Also, she dreaded feeling fatter than any of the French girls who would be there. Most of the time, she tried not to let it bother her that she had a more curvaceous build. But no matter how many men told her that she was desirable and sexy; she couldn't see it for herself. Maybe that, too, was why she had the tendency to cut and run. She couldn't trust that someone would want to stay with her, when there were so many skinny girls in the world. Intellectually, she knew she was fun, and stylish, and sometimes smart, had a lot to offer, and maybe, yes, was a little sexy. But insecurity was a relentless beast.

She checked the address on the invitation Lorenzo had texted her one more time, as if she couldn't trust it not to have changed since the last time she'd checked. The party was being held in an art gallery on one of the side streets that she believed she had been to in previous summers. Chiara, from her lofty perch in the art world, always mocked these galleries. Overpriced art for tourists, she called it. Constance wasn't as snobby as Chiara, at least when it came to her art selections. Maybe there would be some pieces on show that she could scope out for this project. Maybe that would make the Muse come back to play. What did her muse want? Did she need to be fed? Did she need to be taken on vacation? Did she need some music? Constance wasn't quite sure, but hopefully she would figure out what it was, because time was a 'wasting. Anyway, the gallery was secondary. Whatever this magazine was, she hoped that it was one in which perhaps she could feature the yacht. That would make Peter Holmes and Harold happy. But for now, what she really needed was a good glass of wine, and maybe a bit of cheese to calm her nervous stomach. She reminded herself that she needed to go shopping to stock the laughably small fridge on the yacht, and wondered where Peter got his food. Where was Peter tonight, by the way? None of her business, she supposed.

The streets of Saint Tropez were dark, her steps echoing on the damp cobblestones. It hadn't rained, but there was a mist swirling about that made the whole place a bit spooky. Still very beautiful, but also bleak. It was such a departure from how it was the other half of the year. If she was romanticizing her life, she would walk in the very middle of the street and think how lucky she was to have it all to herself. She tried that for a minute. But then she felt ridiculous and got cold. Finally, she reached the intersection she was looking for. Just down the street, she noticed a swath of yellow light pouring out from a storefront, people spilling out into the street as well, their cigarette smoke wafting over to Constance and making her crave one. She could hear laughing, and notes of music as she came closer. Her heart fluttered. Would Lorenzo have some supermodel on his arm? She hated it that she still cared who he was with. But no one would like to have their nose rubbed in the fact that they hadn't been good enough for someone, did they? She hadn't truly been his type. End of story. It happened. Though he could have fooled her. Right from the beginning, their relationship had been hot and heavy, to say the least. And it wasn't just the physical stuff. That could be chalked up to lust. There were also the declarations he had made to her, which had let her to believe that they had a future.

She came closer to the gallery. She could change her mind and just turn around and go back to the yacht and watch a romantic comedy on her laptop. She could order a pizza from that one place that was still open. Stuff her face and drink some local wine that cost nothing but tasted more than passable. No, she needed to force herself to go in. This would be good for her. She needed to start building a support system in Saint Tropez. Maybe there would be someone nice around her age, someone in her industry who wouldn't try to be such a competitor like Penelope was. Maybe she would get some hints on places to go on the weekend to get out of here and actually see something lively. Maybe she would meet a cute guy, one who would make her pass the time and forget Lorenzo once and for all. She stepped inside, relieved to feel that it was warm and dry, peeled off her coat, and scanned the room for a second, trying to get her bearings and locate the bar.

Of course, the first person she saw was Lorenzo. He met her eyes and gave her a warm smile that started to melt her heart, until she remembered. She must have made a face, because his smile quickly transformed into a straight line. What was that about? She was the one who should be upset, not him. And of course, as expected, Lorenzo was surrounded by gorgeous 6-foot tall glamazons. What were girls like that even doing in bleak off-season Saint Tropez? They must have been there just for him. Did he now have a stable of supermodels at his disposal at all times? He'd gotten even worse than he was before. Constance decided to ignore him, because he was obviously otherwise occupied. She might wander by and say hello casually when she was good and ready. Or not. She headed to the bar in the corner and ordered a glass of wine from the attractive, dark haired young man standing behind it.

"Bonjour," said Constance. "Un verre de vin, s'il vous plait."

The bartender startled for a second, seemed to pause, and then said, "Oh. American!"

Constance's French had grown rusty, yes. She had been a pretty good linguist, had held her own in both French and Italian, but ever since she had realized that she would probably never fulfill her dream of living in Europe, she had let them slide. Ever since she'd been back working stateside, she had picked up more Spanish, which was more useful when dealing with installers, but was too bad, because she missed Italian. Its melodious, sing-song qualities. The fact that it described some of her favorite things: food and wine, and love.

"Yes, I'm American," she said, shifting into English. "I'm new here- spending the winter. Are you from here?"

"Yes," said the young man.

"Do you work in the gallery?"

"I work for the magazine. I'm just bartending for the evening."

"Ah, nice to meet you. I'm Constance."

"Sebastian."

Constance was about to ask whether the editor in chief was present, but a couple of girls unceremoniously jostled her from behind, seemingly desperate to get a drink, and she was forced to get out of the way. She headed to the other side of the room, the furthest one from where Lorenzo was holding court. She slowly made her way across the large gallery space, smiling at various people who didn't seem very keen on returning her smile. But maybe she was just being a weird American. She knew that French people took longer to warm up to strangers. Most of the crowd were probably gallery owners, chefs, artists, musicians. She wondered if, after the pandemic, some younger French creative types who were able to work remotely had decided to take advantage of the inexpensive winter rents in places like Saint Tropez and live there year-round. That may have been the case, but she told herself she would not have picked this place. Talk about dead. But maybe they had their own community. Maybe they had a way of keeping it fun. She was hoping that they would let her in to this little secret club of theirs, if it existed. Probably the person who would know the most about that would be Lorenzo, she told herself. Hell if she was going to ask him, though.

She had arrived at the far wall and decided to start focusing on some of the photography on display, pictures of the harbor in St Tropez, but exceptionally well done, with a great balance of shade and light, and attention to interesting details and proportions. Whoever the photographer was, they were very talented. If Lorenzo had ever challenged himself by photographing something other than already beautiful women, maybe he might have reached this level of mastery. Constance was not one of these people who thought that photography was as easy as just point and click. Whenever she heard people talking about how the advent of filters, Photoshop, and Instagram had made everyone a photographer, she would shake her head. She didn't believe that was the case. In fact, she personally was a rather terrible photographer. She could visualize designs in her mind. She could see proportion. She was great at spatial layouts, but for some reason, when it came to capturing her ideas or designs, or even taking an inspiration shot, it all went to hell. The things she saw in her mind's eye absolutely did not translate to the poorly framed scenes she would find in her phone or in her camera. She still hadn't figured out how to create an image that didn't look like a 5-year-old had taken it on their mom's phone. She supposed she should check out the name of the photographer, so that maybe she could buy one of their prints for the boat. Depending on her final concept, there were a few that could work. She leaned in to take a closer peek. Just as she saw the name Lorenzo, she felt a tap on her shoulder. She turned around, smiling, wondering whether she was going to have to apologize to some French person for blocking their view of this honestly spectacular photograph, even though now that she knew that Lorenzo had taken the pictures, she didn't like it quite as much. But it wasn't an annoyed stranger behind her. It was Lorenzo. He was close enough for her to smell that aftershave she had loved, once. The one that smelled of citrus on the Sicilian coast, and cedar, and purely distilled masculinity. It was ridiculous how she responded to Lorenzo, even now. But it didn't matter that her heart did flip flops and that her nether regions started throbbing whenever she was in close proximity to him, because this clearly was not a good idea. However, not for the first time, she started to think that maybe they could have a no strings attached relationship. She'd grown. She'd changed. She had more self-control, now. It could work. Or was it just the addict in her talking?

"I'm glad you came," said Lorenzo. "Welcome."

"Aren't you a little cocky, welcoming me to somebody else's gallery space?"

"This is my gallery," said Lorenzo.

"Oh," said Constance. Ouch. Now she felt a bit embarrassed. He hadn't mentioned that he owned a gallery. Well, wasn't he the enterprising one? She couldn't believe that Mister superficial, globetrotting, modelizing Lorenzo, had settled down to the point of owning a gallery in one of the top vacation spots in the world when she, Constance, couldn't even be bothered to decorate her tiny Miami apartment. She should have been running her own business by now, too. Yet for some reason, she just had never been able to buckle down to do it. Blame it on the ADHD or not, she didn't feel great about it. And now, Lorenzo having this gallery threw all of that into stark relief.

"How was your day?" He asked. "Did things go well with the yacht owner?"

"They went OK," Constance admitted. "Not great. He seems to have lots of demands, but they're pretty vague. I'm going to have to decode what he means and deliver something extraordinary, or else I'm in deep trouble"

"I didn't ask earlier- how's Harold?"

"Same old, same old." Constance could have stopped there, but she apparently needed to vent. "He's got this little mini-me, Penelope, who he gives all the high-profile jobs to at this point."

"That yacht you're working on is not a high-profile job?" Asked Lorenzo, surprised. "Looks it to me."

"I think that this one's an exception because it's in an undesirable location."

"Saint Tropez? Undesirable?"

"Well, in the winter it is," said Constance, feeling a little petty. "And anyway, he gave Penelope the mega yacht in Miami I specifically requested."

"Maybe he's trying to challenge you," said Lorenzo. "Sometimes, you're not really clear on what's good for you."

"How dare you say that?"

"Experience," said Lorenzo. "Observation. But maybe you've changed," he allowed.

"I have changed!" Great, now she was being defensive. She couldn't believe that he was the one telling her about her shortcomings, when he was the one who... Never mind, this was ridiculous.

"Anyway," she sniffed. "Can you at least introduce me to the Editor in Chief or the publisher of this magazine?" She'd had enough of talking to Lorenzo and walking down memory lane every time she looked at him. Images popped into her head of the various things they had done, places they had been, things he'd whispered to her in the middle of the night. It was far too painful, and now she was just going to get down to business and focus on getting this damn yacht decorated, photographed and published.

"If you're thinking about getting the yacht published, I can introduce you to our senior editor. She would be the one who makes all the decisions as to what gets featured."

Constance narrowed her eyes at Lorenzo.

"What do you mean, our?"

"It's my magazine," said Lorenzo. "I'm technically the editor in chief, but I'm more on the business side, even if I still enjoy taking photos. Anyway, Sophie over there- she's the senior editor."

He gestured at a beautiful blonde a few yards away. Totally his type, a little bit less supermodelly. A little bit more spoiled rich girl, Constance decided. But suddenly, she recognized the girl, with a shudder of absolute horror.

Crap. This wasn't just any spoiled blonde Sophie. This was Sophie White. Carlos' daughter. An absolute sociopath. Willing to do anything to get her way, not friendly to other women. And Constance was willing to bet that she would be even less friendly to Constance if she ever put two and two together. Carlos wouldn't have mentioned Constance's name to his daughter, but there was an excellent chance that Mrs. White had mentioned "that slut who decorated our yacht, starting with your father's bed." What the hell was Sophie doing there? Last Constance had heard, Sophie was living in Saint Barts. Not that she'd made it her business to update herself on Sophie's whereabouts. Finding her here in Saint Tropez was very bad luck.

"How do you know Sophie?"

"You've met?" Asked Lorenzo.

"No! Sorry, I meant, how did she get involved with the magazine? She seems quite young for such a job," Constance ad-libbed. The last thing she wanted was Lorenzo telling Sophie, "oh so it seems you two know each other…." And watching the situation escalate from there.

"She applied out of the blue- had exactly the type of experience I was looking for, and she campaigned hard for the job. So far, she seems to be doing great."

Constance bit her tongue to avoid giving Lorenzo her opinion, which was that Sophie had probably fudged her resumé. She didn't recall Sophie having any experience that would serve her as senior editor of a magazine, but the good news was that, according to Carlos, she was intelligent and if she put her mind to something, she was able to get it done. Hopefully for Lorenzo, Sophie would be motivated to produce good work. Or he would learn the hard way to start vetting his employees a little bit better.

"So, you're saying that I have to go through this Sophie character to get anything published?"

"Ultimately, I do have the final say," said Lorenzo.

OK, thought Constance. Between a rock and a hard place, she supposed she would choose Lorenzo's hard place rather than Sophie's rock any day. Stop thinking about his hard place. In any case, that meant she had to be nice to Lorenzo. Dammit.

"Listen," said Lorenzo. "I need to make a little speech. But after that, how about we have dinner? I would love to catch up with you. Let these young people party on. They don't need me."

She made sure to look away from his gaze. She couldn't resist it, but resist it, she must. But she did need to be nice to him. And she was hungry. If Lorenzo was asking her out to dinner, maybe that meant that none of these supermodel types were his wife, or officially his girlfriend. Not that that meant anything.

"OK. You go make your speech," she said. "I'll be right here."

She wasn't one hundred percent sure she would follow through and still be there when he got back, but he seemed to believe her; he gave her a devastating smile and headed off. Constance took advantage of the moment to go get another glass of wine, to calm her nerves.

"How's it going?" Asked Sebastian, the bartender. "I see you met Lorenzo. It's great what he's done in this town in so short a time."

"Oh?"

"He's organized some cultural events. He's mobilized the creative community, especially people staying year-round. And this magazine, it's going to be a great vehicle for showcasing local talent. We're all very excited about it. It took somebody with vision to spearhead something like this."

"Nice," said Constance. "And what do you for the magazine?"

"Features and graphic design."

"And what about your co-workers?" Constance hoped that maybe she would get a little Sophie gossip.

"Camille over there, she is our main fashion stylist." Sebastian gestured at a tall, slim woman with that perfect French-girl bob with bangs and heavy eyeliner. "She's great at what she does. She got burnt out from living in Paris, I think she used to work for some well-known designer, but don't tell her- I can't remember who that is."

"She's very chic," Constance noted. "How about her?" She discreetly gestured in Sophie's direction.

"That's our senior editor, Sophie." The way Sebastian beamed as he said Sophie's name told Constance that Carlo's daughter had claimed another victim. She hoped it was reciprocal. Anything for Sophie to stay away from Lorenzo. What a silly thought, Constance. He's not yours to be jealous over.

Constance turned around as she heard the music stopping. Lorenzo stood in the middle of the room. As soon as he started speaking, all conversation ceased. He had a natural authority that made people not only listen to him, but drink in every word. She couldn't blame them. His body language commanded respect. His looks were arresting. He was so much more masculine than any other man in the room, almost comically so, when you compared him to some of the more effete creatives in attendance. The memory came back, unbidden, of how, in bed, he moved like a wild thing and growled in her ear to communicate his pleasure. It made her tingle just thinking about it. Sex with Lorenzo had been some of the most animalistic, wild, no holds barred experiences of her life. And then, there had been the times that were soulful, almost sweet, so deeply romantic they almost made her cry. That's why he was so intoxicating. That's why she was so addicted to everything about him. And why she'd been so devastated when things had ended.

This time, she would have the upper hand. She decided she would definitely go to dinner with him, and maybe this time, she would seduce him. She would make sure not to fall for him again. And no pretense of friendship. That was for liars, she decided. She listened to Lorenzo's speech with bated breath, as did everyone else in the room. His voice was more intoxicating than the wine in her glass. Lorenzo's French was close to perfect, she knew. But she realized that the crowd was probably international enough to warrant him speaking his precise, just barely accented English. He was also fluent in German. A real linguist, that one. Stop thinking about his tongue.

"I'm so happy to have you all gathered here. This is part of my vision for our adopted town. We were a town of fishermen. We're now a town of creatives. The people gathered in this room are shaping this town in every sense. From the taste to the smell to what we see to how we experience it. I want to celebrate the work that each of you is doing through the magazine. Together we work better. Together, we inspire each other. Help each other to find our muse."

When he said that, Constance trembled. The muse was something that they had discussed together at length, all those years ago. She had told him about her secret frustration that her muse was fickle, as fickle as she was. For Lorenzo, his muse was a constant companion, something he could depend on. A spirit that imbued everything he did. Constance's muse was an irresponsible roommate, who ditched her just when she needed her most. She struggled to start paying attention to what Lorenzo was saying again. Just in time for a disaster.

"And now," Lorenzo was saying, "we have one more creative to welcome into our midst. Someone shaping our harbor, as a yacht interior designer."

Oh shit. If Constance had been hoping to fly under the radar with Sophie, this was not the best way to do it.

"Please welcome Constance. An old friend of mine."

Amongst the spattering of applause, Constance tried to smile at most of the people, to look friendly but not desperate. She avoided looking at Sophie, but her paranoia had her imagining her glare burning into her.

Lorenzo finished up his speech with a brilliant and motivating call to action that had Constance almost ready to join his magazine herself.

"Thanks again, everyone," Lorenzo said, and amongst the hooting and clapping, he made a beeline for her, before anyone could swarm him. She could see everyone's heads pivoting towards him, people wanting to congratulate him on his speech, congratulate him on his project. But he had evidently had enough. Constance remembered that about him. He who looked so confident, so powerful, was, deep down inside, an introvert who could only take small doses of socializing and of being "on." It was endearing.

"I'm so ready," he said. "Let's go."

She was ready, too. Didn't want to risk Sophie coming over or getting any ideas. Lorenzo took her arm, waved apologetically at a few people, and pulled Constance out into the night. Having him hold her arm like this took her back to when they would walk down city streets after an evening out, anticipating what was coming next. The warmth of his body radiated through her coat, making her feel better than she had in a long time.

"Did I tell you you're looking particularly beautiful tonight? Though I don't like your lipstick."

"What? This is my signature color!"

"It is the perfect color on you. And you look ravishing. I don't like it because it makes me worry that if I kiss you, I'll get it all over you, and all over me."

"I don't know why you're assuming that kissing is on the table," said Constance. But of course, the minute he had said it, it was all she could think about. And who was he to decide when he would or wouldn't kiss her? Especially after she had decided that she would have the upper hand in this seduction plan.

"And what do you mean, get lipstick all over yourself," she asked innocently. Before Lorenzo could react, she mockingly planted a kiss on his cheek.

"Like this?" She asked. "But it looks so cute."

She turned his head, holding his face firmly in both hands, and kissed the other cheek. As she did so, she caught Lorenzo's eye. That look of his. Hungry, already. She felt something stirring deep inside of her. Just lust, she hoped, just lust. Don't start to catch any feelings. That would be stupid. Now, she held her breath for a moment, weighing whether what she was about to do was incredibly dumb, but before she could overthink it, she planted a kiss on his lips, a chaste, closed-lip kiss, made satisfying simply because she could picture him getting smeared in red pigment. But then, he put his hands on her waist and pulled her against him, returning the kiss. He started off by tugging at her lower lip with his teeth. She breathed in his scent and her tongue met his, making her lean in closer. Now, he took handfuls of hair in both hands, tipping her head back, exploring her mouth with his tongue. It was as if her body had been waiting for this. She reacted almost immediately, feeling that throbbing ache between her legs, rubbing herself against him. It was even worse because the kiss was so delicious, and she knew how good it could be if she let him have his way with her. As if he could read her mind, he groaned, "forget dinner, let me take you home. I'll cook for you. After."

Irresistible. But if she wanted to have the upper hand, she needed to tease him, make him want her for longer. She wouldn't just give in so easily. Especially knowing that the moment she did give in, it would be damn hard not to crave him at every moment. He kissed her more deeply, now, cupping her ass in both hands, squeezing her against him in a passionate embrace. She couldn't help it. Her mind went straight to all the times he'd held her like that as she straddled him, driving her mad as he dictated their rhythm.

"I love these pants on you," he said. "But I think I would like them better off of you."

She didn't respond, just kissed him back more fiercely. Her fingers traced along his jawline, then she moved a hand under his shirt, running it up his back, relishing the feel of his skin. He shivered, whether from her cold hands or from her touch, she didn't know, but the heat of his skin was intoxicating. She arched against him, her coat open, now, letting him feel her breasts pushing against his chest. Even through their sweaters, she knew that he could imagine what it would be like to have her against him naked. Because she sure could. He ground against her, now, making her feel how hard she was making him. And that's when he let it out. That growl she loved to hear. A low, guttural sound that was the sexiest thing ever.

If they didn't watch it, they were going to put on quite a show in the middle of the deserted street.

She forced herself to disengage from him.

"I don't think we should be going at it in public," she said. "You seem to know too many people in this town. Besides, I'm hungry."

"We can't go to a restaurant. You've got lipstick all over you," said Lorenzo.

"You think you don't? You look like a circus clown." A hot one, but she wasn't about to tell him that. "I've got wipes in my bag," said Constance. "For just such an occasion."

"Really?" Asked Lorenzo as she used a wipe on him to wipe off the worst of the lipstick. Running the cloth over his gorgeous face, while looking deep into his flinty eyes, she could acutely feel that her lips were still engorged. She wanted more kisses from him, but she also needed to take things slowly if she wanted to have any chance of being even somewhat in control of a situation that was quickly going to derail if she wasn't careful.

"God, I've missed you," said Lorenzo.

Haha, she thought. That was rich. He missed her after he'd left her. That simple statement, which was such a lie, coming out of Lorenzo's gorgeous mouth, was beneficial, because it made her quickly gain perspective and yanked her out of the trance that she'd almost fallen into. Yes, he deserved for her to toy with him.

"Your turn," he said, taking the wipe from her and carefully cleaning her face. Even that felt like an intimate act, or at the very least, like foreplay.

When he was done, she allowed him to take her arm again and lead her down another dark Saint Tropez street, towards the one place that had glowing lights coming from it.

"Oh, I've been to this place before, long ago," said Constance.

"Oh? With another man?"

Constance rolled her eyes. Nice try, playing at being jealous.

"Barely. My childhood friend… her parents came here all the time. I loved it."

They entered the restaurant, the warmth drawing them in. The clientele was similar to the demographic in the gallery, with a few older types mixed in. Constance hoped that Peter Holmes wasn't at this restaurant. That would be awkward, especially if the traces of lipstick were still on either one of their faces. She decided that, as soon as they got a table, she would go make sure she looked presentable. They were led to a table in the corner, and Constance excused herself to go to the bathroom. No marks left on her face. But she could see the expression in her eyes, reflected back at her. Hungry. Lustful. Lorenzo had awakened something in her that she hadn't felt in a long time.

To calm down a little, she took the opportunity to check her phone. She had a message from her friend Pam. Art Basel sucks without you. Don't worry, you're missing nothing. But we miss you.

It was good to feel wanted somewhere.

Also, a message from Harold.

I trust you're doing well. An update would be grand.

Sorry- I can't answer right now, Constance texted back. I'm in bed with the client.

Harold wrote back instantly.

You'd better be joking.

OMG relax, Constance wrote back. I'm not interested in him. He's not interested in me. I'm going to do the best job ever.

Phew, Harold wrote back.

If only he knew that she had bumped into Lorenzo. He wouldn't be so relieved.

Now go to bed- you need your beauty sleep, Constance wrote.

She smiled to herself at the banter, but she was genuinely concerned about Harold. He had lived a hard partying life. It was now catching up to him. She'd noticed that his skin tone wasn't what it once was, and he'd had dark circles under his eyes on more than one occasion. She didn't like to admit that her dear Harold was aging. She should be better to him. They were the only family each one really had, after all. She should make him proud of her, instead of just making him fix her messes.

I love you, Uncle Harold, she wrote.

Love you, kid, he wrote back.

Now, she had to go back and face Lorenzo. God, it was awkward. How did one act with an ex, who one was determined to be friendly with, to get a boat into their magazine, but maybe also have an affair with, with no strings attached, even though they were all you could think about? She supposed she would just wing it, just like she did most things in her life.

She sat back down at the table. Lorenzo gave her a brilliant smile. She'd missed that smile. A magical alchemy of perfectly kissable lips, a little scar on one corner of his mouth, from when he'd gotten into a fight as a teenager. And one slightly wonky tooth on that side, just a little bit turned, barely perceptible. But she loved that one imperfection, on a man who was otherwise, to her, at least a Greek god, well, an Italian god. It was as if every part of him had been concocted to attract her. His dark eyes, which oscillated between smoky cocoa and slate gray, depending on his mood. His square jaw. The aquiline nose that some would call big, but which she called perfect. The heavy brows that gave his face structure and masculinity. And that olive skin tone that contrasted so well with her own when they lay tangled together. She was certain that there was no more gorgeous man on the face of this earth, and she liked it even more that he was not everyone's cup of tea. One of her acquaintances had once seen him and had told her, "Are you mad, Constance? He looks like a criminal. An elegant criminal. But he's... I don't know, feral." She knew Lorenzo didn't have a criminal bone in his body, though she liked that someone thought he seemed dangerous, even though he was relentlessly honest and honorable. He'd been born that way, no doubt. And his mother had raised him that way.

"Lorenzo," she said, dreading seeing that smile turn into something darker. "Before we even order, I want to apologize." "Oh?" he said, looking at her. "I didn't dare hope that you'd finally admit…"

"Admit what? What are you talking about? I heard from Chiara that your mom passed away. I wanted to apologize for not sending you my condolences."

"Oh," said Lorenzo. "How could you have? I blocked you. But thank you."

Wow. So, he was admitting he had blocked her. Childish. And what else was he expecting her to apologize for? Well, she had done her part.

They exchanged a few reminiscences about Lorenzo's mother that warmed Constance's heart, but she decided that she would put those memories behind her as soon as they'd finished dinner, because you didn't want any history with someone you were having a fling with, did you? She shifted the conversation, to a debate on the merits of the various pizzas that they might order and share, and finally, they settled on a Primavera and a capricciosa.

Chapter 20

The pizza arrived, as well as a bottle of Nebbiolo, which Constance remembered was one of Lorenzo's favorites. "Here's to your mother," said Constance, raising her glass. "Carlotta was a character. May we all live like she did."

"Yes, she placed the focus firmly on love and happiness," said Lorenzo with a small smile. "I think she was on to something, don't you?"

"Of course," said Constance. But she realized that the way Lorenzo had said it seemed a little judgmental. Did he think that she didn't focus on love and happiness? Well, maybe not the happiness part. And to be fair, maybe not the love part either, depending on how you defined love.

She took a bite of the pizza. It was delicious. There was something about the French version of Italian food that was so charming and tasty in an entirely different way.

"Tell me more about the magazine. I'm fascinated that you decided to do this."

"It was time to settle down, and I wanted to give back. How about you? How is the project going, really? Do you think you're going to get it done?"

"Honestly," said Constance, deciding to just go ahead and tell the truth, "I'm not sure. I'm having issues communicating with the owner so far, but it's only been a day. I have to give it a chance. I was going to invite him to tonight's party, but I just didn't get that vibe from him, you know what I mean?"

"Understood," said Lorenzo. "I'm glad you came alone."

"I am too," Constance admitted. "It's funny, because Harold told me that the owner absolutely wanted to have the yacht published in a magazine, but so far, he hasn't mentioned that to me, so either he's decided it's not a big deal, or he doesn't think I'll last long enough for it to matter."

"If it does work out, I think I know someone who has a magazine. Maybe it's not of the caliber your client would hope for…"

"That's very kind," said Constance, starting to worry again about Sophie. "But I wouldn't want to force you to include something that wasn't a good fit. So far, the Muse is playing hard to get. And it's frustrating."

"I know how that can be," said Lorenzo.

"Really? You've always been relentlessly creative. It's like you just spew out good work without even thinking about it."

"Maybe I'm getting older," Lorenzo admitted.

Constance looked at him, shocked. Granted, he was a few years older than her, almost forty. But he was a man in his absolute prime. Now that she looked more closely, though, there were a few white hairs glistening amongst his dark mane. A few new laugh lines. In her opinion, that only made him more attractive. She smiled to herself, thinking of how angry she normally was when people said that men only got better with age, and women just aged. She hated it when others said it, but she sincerely did think this about Lorenzo. He was the exception.

"I can't believe we're sitting here together like this, after all these years," said Lorenzo. "I feel like no time has passed at all, and an eternity at the same time. Tell me more about you. Where have you been? What have you done?"

"To tell you the truth, I've been everywhere, and nowhere. Done everything, and nothing. Nothing really stands out."

She wished she hadn't admitted that. It was pretty damn depressing.

"Come on," said Lorenzo. "Surely there's something."

Constance wanted to make something up. Make herself sound better. More interesting, more stable. More balanced. But it was all she could do to not start crying right there, at the table.

Lorenzo reached over and took her hand.

"Maybe that's why you're having a hard time designing. You don't take the time to hold on to anything. You don't like to let anything mean anything to you."

"That's not true," said Constance. "I cared about you."

The phrase dropped onto the table like a lead balloon. Damn it, she hadn't meant to say that. She'd wanted to keep it light. Playful. And here she'd gone, spilling her guts out to Lorenzo on their first meal together. Probably the last.

"Did you care about me? Really?" Lorenzo asked, letting go of her hand, which suddenly felt cold, and lonely.

"What kind of a question is that?"

Constance rolled her eyes. This wasn't going anywhere. She was going to go back to the original plan of seducing him, no strings attached. Too bad for the magazine. She would find another one. She would make sure that her design spoke for itself.

"Sorry. That was stupid of me. Tell me about Harold's Thanksgiving. I'm sure it was epic."

It was just the right thing to say. You couldn't think about anything Harold did and stay mad. Lorenzo had always liked Harold. They'd gone on a few trips together. Dinners. Clearly, Harold had had the expectation that the two of them would get married and had been devastated when they'd broken up. In fact, she was surprised that Harold and Lorenzo hadn't kept in touch. It was probably just out of Harold's loyalty to her.

"It was fabulous, as always. Countess Carla, Boris and Natasha, some drama with Ian and his new beau, and Sean. But honestly, I'm a little bit worried about Harold," she said, going serious again. "I don't know. He's getting older."

"Do you think he's ready to retire? I assume you'll take over his design firm?"

"That's just it. I feel like he doesn't expect me to. Maybe he doesn't trust me. That's why it's so important for me to prove to Harold that I can do a good job." She skipped the part about how she sometimes compensated for shoddy work. "And then I think I would love to have my own company, as well."

"I understand what that's like," said Lorenzo.

Constance knew that Lorenzo had worked for a fashion editor who had held him under his thumb for at least a decade of his career. He had made Lorenzo feel that without him, he would be nothing, until Lorenzo had finally gotten the confidence to step out and start photographing, and living life, on his own terms, and it had really marked a turning point for him. His confidence had gone through the roof. He'd gotten assignments all over the world. And maybe that's when he'd decided to leave Constance, because she was no longer good enough for him.

"So, tell me about the people working for you," said Constance.

"Sebastian. He's a graphic designer, a bit distracted sometimes, but he's a fast worker and he'll keep learning," said Lorenzo. "My fashion stylist extraordinaire, Camille- she worked for that guy from Marseille who went to Paris and launched that massive brand- she was his right-hand woman. And honestly, I think that a huge part of his success is due to her, not that she takes credit for it. She's going to be quite an asset for the magazine," he concluded.

Constance felt a stab of jealousy, to hear Lorenzo speaking of someone's creativity in such a reverential way, especially since the stylist was a beautiful woman, just like all the women he surrounded himself with.

"And what about Sophie?" She asked, hating herself for saying her name first. Why had she done that? She didn't want Lorenzo to find out how intimately she had worked with Carlos White. Already, the memories of afternoons spent on Carlos's yacht, fishing and playing cards, lying in bed reading, coffee on the deck, all those things were fading from her memory, starting to feel like they've happened to somebody else.

Chiara had told her she was being stupid.

"Imagine…A billionaire. Married to a billionaire, my friend's married to a billionaire," she'd said, as if testing it out on her tongue. "That would be so cool. We could go wherever we wanted by private jet."

"It doesn't work that way," Constance had said.

And anyway, Carlos's ex-wife was still refusing to grant him a divorce. It would be too expensive. And Carlos was afraid of her. He was a scaredy cat. This was something that not many people knew about Carlos White. If they did, those tech bros wouldn't be worshipping him like they did.

"You seem to be lost in your thoughts," said Lorenzo.

"Sorry, I got distracted, thinking about work."

"Did you just have a wonderful idea?"

Maybe," she lied. "I should go home."

Lorenzo gave her a look. "I'll walk you back to the boat."

Gone was his desire to get her to his apartment, it seemed. It had just been a blip, then. He wasn't really attracted to her, was he? He liked the tall, skinny girls. She had been the strange exception that had proven the rule.

"I can walk by myself," she said.

"No, I insist. It can be dangerous here at night."

"Really?" Constance arched an eyebrow at him.

"French house cats go wild in the off season."

They paid the bill, Lorenzo insisting on covering her part, and walked back out into the night. When he took her arm again, she realized how she'd missed his touch. Even sitting across the table at the restaurant, she'd felt a yearning to feel him next to her. She was being stupid. They'd had a tense meal. Nothing was working out for her. This was so frustrating. Her muse wouldn't visit her, and Lorenzo no longer seemed compelled to visit her bed. Well, not her bed. She would have to go to his place. They walked in silence, as if everything had been said. When they arrived in front of the yacht, Constance stopped.

"Here it is," she said.

"Ohh that one. How many bedrooms is that thing?"

"I can't remember. Anyway, I'm thinking of reorganizing the space. I need to get cracking on it very seriously tomorrow morning." She didn't know what else to say to make Lorenzo stay longer. "What about you? What are you working on?"

Lame, but it worked.

"I'm pursuing advertisers," said Lorenzo. I'll be around, in case you want to meet up for a coffee or a drink, and then I may be in Paris for a few days."

A coffee, or a drink. It sounded like a vague, empty plan. The urgency from earlier in the evening had completely dissipated. A drink would be nice, though. Lorenzo cleared his throat.

"Well, I'd better leave," he said. Was that regret she heard in his voice? "It's weird having you here, Constance. I must admit," he said. "But I'm glad you're here, too."

She stared at him. Weird for him? How about for her? She didn't respond, and let him kiss her on the cheek, a gesture that seemed ridiculously G-rated after their earlier make out session. He started to walk away.

"Wait," said Constance. She was going to get the upper hand now, no matter how hard it was.

"Yes?"

He looked at her expectantly. Closing the space between them in just a few steps, Constance found herself well into his personal space, close enough to smell his cologne. Close enough to feel his heat.

"I just wanted to give you this," she said.

She stood up on tiptoe and kissed him. Mostly closed mouth, just enough tongue and nibbling of the lips to make him a little bit out of breath. Enough to feel him growing excited against her. But not long enough to hear that growl. Because if she heard that, she couldn't be responsible for what she did next. Regretfully, she ended the kiss, and gently pushed him away.

"Well, good night," she said. "I'll see you around."

Forcing herself not to look back, she walked onto the boat and used her key fob to open the sliding doors. She gasped when she noticed Peter Holmes sitting in a chair, almost completely in darkness, with only a reading light illuminating the tome he held in his hands.

"Hi! I didn't see you there."

"Did you have a good time out?"

"Yes, I did. I didn't think you were around, or I would have invited you along," she lied.

"Oh? What was the event?"

"A launch party for a local magazine headed by a friend of mine," said Constance.

"Ah. Lovely," said Peter.

Constance would have thought that he might have picked up on that- that she had a contact who could potentially get the boat published. But he didn't say anything. Maybe he planned on firing her sooner rather than later. Maybe he thought that a local magazine wasn't good enough. Constance decided that she was too tired to delve into it further.

"All right, well. I'm going to turn in," she said. "Tomorrow will be a long day. I'm hoping to make some headway on a design proposal, so that you can have something to look at as soon as possible."

"Oh. Good."

"I thought that maybe if you have any photos of your previous boat for me…" Constance began.

"No," said Peter, shutting her down. "I want something completely different."

"All right," said Constance, dejected. "Well, good night."

She took herself over to the secondary stateroom, undressed, and went into the bathroom to brush her teeth. Her lips were still swollen from the kisses she'd exchanged with Lorenzo, and her eyes burned feverishly, with the kind of excitement she hadn't felt in years. She changed into her silk pajamas and tucked herself into bed. But of course, she couldn't sleep. Her mind was racing. Feeling guilty, she conducted an Internet search on Peter Holmes, trying to gather any information she possibly could about him that could help her to think of a design. The only things she could find were a few reports of him attending charity galas. Maybe that would tell her what he was interested in. But there was no rhyme or reason. It just seemed to be whatever struck his fancy. Maybe she'd finally found the client equivalent of her, or at the very least, found someone else who didn't know what made them happy. Well, that was a unique challenge. If she couldn't help herself, how was she was supposed to help someone else? As she read a few more articles about Holmes and his philanthropy and his business dealings, she started to feel tired, nodding off a few times. She finally put down her iPad, and drifted off to sleep, but not before thinking one last thought of Lorenzo. How he'd been, how he'd smelled, how he'd tasted. How he felt against her. She was lapsing back into obsession. Keep it light, she told herself. Just get him out of your system, she thought. And then everything went dark, and she fell asleep.

Chapter 21

Constance woke to the cries of seagulls outside her stateroom windows, and the smells of the harbor, which were part disgusting, part nostalgic, reminding her of her childhood, waking up on the DeFever yacht. She remembered warding off the chill coming off the water, huddled in front of the Japanese fisherman's fireplace, and drinking hot chocolate made by her mother, wrapped in a blanket, sitting on a chair on the back deck. There was something about being on a boat that soothed her, something that gave her a feeling of freedom and possibility. When you had a boat, you could pick up and leave at any time, and no one thought it strange. Maybe that's why she did this job on boats, specifically. Maybe it did make her happy, even when it filled her with melancholy. What else made her happy? She wondered, as she brushed her teeth and took a quick bird bath. She was anxious to get started on her project, and was feeling reasonably fresh, the jet lag having more or less retreated to a manageable level.

When she emerged from her room, wearing jeans with a colorful silk shirt under a navy cashmere sweater, she was startled to find Peter in the galley kitchen. Her heart dropped a bit, because she had been looking forward to making herself a quick breakfast and a big cup of coffee, without having to talk to anyone.

"Are you one of those girls who doesn't eat breakfast?" Peter asked.

She almost scoffed at him. Did she look like a girl who skipped meals? Was he being sarcastic? Maybe it was an innocent enough statement. Just because her father and her stepmother #2 had always mocked her curves, didn't necessarily mean that everybody found them unattractive, did it? But when she saw him gesturing at a steaming pan of eggs and bacon, she decided not to make a point of it.

"Why don't you have a seat in the main saloon? I'll bring you a plate. You don't have any allergies or anything, do you? I made some French toast, too," he said.

"That sounds amazing," said Constance, not having realized until now how hungry she was, even after last night's pizza.

She sensed a shift in Peter. He seemed happier, more relaxed. That was good. Maybe she would get to talk to him a little bit more about his expectations. She was looking at inspiration photos in her iPad when he arrived with the tray.

"Here you go, my dear," he said. "It was very kind of you, to pick up and leave everything and come here to do my yacht. I really appreciate it. I hope you know that. I'm sorry about yesterday. I was just in a mood."

"I'm glad that things seem to be sunnier today," said Constance. The weather, in fact, had also improved, the sun bouncing off the waves in the harbor. The light was, admittedly, magical.

"I just hoped," she ventured, "that I could talk to you a little bit more about the potential design. Or let's just talk about you. What makes you tick? What is your life like?"

Those seemed to be the magic words. Or maybe Peter had just been in his happy place, cooking for someone. He told her some stories, nothing too personal, but a few details that started to paint a picture. Just when Constance started to think that maybe he would spill a few more intimate details, Peter stood abruptly.

"More coffee?" He asked.

"Sure."

While he has gone, Constance looked at her watch and startled. They had been chatting for over an hour. And it had gone by so fast.

"Wow, I didn't realize how late it is," said Constance, embarrassed, when Peter returned with the coffees. "But thank you for the conversation. I feel like I understand you so much better now."

"No, thank you. I haven't had a relaxed conversation like this in a while," Peter admitted.

"Really?"

"Yes, Constance. Really. Usually, I'm just in the boardroom or on the phone, barking orders at people. I probably need a vacation."

"And that's what I want to give you with my design."

"Thank you," he said, but it was as if a switch had been flipped. The idea of the design was stressing him out, Constance realized. Well, that made two of them.

Chapter 22

Constance got out of her hideous rust colored Citroen and scanned the shipyard. She was certain this was the right address, the one she'd found for a high end, high concept technical upholstery fabric company, but she was currently surrounded by windowless warehouses bearing small, obtuse signage next to dinged metal doors complete with peeling paint. She headed in one direction, with no success, and went to peek around the side of a building, encountering only weeds, when someone shouted out. She spun around. A man wearing a navy-blue jumpsuit, a trendier version of the ones worn by French gas station attendants, waved at her.

"Bonjour! Constance?"

"Yes," she replied, taking in the man's unique appearance. He was tall, skinny, the rolled-up sleeves of the jumpsuit revealing ample tattoos. His longish blonde hair was thrown back in a man bun, and a scruffy beard partially covered an angular face that was rough and ruddy, as if he'd spent all his summers on a sailboat, which he probably had. Constance found herself thankful for the sunscreen her mother had always insisted on slathering her in as a child, and she had continued the habit even once her mother was gone.

"I wasn't sure where I was going," said Constance.

"I know,' said the man, rolling his eyes. "I keep saying we need a better sign, or any sign, really," he said in his strong French accent.

"I'm really excited to see your fabrics," said Constance. "I've been looking for this for years- something that looks like linen or velvet, or like a classic printed wall covering, but that won't be destroyed on a boat."

"I'm pleased for you to see our selection," said the man. "I'm Francois, by the way. We just launched about six months ago, and we are still expanding our collection, but we do have a few good selections."

"I always found that most all-weather fabric is so boring. Everybody's boat looks the same," she said.

"Yeah, it's sad," said Francois. "You get to be a billionaire and then, you still have everything the same as everybody else. It seems completely unfair, doesn't it?"

"Absolutely," Constance laughed.

The man opened a door and led her inside a warehouse space. It was incongruously bright inside, as it was illuminated by a giant skylight in the middle of the ceiling. Racks of fabric lined the walls around the perimeter of the room, and, in the back, Constance noted a conference room with glass walls and a few cubicles with desks occupied by trendy millennial types.

"Wow, this is quite the operation," said Constance.

"Go big or go home, is that what they say in the States?" said the man. "So far, we've been doing well. Our supply chain was impacted by the pandemic, but we're coming back. Also, moving out of Paris has been great for us."

Constance nodded. This was becoming a familiar refrain.

"Do you want to take a look around or do you want me to walk you through the collection?" Francois asked.

"I'll just take a peek," said Constance.

She was embarrassed to have to admit that she had no idea what her concept was yet and was hoping that maybe she would gain inspiration from the fabrics.

"I'll be at my desk. Take your time."

Constance thanked him and walked to the first rack, perusing the offerings. Unlike many technical fabrics, these had color. They had texture. As she had expected, she loved the velvet and nubby linen-like swatches, but there were also some incredible prints, executed in neoprene, that seemed like they would be both water resistant and comfortable. This meant having an option beyond the expected vinyl for outdoor seating.

She snapped a few photos, including pictures of the reference numbers for a few of the more interesting fabrics. It was frustrating to not even have the beginning of an idea of a concept. This morning had gone so well, but if Peter asked for a progress report, she was out of luck. Francois joined her after a moment and said, "well, you're certainly taking a lot of pictures."

"I have a few other clients, too," Constance lied. "How long would take to deliver any of these?"

"We have a few in stock, depending on the quantities," said Francois. "We figured this is the best way to serve our customer. The rest can be ordered, and we use a digital printing process, so, as long as you're not a snob about fabrication, it's not too bad a turnaround. We produce as many of these as we can locally or semi locally."

Constance was impressed with this business model. It was a refreshing change from the way things had gone in the past. "That's great news," she said. "I don't want to commit to anything yet, but I will definitely be coming back."

Once all her questions about lightfastness and waterproofing and cleaning had been answered, she got back into her car and headed to her next stop, an artisanal rug and carpet making facility in the hilltop town of Grimaud. She'd been thrilled that someone had answered her phone call that morning; she had always wanted to visit, and in addition, the place had been highly recommended by Lorenzo the night before. These rugs might give the yacht local flavor. Peter was a traveler. Maybe the key would be bringing in details from all his travels and favorite places. Hopefully, seeing that the carpets, after having seen the fabrics, would start to give Constance an idea of a cohesive design. She started making her way up the hill to the old village of Cogolin, on the way to Grimaud. Maybe it would be a fun place to go for a walk for something new, but for now, she was on a mission. She finally located the rug factory, which was in an ancient building, quite beautiful and regal. She locked the car carefully and made her way inside, opening a heavy wood door to reveal a reception desk, at which sat a woman whose red hair almost matched her own. "Constance?"

"Yes, that's me," said Constance. "Love your hair."

The woman smiled a bit stiffly and didn't say anything. So much for being friendly, thought Constance. Anyway, the resemblance ended at the hair, because this woman was skinny, like most French women. A bit severe, but quite pretty. A little older than Constance herself, but with that Gallic elegance that compensated for so much. Constance found herself tugging at her sweater and deciding that she looked frumpy by comparison to this stylish creature.

"Did you want to see anything in particular?" The woman asked.

"Yes, I just wanted to see anything that would be appropriate for use on a yacht."

"Ah, perfect. Most of our rugs are flat weave and hard wearing, so they would be appropriate for use on any indoor space on a yacht. They are reasonably easy to clean with the steam cleaner. And we would keep your rug on file so that it can be replaced as needed, even if you get a custom design."

"Oh, I can do a custom design?"

"Yes, it will take longer and cost you more, but it is a possibility. But I'm sure you'll find that we have quite a few choices for you."

"Great," said Constance, following the woman down a hall and into a large room. Constance noticed with a start that there was someone else in the showroom, a familiar blonde. Sophie?! Of all people? Well, she would have to play friendly, especially if she wanted to have this boat in the magazine. Maybe Sophie had no idea who she was, anyway. Maybe if she pretended to be delighted to see her...

"Hi, Sophie, right?"

"Have we met?" Asked Sophie.

"Barely. I saw you at the party for the magazine, two nights ago. Lorenzo and Sebastian pointed you out?"

"Oh," said Sophie. "Sorry, I didn't notice you."

What a liar, thought Constance. I was the fattest, red headiest girl there.

"So...you know Lorenzo?" Sophie asked, suspicious. No mention of Sebastian, poor guy.

"Yes, I'm friends with Lorenzo," said Constance, underplaying the relationship, of course.

She wondered if Sophie had been in a relationship with Lorenzo at some point, too, and felt a pang of jealousy. Better to change the subject and show interest in her.

"This is such a great place. What are you doing here?"

"Looking for backdrops for one of my stories."

"Cool."

"What about you?" Asked Sophie.

Constance was so flustered by Sophie's presence that she didn't think twice before answering.

"I'm hoping to use some of these in a yacht design."

Oh shit. Only too late, she realized her mistake.

Sophie narrowed her eyes.

"You design yachts?"

"Yes," said Constance, a feeling of dread subsuming her.

"My dad had someone design his yacht," Sophie said.

Constance's blood started to freeze in her veins.

"Oh yeah? Nice," she said, carefully.

"No, not nice. I hated the design," said Sophie. "Hopefully you'll do better on whichever one you're working on."

"Yes, well, you'll have to come see it when it's done," she said, feeling the chances of the yacht being featured in the magazine evaporating like seawater on teak in the sunshine.

"Which yacht is it?" Asked Sophie.

"The Lombard 4," said Constance, breezily.

"Oh, so your client is like a size queen. That's the biggest boat in the harbor right now, isn't it?"

"I hadn't noticed," said Constance. "Well, I'll leave you to it," she said. "See you around."

"Sure," said Sophie, unconvincingly, going back to her examination of a very boring red and blue rug.

Constance was happy that she had kept reasonably calm during their exchange. Maybe Sophie really had no idea about her father's relationship with his designer. She hoped things stayed that way. She snapped pictures of a few possible rug choices, but she wasn't getting a clear vision yet. What was she going to do? She absolutely needed to find a way to get Peter to talk more constructively, for starters. Maybe getting him around good food again was the answer. It certainly seemed to be his happy place. When she was done looking at rugs and no closer to coming up with the final design, she waved at Sophie, who was still photographing rugs, thanked the redhead at the front desk, and got back into her ugly car.

Chapter 23

It had been cloudy, but now the sun was breaking through, bathing the hills in golden light, and she decided to take a drive through the vineyards around Saint Tropez. Too bad it was winter, and that she was still too frazzled to be in the mood for some nice rosé, she thought. But still, buying some wine to have on the boat would be nice. Maybe she could make Peter a cheese and charcuterie board, pour him some good wine, and get him to speak. Maybe he would finally tell her what had happened with the two other designers he had fired.

But why ask for Peter to tell her? It couldn't hurt to ask Harold to chase up that information for her. So, she texted him, using her voice to text function.

"Hey Uncle Harold, hope you're well- been having a good day checking out some materials. By the way, do you happen to know who those two designers are who were on the project before? I really wish I could talk to them or at least investigate their style." When her phone pinged, Constance yelled at Siri to read the message.

"You sound like a girl who hasn't come up with an idea yet... respond to the message?" Said a digital voice through her phone's speaker.

"Yeah, screw you, Harold," she said.

"Send the message?" Siri asked.

"No, cancel!" Constance yelped.

Another message came through.

"Hey Siri, read the message."

"Yes, I have the names of the other two designers. I just emailed them to you. Respond to the message?"

"Yes. Red heart emoji," said Constance, hope blooming inside of her.

Hopefully, this would help. An idea would come to her at some point. It had to. Surely her muse couldn't play hard to get forever. That was it, she decided. She would go to the supermarket and make an amazing cheese board. Peter would talk.

She stopped on the side of the road to text Peter. She couldn't take the chance of Siri transcribing this one wrong.

Are you in this evening? I was thinking of getting some wine and making a fabulous charcuterie and cheese platter for us, if you don't mind the company.

He wrote back almost instantly.

I would love that. Don't bother with the wine. I have plenty.

Great. If the goal was getting some information out of him, lots of wine would probably help. She headed to a supermarket in the industrial zone just outside of town. She selected a few good cheeses and a few good hard sausages and hams, along with some fig jam and some nuts. She picked up a couple baguettes, too. She would make all of this look beautiful. She drove back into Saint Tropez, strangely finding her spirits lifting as she drove into town. She easily found her way to the parking lot near the harbor. As she was walking towards the boat, heavy bags in tow, she spotted a familiar figure coming out of the hair salon on the corner.

Chapter 24

Constance groaned as she spotted Lorenzo. Would he notice her? Would he try to help her with her shopping bags? Would he say something about their kissing the night prior? Obviously, Lorenzo noticed her instantly. At first, he froze in the middle of the sidewalk and waited for her to approach. When he saw that she was weighed down with shopping bags, he closed the distance between them and relieved her of the bags. She looked guiltily towards the yacht, knowing that it was possible that Peter would be looking in her direction, and she really did not want him to know anything about her personal life. This was, for once, a working relationship.

"It was good spending time with you the other night," said Lorenzo. "What did you get up to today?"

"Sourcing stuff. Oh, I saw your coworker, by the way," said Constance. "She was in the rug factory."

"Oh yes, we are promoting them in our inaugural issue," said Lorenzo. "You have a lot of groceries here. Are you planning on making dinner for someone?"

He almost seemed jealous or suspicious, and Constance thought that that was mighty rich- he had not a leg to stand on.

"Yes, I'm going to try to make a cheese board for my client. Hopefully it's going to make him loosen up and tell me about what matters to him design wise."

Why had she told him that? He didn't need to know.

"Oh," he said. "I'm glad you aren't cooking anything for him. You're such a good cook- you'd seduce him right away."

"You flatter me," said Constance.

But what she thought was, she didn't need to cook to seduce anyone. Carlos White, after all, had seemed to be quite taken by her, even though she was not a blonde supermodel. And Lorenzo himself had seemed rather attracted, too.

"What about you? What are you up to?" She asked.

"Nothing much," said Lorenzo. "The weather was dreary today, and it always drags me down. Do you think your dinner is going to go long? Any way I can entice you into a nightcap?"

"Maybe," said Constance.

After all, if operation no strings attached fling were to go into effect, it might be a good thing.

"Well, I can't very well be entertaining visitors on the yacht," she said. "Do you have an idea of where we could meet?"

"You could come to my place," said Lorenzo.

"Do you live alone?" Fair question.

"What am I? Twenty? I don't have any roommates, and yes, I'm single. If that's what you're asking."

"I wasn't asking," said Constance.

"Well, in any case, I would love to see you at mine when you're done with your client. And cheese isn't a full meal, you know, so maybe I can cook you some pasta or something."

"Sure," said Constance.

Unfortunately, she knew what happened when Lorenzo cooked for her. Again, she wished that she didn't have the memory of all those times. His cooking for her was like a gateway drug.

"Why don't we go out? I'm a girl; for me, cheese is dinner. I'll text you when I'm done," she said. That was safer. Or maybe she would cancel on him at the last second, make him see who's the boss.

"I'll be waiting," said Lorenzo.

And of course, with those words, and the look that he gave her and that masculine face of his and the way he smelled, she knew she wouldn't try to play hard to get. It was impossible. She was hooked already.

"Well, here we are," she said. "Thanks for helping me with the bags."

She took the bags from him, and now she found herself missing his presence the second he walked away. She looked after him for a moment and berated herself. Stop it. You are not going to care about him this time. This time you will love him and leave him.

Chapter 25

She used her key fob to open the door. Again, Peter Holmes was sitting in his chair reading a book. She walked in and cheerfully greeted him.

"You really do love reading, don't you?" She asked without preamble.

"I suppose so," said Peter. "It's an escape. Some people have said that maybe I escape too much, that I'm not in my own life. But I can't help it. There's something so vital about books. I get to see some truths that I can't find in my day-to-day.'

"I understand," said Constance, though frankly, she couldn't find the strength to focus on a single book for very long. However, she thought this was a very interesting thing about her client. Maybe something she could exploit in the design of the yacht.

"Well, I'm going to prepare our charcuterie and cheese dish. I've bought some wonderful things," she said.

"Looking forward," he responded. "Just call me when you need me."

He dove back into his book. Yes, this was something that was important to him.

Constance went into the cramped kitchen of the yacht and again she found herself thinking that it was such a shame that Peter's kitchen was so small and dark. She carefully dug through all the cabinets to find appropriate dishes and bowls in which to display all of the delicious offerings she had collected from the supermarket. Finally, she brought the tray back upstairs.

"Where would you like to sit?"

"I'd been thinking it would be perfect if we sat here. Look, I brought in a little side table for the tray. I've been looking forward to this," said Peter.

He'd been looking forward to this and had been planning ahead. This pleased Constance, but worried her, too. Hopefully he didn't have any thoughts in the back of his mind. All these billionaires spoke to each other, didn't they? Maybe there were rumors going around as to the bonus benefits of hiring Constance as a designer. She hoped not. That would be mortifying. But Peter seemed innocent enough. He brought two wine glasses over, filled them, and handed one to Constance. He clinked his glass against hers.

"What are you reading?"

"Oh, it's some Marcel Proust thing that I always pretended I'd read the entirety of, but in fact, I hadn't. Even now, I think I'm jumping around a bit. I do lose my patience," he admitted. "The way he describes the smell and the taste of a Madeleine, though, is rather impressive."

"Oh, me too," said Constance. "I mean, I lose patience rather easily. Oops. I shouldn't have told you that."

"No, that's human nature," said Peter. "I'd rather know that up front so that we can work around it."

"Thanks for saying that," Constance said. "Cheers to you."

She was glad she wasn't getting any kind of a romantic vibe from Peter at all. But it wasn't just that she felt like there were no sparks. It seemed like maybe romance was not a priority for him, which was interesting because most people got a yacht because of the romance of it. She thought of a good question to ask.

"Peter, may I ask, why was it that you first started yachting?"

"Honestly," said Peter, it might have been some kind of peer pressure. And then I just kept going with it, I suppose."

Constance considered him. He was just as lost as she was.

"You enjoy your book," she said. "I'll be down in the kitchen making you the best charcuterie platter you've ever seen."

"That's a bold claim," he smiled. "But I have no doubt that you will do an excellent job."

As she headed down the stairs to the galley, Constance replayed the exchange in her head. Peter really wasn't that difficult, she thought. Why was it that these other designers had been kicked off the job? It was something she needed to get to the bottom of, especially as someone who tended to run away, and who couldn't afford to do that anymore.

In the kitchen, she took note of how the workspace was too cramped for someone who enjoyed the culinary arts. There wasn't enough storage for the types of platters that many people who entertained on yachts liked to use. Granted, many of the plates used on boats were melamine, but sophisticated clients like Peter had multiple options. She remembered Natasha raving about Peter's yacht in Saint Barts. The Hermès China. Coordinating glassware. The collection of Astier de Villatte ring mugs lined up as usable decor. A pair of Christopher Spitzmiller Aurora lamps custom matched to color of the yacht's hull. The playful House of Hackney pillows on the plush sofas in the main saloon. These things would have simply seemed "nice" to most people, but to designers they were shorthand for "I know what I'm doing." It was odd that there had been such attention to decorative detail when the client was a single straight man. Had there been a woman behind all of this? Natasha had mentioned an intimidating Russian girlfriend, barely out of diapers, but that was a fleeting relationship, apparently. Where were those Hermès plates now, Constance wondered as she sliced up the salami and various cheeses, organizing them on a rather ordinary platter. What if the mystery to all of this was that there had been a woman, and that things ended badly? Constance knew how devastated she'd been when her relationship with Lorenzo had fallen apart. Nothing had quite been the same in the five years since. Granted, she'd had other liaisons, and she'd gotten on with her life, but really, if she looked at the timeline of her existence, it really amounted to before Lorenzo, during Lorenzo, and after Lorenzo. Kind of pathetic. But it was true.

Constance forced herself to stop wallowing and put the finishing touches on her masterpiece. A few little cornichons. Nuts. Dried fruit. Honey. Fig jam. And dried lavender, for effect. Voila. She took a picture of it, for posterity, and carefully carried the tray out to where Peter was sitting, still buried in his book.

"Should we stay in here? It's much cozier, isn't it?" Asked Constance.

"It is, isn't it? I do wish I had a fireplace in here, though. That would make my life complete," said Peter.

Note to self, thought Constance. Investigate fireplaces for yachts. Most fireplaces on yachts were cheesy. She thought back to the Japanese wood stove she'd had on the DeFever as a child.

"I had a fireplace on the yacht I grew up on," she said, cautiously. She didn't know how much Peter cared to know about his decorator's past life, but she figured that maybe this was something they could have in common.

"You grew up on a yacht?"

"Well, nothing as spectacular as this, of course. It was Italian. Designed in the 1960s."

"Wow."

"It was quite beautiful," Constance continued. "It had an original Japanese wood fisherman's stove inside, and well, it was just such a wonderful, cozy feeling to sit in front of that. Everyone thought we were mad, but the Japanese know their design elements."

"Yes, I agree," said Peter.

Her heart leapt. This was a design win, she decided. But she remained cautious about progressing too quickly, lest Peter put his walls back up. Thankfully, he changed the subject himself.

"Your cheese board is spectacular, I admit. I've only seen one or two superior in my life."

"Wow, you've seen better, huh?" Constance was piqued but intrigued.

"Yes," said Peter. "But don't worry. They were created by someone who was beyond compare in the charcuterie department."

"I'll tell that to my pride," laughed Constance.

But as she tried to act all casual, her mind was whirring. This sounded like a woman for sure. How to proceed without being too curious?

"How about that wine you promised?" She teased.

"I was waiting to see what you were going to create, and now that I see that most of the cheeses you selected are from Burgundy, I've made-up my mind. We'll have a Nuits Saint Georges Pinot, slightly chilled. Does that sound good?"

"Absolutely," said Constance.

The man knew his cheese, and he knew his wine. She watched as he headed over to a tall wine refrigerator chock full of bottles. She could tell that he had pride in his collection and decided that the final design should have a larger wine fridge, maybe even two of them.

"Are you familiar with this wine?" He asked, pouring two glasses out for them. A generous pour, not European style. Constance appreciated that.

"I've had it a few times before," she said. "And it's an excellent choice. I'm impressed."

She could have played to his ego and let him mansplain it, but she felt he could take it.

"You're quite a sophisticated woman," Peter observed. "What's your life story?"

"I thought we were talking about you," said Constance.

"I'd rather talk about you," Peter retorted.

"Fair enough," said Constance. She could still find out more about him while seemingly talking about herself. "As I said, I grew up on a yacht as a child, but then my parents had a very messy divorce. My mother got sick and passed away, and my father had other priorities, so at sixteen, I became the ward of my uncle Harold…"

"Your uncle Harold, like the owner of the design company?"

Oh no. She could imagine Peter's thoughts right then.

"Yes. But don't worry. There's no nepotism. He doesn't treat me any better than any of the other employees. So don't think that you're getting a second-rate designer."

She forced herself to smile encouragingly, though she couldn't help but think of Penelope, who was, as they spoke, probably attending an Art Basel event, not that she was even cool enough to want to go and enjoying her job doing a pedestrian redesign on a spectacular yacht in Miami.

"Harold's a wonderful person," said Peter. "We have history, and that's why I wanted to trust his company with this job, despite…you know."

Peter's voice trailed off.

Alarm bells went off in Constance's head. Despite what? What was going on? Had Harold mentioned reservations about her? Or was something worse than she'd thought going on with the firm? She was dying to ask, but she realized that prodding Peter would probably hurt her. Also, they had history. So why couldn't Harold tell her more about Peter and his wishes?

Constance tried to act casual and normal. She was beyond eager to change the subject, and she would have to bring this up with Harold as soon as she spoke to him.

"I wish Harold still had his partner, what a devastating loss," Peter continued, as if it was a logical segue. But Constance was thankful for the non sequitur.

"Yes, Stefan really was a wonderful man."

But now, she was sad. Stefan really had been the clown of the family, and she had loved that. Even though Harold had met him relatively late in life, he had become a natural part of their atypical little family unit. They had enjoyed some memorable adventures together, but they had lost him far too soon.

Now, Constance's optimistic mood was ruined. So, she might as well prod a bit more.

"So, my friend Natasha was a guest on your old yacht in Saint Barts. She raved about it. What happened to that boat and who did that one? Because from what I hear, they were quite talented. Not that I'm upset to have this job. Far from it."

Ugh. She was babbling. This was embarrassing. But seeing how Peter's expression had suddenly changed made her nervous.

"I had no designer for that one," he said. "It was designed by a friend."

The look on his face, and the way he said friend made it sound like it was not a friend at all, but someone who was much more important than that. In for a penny, in for a pound, Constance decided.

"Natasha said you had the most gorgeous tableware. Is that in storage somewhere? I wonder if we could reuse it."

"I sold the yacht furnished," Peter said, his thunderous expression inviting for further questioning.

Oh boy, there was a story here. Constance was sure of it. Most designers would have been thrilled that he'd sold all the contents of the boat, because it meant a clean slate. But Constance was not most designers. She liked incorporating history. Also, this abrupt sale did not bode well. It spoke of some kind of trauma, which was at the heart of the whole issue.

"I'm sorry if you felt like I was prying," said Constance. "Do you want to hear more about me?"

"Yes," said Peter. "I do, actually."

Was she hallucinating, or was there a tear in the corner of his eye?

"Do you want to hear about how I became a designer?"

"Yes, I would like that," said Peter.

"Well, my junior year abroad in college, I was majoring in art history," she said, taking another sip of wine and handing Peter a cheese cracker layered with a walnut and honey. Cheese always made people feel better. "And anyway, I went to Florence. And when I was in Florence, I was invited to the home of local aristocrats, family friends of my best friend Chiara. So, we went to this... Palazzo, I guess you would call it. It sounds pretentious when I say it, but... I don't know. It's hard to express how comfortable and elegant this place was, and for me, being in this place that was full of history, full of layers, I think it made me decide that I wanted to learn to create that for people."

Constance had left the more painful part unsaid. That, growing up on a yacht, then boarding school, and losing the one relationship that had felt like home...she couldn't do that for herself.

"That's beautiful," said Peter. "I'm sure your home is stunning. Do you have a house in Miami?"

Constance blushed.

"Well, I do have a casita in a historic apartment block but... I had the best intentions for it, but I've always got a foot out the door, so I've never really made it my own. I know it sounds crazy, but something's blocking me."

She didn't know why she was being so honest with Peter. None of what she was saying was very flattering to her talent as a designer. She should be able to design things in any conditions.

"Thank you for your honesty," said Peter. "That takes bravery."

"I hope you don't think that this means I can't create a wonderful space for you," said Constance. "I'm confident that I can... it just... There's a lot of pressure on me," she said. "I want to make Harold proud. And I want to make you happy. I can tell that this is important for you. This is not just some show-off toy that you have. This is something that means something to you, which is why I'm trying to understand you better, and, well, I'm not going to lie; I heard about the previous designers who..."

"Don't worry about them," said Peter, interrupting her rambling. "They just weren't right. You get me, much more than they ever did. Listen, I know I'm a difficult man. Hopefully, this will all work out."

"Oh, and I wanted to ask you- about publication- what are your expectations?"

Peter looked at her strangely.

"Why don't we worry about the design, first?"

Damn. That was all the response she needed. She'd thought they were getting warm and fuzzy, but now she saw that she still might get kicked off. And, let's be honest, someone like Peter probably had sky-high standards for the kind of press he expected. Constance's heart sank.

"This really is a delightful charcuterie board," Peter said. "Thank you for doing this for me. But I'm a bit tired. I think I'm going to turn in."

"OK," said Constance. She hoped she hadn't said anything to make him want to leave, but he did seem genuinely tired. "And tomorrow's a new day. I'm going to be exploring more of the local fabricators and resources, the day, after I'll have vision boards ready for you. Does that sound good?"

"I'll be looking forward to it."

Peter rose, gave her a wave, and set towards the stairs leading to his stateroom. Constance took the charcuterie tray back to the kitchen, ate a few more pieces of cheese, and took a last sip of wine. She carefully wrapped the leftover cheese and meats in aluminum foil, so she could snack on them throughout the week. She did the dishes and looked around, feeling empty.

Chapter 26

She thought of Lorenzo. Would she really ping him for a drink? It was awkward to see him, of course, especially after she'd thrown herself at him. But there it was. The old addiction to Lorenzo, coming back. This whole seduction plan of hers, it was a stupid one, wasn't it? Dangerous. She checked the time. It was only 8:00, which, in French time, was positively early, even if it had been dark for eons. As she was still deliberating, her phone pinged. Lorenzo.

So, how did your cheese go? Or are you still preparing it?

No, it's done already, she wrote back. He was tired.

I'm not tired, Lorenzo wrote back.

Neither am I.

So how about that drink before you turn in? He replied, almost before she hit the send button.

I could be persuaded, Constance wrote back.

Why don't I pick you up at the boat in 15 minutes?

Perfect.

She hurried into her suite and examined herself in the full-length mirror. She was wearing pretty much what she'd been wearing all day, but she didn't want Lorenzo to think she'd made too much of an effort. She ran a brush through her hair and added a lashing of mascara. She thought about adding some red lipstick and decided against it. Not for any reason, of course. She threw on her leather jacket and decided to wait on the deck of the ship, but kind of regretted it, because it was now drizzling outside. What odious weather. As she waited, she closed her eyes for a minute, trying to visualize how she could make this yacht truly special for Peter. She needed to strike a fine balance between personal and universal, in case he up and sold this one, too.

When she opened her eyes, there was a vision in front of her. Lorenzo. In his Navy pea coat, his turtleneck sweater, and the jeans that made him look so damn sexy. And an umbrella, thank goodness.

Constance walked down the gangplank, noticing how Lorenzo's eyes swept over her body and then glued themselves to hers. Maybe he missed her a little bit. Maybe he did care. Too bad, though; he'd left her, and now he'd lost his opportunity to be with her, though she realized she was completely lying to herself. Every time she saw him, the only thing she wanted was to be with him all the time. Maybe seducing him would get that out of her mind once and for all. She was probably just wanting to relive a few of their interludes. To get it out of her system.

"I'm glad you were able to come out," said Lorenzo, bending down to kiss her on both cheeks. Even that small touch from him felt so good. She started walking, and he reached out for her arm, facing her on the sidewalk.

"I hope you're not feeling awkward after the other night," he said. "I know it was probably the alcohol talking."

"I knew what I was doing." She looked at him more boldly than she felt, giving him her most charming smile, and batting her eyelashes at him.

"How do you do that?" He asked, groaning.

"What?"

"Drive me crazy just by looking at me- just by being near me," he said.

This made her feel good, but it also made her mad, because if he'd been that into her, why had he left her in the first place?

"Where are you taking me?" She asked, changing the subject.

"There's a little pop-up bar with artisanal cocktails at the Pan Dei Palace."

Constance had forgotten about the Pan Dei. A charming space.

"Why do they bother being open in the winter?" She asked. "There's nobody in town."

"We're here, aren't we? And there are quite a few restauranteurs, hoteliers, artists and decorators who spend the offseason here. After all, that's when things get done."

"You have a point," she admitted. "It would seem like maybe Saint Tropez should be even cooler in the winter months, what with all the creative people here."

"That's how I feel," said Lorenzo. "I'm really trying to capitalize on that with my magazine."

"Tell me more about that," said Constance, as they kept walking. "The other night, we got distracted."

She felt him tighten his grip on her arm. Good.

"Oddly," said Lorenzo, "it's been quite a passion project of mine, and a challenge. But I feel like I'm finally on the right track."

They had already arrived in front of the heavy wooden doors of the Pan Dei Palace. A uniformed doorman stood in front.

"If I were you, I would just hang out inside until someone rings," said Constance. "It's freezing out."

"You can say that again," said the doorman. "But Lorenzo gave me a heads up that you were arriving. Come on in."

He opened the door, and they stepped into an Indian wonderland full of dark woods, sweeping arches, sumptuous fabrics, and colorful art. Legend had it that an Indian princess had fallen in love with a French sailor, and that he had built this palace for her. Constance didn't know how much truth lay in the story, but she thought it was very romantic and charming indeed. She reminded herself that she should spend more time here. She noticed the delightful courtyard ahead, which she remembered from a previous visit, and noticed that the swimming pool was still full, possibly heated. Maybe the hotel had a day pass. That would eat up her daily allowance, but it would be worth it, she decided.

"The bar is over there, to the left," said the doorman. They proceeded through the lobby and to the dark and elegant bar, which was strikingly dim, only lit with tea lights. A few other well-dressed people sat in the club chairs in the corner. There was one couple at one end of the bar, so Lorenzo and Constance took the other side.

The bartender greeted Lorenzo as one greets an old friend.

"This is Hector," said Lorenzo. "Hector was a photographer, as well, back in the day. We were quite the competitors, weren't we, Hector?"

"Impossible to compete with you," said Hector, smiling. "It's fun for us to be working together, now."

"Indeed," said Lorenzo. "We're trying to create a concept that's much larger than just a magazine," he explained to Constance. "It's more of an experiential construct, with all kinds of different creatives contributing. And then we document it in the magazine, so we're creating culture at the same time as we're reporting on it."

"I love that idea," said Constance.

"What would you like to drink?" Asked Hector.

"I think it would be fair to ask you to surprise us," Constance replied.

"Yes, please do," said Lorenzo. "Whatever you want to make us."

"I'll make you two different drinks, and you can taste both," Hector said, winking. Well, Hector was certainly cheeky, assuming that they were on drink sharing terms. Granted, they had swapped spit just the other day, and hopefully that would happen again.

"So how did your meeting go? How was the charcuterie received?"

"He loved it. But he told me that he'd had better before."

"Really? That's a bit rude."

"Actually, it was interesting. There is definitely a woman involved in this Peter's backstory. According to my friend Natasha, his previous yacht had a woman's touch and he sold it completely furnished. Which is odd. I mean, yes, the furniture on yachts is often custom made, but all of the dishes, soft furnishings, and art?"

"That does seem peculiar," said Lorenzo. "But I don't know why you automatically jump to the theory of heartbreak."

"The fact that he doesn't want to talk about it sounds like a sensitive subject. If it had just been a question of simply not liking the yacht anymore, I don't think he'd be afraid to tell me that, especially since I'm his decorator. And also, the fact that he's fired two decorators from this project. That speaks to me of emotion."

"Makes sense," said Lorenzo. "We men don't deal well with rejection. It does affect us."

Constance gave him a look. As if he knew what that was like, unless he'd been dumped in the time between leaving her and now. But it was none of her business, and she didn't want to know about the relationships he'd been in since they had said their last goodbye.

"I've decided the boat needs a library with a fireplace," said Constance, changing the subject.

"A fireplace on a yacht?"

"I had one on the boat I grew up on."

Constance wished that Lorenzo could have seen the DeFever. It would help him to understand what she was about. She had, after all, seen Lorenzo's mother's place, which had told her so much about him. When she'd met him, he'd been so bohemian that she'd been absolutely taken aback when she'd met Countess Carlotta. It was much easier to believe that Lorenzo was a Count now, perhaps, but when he was younger, riding around on a motorcycle in ripped jeans and longer hair, he absolutely looked like a bad boy, much more so than like the scion of two old Italian families. It wasn't like Lorenzo had gobs of money. All that was left from his family was the old Castello, which was really an elegant ruin of a country home, minute fractional rights to a palazzo that was ever sinking into the Venetian canal, and a few beautiful paintings that no one would ever sell. But Lorenzo didn't need money to be compelling. Lorenzo would have been perfect for her. If he hadn't left her.

Hector came back with two glasses, interrupting her negative thoughts.

"This is my twist on the Negroni," he said, gesturing to one. "And this one is like an old fashioned…"

"I tend to like an old fashioned," said Constance.

"Oh, I thought you were a Negroni girl," Lorenzo laughed.

"Yeah, my friends joke that I change favorite cocktails all the time. But the funny thing is, you remember me being a Negroni girl. I actually was a Negroni girl again just a few months ago. I've recently gone back to old fashioned- so you see, everything that's old is sometimes new again."

"Ah," said Lorenzo, lowering his voice as the bartender walked away. "So, is that what you're doing here? Circling back around to me?"

"What? Lorenzo, I'm hardly circling back around. I didn't know I would find you here," she said. "Believe me, I wouldn't have done this on purpose, after what happened last time."

"Pray tell, what exactly did happen last time? In your opinion?" She stared at him.

"You know damn well what happened," she said angrily. "I thought we were having a pleasant evening."

Lorenzo's expression grew serious, and for a moment, she actually thought he might pick up and leave. She didn't want that to happen again. It was up to her to make him stay, if she wanted to seduce him on her own terms. She leaned in and whispered in his ear.

"Now that we're going down memory lane," she said, "I was remembering that one time, near your country house. When we went for a walk in the olive grove?"

She leaned back to see if the recollection had had the desired effect. Lorenzo's eyes flew to hers, a flame burning in them. She loved it that she could still do that with just a few well-chosen words. It was almost too easy.

"You mean the time I took you behind a tree?" He asked.

"Yes," she whispered, as she put her hand on his leg. "I was wearing, I believe it was a blue sun dress."

"Red," said Lorenzo. "You thought I could forget that? Your red sun dress- and you had nothing on underneath it, you naughty girl."

"Well, it was just so hot out," said Constance innocently. "And I didn't think you would find out I had nothing on underneath. It was your fault, for being so forward with me."

"Yes, I did pitch you forward, didn't I?" He growled into her ear. "Do you remember how that felt?"

Oh, Constance remembered. Remembered her hands grasping the rough trunk of the olive tree. Her cheek against the bark. The sun glowing red through the eyelids of her closed eyes, as she savored the feeling of Lorenzo's hands on her hips. How delicious it had felt when he'd first entered her, taking his time, moving his hands slowly to her breasts, squeezing as he thrust inside of her. She'd been on the pill back then, because they'd been supposedly in a committed relationship. And she'd loved feeling the full, hot, hard length of him, without anything between them. She knew that now, if she seduced him, when she seduced him, she'd make him wear a condom. After all, who knew where he'd been? Don't think about that. Back to the memories. His biting her neck, holding onto her shoulders, now, for leverage, as he ground against her. The wave of pleasure that came over her body, halfway between a tingle and a throb. The memory was so vivid, so delicious, that she now found herself squeezing Lorenzo's muscular thigh with her hand, her breathing a bit labored.

"Oh, you do remember, don't you?"

Lorenzo leaned in and gave her a slow, teasing kiss on the mouth. She parted her lips and let his tongue explore and join with hers, the tastes of their two cocktails combined in the most delicious manner. And again, she found herself so hungry for him that she could barely stand it. Who was seducing whom? It was unfair, the effect he had on her. How was it possible that two people could have this reaction to each other, and not manage to make things work between them. It was that thought broke the spell, more than a discreet cough from the other side of the bar.

"Sorry to interrupt," said Hector, "But I think one of your employees is over there. I didn't know if you wanted them to see the boss in such a compromising position."

Lorenzo and Constance both looked over to the corner that Hector was gesturing towards. Constance groaned. Of course, it was Sophie, the worst possible person to spot them like this. Lorenzo noticed Constance's expression.

"Are you sure you don't know her? I don't know why you have so much against her. So far, she's not done anything to make me think that she's anything less than a stellar employee."

"What do you mean? I have nothing against her," said Constance, her heart hammering. If Sophie wanted to, she could absolutely wreck her reputation with Lorenzo. Did she need to preemptively tell Lorenzo about her relationship with Carlos White? No. It was none of his business. Carlos White was in the past. Yes, it didn't speak very well about her, the fact that she had slept with her client, and Carlos White was not the only one. This would open up a whole can of worms that she had no desire to let out.

"Thanks for the heads up," Lorenzo told Hector, smiling. "But I have nothing to hide. Constance and I have known each other for a long time," he said.

"Ohh, this is that Constance," said Hector, his eyes growing wide.

"What do you mean, that Constance?" She said, before deciding that it did not behoove her to make a scene. "Never mind," she smiled. "The past is in the past."

"Well, I'm glad you're back in his life," said Hector. "I know that Lorenzo was devastated when…"

Constance refrained from scoffing and changed the subject.

"Speaking of devastating, you sure do make your drinks strong. Is there anything else that you'd like us to try?"

She picked up her glass and let the large ice cube dance in the bottom of it. She hadn't realized she'd already drained the cocktail. She was feeling a tiny bit tipsy. But just perfectly so. She could handle one more. She wasn't driving anywhere, didn't have anywhere to be.

"Yes, I'll make you something special," said Hector. "How about you, Lorenzo?"

"No, I've got work tomorrow," said Lorenzo.

Constance got the uncomfortable feeling that the flirty part of their evening had just ended. Whether it was something that she had said, or something that Hector had said, or the presence of Sophie, the mood had changed for the worse. Well, she could still catch up with him and talk shop.

"So," she said, as Hector brought her second cocktail. "I'm still struggling with the yacht design. I want to create something soulful, with layers, you know, kind of like your mom's house."

"My mom did have exquisite taste."

I also need something that is going to be high concept and impressive if I have any chance of getting the boat in a magazine."

"There's a chance we could put the yacht in my magazine," said Lorenzo. "But it needs to be the right thing. You understand that, right?"

"Lorenzo, I would never try to force you to help me out like that. If it's not right for your magazine, I would never expect you to include it," she said. She was a little offended, for a second, that Lorenzo was being so negative, but then she talked herself back down. He was correct. This was his professional reputation, after all.

"I'm motivated to make it extraordinary for the client, and not just because of the possibility of getting press coverage. It's just not easy, because the client's not very forthcoming."

"Yeah, that's a challenge," said Lorenzo. "But you'll figure it out. You're great with challenges."

She was worried for a moment that he might say something like "as long as you're not running away from them," but he didn't, thank goodness. He had better self-control than she did in that department. In most departments, probably.

"Well, it's getting late," she said. "I think I'd better turn in. As you said, work tomorrow."

"I'll walk you back," he said.

"No, I'm fine. I could use the fresh air and the thinking space."

"No, I insist," said Lorenzo. "Who would I be if I didn't walk you back? You can think on the deck of the yacht."

Lorenzo waved at Hector.

"The bill please, my friend."

"It's on me," said Hector.

"Absolutely not," Lorenzo retorted. "Business is business, remember, we've talked about this."

"Oh, all right, I know," said Hector.

He brought them a check and Lorenzo put down a €50 bill.

"Keep the change. I'll see you soon," he said.

"Absolutely. See you both soon," said Hector, winking.

Lorenzo and Constance walked out into the night.

"Lorenzo, you've got to stop paying for me like this. I feel like I owe you, now."

"Good," he replied, smiling.

She liked to see him smile like this, hated it when he scowled, especially when she had caused it.

It had gotten even colder than it had been when Lorenzo had picked Constance up, and she cursed herself for the optimism that had led her to wear only a leather jacket. He took her arm; in case she stumbled on one of the slippery cobblestones in the streets. They were indeed slippery, and she almost did lose her footing once, and he held her all the tighter. It felt so good to have the warmth of his body along her side.

She now called up another memory, this one warmer and fuzzier than hot and steamy. They'd gone to Switzerland and stayed in a chalet belonging to friend of a friend, who hadn't bothered to give them the heads up that the place had no central heat. They'd cuddled together under the duvet, not wanting to get out of bed. He'd whispered stories to her all through the evening, about growing up in Italy, and old crumbling palazzos, and princesses and fairy tale animals, and she'd thought to herself that he would make such a good father, even though she'd felt too young to think of children very seriously at the time. And now, well, if she were to be honest, her biological clock was ticking so loudly, it was more like booming. He really would make an amazing father, she thought. Or maybe it was just the idea of him... after all, hadn't he left her? How could she trust a man like that to raise children with, to be with forever? Because having been through the shit show that was her parents' divorce, she had no intention of making the same mistakes as they had. But she also didn't want to find herself in a situation where she stayed alone for so long, maybe only finding her soulmate in the twilight years, like Harold and Stefan had done. She wanted time to enjoy the adventure with someone.

"Sorry- what were you saying?" She said, as something Lorenzo said knocked her out of her reverie.

"I said, I'd love to be able to cook for you at my place."

"I can't believe you'd want to see me again," she said.

"Yes, it hurts to be together like this, but I'll take whatever I can get."

"It hurts you? How can you say that?" asked Constance. "You're the one who left me."

"Absolutely not," said Lorenzo. "How can you say that?"

"I don't want to talk about it," said Constance.

"We're going to have to talk about it at some point," said Lorenzo.

"No. I'm just going to be here for a little bit. I'm going to finish my project. And then I'm going to leave. I'm going to go back to Miami, and I'll just go on with my life, and you'll go on with yours."

"Is that really what you want?" Asked Lorenzo, staring into her eyes, as if daring her to say it. His features a little pinched. Pained. As if she had indeed hurt him. That was rich. He had hurt her. She was starting to realize that having a fling would be impossible. But the thought of not having him, at least once more, was impossible too.

They had arrived at the yacht. She hadn't even noticed. Her head hurt, and so did her heart.

"I guess we're here," she said to Lorenzo.

"Yes."

His voice was lugubrious.

"Thank you so much for taking me out," she said, as a peace offering. "Saint Tropez in the offseason is so much better than I thought it might be- thanks to you."

"You would have found things to do without me," he said.

He backed a few steps away from her. Wow. Not even a kiss on the cheek. No hug. All right, if that was the way he was going to play it.

"Well, good night then," she said.

She backed a few steps away and then turned to walk up the gangplank. She let herself in and turned to see Lorenzo, lifting up an arm to wave at her, as if in a final salutation. What the hell? This seduction was absolutely not going according to plan. But also, it hurt far too much. What was she going to do? This was ridiculous. She needed to focus on her job. Forget the rest of this bullshit. She went to her room, got herself ready, and went to bed.

Chapter 27

Constance woke up feeling deflated, even more unmoored than usual, after the previous evening's argument with Lorenzo. As she brushed her teeth and examined her tired complexion in the mirror, she found herself filled with self-loathing. Why couldn't she just keep it light and cheerful between them? Seduce him and leave him? But, she realized, she didn't have it in her. At least, not the way she was feeling now. She needed to cheer herself up.

As she finished getting ready, selecting her brightest sweater, a Kelly-green Shetland one that matched the Mini Cooper she'd left behind in Miami, she alit on a plan that might make her feel better. The day before, Constance had been delighted to notice that a decor shop she'd always liked was holding a pop-up for the next few days, selling floor samples to make way for new items when the season began. She remembered the place having great pottery, plates, vases, and the like. It would be perfect to lend a bit of personality to the decor of the yacht, even if she still was not crystal clear on the concept. The shop, however, would be good for inspiration. She had noticed some beautiful placemats in the window already, as well as some interesting mirrors that could potentially be a good addition to the bar area.

But first, Constance reminded herself, do your work.

Once she had struggled to put together a vision board, while sitting at her usual table at le Senequier, only partially hoping she might run into Lorenzo, she decided to take a break and to treat herself to a slice of tart Tropezienne before taking herself on a creative date to the store. She had been there before, in the summer, and had admired the taste of the shop owner, who sourced things both locally and further afield. She was looking forward to inspiring herself and maybe even treating herself to something that might decorate her apartment in Miami, though she had to admit that the thought of settling into that place any further nearly gave her indigestion. She couldn't think of how to make it feel like home. If Harold wasn't in Miami, there was no way she would live there by choice.

She walked down the empty street, the heels of her boots clacking against the cobblestones. She took in a deep breath of sea air. It was going to be a beautiful day. She wondered if Lorenzo was going to call her, even though the argument the day before had been completely her fault. She had a feeling he wouldn't call. She would just resign herself to spending an evening in. Peter was out of town for a day or two, so she had the yacht to herself. There were worse places one could be, even if it did feel a little bit lonely sometimes. She'd never had much of a problem being alone. It was just when she was craving being with somebody that the isolation really hurt.

Midway down the street, she found the shop. When she'd been in the summer, the store had been a mob scene, but today she looked forward to having the space to herself and having the time to ask whoever was working there whichever questions might pop into her head. Maybe it would even be the owner. Constance thought she remembered the owner as being a tall, elegant brunette, who had been only too happy to tell her about her inspiration shopping trips in Morocco. Constance grasped the doorknob and swung the door open. A bell tinkled and she carefully closed the door behind her, letting her eyes adjust to the dimmer light. The shopkeeper was occupied with another customer in the back corner of the shop, a blonde woman who had her back to Constance. The back of the customer's head looked suspiciously like Sophie's. Hopefully, Constance was just being paranoid. But the less she saw of Sophie, the better, and she'd already bumped into her two too many times. Third time might be the opposite of the charm, the moment when Sophie finally put two and two together and recognized Constance as the alleged home wrecker who had carried on a so-called affair with her father.

Constance browsed the shelves, carefully keeping her back to the blonde, picking up objects, considering what might work on the yacht, or what might finally be the secret ingredient to making her Miami place feel like home. She jotted down some prices. Would it be rude to take some pictures? She turned to check if the shopkeeper was still busy with the other customer. As she looked over, her eyes met Sophie's. Sophie did a double take, excused herself, cutting short whatever the discussion she'd been having with the shopkeeper, and crossed the store, heading directly for Constance. Oh, no, that couldn't be good.

"Constance," said Sophie, her tone carrying more than a dash of accusation.

Constance knew there were a few ways to play this, innocence being the best option. But that ship might have sailed.

"Do we know each other?" Said Constance.

"I'm Sophie?"

Great, now she was mad at not having been recognized. Oh well.

"Oh yes! I recognize you now! You work for Lorenzo."

"With Lorenzo. But I don't just work with Lorenzo. It appears you know my father- quite intimately, it would seem."

"Oh?"

"Carlos White," said Sophie.

"Oh! Lovely, Carlos, yes. He was a client of mine," said Constance. "What a small world. However did you put two and two together?"

"Doesn't matter," said Sophie. "Listen, you'd better stay away from my dad if you know what's good for you."

"What do you mean?" Asked Constance.

Now, this was offensive. Things were completely over with Carlos. They'd never been that much of a thing in the first place. She'd never had the intention of staying with him, billionaire or not. They just weren't a good fit. The relationship had been one of convenience and had helped her to get away with not fully finishing the job, if she was quite honest with herself. Not a flattering description of a supposed love affair, but there they were. And she knew for certain that we would never use that sort of technique again.

"I'm sorry- yes, your father was a client. But I have no intention of continuing to see him," she said, as calmly as she could.

"You're lying. My dad's a billionaire. He attracts all manner of riffraff like you. And you'd better stay away from him if you know what's good for you."

Constance had to fight with herself so she wouldn't answer the way she wanted to, which would only start a battle.

"Sophie, your father and I are not in touch. I have no interest in a relationship with him, anything other than professional."

"So, is that what's going on with Lorenzo, too?" asked Sophie.

"What are you talking about?"

"I saw you with him at the bar. Is that how you conduct all your professional relationships? I know you want to have the boat you're doing in the magazine. So… what? Are you planning on seducing Lorenzo?"

Constance stared at her, indignant.

"This is absolutely none of your business, but Lorenzo and I have a long history. And no, I don't expect him to take our personal relationship into consideration when it comes to whether the magazine takes on this project or not."

"Whatever. I'm going to make things two things crystal clear," said Sophie. "Number one, I have zero intention of letting you get your little project into the magazine. On principle. And because I don't like you. Number two, if you do anything to make me think that you're approaching my father again, I'm going to tell Lorenzo all about your little affair."

"You're being ridiculous. That is none of Lorenzo's business."

But as she said it, Constance knew how Lorenzo would perceive it. It didn't look good for her. And Lorenzo had always been a little jealous, much as she was. But the good news was, she had no intention of contacting Carlos White. So hopefully, Sophie would not take it upon herself to say anything. Then again, how would a woman like that hold back on divulging such useful information, especially if it felt like leverage? Carlos had always been careful not to say anything critical about his daughter, but from what Constance had gleaned, he did not have too high an opinion of her, especially where her mental stability was concerned. Apparently, she had terrorized one of their neighbors on Saint Barts, and it had not gone well. And now, here she was in Saint Tropez. A coincidence, but an inconvenient one. She felt a bit dizzy and nauseous. All thoughts of the Tarte Tropezienne she'd promised herself were gone now, as the bile rose up in her throat.

"Anyway," said Sophie lightly, "I need to get back to work. Should I say hello to Lorenzo for you?"

"Don't bother," said Sophie. "I can say hello to him myself if I choose to. This has nothing to do with you."

"I'll be the judge of that," said Sophie. "Have a great day." And with that, she turned dramatically on her heel and exited the shop, slamming the door behind her, making the bell jump and clang, jangling in time with Constance's nerves.

"What was that about?" Asked the shopkeeper, as she came up to Constance. It was indeed the owner of the store.

"Hi," said Constance. "Nice to see you again. Oh that? Just a friend of a friend, making threats, you know, as one does."

The shop owner smiled.

"I'm Nicole, by the way, nice to see you again, too. Your name's on the tip of my tongue."

"Constance. Have you been to Morocco lately?"

"I have," said Nicole. "I have a place there, now. And I've been trying to run a little bread and breakfast."

"That's my dream," said Constance. "But for now, I'm decorating a yacht, and I'm looking for a few things that would personalize the decor."

"Of course," said Nicole. "Here, let me show you some good things I haven't had a chance to put out yet."

Constance spent the next hour happily ensconced in discussions of ceramics and decorative touches, selecting a handful of objects that would add some charm and a contemporary feel to the yacht's decor, and photographing them.

"How long are you here?" Asked Nicole.

"Not sure- until I'm done with the yacht," said Constance. "But I would love to stay in Europe for longer. I just don't know how it would feel, you know, as a non-native French speaker. And I don't know if I would want to be in France or in Italy or both…"

"We should have a drink," said Nicole. "As an English woman, it's been a learning curve, but my husband is European, which made it easier and well…What are you up to this evening?"

"Nothing," said Constance. The chances of Lorenzo reaching out were ever narrowing.

"Well, let's have a glass of wine," said Nicole. "What about 5:00? Senequier? We don't have too many other choices right now."

"Actually, I think the bartender at Pan Dei Palace is working this evening," said Constance.

"Well, look at you. I thought I was the local," said Nicole. "OK, I'll meet you at Pan Dei or …it's just down the street. Why don't you come pick me up and we'll walk over together, in case it's closed."

Constance left the shop, smiling to herself. She had made a friend. Her first friend in Saint Tropez other than Lorenzo, and that didn't count much, did it? Bolstered, and feeling lighter than she had in a while, Constance decided to get herself the Tarte Tropezienne after all. Once she had snagged one, she took herself back to the boat and did a solid few hours of work, impressing herself with her ability to concentrate. Between the sugar high and the ample caffeine she'd consumed, it should have been no wonder. But she was feeling optimistic, like maybe she would get this all done after all. Only Sophie's promise of never putting the boat in the magazine darkened her mood. But Sophie wasn't the only one who could decide, was she? If the boat was truly phenomenal, even Sophie would see the merits of publishing it. Anyway, she would cross that bridge when she came to it. For now, there were some design decisions to be made, and fast. She was still scared of Peter firing her like he had everyone else before she even had a chance to show him what she could do.

Chapter 28

The next morning, Constance sat at her favorite second row table at Le Senequier, nursing a hangover and a black coffee. Following a pep talk from Nicole over one too many cocktails, she had finally tracked down the two designers Peter had fired. She didn't feel good about talking about her client behind his back, but she really needed to find out what had happened with each of these people- what had caused his dissatisfaction- because she simply couldn't afford to meet the same fate. He ego couldn't take the hit, and also, she realized that she craved seeing Lorenzo too much to leave town now. And at this point, having gotten to know Peter a little bit better, she genuinely wanted to make him happy by creating something that he would truly enjoy.

She took a deep breath and dialed the first number, for Claire Pierpont, who Constance believed worked out of Monaco.

"Hi, Claire?"

"Yes," said a female voice, the tone a bit cautious.

Constance rushed in to fill the void before Claire could have the opportunity to hang up.

"My name is Constance Morgan. I was calling because I'm working on Peter Holmes' boat, and I was wondering if I could ask you a few questions about your experience working for him. As I understand, you ended up coming off the project."

Constance did not want to assume that Claire had been fired, even though that seemed to be the reality.

The timbre of Claire's voice changed, as she launched into self-preservation mode.

"Well, yes, it just wasn't a good fit," she said. "I proposed a few different designs and Mr. Holmes was not satisfied with any of them. I don't think he really knows what he wants himself, frankly. I proposed the best of the best, all the most modern materials. All the most luxury finishes. And somehow, that just wasn't what he was looking for. But again, I don't think he knows what he's looking for, at the end of the day."

"Fair enough," said Constance. "Well, if it's OK, can you maybe tell me a little bit about the concepts that you presented? Full disclosure, I'm working for him and I'm just trying to make sure I avoid presenting him something that he's already nixed."

"You name it. I tried it," said Claire. "I did a modern design with some silver leafed walls. You know, obviously behind a cover, so that they don't oxidize too fast, but he hated that. And then I did one that had some wallpaper. Again, specially treated and all of that. I mean, I didn't cut any corners, if that's what you're thinking."

"Of course not," said Constance, encouragingly.

"And then I tried a lot of built ins. No go. I tried something with wood, something with carbon. And honestly, it's like I couldn't get anything right. And it's funny, you know, because I'd seen his other yacht- in pictures at least. And well, it's one of the tackier ones, isn't it?"

"You mean the red one?"

"Yeah, the red one. I mean, who has a red yacht?"

Constance pondered this. Most times, when someone had a less than ideal yacht, it was a question of the cost.

"It was crazy, how the designer really went all in with the red theme. The Hermès plates. Balcons de Guadalquivir. The Scalamandré zebras, with a red background, in a powder room," said Claire.

"You don't know who designed that one, do you?" Constance asked Claire.

That would be a useful avenue to explore, because clearly, Peter seemed to have been fine with that design but then, he had sold the yacht, quickly, and at a loss. There had to be something there. This wasn't logical behavior for a businessman like him.

"Yeah, I wish I could help you more," said Claire. "I saw an article, with the photos, and everything, but I can't remember the designer's name. She's not famous, or at least not a traditional yacht designer. It was some woman with red eyeglasses. Maybe she was involved with Peter at some point. That's my theory."

Well, stranger things had happened. Constance wondered why Peter hadn't just hired the previous designer of the red yacht again, but then again, why had he sold it? A breakup? So many questions, none of which she felt she could ask Peter directly. And her conversation with Claire wasn't yielding anything useful.

"Well, I'm not going to waste any more of your time," said Constance. "Thank you so much for answering my questions." "Yeah, good luck," said Claire. "He's very difficult."

Constance hung up and tried the next number, which belonged to Hidalgo Pieres, a popular South American designer who had done a few boats, but who had also created a boutique hotel in Paris and a restaurant in Palm Beach, among other projects. He was relatively high profile, yet he had also been fired by Peter. The phone rang and rang, with no response. It eventually went over to voicemail. Constance knew that she herself never checked her voicemails. So she decided to text.

Hi, I just tried to call you, she wrote. My name is Constance Morgan. I'm the new designer for the Lombard 4, and I hear that you worked on this project for a time. I was hoping to get some insights on what your experience was.

A response came through almost immediately.

Experience? ha. The owner's an asshole.

Yikes. May I ask what kind of designs he rejected or why things ended on a bad note?

He just wasn't satisfied with anything, Hidalgo wrote back. He clearly doesn't know what he wants.

OK, thank you, Constance responded.

She was frustrated. She wasn't going to get anything more from this Hidalgo character. But then she realized, two out of two designers had said that Peter didn't know what he wanted. That was something. A frustrating something, but more than she'd had before.

Chapter 29

Constance put her phone down. Her brain was racing, and she didn't like that. She knew that it would leave her feeling scattered and confused. Usually, when she felt this way, a drive helped to get her settled back down again. She lifted up her hand, got the waiter's attention, and ordered a double espresso. That would also help her to get settled while she figured out a useful destination. Maybe the answer was in the designer of the previous yacht that Peter had owned. That yacht was all the way in Saint Barts, last she'd heard. But it had been published in a magazine, hadn't it? That's what Claire had said. Constance picked her phone back up, sipped her coffee, and went down the internet rabbit hole, searching for images of the interiors of the infamous Red Yacht. And there, finally, four pages down, she found it. An article in one of the regional French design magazines that focused on the South. Was this going to be the answer to the mystery?

There it was. The red and white plates. The floral details. The Scalamandré zebras. Even a Persian rug on the ground, which was atypical for a yacht. And then, a photo of a woman of a certain age- probably around Peter's age. She had chestnut hair with heavy bangs, and yes, red glasses. It was rare for a designer to impose their aesthetic so heavily on a client. Especially when it came to a color like red. Looking at the photo of this woman, Daphne Duplessis, her name was, according to the caption, Constance got a crazy feeling.

What if? What if there was something more between this Daphne and Peter than just the relationship between designer and client? Constance was well placed to know that this happened often. What if their split was something traumatic for Peter? What if that was why he'd sold the boat and needed something completely different, and why he needed the boat to be published, so that he could send a message to this woman? Constance read more of the article. At the end, a short biography of the designer. Constance translated. Daphne Duplessis lives in Bormes les Mimosas, where she owns a home furnishings shop.

Constance's heart started beating double time. Was this town like Saint Tropez? Was it seasonal to the point of everything being closed? She would have to go check. She looked up the store and could find a phone number and an address, but no opening hours. She dialed the number. No response. She double checked the location of the shop on the map on her phone. It was a mere hour away. In her current, enervated condition, she wouldn't be coming up with any cohesive design plans. A drive would do her good, and this might help her to solve a mystery.

She hurried to the harbor parking lot, retrieved her ugly Citroen, and headed towards Bormes les Mimosas. The Village was a hillside town, and Constance unfortunately realized that she had taken the back way, a road called La Mole that was infamous on tourist boards on the region, and which she had sworn to herself to avoid. It felt like she was driving up Space Mountain, navigating this narrow ribbon of asphalt wedged between mountain and cliff, but it was too late to turn around. There were no turnoffs. This would be a terrifying drive in the summer, when cars would be whizzing past in the opposite direction, but today it was deserted, thank goodness. When she finally arrived at the village, she easily found a parking spot in a parking lot near a plaza where a handful of old men played pétanque under a plane tree denuded of leaves. Constance locked the car, and emerged, adrenaline-drunk, making her way on shaky legs towards where she assumed the shop was. Most of the boutiques and restaurants were closed, but there were a few holdouts, and a few apartments and townhomes with open shutters, many of them with laundry hanging out the window, which was a bit of a vain pursuit, according to Constance, considering the damp weather that day. She double checked her phone again. Yes, this was the place. She looked up at the sign above a little storefront. Montagne Rouge. But unfortunately, the shop seemed very much closed. There was not the metal shutter that most shops had over the winter when they were permanently closed, but everything was dark within. The door was locked, the lights were off. But in the window was a very pleasing display; a painted Provençal chair with a tray on it, laden with multicolored glasses. A table with a tablecloth tumbling off of it, its linen folds sculptural rolls against the dark background of the interior of the shop. A taxidermy duck held pride of place on the table, a baroque pearl necklace around its delicate white neck. Very eclectic, thought Constance. Maybe this was what Peter Holmes reacted to. It was hard to express that on a boat. That sort of look could be in danger of weighing it down both visually and literally. That was one of the challenges with yacht design, and many interior designers who wanted to transition to designing yachts were not successful, because they did not understand the constraints. Constance, to her credit, actually did. Perhaps that was why Harold kept her on despite his frustration with her. Maybe she was still a credit to his company in some ways, despite her obvious liabilities. Constance cupped her hands on either side of her eyes and put her forehead against the cool glass of the shop's door, hoping to see more of what lay inside. But suddenly, she heard a cough behind her. She spun around and found herself looking deep into the hooded eyes of the woman whose photo she'd seen online.

"Daphne!"

"Do we know each other?" Asked the woman, visibly taken aback.

"Oh, sorry- that must be kind of creepy," said Constance. "I saw an article about you, and I thought I would stop by and see if your shop was open."

"Ah," said Daphne, still acting suspicious, but letting down her guard somewhat. "Do you want to come inside?" Constance stepped aside, and Daphne unlocked the door, gesturing for her to join her inside.

"My name is Constance. I'm an interior designer, too."

"Too? No. I am just a shopkeeper now," was Daphne's retort.

"Oh," said Constance, slightly deflated but deciding to forge ahead. "The interior design I do is for yachts."

Suddenly, she saw something shift in Daphne's demeanor. She'd touched a nerve.

"Oh, lovely," said Daphne. She pinched her lips together.

"Didn't you do a yacht, once?"

Constance hadn't come this far to get nothing from this woman.

"Yes," said Daphne. "But never again."

"Why not?" Asked Constance, knowing she was being indiscreet, but really needing to know.

Daphne sighed, gestured to two chairs on either side of an inlaid games table.

"Here, sit." Daphne dropped into the chair closest to her, every part of her expressing utter exhaustion. Constance sat down, too. Maybe this meant she would get an answer.

"I did it…for a friend," Daphne said, closing her eyes, as if the very thought was migraine-inducing.

"And you're not friends anymore?"

Constance was sure of it. There was a breakup in this story. Heartbreak.

"I don't know," said Daphne, her glasses steaming up. She removed them; put them back on. "Maybe it was a big misunderstanding. It took me two years to get that yacht exactly how he wanted it and how I wanted it. It was supposed to be for both of us and…Suffice it to say that things ended. I haven't spoken to him since. Now, he's on the other side of the world, in Saint Barts, so I don't need to worry about that."

Oh crap. Constance couldn't possibly let Daphne know whose yacht she was working on. But also, this might be the only person who truly knew what someone like Peter Holmes needed.

"You don't think you could try to go back and fix the relationship? It sounds like you cared a great deal for each other."

Daphne smiled sadly.

"I think it's too late for that, my dear. Too much water under the bridge. Both of us are too proud. We're too old. Listen to me. If you ever are in a relationship with someone you love, don't let that happen to you. There's nothing more tragic."

Constance's mind was reeling. She for a second had considered being mildly disingenuous for selfish reasons, and getting Daphne's input, without telling her who the client was, just to capitalize on her aesthetic. And then, in the next split second, had realized that she couldn't live with herself if she did that. But now, she had another idea in mind. She couldn't fix her one great relationship, but maybe, just maybe, she could have a little something to do with fixing this one. Time for reverse psychology.

"Oh. Then I imagine it's no use me begging you to help me to decorate a yacht for a client in St Tropez," she said, sadly. "It's a pity, your design for that St Barts client was so similar in mood to what I had in mind. But I understand if…"

"Wait- now that you're here, you might as well tell me about the job," said Daphne. "I don't think I would take it, but I'm curious. Who's the client?"

"Ohh, you know, just one of these billionaire types, I can't really give you the name. Security concerns," Constance lied through her teeth, feeling guilty about it but not seeing any way around it.

"All right," said Daphne. "I mean, it would be nice to know something about the client, wouldn't it?"

"Maybe, eventually, but really, since you're not coming on board…" said Constance, making a quick calculation. Daphne was on the hook. Once she was onboard, she might be OK with the project, even if she found out the client was Peter. And then, Constance might not only gain her design acumen, but also be able to play matchmaker. But that discovery needed to be delayed as long as possible, for both reasons.

"I haven't officially said no yet," Daphne pointed out.

"But you seem unsure. I can't take the risk, and even if you were to join the project, I feel like it would be best to get your unfiltered initial ideas and thoughts, you know, before you let any knowledge about the client shape your creativity," said Constance.

"Is he that famous?" Asked Daphne.

"I would say he's known. You've probably heard him of him," Constance said, shrugging.

"You're being very mysterious," said Daphne.

"You know how it is." Constance held her breath. Was she really going to do this?

"OK, so tell me more. Is it a sailing yacht or a motor yacht?"

"Motor," said Constance. "But classic, elegant. New. But with thoughtful details."

She pictured the Lombard 4 in her mind. Seeing it not only as it was, but also as how it could be, and tried to express these things to Daphne, without mentioning any details that might tip her off as to the actual identity of the boat and of its owner. From what she'd gleaned from Daphne so far, it seemed like she was a bit isolated, probably not keeping track of yacht sales and who owned what, but she couldn't take any chances.

"There are a few challenges, one of them having to do with the color scheme. I don't want it to be the usual blue and white," she said.

This, after all, was the truth. It would be impossible to make it the usual blue and white due to the green on the hull.

"I'm used to doing boats with interesting color schemes," said Daphne.

"Yes," said Constance, thankful to be speaking truthfully again. "Part of the reason I contacted you is that I love how you incorporated the red and white into the decor of that yacht you did."

"Yes. I'm sure the owner is still enjoying those Hermès place settings I had to track down from the four corners of the earth," Daphne said bitterly.

"I know a little bit about how you feel," said Constance. "I've had relationships with owners before. And it hurts, to know they're still enjoying the fruits of your labor."

Lie. She couldn't care less about those past clients, and she mostly flushed her designs out of her head as soon as she had completed them, or, let's be honest, mostly completed them. And she now realized that part of Peter's problem was that he was still reeling from the sale of his beloved yacht following his breakup with Daphne.

"So, what would you say you did to be so successful with that one project, when you were new to yacht design?" Asked Constance, now very much in interview mode.

"I would say that a big part of it was that I knew the yacht owner intimately," Daphne admitted. "And that wouldn't be the case with this project, so I'm curious as to why you are so intent on having me help you."

She looked at Constance with a shred of suspicion in her expression. Constance froze. Had she already given away her hand?

"I told you- it's your sense of color. Your strength with accessorizing. I'm a bit of a minimalist. You're more of a traditionalist, but with a fresh angle. I don't know why, but I got a gut feeling."

"I see. Other than the consulting fee which I assume you would be paying me, what's in it for me?" Asked Daphne. "I have a simple life that works for me. I don't need to add anything to it."

Constance could see her point. Daphne was busy with the shop, and she also evidently valued her peace and quiet. Why should she want to help Constance? Constance wasn't exactly offering her a king's ransom or a full-time salary. Constance might have known that she was going to try to gain back Daphne's lost love, but Daphne couldn't know that yet. What were the benefits of working for Constance? Then the answer came to her. She would have almost thought it was a lie, except that when she said it, it resonated, so sure, and so honest, that she realized that it was the truth, and nothing but.

"As I said, I just got a feeling from you. Your work, your shop, the way you live…I'm considering relocating to Europe," she said. "And if I did so, I would need a design partner. My Uncle Harold has a design company, and I would like to run the European branch of it. If we work together as well as I think we might, I feel that having you on board would be a great advantage for me. And admit it, you have a full life, but isn't it missing just a little bit of excitement?"

That seemed to have stirred something in Daphne. A spot of color rose to her cheeks. Her hooded eyes started to shine more than before.

"If this happened, we would become… partners?"

"Yes. If that's what you wanted, and how it worked out, we would have an equal pay structure."

Daphne looked at Constance, as if trying to determine the honesty behind her statements, and finally nodded, satisfied.

"All right. I'll do it. When do we go see this yacht?"

Constance wracked her brain. She couldn't have Daphne come onto the yacht when Peter was there. She was going to have to get rid of him, and be able to sanitize the paltry decor, so that Daphne wouldn't have any suspicions.

"Let me see when the client is leaving next. He's a very private man. I don't want us to disturb him. But time is of at the essence, so I'll try to make something happen in the next few days. How does that sound?"

Chapter 30

Early the next morning, Constance gave Daphne a call. In a fortuitous twist, Peter had announced via text the night before that he would be extending his trip and be flying to Monte Carlo for a few days, for a yachting convention. He was looking for a new tender for the boat. Constance would have liked to have a say in the design of the tender. She had even risked texting so much to Peter, who had responded with, as long as I'm happy with your design. That was a bit ominous, but fair enough. Worst case scenario, Constance supposed she could work her magic with upholstery and other details aftermarket. She still hadn't heard anything from Lorenzo, which made her sad, but she tried to put it out of her mind. Daphne answered on the first ring.

"Hi," said Constance. "So, the client's out of town. I know it's last minute, but any way you can come by this afternoon?"

"Sure," said Daphne.

Constance gave her the address, hung up, and went to work, hiding any photographs or personalized decor from the yacht. She took a quick lunch break, heading to the one sandwich shop that was open all year round. She chose a tuna sandwich, a Pan Bagnat, that she wasn't much in the mood for, but there were not that many other choices. As she was walking back to the boat, she thought she caught a glimpse of Lorenzo, walking up ahead, but then he turned into a street, and by the time she got to the intersection, he was gone. She wondered if he would ever reach out to her. Ever invite her out again. She could call him, too, she decided. She didn't have to be the1950s housewife, waiting for the man to make all the decisions.

After all, if she was going to make a game of seduction, she had to take the reins once in a while. She paused, in the middle of the sidewalk, and sent him a text.

Hi. I don't know what you're up to tonight, but I've got a design assistant coming in the afternoon, and after that, I really had a hankering for a cocktail or two (with you).

Lorenzo answered almost immediately.

I'll pick you up. Let me know when you're ready.

I'm looking forward to it, Constance wrote back. She was thankful that Lorenzo hadn't held a grudge, after she'd picked a fight yet again. Now she had something to look forward to.

She was measuring and visualizing a few potential design directions, when Daphne walked up to the boat. Her eyes narrowed behind her red-framed lenses, taking in the green color of the hull.

"See, you said you did a red boat, and here's a green boat," said Constance, a bit nervously. Daphne had lost contact with Peter. But did she really know nothing about him and about his current life? No, Constance decided. Not everyone was uber-connected to social media like she was. She let Daphne on board.

"Would you like a glass of wine?" She asked.

"I would say I don't drink during the day, but that would be a lie," said Daphne. "Sure. Whatever you have."

Constance poured them both a glass of white from the side of the wine fridge that Peter had said she could have, a nice Pouilly Fuissé, and gave Daphne a tour of the boat. As they walked through, Daphne seemed to gain enthusiasm.

"It's got a challenging layout," she said. "I think that could be optimized."

"Yes," said Constance. "That's what I was thinking, too. The owner of the boat likes to cook…." She almost beat herself up for saying this. But plenty of people liked to cook. "I was thinking of keeping the galley, but also having an entertaining kitchen up top."

"Brilliant," said Daphne. "I've never seen anyone do that, but I think that's a great idea. What other things were you thinking?"

"Well, I'm sure that you could be the one to help me to bring the color scheme together."

"Yes, absolutely," said Daphne. "I'm envisioning all different shades of green, from malachite to eau-de-Nil and celadon…and sand. And then perhaps some touches of a warm, complimentary color, like Hermès orange for balance."

"That sounds perfect," said Constance. "So, if we're talking division of labor, I would be focusing on the main finishes and layouts, and some of the technical stuff, and you would be doing the soft furnishings and many of the decorative accessories."

Daphne just nodded, still looking all around. Constance imagined that, if she was anything like her, she was visualizing the boat as it might be.

"Alright, let me show you the cabins," said Constance.

She first led Daphne through the two upper cabins, including the one that she was using as her own room. And finally, the guest cabins and bunk rooms.

"Now, the main stateroom," she said, leading Daphne into Peter's bedroom. She thought she noticed a strange change of expression in Daphne, a wrinkling of the nose. Her skin growing paler. Daphne leaned against the wall.

"Are you OK?" Asked Constance. "You look like you might feel ill."

"No, don't worry. Just the wine. I shouldn't be day drinking, at my age. And there was a little wave, I guess… I do get seasick sometimes," she said.

"Oh, sorry," said Constance. "I don't know anything about that. I grew up on a boat, and I get land sick sometimes, to tell you the truth."

Constance showed Daphne the remaining areas, but Daphne was quieter than she had been before, simply listening to Constance's ideas and occasionally nodding. Constance knew what that was like. Finding yourself in the creative zone, not wanting to speak, for fear of the muse getting scared away.

"Are you being visited by the muse?" Constant smiled.

"Yes, my creative juices are flowing," said Daphne. "In fact, I'd better go. I've got some ideas I'd like to sketch out, and some things I'd like to look into. Is there a budget for this job?"

"No, not much of a budget," said Constance.

"Must be nice," Daphne smirked.

"Right? But of course, we don't want to make the client feel that we're taking advantage."

"All right. We'll talk in a few days. What if I need to revisit the boat? Do I contact the client, or do I contact you?"

"Me," said Constance, quickly.

"Once we get into the swing of things, we'll have to be on the yacht more frequently, doing measuring, and install, and staging…or just getting the lay of the land a little bit more," said Daphne.

Constance's head was spinning. She was having a mini panic attack by this point. But it would only be normal for Daphne to visit the boat frequently, bringing things on board, trying things out.

She needed to get rid of Peter. She couldn't possibly have him in town, risking his seeing Daphne, at least not before the big reveal. "You know, I'm thinking that it's problematic that the client is planning on staying aboard. I'm going to need to get him off if we want to go full steam ahead," said Constance. "I don't know if he'll go for it, though, because he wanted to supervise the work, and he wasn't even very sure about keeping me on."

"I've seen your vision boards. They're impressive. If you showed them to him, and then told him that you needed to do everything at once, because there's a deadline for the magazine? You said he wanted it published, right?"

"You're right," said Constance.

She hoped she would manage to get him out. With Peter gone, he wouldn't have a chance to be critical about her design, he wouldn't be so quick to fire her. She felt more vulnerable, now that taking the so-called easy way out was not an option, wouldn't be ever again. Having experienced being in Lorenzo's presence again, she couldn't even imagine being with anyone else. Well, she would have to have another relationship one day, because Lorenzo wouldn't work out. She knew that from experience. But for now, there was no one else she could even think of.

There was a pinging noise from her phone, and she startled. A text from Peter.

I'm coming back early. There's nothing promising at the yacht convention. And you're right, I will wait for you to weigh in on the tender.

She sent him a celebratory emoji.

When will you be back?

About half an hour away.

Constant gulped. She needed to shuffle Daphne out.

"The client is on his way," she said. "I would just as soon he not see you until we've got more of the design decided," she lied. She cringed. That made zero sense.

"You're not going to cut me out of the deal or take credit for my work, though, are you?" Asked Daphne.

"No. Of course not," said Constance. "It's just... I didn't exactly ask him if it was OK to have someone else on board and considering that he's been so difficult with other designers, I just don't want to rock the boat, so to speak."

"Alright," said Daphne. "I'm trusting you. You're telling me everything, right?"

"Of course," Constance lied, feeling horribly guilty about it. But it was for the best, wasn't it?

Constance was just putting back the personal objects she had hidden away when Peter came on board.

"I hope you had a more productive day than I did," Peter said by means of greeting.

"Actually, I did," said Constance. "I've got good news. And bad news, I would say. I've been working on the concepts…" She handed Peter her iPad, showing him her sketches and vision boards. His eyes darted from side to side as he took it all in. He seemed to like what he saw.

"These look good. What's the bad news?"

"Well, it's going to be a bit more involved than you might have thought at first. I'm talking about reorganizing the spaces and planning on a whole ceiling and lighting element and…well, I know time is of the essence."

"Time is of the essence?" asked Peter.

"We need to have it done before the deadline."

Peter simply looked at her blankly.

"For the magazine- for publication," she clarified. Not that she even knew what the deadline might be, and not that she and Peter had discussed it. But businessmen like him had so much going on, she knew, that they sometimes had to pretend to remember things, for fear of looking weak.

"Ah," said Peter. "Yes. Do you think you'll get it done?"

"I really hope so,' said Constance. "But I think that to maximize our chances, we would both need to move off of the boat, unfortunately, so that we don't need to tiptoe around the construction."

"That makes sense," said Peter. "I do have an apartment in Monaco that I can go back to. And that way I can be on hand, if you ever have a question. You know that I'm trusting you on this, right? I'm trusting you on the basis of your vision boards, and I hope that you follow through. I'm doing this in part as a favor to your Uncle Harold, who believes in you."

"I appreciate that," said Constance, feeling acutely embarrassed. So that's what it was. She hadn't built a professional reputation for herself at all. The only job she had gotten was because Harold had had to beg people to take her on. It was embarrassing. It was proof that she'd been doing things very, very wrong, and that things needed to change. Having the yacht published in a magazine could be the turning point in her career. Her design for the Grace Kelly yacht might also speak for her, but that didn't help the fact that people knew that she wasn't a great project manager. In one of the bigger firms, she might have been able to simply design and never have to follow through on things; that would have been easier, but unfortunately Harold believed in getting one's hands dirty, and taking care of everything, A-Z. If Constance ever took over, she might change the way things were run, but she could see the benefits of doing it the way that Harold did. Perhaps she had to adapt to fit that model rather than the other way around, especially since the whole company was Harold's vision and not hers.

"Speaking of Harold," said Peter, "I guess you're going to have to ask him for a higher per diem, because I don't have a local place for you to stay on land."

"I know that," said Constance. "I'll figure something out. I'll talk to him."

Once Peter had gone below deck to his stateroom, Constance tried to dial Harold. He didn't pick up. She would try him again later; she didn't want to leave a message conveying such sensitive information. She went back to her room, wondering where she would be staying, starting just a few days from then. More instability. But she didn't have a choice.

Chapter 31

Constance checked her makeup in the mirror, having a little panic attack over what had just gone down. Maybe this was a very bad idea. Her phone pinged. Lorenzo, responding to her message.

Want me to pick you up?

She smiled. Speaking with Daphne about long lost loves and misunderstandings had perhaps prepped her to be more lenient towards Lorenzo and his transgressions. But it also had filled her with a little bit of sadness.

She shot back a message.

I thought I might meet you there. I need a little inspiration walk, and I need to try to call Harold.

Ok.

Lorenzo sent her an address, for yet another concept restaurant or bar, she imagined.

She left the boat and walked down the cobblestone streets. In the waning light, the pastel colors of the houses were soothing. Muted. She should maybe spend some time here this summer. After all, she deserved it after doing her time here, serving her sentence in the offseason, when things were less than optimal. Still, she found that she was starting to fall in love with this town. In a strange way, St Tropez at its worst had woven a soulful spell on her. Miami couldn't hold a candle to it. As she was walking, waxing poetic, her phone rang. Normally, she would have been disinclined to respond, but it was Harold.

"Uncle Harold," she said, once she picked up.

Harold coughed into the phone.

"Yikes. Are you OK?"

"I'm fine," said Harold. "I saw you tried to call. I'm just checking in on you. I know that you've been having a bit of a struggle, and I wanted to know if you needed me to send Penelope over to help you out."

"I thought Penelope was busy."

"She is, but she can multitask," Harold shot back. Which felt a little cruel. But the weakness in his voice worried Constance, so she didn't deal him a stinging retort, as she normally would.

"I don't need Penelope."

'You don't? So, you've made progress?"

"I discovered something interesting."

"Oh?" said Harold, sounding a little wary.

"Well, I decided to reach out to the designers who've been fired by Mr. Holmes."

"That's a waste of time," said Harold.

"Hmmm," said Constance. "Basically, what I found out was there wasn't any real reason that either of them was fired."

"I rest my point."

"Get your lazy ass point back up, darling uncle. And listen on. They were all doing their jobs. They're all reasonably good at what they do, so it's not that that got them fired. And so, then I looked up who had done his previous yacht, the one he suddenly sold in a fire sale? And I discovered that there's a woman behind all of this."

"Oh?" said Harold. She clearly now held his attention.

"Yes, a woman named Daphne. She has a shop in Bormes les Mimosas. And it seems to me like they had an unresolved love affair."

"Oh, that actually makes sense," said Harold. "But how does this help you?"

"I thought you would never ask. I hired Daphne to help me with the design."

"You did what? I didn't authorize another designer on this project!"

"It'll come out of my fee," said Constance. "It's worth it."

"Why?"

"Because she's a good designer and stylist, and if I can play matchmaker on top of it, all the better."

"You're crazy. I hope you know what you're doing," said Harold. Now about the press coverage. Do you think you're going to be able to get that done? Are there any magazines you can think of that would publish such an article?"

Constance paused for a minute. She didn't know if she wanted to reveal the ace she had in her pocket. Better to let Harold wonder.

"I'll figure it out," she said. But before I can have anything published, I need to have a finished design."

"Yes, you'd better hurry. Manufacturing always takes a long time. Longer than you think," said Harold, coughing again.

"Do you have a cold again?"

"Yeah, just some crap I picked up at Art Basel. I hate going to that thing," said Harold.

"Well, I miss it, personally," said Constance. "I would have loved to be there."

"I know," said Harold. "But I went for you."

"OK," said Constance. "You'd better get better in time for Christmas."

She needed to mention that she needed to find a place to stay other than the boat, but she lost her nerve. There was always tomorrow.

"Well, I've got to go. I'm going to some pop-up thing or another."

"Enjoy," said Harold.

She felt stressed that she had left some crucial things unsaid. But she had just arrived at the address that Lorenzo had given her, and sure enough, here came Lorenzo, out of the doorway, as if he had a sixth sense that warned him of her arrival.

"Constance," he said, taking a step forward.

As always, he looked devastatingly handsome, this time, in black jeans and a thick olive-green polo neck cashmere sweater. She could already imagine what the soft knit would feel like under her hands, his hard muscles underneath. She suddenly felt self-conscious. She hadn't paid much attention to what she'd put on that morning. She mentally went over what she was wearing. Not too bad. Some velvet culottes. Black boots, and a cashmere V-neck. She hoped she didn't look too chubby in the ensemble, and almost immediately mentally rebuked herself for thinking that way. She really needed to stop. She was what she was. This was her body. Chances were slim, ha, ha, that it would change anytime soon.

"You look gorgeous," said Lorenzo. "Did something happen today? You look different, like you've got a secret. Very naughty," he said.

The way he said naughty made Constance think of all the naughty moments they'd shared together in the past.

"Actually, I do have a little secret," said Constance. "And I will keep it to myself for now, if you don't mind."

"Oh, I don't mind. I like this side of you." He gave her a lingering peck on both cheeks, giving her the opportunity to breathe in his Cologne, that same reassuring, but dangerous, manly, citrusy scent. God, she'd missed him these past few days.

"Come on, let's go inside."

He took her arm, and she shivered. Why was it that whenever he touched her, even in the most innocuous way, she felt somehow aroused and appeased all at the same time? Why was it that every time he touched her, it felt like coming home? She needed to stop feeling that way. It didn't make any sense. They walked into a basement with vaulted stone ceilings.

"Wow, this is cool," said Constance.

"Yes, this is an old wine storage area. A caveau, as they call it here. Back in the day, they would have jazz clubs hidden in here, like speakeasies. Not that they had a prohibition in France."

"Yeah, Europeans are smarter than that."

"This is my friend Felix. He's the bartender and hopefully future owner of this concept space." Lorenzo extended his hand towards a dark-haired Frenchman with angular features and sparkling chestnut eyes. He was on the short side, but he exuded a brand of confidence and power that Constance found impressive.

"I can't wait to check out your cocktails," said Constance. "This is so exciting. Is this your first bar?"

"No, I had one in Marseille, a few years ago. My ex-wife got it. And then one in Montpelier. Too many students there. And well, I thought, let's try this out now," he said. "What shall I serve you?"

"Surprise us," said Constance and Lorenzo at the same time. They glanced at each other and laughed.

"Chips!" Said Felix.

"What? You serve chips?"

"No, it's something we used to say as kids. When two people would say the same thing, one would say chips, and the other one would not be allowed to speak for a certain amount of time."

"Oh, like jinx," Constance laughed.

"Good luck keeping that one silent," she and Lorenzo both said at the same time, pointing at each other, setting off another spell of giggles.

"You know what they say," said Felix. "Saying the same thing at the same time is a sign of synchronicité amoureuse."

Now, Constance and Lorenzo each seemed intent on pretending they hadn't understood that, let alone heard it.

"Anyway," said Felix, once the silence had grown awkward, "the specialty here is that I serve you little snacks. To pair with each cocktail, or each glass of wine."

"Oh, yay," said Constance.

She hadn't realized how hungry she was. She felt self-conscious being seen eating too much in front of anyone. She assumed that they would jump to conclusions about her gluttony, compared to the skinny French girls who had some self-restraint. But too bad. She was starving. And so, when her cocktail came out, along with a little plate, she pounced on the dish.

"This is delicious," she said as she sampled an olive stuffed with blue cheese.

"It is delicious," said Lorenzo. "But I would love to take you out for a real dinner after this as well. There's a…"

"Let me guess," said Constance, "a pop up?"

"Yes, this one is a pasta concept."

"I…" Constance hesitated. She needed to keep a clear head tonight, turn in early, and strategize for how she would emerge from the mess she had made for herself unscathed.

"Unless you think that your client needs you there with him this evening?"

Was Constance imagining it, or did she detect a little bit of jealousy?

"No, I don't believe he expects me to be there," she said. "The wine and cheese the other night was just a polite thing, Lorenzo. I was just thinking that I have a lot to do. The project is finally starting to move forward."

"Have you figured out a little bit more about how to make him happy, then?"

"Yes, I think I have a trick up my sleeve," said Constance. "But I still am going to need to come up with something extraordinary, because I need this thing to be published. The client is one thing, but what will impress a magazine is quite another."

"If only you knew someone who owned a magazine," said Lorenzo, winking at her.

"We've already had this talk. I don't expect you to help me because of our…relationship. Not that we have a relationship, but you know what I mean."

"We would still have a relationship if you hadn't left me," said Lorenzo.

Constance almost spit out her drink. She'd left him? That was hilarious. She was about to lay into him when she was interrupted by Felix, who was bringing them a second plate of little snacks. And she was glad of the interruption, because Lorenzo didn't even deserve for her to spell it out. He knew what he'd done, and no matter how he tried to spin it, it didn't change the truth. He had run off with a supermodel. Right when things were getting a little bit messy, and she'd been a little bit scared, and when she needed reassurance, he had been out the door. That was what had happened, wasn't it? He couldn't gaslight her into believing otherwise.

"Listen," said Lorenzo. "I can see all the thoughts going on in that gorgeous head of yours. I don't want us to fight. You know how I feel about you, so… if you need to take some more time, I understand, but…"

"You're saying that I have a choice in the matter?" Constance snapped. "You're saying I'm the one who makes this decision?" A bitter laugh escaped her lips and Lorenzo recoiled.

"I'm glad you think it's funny," said Lorenzo coldly, the former warm ambiance between them evaporating. Constance felt guilty, all of a sudden, for rewarding his invitation, and his patience with her, with this unpleasantness.

"I'm so sorry," she said. "I'm an idiot. Can we talk about something else?"

"Please," said Lorenzo, rubbing his eyes.

"OK. What would it take for you to want to have a yacht in your magazine? I'm not talking about something that you would do as a favor for me, but something that would be mutually beneficial to us."

"That's a good question," said Lorenzo, considering it. "Well, it needs to be something different, something novel, something visually arresting, something with a big concept. Something that can inspire. Something with a story…"

He rattled off all of these qualifications almost without thinking, and Constance found herself impressed by his passion and by his innate grasp of his editorial mission. She had almost never found him hotter.

"All right," she said. "Then I have my work cut out for me."

Lorenzo smiled.

"I suppose you do. So where are you on that? You seemed to be excited about something earlier this evening."

She decided to leave out the part about her matchmaking plan.

"I think I'm making progress. I've found some great local resources. But I still have a few challenges. And I don't have much time left because fabrication does take quite a bit of time. By the way, what kind of a lead time would you need for the magazine? If, and only if, you decided that the project was appropriate for your premier issue?"

"Time is of the essence," said Lorenzo. "I've been working on editorial content for the past few months already. I still have pages left for last minute inclusions, some of which I could possibly assign to you. But I also am working on an alternate plan, in case it doesn't work out."

"Sounds fair," said Constance, panicking a little bit. "So I spoke to my uncle Harold today."

"Oh, please say hello for me next time you talk."

"I haven't told him you were in town," Constance admitted.

Was that a hurt expression on Lorenzo's face?

"He always liked you," said Constance, hurriedly.

"Well, how's he doing? I would love to see him again."

"He's coming for Christmas," said Constance. We're staying in Cannes, so maybe…depending on your plan…"

"I don't have a plan yet," said Lorenzo.

"Well, I'm a little worried about Harold, to be honest," said Constance. "He's had a bad cold."

"Well, it is cold season," said Lorenzo.

"Yeah, but…I don't know. He's slowed down. I'm a bit worried. I don't know what it is. Maybe it's just the mood I'm in…"

"Well, definitely check back on him then," said Lorenzo. "Trust your intuition."

Yes, she always had been intuitive. And something was telling her that something was up with Harold. But why she hadn't found out sooner that Lorenzo was about to move on with a model, five years ago? She shook that thought out of her mind.

"So," said Lorenzo, shaking his glass, which was empty save for the ice cube and a sprig of herbs. "Are you ready to go to the next stop?"

"Honestly," said Constance, I'm pretty tired."

She wasn't lying. She felt emotionally exhausted.

"Me too, actually. Why don't we do a carry out? You need to eat. We can walk there, put in an order, and I'll walk you back to the boat. How does that sound?"

"I would like that," said Constance.

They stepped outside. The drizzle had returned. She thought of what this meant for her hair. It would be frizzing out of control by now. Lorenzo had always claimed he'd liked it that way, but she certainly didn't. Lorenzo had taken her arm again, and she felt that warmth permeating her.

Suddenly, a barrage of emotions hit her. Everything that had happened on in the course of this roller coaster of a day had decided to come back to the surface, all at once. A tear popped out of her. Then another. Then a sob.

"Are you OK?" Asked Lorenzo, turning to face her and brushing the tears away gently with the finger.

"I don't know what's wrong with me," Constance hiccupped.

"Talk to me," said Lorenzo.

"I don't want to burden you," she said. "I don't even know what it is. It's just… everything. I'm a wimp."

"You're not a wimp. What's going on? Are you scared you're not going to get the project done?"

"Maybe."

"Maybe?" He squeezed her against him, and she resisted the urge to completely burrow into his warm chest. It set off a whole new flood of tears.

"And I don't know," she mumbled into his sweater, "maybe it's a lot of other things. Maybe it's seasonal affective disorder. I should be in the sunshine."

She laughed, a little bitterly.

"Come on," said Lorenzo. "Don't make light of it. If you need to talk to me, you know I'm here."

He pulled away and kissed her gently on the nose, and her heart felt like it was about to burst. How was it that these innocent gestures from him could awaken so much emotion in her? She thought of Daphne and Peter. What if Lorenzo had been the right person for her, and she'd let him get away? Dammit, of course he'd been the right person. But then again, he'd her get away, too.

"Lorenzo, have you ever thought…" she paused. Sniffled. Normally, she wouldn't say it, but she was feeling turned inside out, and she wasn't in the mood to hide anything. Not like anything could hurt more than she'd been hurting this whole time. "It's stupid, but have you ever thought that there's just one person for each of us? That's a really American thing, isn't it? The idea of 'the one?' Your soul mate. Whatever you might want to call it…how would you say that in Italian?"

"I don't know what we would call it," said Lorenzo. "Maybe Dante or someone had a word for it… But I do know that there are some people from whom simple touch feels magical. A simple look is enough to make you feel a million emotions, live a thousand lives."

Constance stared at him; her eyes wide. That was how she felt. Was he just saying that in general, or did he feel that with her, too? She didn't dare ask.

"That's a thing, right? I guess every couple thinks that is the case with them."

In which case she was broken, because she'd only felt it with one person.

"No. I think it's a rare gift," said Lorenzo. "I think that when that happens, one needs to preserve it at all costs. One needs to respect it."

"So, if it's real, it can't be broken, right?"

She'd only thought they were soulmates. If it had been true, they would never have been apart.

Lorenzo shook his head.

"Sometimes there's something that... Sometimes maybe it isn't the right time, and then it's important to try to see if there's a second chance, and then, you have to take it."

Constance looked up at him. His gaze pierced deep into her soul. She felt shy, all of a sudden. She didn't want to talk about herself. Didn't want to talk about them. "Well, this Daphne woman I met. I think that maybe she and my client are that for each other. So… that was my secret from earlier. I'm playing Cupid. I just want to see somebody happy," she said. "Because maybe it's too late for me."

"Why would it be too late for you?" Lorenzo asked, as if surprised.

As if he didn't know that it was too late for her, because her person had chosen someone else. He'd decided she wasn't good enough. Constance didn't know what had happened to the supermodel that Lorenzo had gone off with, and she didn't want to know, didn't want to ask. Just thinking about it made jealousy burn deep in her heart. She shook her head.

"I'm being silly. Must be hormones."

He took her chin in his hand and tilted her head up, forcing her to look at him. She tried to turn her eyes away, but then of course, found herself caught in his magnetic gaze.

"You know you're special to me," he said. "Never doubt that."

"OK," she said.

But she did doubt it.

"Here," he said. "The pasta place is right around the corner."

"All right," said Constance.

She was in a bit of a haze, barely paying attention to what Lorenzo was ordering for her. She just put down her card, which he swept away.

"No, it's on me," he said. "I'm the one who's the bad influence, taking you to all these places."

"I can afford it," she protested.

"That's not the point," he responded.

They waited near the doorway, a propane outdoor heater making it surprisingly comfortable. Still, she shivered at the thought of the kiss he'd given her earlier on. Why did it have to be so complicated?

"Are you cold?" He asked.

She nodded. It was easier than expressing how she really felt.

"Come," said Lorenzo.

He opened his pea coat, wrapped it around her, tucking her in against his chest. She leaned into him, breathing in his scent. This. This was where she wanted to be. All the time. Could anything feel this good? They stood there together, and time melted away. As attracted as she was to him, it was these moments, too, the ones where he was just taking care of her, being himself, comforting her, making her feel safe…those moments were what really made a difference. She didn't know how long they stayed there, wrapped up in each other. But she didn't want it to end. When Lorenzo's name was called out, they regretfully disentangled themselves from each other.

"That felt so good," she whispered into his ear.

"If you're ever cold again, you know where to find me."

His voice had gotten that gruff tone again, the one she loved so much. And then she realized: it wasn't just when he was aroused that he sounded like that. It was when he was emotional, too. Lorenzo retrieved the bags with their orders, and they headed back down the street, towards the harbor.

"You don't need to always be walking me back," she said. "I'm a big girl."

"Of course, I need to walk you back. Unless you want to go back to my place instead," he said.

She contemplated this. She really did want to go back to his place. Had been planning on it as part of her seduction strategy, in fact. But now, she knew that her heart couldn't handle any games.

"I might be tempted. But I have to work in the morning," she said. "And I might try to see if I can get a little bit of input from Peter on my new direction, before he leaves."

"He's leaving?"

Constance could hear the relief in Lorenzo's voice. He had been jealous, after all.

"What do you think he's going to do when he finds out that you've found this Daphne woman?" He asked, acting all casual, now.

"I don't know. It could be great, and it could be horrible. I'm a little scared, honestly, but I can't think of anything else I could do that's going to set me apart from any other designer."

"What are you talking about?"

"Once in a while, I've got these moments of genius, and then I can't keep that inspiration to the end. I swear my creativity is broken sometimes. My fricking muse has ADHD, too."

"That's the nature of creativity, silly," said Lorenzo. "You're not the only one. I just think that your highs are higher, and your lows are lower. Maybe that's a gift."

"Yeah, great gift," Constance scoffed.

She was now fully focused on her shortcomings as a designer, no longer enjoying the simple pleasure of feeling Lorenzo's warmth against her side. They were about to come into view of the harbor, when Lorenzo tugged her by the arm.

"Here, come here. Before your client sees us," he said.

And he swept her up into a passionate embrace. He put their delivery bags down and pulled her closer to him, running his hands all over her body, over her clothes, making her wish that they were somewhere where they could be completely abandoned to each other, but also making her relieved that they weren't anywhere near a bed, because she didn't know how much self-restraint she might possibly muster at this moment. Silly her, though. They had never needed a bed. The memory of them going at it in the shower popped into her head, almost making her want to wrap her legs around him, there and then.

"I want you so badly," he said in his gruff voice, growling in her ear.

She ached for him, too. Her body tingled. She could almost taste her desire for him in the back of her throat. Feel her need for his hands on her. Feel herself craving him. But she had to be the voice of reason, the responsible one.

"I have to go," she said.

"All right." She could hear the disappointment in his voice. "I'll see you soon?" He asked.

"Of course," she said, faux casually. As if she didn't care one way or another, when of course, she was addicted to him, always had been. She'd tried to shake the feeling away, but it was no use. "I'll see you soon," she said, more forcefully.

He handed her one of the takeout bags, squeezed her hand, and she turned and walked towards the yacht, feeling cold and alone. She turned to wave to him. But he had already left. No surprise there. She went up the gangplank and entered the yacht. There was Mr. Holmes, in his favorite chair, reading a book. He wasn't really reading, though, was he? He looked pensive. In fact, he was playing with the pages, folding them in on each other, creating a design of undulating paper. It was quite beautiful, quite sculptural. But he was ruining the book.

"What are you reading?"

"Tropic of cancer."

"Oh," said Constance, taken aback. That was quite an edgy read for somebody like him, wasn't it?

"Did you have a nice evening? And did you find a place to stay?" Peter asked.

Shit. She'd almost been hoping that maybe she could convince him that she should stay on the boat to supervise things, but now she realized that a man like Peter was a man who liked control, and if he wasn't on the boat, it would be weird for her to be there.

"I'm figuring it out," Constance lied.

Where was she going to go? She worried. Her daily fee was ridiculously low, pretty much because Harold was at the end of his rope with her. She couldn't ask for more. She would suck it up. Be an adult. Dip into her savings, if need be.

She needed to prove herself.

Chapter 32

The sound of the ringtone as she waited for Harold to pick up the phone set Constance's nerves on edge. He used to pick up immediately, didn't he? Always had his phone on him. Was always on the ball. Was Harold slowing down? How old was he? She used to calculate it from her dad's age but couldn't remember what that was anymore. As if her father had ever remembered hers. Harold was probably something like 75. That was a bit old. He'd always kept himself in shape. But she had to admit that things had been changing of late. It was a slippery slope, age. No, he was fine, she reasoned with herself. Come on, answer, Harold, she thought. It was a good thing she hadn't asked about increasing her per diem yesterday. Today, she was no longer asking for permission, she was just keeping him apprised. Like an adult would do.

Harold picked up the phone after what felt like an impossible number of rings.

"Constance?" He asked.

This was punctuated with a disturbing cough. It hadn't gotten any better.

"Uncle Harold, you really need to take care of yourself."

"I'll be fine. Everything OK? Please tell me you haven't gotten kicked off the

project."

"No, nothing like that," she said. "In fact, I think I've finally found a basic concept that does make him happy. And I've got a couple details that are a surprise. So, here's the thing… I can't stay on the boat while this is being done. It's full steam ahead, especially if we want it in the magazine."

"The magazine?"

Shit. She'd said the.

"Are you saying that you've found a magazine that will feature the boat?"

"Well, kind of. There's a new magazine here. But you know better than anyone what the editorial process is like. I need to get it done by the deadline, and the editors need to be ok with featuring it."

She cringed for a minute, wondering if Harold would be OK with a
local magazine, but he didn't seem to react one way or the other. "All right. I hope it works out," he said. "Do you happen to have met the editor in Chief? Maybe try to woo them over," he said. "You're charming when you want to be."
"Yes, I'm on that," said Constance.
Of course, the image of her on top of Lorenzo, riding him as he thrust into her, popped into her mind. Stop it, Constance.
"So, as I was saying, I can't stay on the yacht anymore," Constance said. "I need to find a place to stay." She said this more to banish the image from her mind and force herself to focus on the shifts how of her own creation which she was not running.
"Constance, that was a bit impulsive of you. There aren't that many hotels open in this season, and any that are, are going to be a fortune. Have you tried to negotiate
anything with any of the local spots? I can't raise your per diem."
"I wasn't asking you to."
Constance was expecting to feel a bit triumphant as she said this, but instead, a weight started to crush her, hitting the back of her neck, coming down like a vice on her temples. She had been impetuous. And she had screwed herself in the process. What was she going to do? If anything, she would have to find some horrible studio apartment, miles away.
"Maybe you can see if you can be someone's roommate?"
"Maybe, yeah. I'll figure something out," she said.
But would she? Once they had disconnected, she realized she hadn't even asked Harold when he was arriving. She hadn't asked what was going on in Miami, either. She didn't want to know how Penelope was doing, anyway. Probably going from strength to strength on the big yacht project she had scored out of her own merit.
Constance tried to project her imagination forward a month, to when this yacht project would be over. What would be waiting for her in Miami? She found herself dreading the return. That wasn't her full-time home, was it? It just didn't resonate. What did resonate? Where did she want to live? What did she want her life to be? She needed a life with more adventure. Europe really was the place for her, wasn't it? Enough wallowing.

She looked around the yacht. She owed Daphne a visit. They were going to have to work on the final concept, and she was going to have to get the fabricators on board. And then, there was the ceiling detail. She was quite proud of herself for coming up with it. Better to keep it a secret for now. She had found, at last, the arresting moment that she hoped would be enough to gain the yacht entry into the pages of the magazine, on its own merit. Was it the muse? Was it her? Hard to tell, but she didn't care. It was a damn good idea.

Chapter 33

After jotting down a few more notes and making sure she had considered all of the things that needed to be discussed with Daphne, Constance decided to leave the confines of the boat and go sit at Le Senequier. It would be nice to get a hot chocolate. As she made her way to the cafe, she mulled over her situation. Even if she found a tiny, depressing spot to sleep, it wouldn't be a huge deal. She was well within her rights to spend her days on the boat, ostensibly supervising the work. She would have to start asking around to see what she could find. No time like the present. She paused along the sidewalk and texted Daphne to set a meeting time, but Daphne responded almost immediately, saying that she could only meet the next day. She was delivering a table to a client a few hours away.

Alright, Constance wrote back. I'll bring you coffee in the morning. And
we'll get started.

Now, Constance's mind went back to her living arrangements. Must be nice to be someone like Peter, with his choice of luxurious apartments that he could go to. He could jump to any of his homes throughout the world. She thought she'd heard him mentioning that he might go to New York for a time, before returning to Monaco, as well as making a stop in London.

It started raining again. Not rain, exactly. An icy mist had descended on the town, muting out the colors of the pastel facades that normally gave Saint Tropez a cheerful vibe. It was amazing how fast it could go from happy to dreary, in just a few minutes. Just like her mood.

She arrived at the cafe and sat down in a chair in the 2nd row, where the rain couldn't reach her. After ordering a hot chocolate, she wrapped her cashmere shawl around herself more tightly, and took out her phone again, attempting to navigate the personal ads on the regional boards. But, as she had pretty much expected, nothing was immediately apparent. The French had a frustrating way of not conducting much of their business online.

On a whim, she texted Nicole, the shop owner, both to see if she had any ideas, and to plan another outing, but she replied that she had gone on a last-minute trip to Morocco and was subletting her Saint Tropez place to a family, or she would totally have let her stay there. What was Constance going to do? Wander through town, looking up at windows to see if there were any for rent signs, while knowing that none of the owners of the apartments actually stayed in town in the winter and it would be difficult to reach them?

Just as she was starting to feel pretty sorry for herself, she noticed a pair of boots coming into her field of vision. She lifted her originally downcast eyes, her gaze traveling up a set of muscular legs encased in vintage blue jeans. By this point, she was pretty sure who those legs belonged to. Her eyes kept, traveling up, to a beautiful cashmere pea coat. Loro Piana, she knew. Gifted to him on a shoot. And then, of course, her eyes took in the stubble-dotted chin. The sharp nose. The intense look. Lorenzo.

"Hi," he said.

He looked concerned, she thought. Was that possible? Did she look that
pathetic?

"I thought I might find you here. Are you OK? Can I sit down here?"

"Sure. Have a seat," Constance mumbled.

"So... what's going on? You look frustrated."

"I'm just looking for a place to stay."

For some reason, Lorenzo looked more uncomfortable than shocked. Had he been expecting her to fuck up?

"What happened? I thought that you had a bedroom on the yacht."

Constance sighed dramatically.

"I didn't get fired, if that's what you're thinking. Yesterday, when I started to tell you that Peter was leaving, I didn't get to explain. Now that we're moving into the execution phase, I think it's going to be difficult to stay on board. Also," she admitted, "Yes. I needed to get Peter away so that he wouldn't fire me. And well, I guess I told him that no one could be on the boat. I've done this to myself. I do realize. But do you know anyone who's renting out an apartment? Or even a room in an apartment?"

Lorenzo paused, as if making some mental calculation.

"Yes, actually, as a matter of fact, I do."

"Really?"

Lorenzo looked away for a moment, then back at her.

"Yeah. I'm sure I could get you in there to take a look. Probably later this afternoon or early evening; we could meet there and then we could go for dinner."

Constance looked at him. Going to dinner with him sounded great- but it would be dangerous- she had been so close to throwing caution to the wind and begging him to take her home the night before; seeing him again, so soon, was just feeding the addiction. But she did want to reward him for maybe finding her a place to stay.

"Whose apartment is it?" She asked, as if she had much of a choice.

"Oh, a friend's," Lorenzo said, noncommittally.

Probably a girlfriend, then, knowing him; probably some model who only used the place in the summer. But again, beggars couldn't be choosers, and as long as the apartment was the right price, she would accept it.

"How much is it? Is it a full apartment or a room?"

"A room. With a bathroom. You would share the apartment with someone. Have use of the kitchen. I think it's like €500 a month."

Constance was surprised. She did a quick calculation. Yes, that sounded more

than reasonable. In fact, she could even spring that on her paltry per diem.

"Wow. OK. Thank you. I would love to take a look at it. Are you sure it's really available?"

"I'll make sure, and confirm it with you later this afternoon," said Lorenzo. "Then I'll send you the address and we can meet there."

"Thank you so much," said Constance.

"Don't thank me until you've seen it," said Lorenzo. "So…do you think you're going to have the boat ready in time for the spring issue of the magazine?" Lorenzo asked before he left, almost as an afterthought.

"I hope so," said Constance. "You never told me an exact date."

"Beginning of February?"

"I hope so." She didn't say what she was thinking, which was, as long as meets with Sophie's approval.

"I hope so too," said Lorenzo. "OK, I'll see you later."

She watched him walk away. He seemed a bit on edge, and this worried Constance. What was he thinking? What was going on behind those dark eyes? She allowed herself to think of where they might go to dinner together. She would make an extra effort to be charming. And she would carefully choose her outfit, and do her makeup, to compensate for the other day, when she'd been all basic clothes and snot bubbles. Why was she trying to impress him, anyway? Their relationship had fallen apart, despite the supposed soul mate feelings. And it probably would not be stuck back together, no matter how fast her feelings threatened to run away with her.

She spent the rest of the afternoon sketching out her top-secret ceiling idea and reaching out to potential fabricators. This was something that she didn't want to share with Daphne, or even with Harold. It was going to be her surprise to them all. Something that would be all hers. Her way of showing that she did bring something to the table. She wasn't just cheating by bringing Daphne in, and she hadn't just hired her to play matchmaker. She was being strategic. Capitalizing on her strengths.

She realized that she actually appreciated not sleeping with the client for once. It leveled the playing field, made her depend more on her own creativity and ingenuity, even if that damn muse refused to show up when she was supposed to.

Constance checked her watch again. She was growing impatient, waiting for Lorenzo's message. Had his mysterious friend decided that they didn't want to rent out a room after all? She started growing a bit paranoid.

There had to be other places available, no doubt, but if this one didn't work
out, she would probably have to check into a hotel while she found a replacement. Finally, her phone pinged, a message, long-awaited, from Lorenzo.

Here's the address.

She looked it up in Google Maps. It looked like a great location, in the charming older part of town. She thought she might be sneaky and try to figure out who owned the place, but this being France, she couldn't find any information online. Shall I meet you there in half an hour? Lorenzo wrote.

Constance wished she'd had more time to get ready, but she was impatient to see the place. And Lorenzo.

She slipped on her leather trousers and put on a petrol blue Cashmere sweater with a deep V-neck that afforded a peek at her lacy black bra underneath. She threw on her heavy coat, wrapped a scarf around her neck, and went to head out the door. She ran back to the bathroom and swiped on a fresh coat of her signature red lipstick. There. That might keep her under control.

The rain had stopped, but the temperature had dropped. It felt positively frigid in the gathering gloom of evening. When she arrived closer to the designated address,

she noticed Lorenzo standing in front, waiting for her. She tore her eyes away from his and looked up at the building, an apricot painted stucco facade with moss green shutters. Very charming, with balconies on the front. She allowed herself to hope for a moment that this might work out. Maybe, she dared hope, she could hold onto this place for a little while. She wondered about the roommate. Lorenzo hadn't been very forthcoming this morning. She hoped they would get along.

"So, I need to be honest with you," said Lorenzo, as he turned the key in the

lock of the front door.

His heart sank. Great. He was going to tell her that the apartment belonged to his girlfriend, wasn't he? Well, she needed a place to stay anyway. She was an adult. She could. Deal with this.

"Is it about my roommate?"

"Yes," said Lorenzo, eyes downcast.

"She's your girlfriend, isn't she?"

Lorenzo said nothing, but she thought she saw him sigh as he fiddled with the keys, opening the door to the apartment. Constance held her breath. She'd hit a nerve, hadn't she? He'd been toying with her. Toying with this other girl too, apparently, because he'd been the instigator as much as she in their make-out sessions. She didn't wanna be disappointed, but she was. She'd been pretending to herself that she was teasing him as a game. But, in reality, she'd been falling for him. Head over heels. Just like before. It made her want to run away. But she couldn't run away. She needed to finish this job. And she needed a place to stay. She looked around the apartment. The space looked a bit masculine for your typical model, decorated with black and white photographs. Of course. That made sense. Someone he was dating might want to have some of his work. he was insanely talented. Most of these works were from the harbor series she'd seen in the gallery. And then she noticed a large portrait in the corner. A photograph of a girl. Her hair flying around, obscuring most of her features.

Her heart seized up.

"Is that…"

Lorenzo looked at the photo, too, then back at her.

"That's a photo of me."

"Yes," said Lorenzo, looking down. "Remember? I took it when we went on that weekend to Camargue, to see the wild horses."

"But…I don't understand."

"This is my apartment."

"Oh. I don't think it's a good idea for me to…" her heart was racing, her mind too. This was a dumb, stupid, very bad idea. Lorenzo interrupted her.

"It'll be fine. Your uncle Harold reached out and asked me if I could do him a favor. If you stay here, it can be just as friends. I have a room for you. It's going to be on the up and up."

She didn't like that idea of just friends, but she didn't like the idea of Harold rescuing her once again even more. She looked at Lorenzo warily.

"You and Harold have been talking? Forget it. I don't want to know. Just show me the room, I guess," she said, deflated.

What would it be like, sleeping on the other side of the wall from Lorenzo, if he even spent his nights here, that is. He probably had a bevy of girls that he stayed over with. What if he brought someone home? What would that be like for her? It would be torture. Lorenzo opened the door to a smaller room off of the hallway. Even in the gloom of the late afternoon, it was light enough. Simple, with a large bed, a few more black and white photos, and some vintage furniture. Mid-century, a style Lorenzo had always liked. There was even a desk in the corner.

"You could redecorate, if you wanted," he said. Constance held her breath and bit her tongue, to keep from saying, "I won't be here long enough to bother."

"You would have your own bathroom," said Lorenzo, opening another

door and showing her a small but well-appointed bathroom.

"It looks good," said Constance, a dubious expression on her face. "I'm just worrying about the logistics," she said.

"Logistics?"

"I mean, what are the rules about bringing someone home?" Lorenzo gave her a look.

"Are you planning on bringing someone over?" He asked.

"Well, not me, but you, I'm sure."

"Really? I guess we'll cross that bridge when we come to it," Lorenzo said, looking annoyed.

"Well, I think it'd be nice to establish some ground rules," said Constance.

She wanted to punch herself. Why was she being like this?

"Alright, so if one of us plans on entertaining anyone, we need to give the other a heads up, how's that?" Said Lorenzo.

"Perfect," said Constance, even though she didn't like the idea of him entertaining anyone else. Not at all. And not like she was planning on it, either. Better to lock it in before she annoyed Lorenzo into changing his mind. "500 a month, you said? I'll take it. When can I move in?" She asked.

"Tomorrow, if you like," he responded.

"Great."

She didn't know why she wasn't happier about this. Well, of course she knew why

she wasn't happier about this. She was going to be living with her ex-boyfriend,

as friends. Her ex-boyfriend that she'd never really had gotten over. Her
ex-boyfriend who had walked out on her and shacked up with a supermodel, her
ex-boyfriend, who for some unexplainable reason had a portrait of her on
the wall of his apartment. Her ex-boyfriend who held her fate in his hands, having the power to publish her work or not, pretty much dictating whether she stayed in Harold's employ or not.
It was acutely uncomfortable. She found herself fantasizing about running off to the Seychelles, or maybe Morocco. Did Nicole have a spare room there, perchance? Surely, she could build another life there before jumping to. The next spot? But that was what she'd always done, wasn't it? And it hadn't really worked for her, had it?
"Yes, I'll move in tomorrow," she said, since Lorenzo still hadn't responded. "Thank you."
This going to be horrible, she decided.
"Shall we celebrate somewhere nice?" Asked Lorenzo.
"Sure," she said.
But she only accepted because she was hungry and really needed a glass of wine or three. She wasn't in a celebratory spirit at all.
"It's Thursday today," said Lorenzo. "More of the restaurants are open, which is a nice change. Would you like Italian or Asian?"
Constance's stomach growled despite being tied in knots. They left the apartment and set off down the street, Lorenzo, taking her arm, as she had come to crave. Her heart hitched again. She reminded herself to breathe. Where was this roommate situation going to go? She didn't see it going anywhere good.
Before she knew it, they were at the restaurant, a dark space with vaulted stone ceilings. She let Lorenzo do the ordering. She was ravenous, but more than that, she needed a drink. The evening went by in a blur, she asking him a few questions and listening to him talking about the ups and downs of starting a magazine, and also sharing about his struggles to maintain the family property in Italy, now that his mother was deceased.
Constance could see the property in her mind's eye. The allée of Cypress trees, majestic, leading as far as the eye could see. The distant mountains, bluish in

the light of dawn, golden hills, lavender, olive trees... If you asked Constance what her idea of Paradise was, that might be it.

"Have you ever thought of just moving there and making a go of it?" She asked.

"Me? A gentleman farmer?"

"Well, I was thinking more a real farmer, or at least earning a living from the property...you know, doing photo shoots, throwing events."

"I have thought of it," said Lorenzo. "But it's a lot. I would need a partner to help me with that. These ideas sound like paradise, until you're there by yourself, trying to make it work."

Constance stopped asking questions then, because she didn't want to imagine him

moving into that property with another woman. One who would support him. One

who could be stable and help them with building a life. Would she ever change? Would she be able to put down roots at some point?

"What's wrong?" Asked Lorenzo, concern making his charcoal eyes even darker.

Don't cry, Constance. You already blubbered all over him last time.

"Nothing. I just..."

Oh, to hell with it. He probably already judged the hell out of her, might as well have a sounding board. She sighed and went on.

"Do you ever worry that you're never going to figure out what you want to do in life, and that you're just going to look back one day and realize that you never built anything?"

"No," said Lorenzo. "Is that how you feel?"

"Yes," Constance admitted. "I don't want to be this way," she said.

"Then change," said Lorenzo.

"How am I supposed to do that?"

Maybe she needed someone to motivate her to change. She had thought that Lorenzo would be that person at one point. She had believed that, but once it had been over between them, it had felt like part of her had died, and withered, and would never come back.

"You can't expect someone to change you," said Lorenzo. "It has to be something you decide."

The old Constance would have snapped at him for saying that, but he was right. Lorenzo leaned forward and took her hand across the table. Just that simple gesture made her heart melt. She noticed that his knees were now touching hers under the table. She looked into his eyes. Oh my God, Constance, don't cry. The lump in her throat grew.

"I'm sorry," she said finally. "I don't know what's wrong with me. I'm just feeling so melancholy. You must be so bored with me."

"I'm never bored with you," he said. "I like that you're being real with me."

"It's messy," said Constance.

"I like messy."

Constance thought back to how their relationship had been, before. They had never really discussed their feelings. They'd tended to show their feelings more through actions than through words. Physical touch had been their love language. And that had been enough. Until the misunderstandings had dug a gulf between them, so wide that it couldn't be crossed.

"Constance," said Lorenzo, "we've both grown up, you know. And we're both
growing up still."

"I'm 32," said Constance. "I should be grown up already. I should have a
family by now."

"What about me?" Asked Lorenzo. "I'm older than you. I don't have a family."

His statement dangled in the air between them. Where was he going with this? Long ago, she had thought that they would have those things together, but that ship had sailed.

Tears came to her eyes again. She pulled her hand away from Lorenzo's and wiped them away.

"I'm so sorry," she said. "This is lame."

"It's OK," said Lorenzo. "You don't need to be cheerful every time you're with me. You can talk to me, you know."

"I know," said Constance. "I just don't know how."

"That's OK, too," said Lorenzo. "Come on, let's go," he said. "We're both tired."

He paid the bill, refusing to let her put down any money, again, and walked her out of the restaurant. The drizzle had started up again.

"I suppose it's no use saying you don't need to walk me back," said Constance. What would it be like, living with him? How often would they be in the same space, she wondered.

"You know I would never let you walk alone," he said.

They strode down the cobblestone streets, falling in step with each other easily. Their bodies had always been in sync. He moved his hand from where it held her arm, and wrapped his arm around her, sheltering her a bit more from the elements.

"You know I'm here for you, right?" He said, his voice just as gruff as it was in the

throes of passion. Constance remained silent. Lorenzo stopped. Faced her. Put a finger under her chin and forced her to look into his eyes.

"I'm here for you," he said, more firmly.

She gulped. He looked like he was about to kiss her. He had that feverish gaze that she knew so well. She could feel her own cheeks growing red and flushed. Feel her

desire to kiss him. She started to lean forward, but he kept her chin in his grasp, just looking deep into her eyes, into her soul, in that way that she couldn't look away from. God, she wanted him so much. She felt an ache all over her body, wanting to be claimed by him. How did he have this effect on her? She was sure he knew it, too. After a moment, he broke his gaze, making her feel as if an icy gust of wind had just swept over her body. It was agony.

"Come on, I'll take you home," he said.

Chapter 34

Constance walked up the gangplank of the yacht. Her heart hammering in her chest. She looked back over her shoulder, noting Lorenzo giving her a small wave. Once he saw her open the glass door to the saloon, he turned on his heel and headed back into the center of the town. Constance jumped as she noticed the presence in the chair in the corner. Peter was there, reading his book as usual.

"You're back," said Peter.

"I thought that you had left already," said Constance.

"Tomorrow morning. I trust you found a place to stay."

"Yes, I did," she said. "It's going to be full steam ahead starting tomorrow. I think you'll be pleased."

She wondered, not for the first time, how Peter would feel when he knew that Daphne was involved, but she decided that she would cross that bridge when she came to it.

"Who was your friend?" Asked Peter.

Constance looked outside and realized that, from where he sat, considering the dim light from his reading lamp, he had a perfect view of the sidewalk along the front of the harbor, illuminated by streetlights.

"You make a nice pair," said Peter.

"He's an old friend," said Constance.

"Don't you mean a boyfriend?" asked Peter, with an avuncular tone. Not dissimilar to how Harold would treat her, but maybe a little bit less sarcastic.

"He was a boyfriend," Constance admitted. "But that's over now."

"You know," said Peter. "Don't let a misunderstanding ruin something that's potentially good."

"It was no misunderstanding," said Constance.

"All right, just take it from an old guy who's lived a long life," said Peter.

"You're being ridiculous. You're not that old."

"Well anyway," said Peter, "mistakes have been made."

Constance looked at him. Was he talking about Daphne? She had a feeling he was. This comforted her and made her feel like maybe her plan to get them back together was a good thing. If it worked, the good karma that resulted might help her.

"All right," said Constance. "Anyway, I'm going to go off to bed, I've had a long day."

She noticed again how Peter was folding the pages in his book as he chatted with her. She saw the way the light filtered through the paper, making the pages glow gold and throw shadows on each other. It was hypnotic.

"I leave early in the morning," said Peter. "You know you can reach me anytime. Keep me apprised of whatever's going on. I'll sign whichever checks I need to sign. I'm going to trust you on this…There's something about you… You're different than the others. Don't undersell yourself, Constance."

"Thanks," said Constance.

She hoped she wouldn't disappoint him. Peter seemed to be the first person in a long time who had trusted her to do what was right to complete her work. She owed him her best. And she couldn't disappoint Harold, either. Again, talking to her uncle today, she had had the most disconcerting feeling that there was something he wasn't telling her. To stop the negative thoughts, she thought again about Italy. About Lorenzo's property. But then she drove the vision away. She was being ridiculous and sentimental. That was all fiction. The reality was going to be sleeping wall to wall with Lorenzo. This town was barely big enough for the both of them, and now they were going to be sharing a not so big apartment? Stop thinking about it. She went to sleep, dreaming of cypress allées and olive trees, their silver leaves shining in the sun.

Chapter 35

The next morning was sunny and disconcertingly warm and beautiful. What a sad day to be moving off of the yacht in the harbor, thought Constance as she got herself ready and packed her bags. She would leave the bags on board while she drove to Daphne's. Daphne had promised her a working lunch, and then she would come back and go through the awkward process of moving into Lorenzo's space. Even when they had been dating, they hadn't truly lived together. Yes, they had stayed at each other's places. They'd found it difficult to spend time away from each other. But the distribution had been more or less even, and Lorenzo had often been traveling for business, as had she, so it had never become fully domesticated. She found herself craving that a little bit. Domestication. The idea of cooking with someone, of coming home to someone. For the first time in her life, that was starting to feel like a goal. Behind the wheel of her ugly car, missing her Mini Cooper, she visualized some of the details of the construction and decor. She organized her thoughts in her mind to best communicate to Daphne what they should do, and Daphne would hopefully fill in the blanks with some of the similar details she had used in Peter's previous boat.

How would she reintroduce them to each other? She wondered. Clearly, Peter was regretful about the whole thing, but was Daphne? It had certainly seemed so.

She arrived in Bormes les Mimosas, where it seemed like the whole population of the village was out enjoying a spectacular day, parked, and made her way to Daphne's shop. She knocked on the window and waited as she saw a light turn off in the back and noticed Daphne's form shuffling towards her. Daphne was wearing a cherry red cashmere sweater. The bangs of her brown, chin- length bob were swept over, and not for the first time, Constance decided that she looked like a mix of Jane Birkin and Charlotte Rampling. She had that Franco-English thing down pat. Constance could see how someone like Peter would fall in love with that. Daphne offered Constance a cup of tea and served it to her in a porcelain cup that was so thin, the light shone through. Constance cradled the cup gingerly, blowing on the tea, and started to do a recap of their design ideas. They spent a delightful morning, conversing about design concepts and nailing down all the final details, Constance pleased to confirm that they did make a great team. Harold had often talked about expanding to Europe and had just never really had the bandwidth to do so. Maybe it was finally time. She forced herself to focus on the matter at hand. After just a few hours, everything was set, a rough timeline established. Each woman had a list of tasks. If they were able to stick to this, the boat might actually be ready for publication. If not, it would be a disaster. It was going to take every shred of concentration and finesse to make sure the project got done. It was ridiculously ambitious, in fact, and Constance couldn't believe that she had fooled herself into thinking that it would be easy. No matter. She forced herself to push down the overwhelm and focus on a positive outcome.

Over lunch. Daphne gave Constance a perplexed look.

"So, you've mentioned a magazine several times," she said. "Who's insisting on it being in the magazine? The client, or your boss?"

"Well, I think it's the client," said Constance.

"You think?"

"He never mentions it, but my uncle has been keeping on me about it."

"No matter, I suppose," said Daphne.

"Yeah." Constance was pensive.

"I want to thank you," said Daphne, "For taking me on. I'd missed this more than I'd realized."

"My pleasure," said Constance. She hoped Daphne wouldn't kill her when she revealed her secret plan. If only she could know that their breakup had been due to something fixable.

"How have things been for you in St. Tropez, all alone in the low season?" Daphne asked.

And there Constance saw it: her chance to get to the bottom of the mystery.

"It's weird," she said, cautiously. "I'm not really that alone."

"The client?" Asked Daphne, sharply.

Constance froze. Was she judging her? Thinking she was in a relationship with the client? Who was she to judge?

"God no." She pressed on quickly, afraid that Daphne would ask her again who the mystery client was. "I discovered that my ex-boyfriend happened to be in town. It's weird to see him again. After things ended as they did."

"How did they end?" Asked Daphne.

Well, that was what Constance wanted to know from her.

"A silly misunderstanding," she lied. "We never communicated much about our feelings." OK, maybe not so much of a lie, there.

"That's what happened to me and …my previous yacht guy," said Daphne.

"Oh. I wonder to myself," said Constance. "What would it take for me to forgive and forget? What would it take to fix things? But I can't think of anything."

"Really?" Asked Daphne. "I would think it would be easy. I know what I would have needed."

"You do?"

"Probably just an apology."

"Just…an apology?" Asked Constance.

Daphne nodded, smiling to herself.

"Yeah. Isn't that pathetic to say? Just an apology and an explanation and a promise to do better."

"That's it?"

"Listen, in my case, I believe that neither one of us wanted to hurt the other," said Daphne. "We just felt that we knew each other so intimately that the other one knew what each one was thinking… and well, a tiny thing here, a tiny thing there, and then, there we were, at an impasse. And now, I feel stupid. We wasted so much time. But my pride won't let me go back to him. And him? He's probably not even thinking about me."

"What if he is?" Asked Constance.

"I guess I'll never know," Daphne sighed.

"Does it ever get easier?" Asked Constance.

"I don't know."

That was the last thing Constance wanted to hear. She had wasted the past five years of her life. How would things be different if they had never separated? But it wasn't on her, was it? He had left, granted after she'd yelled at him and gone on a few business trips without letting him know, and run away a few times, and…maybe he wasn't completely to blame. Maybe she had abandoned him, not let him in, especially towards the end. Had she been the one who had left him? She wouldn't be self-sabotaging that badly, would she? But of course, she had a pattern of not being kind to herself. She'd done that her whole life. From punishing herself for eating an extra slice of pizza, to berating herself for not being able to concentrate on a project, to undervaluing herself and jumping into relationships with clients that were inappropriate. She hadn't respected herself at the end of the day. Maybe she would talk to Lorenzo. The very thought made her insides clench and a feeling of dread descend upon her, but also, it was a little bit exciting. Was there something salvageable between them?

"I'm sorry. What were you saying?" Said Constance.

Daphne had been speaking, and she had been in the clouds.

"You're thinking about him, aren't you?" Asked Daphne, smiling. "Fix it. While you still can."

Chapter 36

As she drove into Saint Tropez, her phone pinged. Lorenzo, of course.

Are you about ready to come move in?

Yes, just getting back into town, she responded.

Why don't I meet you down at the boat? Lorenzo wrote. That way, I can see the before, before you transform it. And I'll help you with your luggage.

She was just doing a final sweep of the boat to make sure she hadn't forgotten any of her things when Lorenzo arrived and rapped at the glass door to the saloon. She let him in. He gave her a kiss on each cheek, allowing her a whiff of his aftershave and bringing a flush to her cheeks.

"You look happier today," he said. "Did you get some good work done?"

"I did," she replied. "And I still have that sneaky little side project."

He looked at her, one eyebrow raised.

"You're not getting distracted with something else, are you?"

"No, just a little matchmaking," said Constance.

"I don't want to know, do I?"

"Maybe not," Constance admitted.

Constance gave Lorenzo a tour of the boat, visualizing the spaces as she had designed them with Daphne. She could imagine how it would look when the work was done, and she already beamed with pride as she imagined the final effect, and how Peter would react.

"I love seeing you like this," said Lorenzo. "You're in your zone. You know, you really are very good at what you do. Don't ever let anyone make you doubt that."

"Thank you. That means a lot."

She led him upstairs, to the upper saloon.

"So, this is kind of a crazy idea," she said, "but I'm thinking of making this area into kind of an exhibition kitchen, instead of just having the small galley downstairs. I'll of course have a traditional galley downstairs for entertaining, or a private chef. But Peter loves to cook. And I'm thinking that he can entertain his guests or a lady friend, by cooking up here with the view and the sunlight."

"That's a wonderful idea," said Lorenzo. "I've never seen that done before. It's brilliant, actually."

He came closer to her, as she was gesturing to the windows on either side, showing him how the kitchen counters would fit flush under them.

"You're my decorating genius," said Lorenzo, taking her into his arms. Before she knew what he was doing, or what she was doing, she had reacted to his embrace, leaning into him and tilting her face up to be kissed. He claimed her mouth and started running his hands down her back as she pressed herself into him. She could feel his body reacting, as well, feel something hard pressing against her belly. Feel the heat rising between them. Her breath coming in gasps. He started growling into her mouth as he took handfuls of her hair and tipped her head back further to devour her neck. He lifted her onto the dining table that currently occupied the space, spreading her legs and grinding between them. He ripped open her cardigan and shirt and nuzzled her breasts, moving aside the lace of her bra so he could tease a nipple. She gasped. It had been so long since he had done this to her. He knew it got her going, made her so wet for him that she would soon be begging for it. She reached for the zipper on his jeans, fumbling, and he moved her hands aside and undid the top button himself.

"I've missed you so much," he said.

"I've missed you, too. I've missed this."

"Are you sure?" He asked, his mouth on hers, now, struggling to remove her sweater and her shirt. "I wanted to make it special, but..."

"No," she said, against her will.

"What?"

"Not now. There might be a security camera."

He groaned, biting her neck in frustration. Even that felt so good that she was tempted to throw caution to the wind. But this was her job that she would be impacting. She couldn't betray the client's trust like that, couldn't be seen going at it like a wild animal the minute he left town.

"You know there's a chance I might actually explode, right?"

"I didn't want to stop either, but it's for the best."

Also, her heart was hurting. She was better at no-strings attached sex than most of her girlfriends, but with Lorenzo, it never happened that way. And just now, they hadn't gone all the way, but it had been enough to bring back all the old feelings, as if they had ever gone. She couldn't possibly handle having him inside her, breathing with her, giving her the sort of pleasure that no one else could. It would break her heart in a million pieces.

"Listen," said Lorenzo, readjusting himself with a pained groan, "let's take your things home before it gets too dark. I'm cooking for you tonight, remember?"

She nodded, her heart feeling fragile and hollow. Moving in with Lorenzo was a stupid idea, wasn't it? She wouldn't be able to stick to this just friends program, but judging from how he reacted to her, how could he pretend to want that, either? This whole thing was just going to end in heartbreak again. Nothing had changed between them. There was still the same attraction, the same passion, but the same inability to tell each other the truth of what was going on in their hearts.

"Come on," said Lorenzo.

She nodded, and they made their way downstairs. She took one last look around the yacht, locked the door, and they set off towards the apartment.

Chapter 37

The next morning, Constance poured herself a cup of coffee, listening intently to hear whether Lorenzo was up yet. She felt bad that they'd had an argument again the night before, right at the moment when she thought they might make a mistake and finally fall into bed with each other. She clutched the delicate China mug, remembering that Lorenzo's mother had owned the same ones. Maybe this was her set. Or maybe he had sourced some from elsewhere, considering them a comforting touch of home. He was sentimental, that way. She loved that about him.

She heard the door to Lorenzo's room open. She held her breath. She didn't want to look in that direction, knowing that seeing him would make her heart soften and make the guilt all the more intense. But of course, she looked towards him, because she couldn't help it.

"Lorenzo. I'm… I'm so sorry that…" she started to say, but then she noticed the roller bag behind him. Her heart sank. "What? You're leaving? I'm sorry about our fight, but I didn't mean…Wait a second. This is your apartment. I should be the one leaving, not you."

Lorenzo smiled, a little grimly.

"You want to leave? Is that what you really want? Or are you just scared?"

"I'm not scared." She set her mouth in a stubborn line, facing him. Daring him to contradict her. But she was a total liar. She was terrified.

"I'm not leaving you forever. I have a business trip to go on. I'll only be gone one night."

Constance's heart seized up. She'd been looking forward to making up for the disastrous evening before.

"Oh. I was hoping we could talk," she said.

"About your feelings? I would love to do that. We'll talk as soon as I'm back."

"Where are you going? Sorry. You don't need to answer that. It's none of my business."

"I'm going to Barcelona," said Lorenzo. "Interviewing an architect for the magazine."

Constance nodded, as if that was cool, but she couldn't help it: she had to wonder whether this architect would be a beautiful female architect. Why couldn't Lorenzo conduct the interview on the phone? She had to stop thinking this way. He wasn't hers to be jealous over. And even if he was hers, her jealousy wasn't going to be doing her any favors.

"All right. I guess I'll see you on Friday morning then," said Constance.

"Yes," said Lorenzo.

"Safe travels," said Constance.

This was so awkward. The memory of the fight they'd had still remained on her like a fingerprint. Indelible, difficult to erase. Creating a sensitive bruising around her heart.

"See you tomorrow," said Lorenzo.

And then, he left. Without so much as a second glance. Constance's mind was racing. He was mad at her, wasn't he? This was just too painful. Why did she do this to herself? No matter. She needed to focus. She had some work to do. She needed to find a way to get that ceiling installation idea of hers to become a reality. The original fabricator had all but given up on the whole concept, and it was now up to Constance to make it happen, if she wanted any chance at getting the yacht into the magazine. She would go to the coffee shop. She could focus more there, surrounded by empty chairs, with squawking seagulls as background noise, knowing that she wouldn't see Lorenzo, than she could in his space, missing him like crazy already.

It was warmer out today. Almost balmy, really. She enjoyed the sunshine on her face as she walked down the street towards the harbor. She might even need to peel off her jacket when she got there, she thought. What a treat. It had her thinking ahead to what the spring might bring, and how she was going to break it to Harold that she had every intention of staying in Europe. She had to prove herself so that he would be OK with her building his company abroad. Would he trust her to do that? The best way to get him to trust her was to do the work, she decided. She looked at her schematics and sketches, and then her phone pinged. Dammit, she'd been getting in the zone, only to be distracted by this. It was the ceiling fabricator.

I'm sorry, but we don't think we can translate your vision. Seriously? Old Constance would have fired off an insulting message, but instead, she decided to be strategic. There weren't a thousand fabricators in town. She should help these people help her. She thought of all of the resources she had at her disposal. And then she remembered, one of the pop ups that she had been to- a multimedia studio that specialized in shop displays and art installations. They had a machine to melt large sheets of plexiglass, to bend it, didn't they? If she could obtain thin sheets of vellum-like plastic, could she potentially have that machine create the folded effect? The ceiling could be constructed in panels, and then all the fabricators would need to do is create reinforced holes to bolt it all to the ceiling, creating a system so it could be easily detached to replace the light bulbs. And hide the seams with detachable molding. That was the way to go. Not that complicated at the end of the day, she decided. She quickly made some phone calls, described the process to the studio and got a verbal OK from them. They had many client projects to work on first, but they could do an experimental first run to see if it would work, and then schedule her from there.

Constance texted back the fabricator.

Don't worry, it's all sorted. I'll come over and explain soon.

She paid for her coffee and her croissant. Walked to the harbor parking lot to pick up her car and drove herself to the industrial zone. After picking up a sheet of the vellum plastic material at one warehouse, she brought it to the multimedia studio, and after a few false starts, they figured out a technique that worked. Thank goodness. Constance breathed a sigh of relief.

"Yeah, it's not easy, but I think we can figure it out. We just need a couple weeks before we can get started on it," said the manager of the studio.

"A couple of weeks? Is there any way you can expedite it?" Asked Constance. "No, forget it, I understand. Just let me know when you can get to it, and if you have any cancellations, I'd love it if this could get bumped to the front of the line."

She just needed to get everything else done, and then she'd just be waiting on that one detail. Granted, the one detail that was the pièce de resistance. She couldn't have the yacht photographed without it.

She spent the rest of the day communicating with Daphne about details, waiting for a delivery of dual wine fridges, checking in on the progress of the fittings for the kitchen- she'd hoped it was coming along swimmingly, except that there was a scratch on one of the cabinets she had sourced, and it had to be re-finished. This needed to be perfect. Attention to detail had been Constance's weak point, and now she was going to make sure she never overlooked anything again. For now, at least. At the end of a frantic day, she went back to the apartment, sad to feel the emptiness of it.

Chapter 38

She sat at the kitchen island in Lorenzo's apartment. It was pouring rain outside, and she wasn't in the mood to repair to her usual table at Le Senequier, even if she felt awkward about the possibility of his coming back home and seeing her trying to work in his space.

They'd been trying to coexist peacefully since he had returned from Barcelona, but it was a little weird. They hadn't fought again, but their roommate arrangement was more awkward than she'd even imagined it would be, which was very awkward. As she sullenly tried to put the final touches on her design for the yacht's kitchen backsplash, her thoughts went to Harold. He still hadn't gotten back to her with details about their plan to spend Christmas in Cannes, she realized. She kept expecting him to let her know when he would arrive, yet he still hadn't updated her, which was strange. Yes, Harold tended to keep things for the last minute, but with some things, such as Thanksgiving and travel, he tended to be hyper organized. She was looking forward to seeing him, and quite frankly, really looking forward to a nice stay at the Martinez. Should she reach out to him and ask him what was going on? Why not? Once she was set on those plans, she might be able to concentrate a bit better on the boring task of figuring out more technical details for the yacht. The lighting, for example, was giving her so many issues that she almost questioned whether it was even worth it.

Of course, it's worth it, silly, she told herself. It's the focal point. It's never been done before. Stop quitting when the going gets tough. This ceiling was going to be the most spectacular detail, the most memorable one. The thing that most likely would get the boat into a magazine. Without it, it was lovely yacht decor, but nothing that special.

Hey, Uncle Harold, she texted. When do you fly in for Christmas? Maybe you forgot to let me know the details.

She stared at her phone, as if willing Harold to write back. Usually, he was a pretty good texter. He was as attached to his phone as she was to hers. She saw the three dots on her screen and waited. Then the three dots went away. This was something that they had joked about detesting. There was nothing more frustrating than seeing that someone had written something, then reconsidered, then started writing again, then reconsidered again. What a waste of time. What an emotional roller coaster it was. Come on, Harold, she thought. Shit or get off the pot.

Finally, a message came through.

Sweetheart, I'm so sorry, but I'm not able to make it to Europe, he'd written.

What???

Constance had been far from imagining that he would scrap the trip altogether. She'd been afraid that maybe he hadn't been able to score the hotel she wanted, or that maybe his flight came in late on Christmas Eve, or something of that nature. But not coming at all? And it just wasn't realistic for her to fly back to Miami. Still, she thought maybe she would give it a try.

So, what, are you flying me out to Miami? She asked.

The thought made her sad. She didn't want to go to Miami. She wanted to be in Europe, but for Uncle Harold, she would do pretty much anything.

Sweetheart, I would love to see you. You know that. But it makes no sense. You're on the last stages of this yacht design. I don't want you to fall behind.

Not to pry, but why aren't you able to come out? Constance started to write, but then she deleted it. What was going on? Did she dare ask? Was Harold sick, or was he missing Stefan? Sometimes, around the holidays, he did tend to get down, which was why the trips were such a great idea.

But if Harold didn't want to tell her why he couldn't make it, it wasn't like he owed her an explanation. He didn't owe her anything at all, in fact. Well, he kind of did owe her, as her legal guardian. Not that he was her legal guardian anymore, she reminded herself. She was her own person, an adult. But for heaven's sake, she didn't have anyone else. Still, if Harold had cancelled on her, he obviously had his reasons.

OK, Uncle Harold. Well, I'll miss you, she wrote.

As she put down her phone, tears started running down her face. What was she going to do alone, in the South of France? Maybe Daphne was alone too, but she had the feeling that Daphne quite enjoyed her solitary time, or at least pretended to. They weren't close enough that she would ask her to spend an important holiday like that with her, anyway. Maybe she would take herself to a spa. But she didn't have that sort of time or money to waste, and it felt kind of pathetic. Maybe she could beg Chiara to come visit. But Chiara had always spent Christmas with her family, or with Sven's, and Constance didn't want to be a third wheel.

She was still sitting there, sniffling, with a pathetic look on her face, no doubt, when Lorenzo walked in, looking purposeful. When he saw her, he did a double take.

"Are you OK?"

"No," she admitted. "But I'll be fine."

"Do you want to talk about it?" Asked Lorenzo.

"It doesn't look like you have time," said Constance. "You look like you're in a hurry."

"Yes, I unfortunately need to leave town. Another business trip."

"Oh."

Why did Constance always assume that business trip was coded language for a romantic escapade? Not that she had any right to ask, not that it was any of her business. But it still made her feel like crap.

Lorenzo paused.

"Constance, Are you sure you don't want to talk about it? You really look sad."

She looked at him, hesitating, and finally broke down. Who else did she have to talk to?

"My Uncle Harold was supposed to come for Christmas and, well, he's not coming."

"Why? Is he OK? Is it his health?"

"I don't know. He wasn't really forthcoming about it. And for some reason. I didn't feel like it was the time to ask," Constance admitted.

"Then it probably wasn't," said Lorenzo.

That was one thing about him. He'd never doubted her judgement. Not even when she was being stupid.

"Maybe you want to come on a little trip with me for Christmas? Would that make you feel better?"

"A trip with you?" Constance exclaimed. "We can't seem to get through a single evening without fighting!"

"Without fighting, or without falling into each other's arms," Lorenzo corrected.

"I wouldn't want to ruin your holiday," said Constance. "Clearly I'm incapable of controlling myself."

"Controlling yourself when it comes to pouncing on me, or controlling yourself when it comes to fighting with me?" Asked Lorenzo, smiling.

"Both, probably," Constance admitted.

"OK, how about this?" Lorenzo proposed. "How about a truce?"

"A truce?"

"A truce. I take you somewhere over Christmas, a surprise. I promise to make it fun, and you in turn promise not to fight with me. Even the Germans and the English were able to do this in World War 2- to have a detente over Christmas. If they could not shoot at each other, surely you can avoid fighting with me while I feed you and pamper you."

Constance smiled. It sounded heavenly. Was she really able to do this? The idea of a truce might actually make everything so much easier- if she wasn't allowed to say anything about their past, they wouldn't fight. She could stay quiet, couldn't she? She'd always been good at the quiet game as a child. Until she'd realized that it was just her parents' way of getting her to shut up.

"Alright, truce," she said.

"OK. Well, I'll think on where we're going. I'll let you know what types of things you should pack. I should be back in just a couple days," he said.

She looked at her calendar. Wow. Christmas was just a few days away. Harold really had left her dangling until the last minute. She supposed that he hadn't wanted to disappoint her. Or maybe whatever had come up was an emergency, something he hadn't been aware would happen, until the last minute. Just then, a text message from Harold came through.

Darling, I did make a reservation at the hotel in Cannes. Please feel free to use it. I know it won't be the same but consider it my Christmas gift to you. Unless you have a better plan, in which case I think I can still cancel.

So, it was a last-minute thing, thought Constance. She considered the text message, thought about her favorite hotel, the large Christmas tree in the lobby. The pool heated up so that one could swim even in the winter. The spa, which she adored. And then she looked up at Lorenzo. Yes. She had a better plan.

"Everything all right?" He asked.

"Yes. Let me know when you decide where we're going."

"Will do," he said. "I just need to pack and I'm out the door, but I'll be looking forward to seeing you as soon as I get back."

"OK," said Constance.

She went back to trying to work on her, lighting her mind racing. She was glad that her being busy prevented the jealousy from bubbling up. Where would Lorenzo take her? What would it be like, just the two of them over Christmas? Was this going to be a friendly trip, or a romantic one? Would share a room on this mysterious trip? What did this mean for their relationship, if indeed they had a relationship?

Chapter 39

Constance was sitting at the bar in the kitchen, nursing a second coffee, when Lorenzo came through the door, wheeling his travel bag behind him.

"You're back," she said, trying not to act too pleased, even though she was ridiculously excited at the prospect of going on a weekend trip with him. He closed the space between them in a few steps and swept her into his arms. Well, that was felt nice. She breathed in his aftershave.

"I've missed you," he said. "I got used to having you around every day. Are you all packed?"

"I am."

"All right, just give me one minute, and we'll be off. By the way, truce starts now!"

She smiled.

"Damn, I didn't even have the chance to fight with you over your business trip."

"I'll tell you all about it on our way. We need to hurry. I don't want us to miss our plane."

"We're taking a plane?" Asked Constance.

"Oh, I should have mentioned. Yes. Bring your passport."

"Good to know," said Constance, rifling through her bag. Sure enough, her passport was there. She didn't know where else to put it. She finished off her coffee and put the mug in the dishwasher, by which time Lorenzo was already out of the room, with the same bag, wearing a beautiful cashmere turtleneck sweater under his pea coat. She gave the sweater an appraising look.

"What?"

"Nothing. You look good."

"Ready, my dear?" He asked.

"Definitely. Are you not going to tell me where we're going?"

"No, not yet" responded Lorenzo. "I like to keep a little bit of suspense and a little bit of mystery alive between us."

Mystery had never been his problem. And he had definitely surprised her by leaving her after a year and a half. But she couldn't say anything about that. The truce was on. She shook her head to clear those thoughts.

"Come on, let's go. The car is double parked outside," said Lorenzo.

He still drove the old BMW 2002 he had already owned back when they were first together. He did have a tendency to keep his things for the long run, except for one thing: Constance.

He threw her weekend bag into the trunk along with his, and they were off.

"So, we're taking the plane."

"Yes, we're going to nice airport. I hope I'm not cutting it too close," he said.

"Didn't you just come from the airport?"

"Yes, but it was worth it to come pick you up," he said. "I didn't want you to have to taxi." That was very thoughtful of him. She realized that he remembered that taxis were not her favorite place to be. She'd been harassed one or two times in Miami, had finally gotten used to ubering again, but when she was abroad, she always hesitated to get in a cab, especially not speaking the language well.

They arrived at the airport and Lorenzo parked the car. He took her travel bag in one hand and dragged behind his bag with the other. They swept through security and ended up at the gate.

"Ha, now I know where we're going," said Constance. "Are we staying in Rome or are we…"

She interrupted herself. She didn't dare to hope. Were they going to go to Lorenzo's mother's house? Constance had loved that house. Had dared to dream that she might spend more time there, fantasized about running a hotel in the home, pictured throwing elegant dinner parties. Entertaining people from around the world. And of course, redecorating. Lorenzo's mother had had extraordinary style and a fantastic taste level. There were still some things that Constance could see herself doing to update the property. Not that she would ever get the opportunity to do that after they'd broken up, but it had been a beautiful dream as long as it had lasted.

"Are we staying in the city?" She finally asked.

"You know where we're going," said Lorenzo.

"Your mother's house?"

"Well, technically, my house now," said Lorenzo.

"That's true," said Constance. She hadn't really thought of that. "I forgot. I guess you're officially a count, now. That's sexy."

"I've been a count for a while. Since my father died," he reminded her.

"Oh. Yeah. How often do you go? What's happening with the house right now?"

"I don't know," said Lorenzo. "I told you. I've had a hard time going back. But it's time for me to think of ways to make it pay for itself, or I'll have to get rid of it."

"Get rid of it? No, that would be a tragedy," Constance exclaimed. "You could have a wonderful hotel. You could have an event space. You could rent it out for movies…."

Lorenzo smiled grimly.

"You've said that. You have a lot of ideas. But I would need someone by my side to make those happen."

Constance wanted to say, I could be that person, but of course she stopped herself, feeling awkward.

"Well, I can't wait to see it again," she said. "Has it changed at all since the last time I was there?"

"Most things about that place never change."

"That's a good thing," said Constance. "I love it so much there."

"I'm glad," said Lorenzo.

They made their way onto the plane. Lorenzo ordered them two flutes of champagne clinking his against hers.

"To us," he said.

"To us," Constance echoed, wishing that it could be true.

"Tell me, Lorenzo, you talked about wishing you had a partner to do things. What kind of woman, what kind of person, I guess, are you looking for?"

Lorenzo gave her a look, as if saying, remember the truce.

"I don't mean to fight- I'm just curious, I mean, I know I was not what you were looking for, but what are you looking for?"

"What are you talking about, Constance?" said Lorenzo. "You were everything I ever wanted. You were the one."

"You know?" Said Constance. "I'm so sorry. We have a truce. I want us to just have fun. So, cheers to us. Having fun and not having a fight and getting along and having a wonderful weekend."

"All right," Lorenzo smiled. "I can do that."

He clinked glasses with her again and they settled in, she holding his hand, feeling the heat of his palm against hers. It was soothing. He leaned closer against her, and she snuggled against him as much as possible. It felt divine. What would it be like once they got to the property? Would they have separate bedrooms like they did in the apartment, or would he assume that she was going to be with him? She closed her eyes for a moment and was shocked when she was shaken gently awake by Lorenzo.

"You must have been exhausted," he said. "Did you have go out and party while I was out of town?"

If it had been any other day, she would have told him about how she'd stayed up at night because he never texted her during his trip. But since she'd promised to be pleasant, and since it wasn't actually true, she just smiled and told him about her ceiling woes over at the yacht.

"I'm really sad about it, but I don't think I'm going to have the place ready for you to photograph in time for the issue. I feel like I've failed, but I don't want to tell Peter until he sees the yacht. Once I spring my surprise, and he sees my design, he'll be so happy he won't care if it wasn't photographed."

"You can get it in the next month," said Lorenzo. "I can talk to Sophie about it. I'm sure she'll be open to that."

Constance shuddered at the mention of Sophie. Sophie, who had only bad things she could possibly share about Constance. Not that it mattered if Lorenzo knew that she'd had an affair with Sophie's father because, well, they hadn't been together. But still, this was something she would rather Sophie not mention. According to Sophie, it was something of a character trait, and, well, that wasn't very flattering, was it?

"Yes, it would be great to have you both come look at it," said Constance, more lightly than she felt.

They got off the plane and exited the airport. Once on the curb, Constance noticed the old Mercedes that had once belonged to Lorenzo's mother, Alberto at the wheel. Alberto called himself a butler, but he had been Lorenzo's mother's factotum. Gardener, chauffeur, sometimes chef and definitely an old friend to the end. Constance had always loved his sense of humor. Even if she couldn't understand everything he said, his hand gestures made the meaning of everything abundantly clear.

"Alberto, so nice to see you," said Constance as she slid onto the leather seat in the back of the Mercedes, Lorenzo taking his spot in the passenger side up front.

Alberto said something rapid-fire, which Constance understood as an expression of happiness at seeing her, too. Now, Lorenzo and Alberto caught up in Italian, and Constance sat back, hypnotized by the vision of branches and landscape whizzing by, and by the sounds of the sing-song Italian vowels. Within an hour, they were pulling up to majestic wrought iron gates. This was Lorenzo's now. Constance looked around, imagining how it could look with a few extra flowers here. A symmetrical allée of trees there. On the approach, she noticed how a statuary on either side would help to define the space. How a motor court up front could accommodate bigger groups and even a wedding tent. She knew the view in the back was gorgeous as well, but up front had its own merits, with beautiful, verdant hills full of cypress in the distance, a few other castellos dotting them like something out of a fairy tale. They stopped in front of the house and got their bags out of the car. You'll have your usual room, Mr. Lorenzo?" Asked Alberto, proudly demonstrating his vastly improved English.

"Yes, of course, said Lorenzo. "My mother's room is still hers, as far as I'm concerned."

"What about Miss Constance?" Asked Alberto, blushing when he realized the insinuation behind the question.

"Don't worry, Alberto, I'll figure it out with her."

"All the rooms are ready, in any case," said Alberto. "I'll go back to my lodges and just call me if you need anything."

Once Alberto had gone, Constance looked at Lorenzo expectantly.

"So, what was your plan? Which room am I to be in?"

"Whichever room makes you happy," said Lorenzo.

Constance debated on whether she should tell him that the room that would make her him her happiest was with him.

"Why don't we decide that a little bit later on then?" She said.

"All right. Why don't we go for a little walk and then I'll make you some lunch?"

"Why don't I go to the pink room? Is it still pink? Just to freshen up?"

"Yes, absolutely."

She went up to the pink room, which she had stayed in a few times, back when she and Lorenzo would visit and his mother, an old-fashioned sort, liked to keep up the pretense that she wasn't sharing a room with her son. Constance looked at herself in the full-length mirror, smoothing down her sweater and raking her fingers through her russet curls. She got some walking shoes out of her suitcase. And laced them up. She was glad they weren't going to be talking about any painful subjects but found herself wondering what the heck they were going to talk about instead. What did they used to talk about? Nothing much. They spent much of their time in bed. Maybe it would be good for them to figure this out.

She came back downstairs, holding her coat and her scarf in her hands.

They set off, through the field at the back of the house and towards the woods, where Constance knew that beautiful paths intersected each other, capitalizing on different views on the mountains and the valleys. She had crisscrossed these woods so many times, she felt she knew them by heart. She and Lorenzo had had a few little dalliances at multiple different spots along here, as well. She decided to remind him whenever they came across one. The first one was a bench.

"Remember this one, Lorenzo?" She said.

"How could I forget?" Lorenzo responded, the gruff tone already coming into his voice. He squeezed her arm and pulled her closer to him. "I had never pegged you as such a nature girl," he said. "But now that I think of it, the number of times that being in nature seemed to make you more amorous…"

"Yes. Those are some of my favorite memories."

"We could have been caught so many times," he said.

She looked at the bench, remembering that afternoon.

"We could have been caught, but considering the position, you would have been far more exposed than I to any interloper who might have surprised us in the heat of the moment," she smiled.

"You sure? If it wasn't so cold, I would recreate it, to refresh your memory," said Lorenzo.

"If it wasn't so cold, I might let you," Constance replied.

She could almost feel it as she replayed the episode in her mind. The rough stone under her bare ass. Feeling him pumping between her thighs. The waves of pleasure. The fear that someone might catch them adding to the excitement.

Now, back in the present, he nuzzled her neck.

"Too bad it's so cold. I'll have to bring you back in the springtime if you're still here."

She remained silent. She didn't know if it would make a difference if she told him she was planning on staying in Europe. She had to remind herself that this was just a fake truce. They weren't getting along better. They were just avoiding talking about the bigger issues. But still it felt wonderful.

Chapter 40

Constance leaned back against the kitchen cabinets. Countess Carlotta, Lorenzo's mother, had had this kitchen painted an arsenic green, which apparently had been the last straw for Lorenzo's father, an impoverished aristocrat himself, who had left when Lorenzo was a baby. Paired with the old Italian tiles featuring exotic beasts and the old cotto tile floors, the effect was both jaunty and sophisticated. Carlotta's collection of copper cookware and fantastical majolica plates rounded out the look. Constance wouldn't have changed a single detail in this room. Especially not the man who stood at the old Ilve range, woolen slippers on his feet, perfectly fitting jeans hanging off his hips, stirring a steaming pot of Minestrone. He noticed Constance looking and picked up his glass of Montepulciano, lifting it towards her. She smiled and took a sip of her wine. Delicious. It felt good, this temporary truce between them. Being able to spend time with him. Enjoying his company. But it hurt, too, knowing they would go back to reality at the end of the weekend, and that she would feel compelled to bring back the subject of how he had left her. She held her breath and silently counted to ten, biting her tongue to keep herself from saying something she would regret.

"You ok?" asked Lorenzo, looking up from his soup.

"Just enjoying being here. I've missed this place."

"I have, too."

At this, Constance had to bite her tongue again, to keep from asking who else he had really visited with since she had been there last.

"You really haven't been able to come back often?" she asked, instead. Did she even want to know the answer?

"No."

"No?"

Lorenzo sighed and gestured for her to come closer. She tucked herself into the space under his arm and sighed contentedly as she smelled his aftershave, felt his warmth against her. But she still wanted to know, even though she didn't. She waited, not wanting to fill the silence with any chit chat. Sure, they had a truce. But they had to talk about something, didn't they?

"I came to settle my mother's affairs. I was here for two weeks. Everyone was coming out of the woodwork. Farmers to whom she had supposedly promised they could farm the back fields at no cost to them. I let them. What could it hurt? The antiques dealer who swore that she was going to sell her the silver for a song. I resisted, there…."

Constance tipped her chin up, to look him in the eye.

"I'm so sorry, that's horrible."

"Oh, and I didn't mention the supposed best friend to whom she supposedly owed money, the seamstress who had a bill for me, and the grocer who had apparently been extending her a credit for the past year."

"Do you think any of it was true?"

"No idea."

"But you can't keep hemorrhaging money, either. This property must cost you a fortune."

"I know. And yes, it does."

"You wouldn't get rid of it, would you?" asked Constance. She didn't know why she cared. That was a lie. Yes, she knew why. She hadn't been here in five years, but the idea of the villa had remained with her, a golden dream, almost a promise, despite the fact that she had had no expectation of ever seeing Lorenzo again.

"I don't want to. But…"

"But it's your birthright!" Constance cried.

"Nothing is truly a birthright. There's a funny little thing called reality, and it has a way of infringing on the fairy tales we tell ourselves."

"I refuse to accept that," said Constance, setting her lips into a pout.

"You do? Look what happened to…" Lorenzo stopped short.

"What happened to what?" asked Constance. He wasn't going to say what had happened to them, was he? She needed to stop him before it ruined their night.

"What could you do to make this place pay for itself?" she asked, to make damn sure that Lorenzo didn't finish his sentence.

"I've thought about it," he said, giving her a squeeze. "But it's not super realistic. I told you- I would need a partner to help me with it."

"Surely there's something you could that wouldn't be too difficult," Constance protested. "I've always thought..."

"Oh? Have you thought about it, too, then?" Lorenzo asked, pulling away so he could look at her, a wry smile playing at his lips.

She could have lied, could have protected her ego, but they had a truce. After this weekend, they probably wouldn't spend any significant time together again. So, she might as well put it out there.

"This place is magical. When we were together, I used to fantasize about what one could do here."

"Oh really?" Lorenzo asked. "What were your best ideas?"

"Bed and breakfast. Photoshoots. Writing retreats. Cooking classes. Movie set. Wellness retreat. Weddings. Truffle hunting," Constance rattled off in a single breath. Lorenzo laughed out loud.

"That would never work," he smiled.

"What the hell do you mean?"

"There are no truffles here, and I'd be terrible at training truffle pigs."

"Come on," said Constance. "You have to admit the other ideas are genius."

Lorenzo pulled her back into a hug and squeezed.

"Yes. Genius. But I couldn't do any of them alone."

"What if you didn't have to be alone?" asked Constance, boldly.

"You've been tiptoeing around that, teasing me with it. Are you offering your services?"

"What if I was?" she asked.

A girl could dream. Even knowing that it would never work, because she had given herself wholly to him and it had failed miserably once before, this weekend was for fantasy. For what could have been. Even if it made it hurt more.

"You? Staying in one place? I can't imagine," Lorenzo teased.

Any other day, her hackles would have raised at this dig, but she decided to go with it. Not only because of the truce. Because he was fundamentally correct. Constance pulled away, to look him in the eye. Did she dare tell him about the dream that had been building since she'd been in Saint Tropez? Did she dare tell him that Europe was where she wanted to be, wanted to stay? Did she dare admit that Miami was just a place she had landed because she'd been escaping Lorenzo, and because Uncle Harold was there, and was all she had left in the world? No, Constance, she decided. Keep it light. This truce is just a game. You're loving him and leaving him. This time, you'll have the upper hand.

"I would make an exception for this place," she shrugged.

"You would live here, in the middle of nowhere, in Italy, where you don't speak the language, full time?"

"I might have a pied a terre somewhere," Constance admitted. "I know a hot guy in St Tropez who has a pretty sweet crash pad. I could maybe stay there once in a while, if he would have me. Or maybe when he's out of town."

"Don't tease me with that scenario," said Lorenzo, looking hurt, all of a sudden.

"You don't like the idea?"

"I like it too much."

Lorenzo suddenly turned his attention back to the pot on the stove.

"Looks like it's almost ready," he said. "Why don't you pour us some more wine?"

Constance obediently splashed more of the ruby liquid into their glasses, glad for the distraction. Things were getting awkward. Time to steer them back to where she knew there would be no misunderstandings.

"The minestrone smells amazing," she said, sidling up to him and giving him a flirtatious glance. She slid her hand down his back and grabbed his right butt cheek. "Not as amazing as you, though."

"Don't distract me. I'm going to burn myself."

"Maybe the soup is too hot and needs to sit for a moment?"

"Not Minestrone," he laughed. "It's ready now. Here, cut the bread, and I'll fill our bowls."

Constance sliced a few pieces of Ciabatta and placed them in one of the baskets she remembered from her previous visits.

"Dining room, or kitchen?" asked Lorenzo.

"The kitchen is so cozy," said Constance. "It's always been my favorite room. Imagine a cooking retreat here. You could charge a fortune."

"Tell me more," said Lorenzo, as they sat down at the farm table that anchored one side of the room.

They spent the next hour drinking far too much wine and laying ambitious plans that Constance knew full well would never come to fruition. Much as her plan had been to seduce Lorenzo, the soup was so delicious, the wine so drinkable, and the conversation so intoxicating, that before she knew it, her head was gently spinning.

Chapter 41

Constance awoke in the pink bedroom, alone. Not what she had been planning at all. Not only were her eyes crusty and her mouth dry, but she had a pounding headache. She would have to do better today. She hoped she hadn't made a fool of herself. She took herself to the en suite bathroom, brushed her teeth, and splashed water on her face, using one of the washcloths to dab the mascara from under her eyes. Should she get dressed, or come down in the silk dressing gown that was hanging on the back of the bathroom door? Carlotta had collected these from her travels and had been in the habit of selecting specific ones for her guests according to their coloring and personality. And the one hanging on this door had been Constance's personal favorite. A teal peacock print not unlike the one she had tracked down and purchased for herself in a fit of retail therapy after breaking up with Lorenzo, and which she never traveled without. Carlotta's version was so much better, she realized now. She hoped that none of Lorenzo's supermodels had worn this one. She couldn't stand it. In fact, forget the robe. She would just take a quick shower and get dressed.

When she came downstairs, she found Lorenzo, in a dressing gown and slippers, on his laptop at the kitchen table, a grim expression on his face. He lit up, at least, when he noticed her, closed his laptop, and stood up, closing the space between them in a few long paces.

"How did you sleep?"

"Like the dead."

"We did have almost two bottles of wine."

"Ugh. Don't even say the word wine." Constance put her hand to her aching forehead. "Did I say anything I might regret?"

"Of course not. Did I?"

"No. We could have shared a room, you know. You could have taken advantage of my condition."

"I would never. When I take advantage of you, I want you to be fully present," Lorenzo growled, taking her into his arms. Constance melted, feeling immediately better. He gave her a kiss on the nose, then on the forehead.

"You showered and got dressed already," he said regretfully. "I was thinking we could have had breakfast in bed."

"My clothed state could easily be reversed," Constance observed.

"Let me make you breakfast first," said Lorenzo. "I don't know about you, but I'm famished."

"Same," Constance admitted. As much as she was hungry for Lorenzo, her stomach was growling.

Chapter 42

"So, what's on the menu for today?" Asked Constance, a smile playing on her lips.

"It's Christmas Eve. I thought we would go to the special Christmas market. We could pick up a few extra ingredients for the feast I'm planning on making you. There is a cocktail party at the neighbors', then midnight mass. Then, I take you home and have my way with you. After, of course, Champagne, oysters, and a few other delicacies."

"Sounds like a plan," said Constance.

"Oh, and I've drawn you a bath," said Lorenzo. "Or actually, the butler did, but I told him to. So, I think that counts, doesn't it?"

"Of course that counts," she smiled. "Are you going to be joining me in said bath?"

Lorenzo's face fell.

"I wish I could, but I actually need to go distribute gifts to the farming families around. I thought this would give you something nice to do while I'm gone, as long as you promise to think of me while you're in the bath."

Oh, she would think about him all right. She nestled in closer.

"When you said that I could undress again, I wasn't thinking about taking a bath alone," she whispered.

"Neither was I," he said. "But unfortunately, here we are. I promise that as soon as you are out, we'll have the rest of the day together."

After breakfast, Constance made her way upstairs to the guest bedroom, the one with the deepest tub. The butler must have been in just before and had refreshed and warmed the water. Citrus-scented bubbles played on its surface. She went to grab her book; she rarely had time to read and loved to read in the bath. She undressed and gratefully slipped into the water.

Just as she started reading, the door cracked open slowly.

"Do you mind if I come in?"

"I thought you said you were going to be distributing gifts to the poor little children," said Constance.

"I couldn't stay away. I just wanted the image of you to take with me. It's cold out there. I thought it would warm me up."
Constance smiled as Lorenzo stepped into the bathroom. She sat more upright in the tub as he bent down to give her a kiss. As always, the feeling of their lips meeting was electric. Soon, his tongue was twining with hers. His fingers were trailing down her cheek, down her neck, over her shoulders, and down under the water, so he could better stroke her breasts. She gasped as he pinched a nipple between his fingers.
"Don't start anything that you can't finish," she warned.
Lorenzo groaned.
"Why did I do this to myself? Maybe the children can wait until next Christmas for their gifts." Constance pulled his face towards her, kissing him passionately, whispering, "you can't possibly do this to me and then leave me to my own devices. What am I supposed to do now that you've gotten me all hot and bothered?"
 Lorenzo groaned again, kissing her back, and squeezing her breasts harder.
"God, if you weren't soaking wet, I would take you right now."
"Empty promises," Constance teased.
"You drive me crazy," he said. "I have no choice. I have to go now. Why did I decide to go see those kids today of all days? They probably don't even deserve anything. They've probably been very, very naughty."
"Not as naughty as the thoughts I'm having right now," said Constance.
"You tease," said Lorenzo.
"I'm not the tease, here. I fully intended on following through. It's not my fault you have this busy schedule as hot Santa," said Constance. "I thought you were all mine today."
"I am," he said. "After this."
"We are just not alone until after mass. That's far too long to wait," said Constance.
"It is," said Lorenzo. "But I want us to be able to take our time. I don't want to love you and leave you."
Because they had a truce, Constance didn't say, But you're so good at that.
Instead, she said, "sometimes even a quickie can be of high quality."

"Yes," Lorenzo groaned. "You're right. It can be. And no one ever appreciated a Santa with an erection."

"Except for me," Constance smiled.

Lorenzo started to unzip his pants. Constance's eyes were glued to his strong hands as he pulled down the zipper. Just then, a voice called out.

"Oh fuck," said Lorenzo. "That's Alberto. He's supposed to drive me. That's it. I'm going to tell him that I've got some business with you first."

"Absolutely not," Constance laughed. "I would be mortified. Come on, you go and come back soon."

"I don't want to," said Lorenzo.

"I don't want you to, either" Constance said. "But you don't have a choice. Now go, Santa Claus. I'll see you when you're back. I'll be ready for the Christmas market."

"All right," he said. "I can't wait to give you the gift I have for you," he called out as he left the bathroom.

"You almost just showed it to me," said Constance.

He popped his head back into the bathroom.

"No, I have another one as well," he said.

Constance smiled. She was glad that she had convinced herself to buy him a gift, even though she'd been worried that it would not be reciprocated. She sank down into the bath, thinking of Lorenzo, frustrated that they'd been interrupted, wondering whether she should do something about the pent-up sexual energy, but deciding that the deferred nature of the act would make it all the more delicious, when they finally did come together. She liked this truce. It was wonderful to be able to just enjoy each other without recriminations and accusations. And not being in bed 24/7 meant that they were actually talking. She loved talking with Lorenzo. She had, she realized, shared more with him about how she was feeling, even without the truce, than she ever had when they'd actually been together.

Eventually, she started feeling guilty about. Using too much hot water and emerged from the bath, wrapping herself in a fluffy bathrobe and going back to the pink room to select a warm but festive outfit, deciding on an emerald green cashmere sweater dress, which she had found on sale in the same shop where she had purchased Lorenzo's gift. She added warm stockings, her knee-high boots, and a swipe of red lipstick. She smiled to herself. She was going to make him wait and work for it. She spent the rest of the time until Lorenzo returned corresponding with Daphne over some of the details for the yacht. She wondered again what Daphne was up to today. Other than working, was she really so content being alone, or did she miss the idea of having a loved one with her? Had she ever spent Christmas with Peter? Constance couldn't ask about this, of course. It would be suspicious.

Chapter 43

When Lorenzo returned, a warm smile was lighting up his face.

"How did it go?" Asked Constance.

"You should have seen them," said Lorenzo. "I'm glad I didn't make them wait for a year. They were all thrilled."

"They count on you," said Constance.

"No, not really," said Lorenzo. "But it's tradition, and it's just a special time, I think, for all of us. Their families have been working for mine for generations, and I so appreciate the support. I've known these kids for so long that I feel like an uncle to them. Especially since I don't have any children of my own yet."

If they hadn't been under a truce, she might have said, Whose fault is that you don't have kids yet?

But instead, she smiled at him and said, "One day, you'll be such a good father, Lorenzo."

This made him grin even wider, exposing that adorable wonky tooth of his, and it was the sweetest thing she'd seen in a while. His expression, though, then turned wolfish, as if he was thinking of exactly how one makes a baby. Until he noticed the red lipstick.

"Damn lipstick. You do look beautiful, though. Are you ready for the winter market?"

Constance remembered the time they had gone to the market with Carlotta. She and Lorenzo's mother had picked up a few little delicacies, and Carlotta had pointed out some of the traditional decorations. Constance thought she would like to pick up a few decorations for her future Christmas tree. She smiled to herself. She had never thought about a Christmas tree of her own before.

"What are you smiling about?" Asked Lorenzo. "I love to see it."

"Just happy," she said.

At the Christmas market, they strolled around the stalls, their breath coming out in puffs. It was frigid outside. She was glad she'd brought her thick scarf, and that she'd layered up underneath her coat. Lorenzo took her gloved hand and put it into his pocket, warming it up further.

"I love doing this with you," he said. "I wish we could do it always."

She did too. But she was having such a hard time vocalizing that- it seemed too intimate, somehow. Too vulnerable. But if Lorenzo could say it, she could extend herself.

"I love it, too," she said. "Remember when we came with your mother? All those pretty decorations- I regretted not buying any for myself. I'd like to pick up some of those this time," she said.

"But you told me you've never had a tree in your adult life," said Lorenzo.

"Maybe next year I will. I would like to have them now, just to make sure that I get one."

"Where will your tree be?" Asked Lorenzo.

"Who knows?" Constance shrugged again, embarrassed to say, wherever you are. And also, wasn't that an artificial response, just a byproduct of the truce?

"Come on, I'll lead you to the stall that I think you're talking about," said Lorenzo. They arrived, and sure enough, that was it. A beautiful market stall full of stunning mercury glass decorations, some of them depicting woodland creatures, others in the shape of exotic mushrooms, or birds with flamboyant plumage.

"Aren't they perfect?" Constance cooed, starting to try to make a selection.

"You're perfect," said Lorenzo, kissing her in the space between her scarf and her jawline. "Except for that lipstick. Why did you have to put on that lipstick?"

"Just to tease you," she said, smiling.

"It's working," said Lorenzo.

Constance thought back to that morning, when he had started unzipping his jeans. How she would like to decorate his member with lipstick. Maybe she would do that tonight.

"You've got a very naughty expression on your face," said Lorenzo. "What are you thinking about?"

"Just the places where my lipstick could go," she said faux-innocently.

Lorenzo groaned.

"You'd better be careful," he whispered in her ear, "or you may get a big hard… lump of coal in your stocking."

Constance's breath caught in her throat. She knew that Lorenzo had noticed that the way in which he'd said big and hard had had the intended effect.

"Two can play this game," he whispered.

"You're a bigger tease than I am," Constance retorted.

"Impossible," said Lorenzo.

Constance purchased a few decorations, picturing them on their first Christmas tree together. Wishing that it could be true. That the secret life she had dreamed of for herself could be a reality. She caught the scent of something delicious.

"Chestnuts," said Lorenzo, "should I get us some?"

"What kind of a question is that? And where's my spiced wine?"

"You poor dear," said Lorenzo. "I've been starving you."

Once they had their chestnuts and their wine, they wandered around some more, purchased a few more small items, and made their way back to the car.

"It's almost time for the cocktail party… and then mass," said Lorenzo regretfully.

"You're really into this whole delayed gratification thing, aren't you?" Constance smiled. "How much trouble would you get into if you didn't go to the party?"

"Loads of trouble," said Lorenzo. "I wouldn't hear the end of it. And I think Chiara's parents might be there?"

"No, they're all in St Moritz, but I guess we still need to go," said Constance. She was a little relieved that Mr. and Mrs. Ludovisi were out of town, as she was feeling guilty for not filling Chiara in on the details of what was going on with her life.

"I suggest we get dressed separately," said Lorenzo. I don't think I could bear being in the same room with you if you take off a single thing."

"Fair enough," said Constance. "And I don't want you to mess up my hair or my lipstick," she said, smiling.

They retreated to separate rooms, and she got into the same dress she'd worn for Thanksgiving with Harold. It was her most flattering one, and she knew it wouldn't be out of place with Lorenzo's fancy neighbors. She slipped on an elegant pair of high heeled knee-high boots, another purchase from her shopping expedition while Lorenzo had been away. They both stepped out into the hallway, admiring each other in their holiday finery. Lorenzo was wearing an Austrian hunting jacket. His father's family had roots in the norther part of Italy that might as well be Austria. He looked so handsome in the tailored garment that she could barely tear her eyes off of him.

They drove off to the party, Constance gasping as they pulled up to a romantic palazzo with candles in every window.

"It's magical."

"Even more magical being here with you."

Chapter 44

The next thing she knew, Constance was opening her eyes, blinded by dazzling sunshine blasting through the window.

"What time is it?" She groaned.

"Merry Christmas," Lorenzo whispered into her ear, nuzzling her neck and scooping her up so she nestled against him, her back to his front.

"That's right, Merry Christmas," she said.

She couldn't remember clearly what had happened the night before. But then it came back to her. A beautiful midnight mass. Too many glasses of champagne. And...

"I'm sorry, I had too much to drink last night. Said Constance. Did I throw myself at you?"

"It was mutual…"

She wrinkled her nose.

"No, I'm joking," Lorenzo whispered into her ear, giving her the chills. "I want our first time in five years to be something to remember. And, I have a gift for you."

"I know. I can feel it." She raised an eyebrow. "Wait, I'd better go brush my teeth."

That's not the gift I was talking about, but if you want this one first, I'll be right back, too, he said," leaping up and heading to the bathroom the hall.

Constance got up and brushed her teeth, splashing water onto her face and trying to tame her hair a little bit. She readjusted her negligee and casually got back into bed, just as Lorenzo returned, wearing only his thin boxer shorts and holding a box wrapped in shiny paper, tied in a ribbon.

"Oh Goody," said Constance. "Do I get to open it now?"

"If you like," said Lorenzo. "Or you can wait."

He got back into bed, placing the box on the nightstand, and took her back in his arms. Yes, the gift could wait. She had her gift to him in her suitcase. It was a soft, emerald green cashmere sweater that she knew would look amazing on him. And it was her color, too. So, he would look all the better standing next to her.

If only this truce lasted forever.

Lorenzo kissed her cheekbone, then her chin, then her nose, then took her face in his hands and devoured her lips, rolling on top of her and pressing himself against her, awakening her desire just as quickly as ever.

"What if I forgot to bring you a gift?" She teased.

"Well then, I suppose you'd just have to show your gratitude for the gift that I got you in some other way," said Lorenzo. "I have a few ideas for how you might do that."

"I think I remember what you might like. But it's been such a long time," said Constance. "I think I remember you liking it a lot when I was on top," she said.

Lorenzo moaned at the mere thought of it and kissed her again. "I seem to recall that you mostly doled that out on special occasions… but I think that Christmas morning counts as a special occasion, doesn't it?"

"It does," Constance smiled.

Back when they were first together, she was more self-conscious than she was now about her curves and didn't like the idea of a man looking up at her and seeing her large breasts and her tummy as she moved on top of him. But with time, she had realized the advantages that the position allowed her. How she could control her own pleasure. How she could also hold down a man's hands, look into his eyes and take control. She had learned to appreciate it. And besides, she'd been this way for years now, had found men who clearly appreciated her, had learned to appreciate herself. She was unlikely to change and wasn't going to ruin her own life because of a few extra rolls of flesh. Flesh that Lorenzo was currently kissing and caressing. He propped himself up on one elbow, taking her in as she lay back, her eyes locked on his.

"You're so beautiful," he whispered. "You've always been the most beautiful woman in the world to me. Do you know that?"

"I have?" she asked, genuinely surprised.

"Of course. You know that," he responded.

If they hadn't been under a truce, she would have countered with something about how she thought he preferred supermodels. But instead, she decided to take the compliment, which, she had to admit, sounded sincere. She wanted to believe it, so badly.

"You're not so bad yourself," she responded. "In fact, you might be just my type."

"Oh, yes?" he smiled. "That makes me happy."

She kissed him back more deeply this time, stroking his body, loving the feel of his hard muscles. She'd always loved the contrast between his olive skin and her soft, pale flesh. Opposites did attract.

"Lie back," she said.

He complied, rolling onto his back, his abdominal muscles rippling. She ran a finger down his chest, tracing the little valley between his stomach muscles, continuing further down to where the happy trail began, and further still. He was already rock hard. As she stroked the length of him, gently at first, then wrapping her hand around his member and giving it a squeeze, his soft groans turned into a feral growl. She loved that noise. It was one of her favorite sounds on Earth. She would do anything to hear it again. She was addicted to it as much as she was addicted to the way he looked, the way he smelled, and the way he felt.

She straddled him, planting butterfly kisses down his chest, tickling his skin with her tongue, moving down... down... until he could take no more, and placed his hands on her shoulders. She heard his sharp intake of breath as she took him into her mouth. He shuddered, and then growled again, more deeply, as she worked her tongue around the tip of his cock, then took as much of him as she could into her mouth, using her hand to stroke the base of him.

"That feels so good," Lorenzo moaned. "There's nothing better."

"Oh really?" Asked Constance, coming up for air for a second, then going back to teasing him, sucking on him while using her tongue on the head of his member, feeling him grow even harder in her mouth. He writhed on the bed under her. She could tell he was close, but she wasn't going to let him get away with climaxing too quickly.

"Nothing else better than this? Really?"

She paused for a moment, looking up at him, her desire to tease him at odds with her desire to just have him inside of her, already.

"I don't know is there something better?" He tried to say, but he interrupted himself with a groan as she took him back into her mouth.

"You'd better be careful if you don't want me to lose control," he panted.

"But I do want you to lose control," she said. "Just not now." She ran her tongue up and down the length of him one more time.

"Did you happen to bring anything that we might need? For my gift?"

"Fuck," said Lorenzo. "Yes. Wait. one minute."

She enjoyed the view of his gorgeous ass as he rolled over and opened the drawer of the nightstand, rummaging around and bringing out a small gold packet.

"Got it," he said. "I almost didn't bring any. I didn't want to assume, but then I told myself that Christmas miracles do happen."

"Stop talking," said Constance. "And put that on."

She was more than ready. She could feel the throbbing between her legs, almost taste her impatience to have him inside of her. He lay back, opening the foil wrapper and taking out the condom. She admired him as he unrolled it down the length of him. They locked eyes, and she clambered on top of him, slowly lowering herself on him, taking him all in, until he was completely buried inside of her, to the hilt. This time, they both groaned.

"I'd forgotten how good this was," she sighed.

He fit inside her just right. They were like two puzzle pieces, made for one another. She started moving, undulating her hips, savoring the feeling of his cock inside of her, while he thrust up to meet her movements.

"I've dreamed of this," he moaned. "So many times. You have no idea."

She smiled and ground against him harder, little cries coming from her lips as he hit every secret spot Feeling the waves of pleasure already building up inside her body. He reached up and cupped both of her breasts in his hands, and arched her back, throwing her head back in ecstasy, moving faster now. She wanted this to last, but she also felt the imperative of her climax approaching.

"Slow down," he said. "I want to make it last."

"Speak for yourself," she said. "This is my Christmas gift. You'd better not disappoint me."

"If I do, we can go again," he said, thrusting into her harder. She ground against him, too, leaning forward to let him suck on her nipples while he grabbed her ass, dictating her rhythm and helping her to grind against him even harder. That did it. The pleasure came over her in waves. She felt herself clenching around him, and him throbbing into her, his growling matched by her gasping. An X-rated symphony. She realized that the butler was probably somewhere in the house. But at this point, she didn't care. She was too involved in her own pleasure, and Lorenzo's. She hadn't lied. It had never been this good with anybody else. And she knew he wasn't lying to her, either. He was as attracted to her as she was to him. Why couldn't they make this work? But she couldn't think about that. She just rode out the orgasm, feeling wave after wave of it, until she finally collapsed in a heap on top of him, his breath tickling her sweaty neck as he recovered from his own climax.

"That was amazing," he said. "Thank you for being here. It's the best gift ever."

She simply kissed him, forcing herself not to cry. They lay there, afterwards, holding each other, savoring the moment. Once their breathing had returned to normal, Lorenzo nudged her gently and said, "OK, now do you want your other gift?"

"I don't know how it'll compare to the one you just gave me, but all right."

He passed her the box. So beautiful, with gold and silver moiré paper and a silk bow in a gorgeous shade of rust that she noticed exactly matched her hair. She pulled on the ribbon and opened the box, revealing glimmering silk fabric with a gorgeous print. Was this what she thought it was? She lifted the item out of the tissue paper. Yes. It was a beautiful silk dressing gown. The same kind that Carlotta used to buy. The ones that Constance had never been able to source herself, because she hadn't had the opportunity to ask Lorenzo.

"Was this one of your mother's?" Constance asked.

"No. I had this one designed just for you," said Lorenzo. "By the same place she had make hers. I can have more designed for you, anything you like, as long as you stay with me," he said.

She held back the tears that threatened again. What the hell was wrong with her? And kissed him.

"I love it," she said. "Thank you so much."

"You're welcome. Is it the right color or… do you like…?"

"It's beyond perfect. I love everything about it," she smiled.

It was true. He still knew her best, even after all these years. She held up the dressing gown again, admiring the shimmering jade colored silk, the playful but elegant design featuring cheetahs, with leaves in the background executed in a way that was both graphic and subtle. It was the most beautiful thing she'd ever seen. If she could translate this into wallpaper, she would be famous.

"Why don't you put it on?" Smiled Lorenzo. "You can wear it while I make you breakfast. I gave the Butler the day off- you know, it being Christmas, and all."

"Oh! And here I was, being quiet for Alberto's benefit," Constance smiled.

"That was you being quiet?"

She nodded, giggling.

"Well, we'll have to go again. And you'll feel free to be as loud as you like. Just don't shatter my eardrums," he smiled.

She wrapped herself into the dressing gown and they went downstairs, hand in hand. There was frost on the ground outside. She could see it through the kitchen windows, glinting in the sunlight. It was magical.

"Wait, I have your gift too," she said.

She ran back upstairs to retrieve it, handing him the gift bag, its handles tied with a ribbon.

"May I open it now?"

"Of course."

When he held the sweater up to himself, she drank him in with her eyes. It was perfect. It suited his skin tone perfectly.

"Does it look OK?"

"More than OK," she responded.

"I think it's your color too," he noted. "You'll look all the more beautiful standing next to me."

She simply smiled and kissed him.

"All right, breakfast, my darling. And then we'll go for a walk. How does that sound?"

"It sounds perfect," said Constance.

The rest of the day was magical. A walk. A bath- for two, this time. Making love again, in front of the fire, and then, a wonderful dinner. Simple, but full of the Italian flavors that Constance had missed so much.

"Do you know that I haven't looked at my telephone all day?"

Constance smiled. "That never happens."

"Neither have I," Lorenzo grinned. "Let's throw our phones away."

"I wish I could," Constance groaned.

"Well, don't check it now. It's Christmas," said Lorenzo.

"Nobody's going to be trying to reach you."

"All right," said Constance, even though she knew she should call Harold. "I won't, but you have to distract me."

"You've got a deal," he responded. And he kept his promise.

Chapter 45

The next morning. They woke up, still snuggled in bed together, but the atmosphere soon changed. Lorenzo grabbed his phone off the nightstand and frowned at it. "Crap. There's a bit of a business emergency in Paris."

"The day after Christmas?" She asked.

"One of our biggest advertisers is threatening to pull out. I have to go wine and dine this fucker, to convince him again."

"Do you have to?"

"Having a big advertiser for the first issue is crucial. It convinces all the others to trust us. If this one jumps ship, I'm sunk to begin with."

Constance nodded. Intellectually, she understood. But emotionally, she resented Lorenzo being ripped away from her again so fast and going to Paris.

"Do you have to stay in Paris overnight?"

"No, maybe I can take this jerk to lunch and be back by evening," he said.

She remembered now all the times that Lorenzo had left her for a last-minute photo shoot, or some such thing, and how resentful she'd been. She realized now that she'd felt that his career was more important to him than she was, or that it was progressing faster than her career, and every time she thought she had proof of that, it hurt a little bit more. Now, she saw that it was an obligation. But she didn't have to like it.

"Can I come with you to Paris?"

"I would love you to, more than anything. But it makes no sense. I'll be hand-holding this guy, and then hopefully be back tonight, with you. I'm sure you have more than enough boat-related things to keep you busy in the meantime."

He was right. But still, she was bummed. She'd been hoping for a few more days outside of reality, enjoying being together, before it was snatched away from her again. Constance packed up her things, and they rode to the airport. They couldn't even talk then, because Alberto had last minute things to talk to Lorenzo about, and then Lorenzo had to run for his plane to Paris, barely giving her a peck on the lips before hurrying to his gate. Constance got to hang around the airport for an extra hour, feeling sorry for herself, before taking a solo flight back to Nice.

Chapter 46

Constance tapped her fingernails on the glass surface of her table at the terrace of Le Senequier. It was sunny, but chilly, the masts of the boats parked at the harbor glimmering, seagulls spiraling in the sky, their squawks filling the air. A crystalline quality to the light held a promise of, maybe, an early spring. Constance found herself wishing, not for the first time, that she could spend some more time in Europe, even once she was done with this project. She wondered how Lorenzo would feel about that. Not that it had anything to do with him. Well, not really. After all, it was highly unlikely that they would end up together, no matter their chemistry. On top of that, he had ended up letting her know late afternoon the day before that he needed to stay in Paris for the night, after all, and then, that morning, had let her know he was on his way back, but urgently had to stop by the office.

She didn't have time to worry about it. For now, she needed to focus. She took another shot of coffee and grimaced as she swallowed the bitter liquid.

If she wanted any chance at getting the boat featured in the magazine for the opening issue, she needed to pay attention. Harold had suggested, last time she'd spoken to him, hiring an expediter, but Daphne had reassured Constance that they had it all under control. For the first time in her career, she had created a complete list of all of the fabricators, so she could keep them on task. The carpet makers were already in the process of weaving a custom design and, as of right before Christmas, they appeared to be on schedule. The woodworkers were slow, but steady, and didn't have too many complicated pieces to execute, so she decided they would make it. In terms of the fabrics, she'd had to revise the original plan, but she'd found a solution that would work. Now, it all boiled down to install and staging. She would have to be onsite every day starting January 2nd. Some of the appliances were on back order, but she'd been reassured as to the fact that they were coming in. Some of the artisans, such as the tile installer, were on standby, waiting for the right time to come in.

She felt her heart sweet with pride at herself. She had managed to stay on track singularly well on this project, pushed by multiple motivators of not disappointing Harold or Peter, getting Peter and Daphne back together, and not looking bad in front of Lorenzo and Sophie.

She went back over her plans, and her calendar, looking at the ever-shrinking window of opportunity to set everything up. Daphne was busy sourcing some of the special books, objects, and antiques that would make the client Constance had carefully described feel at home in the space. The two women had agreed that they wanted to deliver something absolutely turnkey.

As Constance tried desperately to maintain her focus on the columns of numbers and dates, struggling with them, to be sure, her phone rang.

Harold's number.

She picked up right away.

"Uncle Harold," she said, delighted to be able to let him know how well she was doing, for once. But she was shocked to hear a familiar voice on the other end of the line that was not Harold.

"Penelope, what are you doing with Uncle Harold's phone?"

"You need to come quick. Your uncle's in the hospital," said Penelope.

"What happened?" Constance's heart was beating out of her chest, panic rising in her throat.

"He collapsed at the office. They say it's his lungs. Just come fast. I think he's going into surgery. At Miami General."

"I'll be there as fast as I can," said Constance.

She sat there in the café for a second, stunned. She squinted, looking outside, noticing how the disconcertingly bright day was now so at odds with her mood. Minutes ago, she'd been feeling in control and optimistic, and now, with a single phone call, everything had changed. Harold. Harold was all the family she had left. Her dad didn't even count, ever since he'd run off with her stepmothers. She couldn't do it without Harold. Couldn't lose him. She'd been worrying about him, that strange cough of his for the past few months, but she hadn't thought enough of it, because he hadn't made a big deal of it. Had he been hiding something about his health from her? Was this why he was pushing her? To challenge her, so that he could see if she would be able to take over once he was gone? The thought was too terrible to consider. No time to think about those things. She needed to get on the first flight to Miami. She logged onto her airline app and booked a plane leaving out of Nice that afternoon. She needed to hurry. As was, she would just have time to pack and go. She threw a bill and a few coins on the table and gathered up her things, hustling over to the apartment. Lorenzo still wasn't home. She should let him know that she was leaving town. But it was too complicated to get into. She hadn't even gotten a return ticket. She didn't know what she would find when she arrived in Miami, how long she would need to stay. This might mean messing up the whole Lombard 4 project, but Harold was more important. Still, she made the decision not to pack all of her things- just her carry on. She still had clothes in her apartment in Miami, and she fully intended to come back here once things had settled down. For once, she was not going to just run away. For once she was going to finish what she had started. She just wasn't sure whether that applied to whatever she had with Lorenzo, or not.

Chapter 47

She was just starting to wheel her carry-on out of the room when the front door to the apartment opened. Lorenzo walked in and stared at her with hurt expression. "Where do you think you're going?" He asked, his tone concerned, but also frustrated.

"What's that tone supposed to mean?" Asked Constance. She had no patience for this right now.

"That's it? You're running away from me again? We get close, and you just cut and run?"

"What do you mean, again? I'm going to the airport. My Uncle Harold is in the hospital."

"Oh no! I'm so sorry. Why don't I drive you to the airport, so you don't have to worry with the parking?"

"I'm sure you have a million more important things to do," said Constance.

"No, I absolutely don't." He retorted. "Here, give me your bag. What time is your flight?"

Constance told him.

"You're cutting it close. Let's go," he said.

They hustled to where he had parked his car. He put her bags in the trunk, and she got into the front seat and clicked her seat belt, her heart still hammering in her chest worry for her uncle taking hold of her.

"Is it his lungs?" Asked Lorenzo as he started the car and navigated down the narrow streets.

"Yeah. How did you know?" Asked Constance.

"I didn't tell you? we chat once in a while," said Lorenzo, as if he had told her. "I'd noticed he had a bad cough. I've asked him about it, but he never wanted to discuss. In any case, I hope you keep me posted."

"OK," said Constance, too upset to delve into why Lorenzo had been keeping in touch with Harold, and why no one had told her.

"You're coming back though, right?" Asked Lorenzo.

"I don't have a choice," said Constance. "I have the project to finish. I'm going to finish something for once. And I understand if this sets me back, and I don't make it into the magazine. I'm so thankful that you even entertained the notion, and so sorry that I'm going to let you down."

"Constance, you're not letting me down. You've been doing an amazing job. Delays happen. Life happens. I'm going to hold the spot for as long as I can, and we have a potential replacement. And if it's not in the first issue, maybe it can be in a future issue, right?"

"I guess so, said Constance. But I don't want to disappoint the client either. Harold had mentioned he wanted it published before summer for some reason."

"Have you discussed it with him?" Asked Lorenzo.

"No. Maybe I should," said Constance.

"The magazine will always be there to put your project in, especially if it's going to look like the vision boards you showed me. It's a stunning concept."

"What if Sophie says no?" Constance wasn't too upset to be a little petty.

"Believe me, I will fight for you."

She almost started crying at this kindness from Lorenzo. She was so emotionally overwhelmed. And then, like the idiot she was, she decided that, since the truce was over and she wasn't going to see Lorenzo for God knew how long, the best thing to do would be to start a fight.

"Funny, you didn't fight for me five years ago."

Lorenzo gave her a side glance as he merged onto the highway.

"You and I have two vastly different versions of what happened."

"My version is the truth. You left me. You walked away."

"Bullshit. I was going to propose. I had a fucking ring, Constance, and you walked right out the door."

"You left me for a model."

"You can tell yourself, that, but the only thing I'm guilty of is thinking that, if I loved you enough, I should let you go. I should have told you that you were being an idiot."

Constance stared at him, clenching her jaw.

"Wow, I wished I lived in your reality. How fucking romantic. Compared to the truth."

Lorenzo sighed.

"Constance. Why would I bother lying to you at this juncture? We've been apart for so long. We barely manage to be civil to each other when we're not making out, or in bed, or have a truce. There's no reason for me to lie to you other than…I'm stupidly, desperately, in love with you. Still. Despite the fact that you broke my heart in a million pieces when you ran away for the final time."

Constance just stared at him, her heart beating. Aching in her chest. She thought back to that time. Screwed her eyes shut for a moment, trying to see more clearly, somehow, looked back at Lorenzo. Yes, she had been looking for a way out, hadn't she? But not because she bored with Lorenzo. Not because he wasn't good enough for her. Because she was scared. Scared that he would get bored, the way she always had with everyone else. Scared of staying put, when she'd spent a life moving around. He was the one thing that she had never wanted to lose, and stupidly, she'd decided it would be easier to cut and run, to ruin it herself. Because otherwise, Lorenzo would have left her one day, just when she'd started trusting him to stick around. She looked at him again. His hands were gripping the steering wheel.

"It's easy for you to spin your version of the truth now, after the fact, when I can't prove that you were cheating on me," said Constance cruelly.

That old instinct of cutting and running was back with a vengeance. Her feelings for Lorenzo were just too overwhelming.

"Great. Believe whatever you want," said Lorenzo. "I thought I would just put it out there anyway, tell you how I felt, because if I didn't, I would have regretted it my whole life. I thought that maybe we had a chance. But now, I see that you're absolutely serious that we're never going to be together. And I guess I have no choice but to accept."

"Good," said Constance, her teeth gritted.

But inside, she felt like sobbing. Why was she being so stupid? Why was she being so stubborn? She thought back to the magical days around Christmas. Thought back to the way he'd looked at her, too many times to count. Thought about how he often put his hands on her cheeks as he kissed her. How hard it was for her to resist pouncing on him at every moment. Why did he have this effect on her? Why him, and nobody else? She risked another glance at Lorenzo. He looked deeply unhappy, and it broke her heart.

"Lorenzo, I'm sorry. I'm crazy. I don't mean what I said. I think. Can we talk about this when I come back?"

"I don't think there's anything left to discuss, Constance. You've made your stance abundantly clear," he replied. It came out in a growl. So similar, but so different to the times he had growled in her ear during lovemaking and between kisses. Suddenly, she wanted nothing more than to feel his skin on hers, to at least hold his hand. To wrap herself around him and make him stop looking so sad. It was all her fault that he was sad, wasn't it? She had been the one to run away from him, and not the other way around. Here she was, trying to fix the relationship between Peter and Daphne, when her relationship was the stupidest misunderstanding ever. Was it best to let Lorenzo go? Let this beautiful man go on and have a pleasant life with somebody better? Lorenzo, who always made her feel like the most beautiful woman on earth every time they were together?

They rode the rest of the way to the airport in silence, she with tears running down her face. When he pulled in front of the terminal, he simply hopped out of the car and retrieved her bag from the trunk. He held it out to her, his face grim.

She wanted to say, I love you. I'll be back. I'm sorry. I'm an idiot. A million other things, none of which would change anything. But seeing his resigned expression, she thought to herself, Let it be. Let it break off now. I'll put some distance between us, and by the time I come back, he'll be better off. Would that jeopardize the placement of the yacht in the magazine? She hoped not. Her work spoke for itself this time, didn't it?

Lorenzo stood there as she took her bag, looking unsure as to what to do, whether to hug her or give her a peck on the cheek, and finally, he just quietly turned around and walked back to the car.

She was such a fucking disaster. She would never deserve someone like Lorenzo anyway, she told herself. Why did she do this? She watched the car pull away and walked towards the terminal with a heavy heart. She checked the time and panicked. Good thing she had only a carry on. She hustled through security and just made it to the gate as it was boarding. The minute she got into her plane seat, she fell into a deep sleep, only waking up when the plane landed in Atlanta.

She tried to call Harold's number again, but this time, no one was responding.

Hold on, Harold. Hold on.

She checked her phone repeatedly. No messages. How could no one keep her posted on what was going on? Before she knew it, she realized she needed to hurry to make it to her connecting flight to Miami. She grabbed herself a coffee and had to break into a jog to make it to the gate.

On the plane, she fell asleep again. By the time she landed in Miami, it was late afternoon already. She didn't know what time visiting hours were, but too bad. They would have to accept her at the hospital. She jumped into a cab, barely even caring that the driver seemed a little edgy and held her breath as the car made its way through Miami afternoon traffic to Miami General.

Chapter 48

After sweet-talking her way into Harold's section at the hospital, Constance knocked lightly on the door jamb of Harold's room. Thank goodness he was no longer in intensive care, but rather in recovery, having already gone through surgery.

"Hey," she said softly, walking in.

"Hey yourself," Harold, croaked.

The surgery had taken out a lobe of his lung that had a large tumor in it and was impacting his breathing and had drained an impressive amount of liquid. They were currently doing a biopsy on the mass to check if it was cancerous, but there was some hope that perhaps it wasn't. Perhaps it was just scar tissue caused by Harold's numerous bouts of pneumonia over his lifetime. Still, this was no laughing matter, and it hurt Constance see him looking weak and pale, greatly diminished.

"Uncle Harold, why didn't you tell me that you were feeling bad before it got to this level?" She asked.

"I was fine. You were where you needed to be. I didn't want to distract you," he said.

"Distract me? You're the most important thing in my life! Designing a silly yacht is secondary. And besides, you know that anything is capable of distracting me, from a squirrel to another project, to a man." She was dying to tell him about Lorenzo, but decided it was not the time. Anyway, she'd ruined it, again.

"I guess I was in denial about how I felt. And I don't want to be the most important thing for you- I thought that maybe in France, you were maybe starting to build a life you wanted."

"Sorry, nope. And what? You thought you would magically get better?"

Harold shrugged, weakly.

"When do they say you're going to be able to get out of here?" Asked Constance.

"As soon as they have the results of the tests, and as soon as I'm more stable," he replied. "There's still fluid building up, so they're going to remove that a few times, and we'll see what happens. I might have a chic little oxygen tank to tote around for a while after I go home."

"I know you'll rock it," said Constance, smiling. "If anyone can make an oxygen tank look fab, it's you. Just remember oxygen's super flammable, so no smoking."

"Damn it, you're right," said Harold. "Well, I always wanted to quit. So enough about me. There's nothing more boring than an old guy in a hospital. How's the project going?"

"Everything is really great," Constance said, happy to switch her focus to something happy. She described where she was in the process and explained the ceiling detail. She'd almost lost him. She wasn't about to withhold anything from him.

"Darling, that all sounds brilliant. I'm so proud."

"Well, I have to admit something to you, though, Uncle Harold."

"Oh oh," said Harold.

"No, don't worry! I'm not sleeping with the client," she said, smiling.

"Thank goodness," said Harold. "I don't think I would have been able to handle that. Especially since Peter is a friend of mine. Good thing I'm in the hospital for whatever you need to tell me, though, in case I pass out and need reanimation."

Constance smiled. She was glad to see his humor was intact.

"OK, you know how I was saying I'd brought on somebody to help me with the details?"

"Yes. The local woman," said Harold cautiously.

"She's Peter's old lover. The woman who broke his heart, the woman who decorated his yacht in Saint Barts, the one he ended up selling. The one he wanted to impress with the magazine feature. Oh, and Uncle Harold, speaking of magazine feature, I'm so sorry, but with the ceiling detail, the work might take longer than we'd hoped. We really had a tight timeline, and I might not be able to get the boat in the magazine before summer, and I know how important that was to Peter, but maybe if it works out with Daphne…"

She stopped talking, noticing that Harold was looking at her strangely.

"Right, right, OK," he said, distractedly, "and what does Lorenzo say about that?" Constance froze.

"Wait a second. You knew that Lorenzo was in town, didn't you? You knew that he owned the magazine?"

"Uh, yes, I did," said Harold, looking like he wished he could hide under the bed. "Uncle Harold. Did Peter actually want his boat in a magazine?" Constance asked, realization dawning upon her.

"Not exactly," said Harold.

"You sent me to Saint Tropez in the damn winter and cooked up the whole magazine thing because you wanted me to get back together with Lorenzo? Is that what you did?"

Harold looked at her guiltily.

"An old man can dream," he said. "You two were the most beautiful couple I've ever seen, you and Lorenzo. He had asked me for your hand in marriage, and I was already looking forward to the wedding- not the paying for it part, but the walking you down the aisle part- and then next thing I know, you've broken up, and I never found out what happened."

"You talk to Lorenzo all the time, it seems," Constance accused. "Didn't he tell you?"

But while she said it, she mind raced. So, it was true. Lorenzo had bought the ring. He'd even asked Harold. And Harold had loved her enough to not question her when she'd ruined the most beautiful thing in her life. He'd stood by her, thinking that that's what she needed.

And Lorenzo had done the same thing. Respected her wishes enough to let her make her own mistakes, even if they hurt him. She wanted nothing more than to pick up the phone and apologize and tell Lorenzo that she was so sorry for what she'd done and how she treated him, but she had a horrible feeling that this time, it was too late. She'd seen the broken expression on his face.

"I think I've made a terrible mistake," said Constance, blanching.

"What do you mean a terrible mistake? Did you did you get involved with Lorenzo again? Wait, you didn't break up with him again, did you?"

"Well, not exactly involved, but maybe a little bit. And yes, I'm afraid I've... I'm afraid I've broken things... irretrievably."

Harold closed his eyes. He still didn't look so good, and Constance felt horrible for paining him like this.

"Constance, can you just let an old man see one happy ending in his life? Can you do that? Do it for me. If not for you."

"I'm sorry. I think it's too late, Uncle Harold. I don't think he wants me anymore. I think I've pushed him too far."

"Get on a damn plane! Now!"

"I can't leave you like this," Constance replied. "That would be running away, too."

"I just want you to have a happy life," he said simply. "Can you promise me you'll try to do that?"

"I promise," said Constance.

"The minute I'm out of here, you're back on the plane, kid."

"Gladly," Constance smiled, holding his skinny hand.

The nurse Constance had sweet-talked earlier tapped on the door.

"Sorry, extended visiting hours are over," she smiled.

"All right. I'll come back tomorrow," said Constance, rising from the chair next to Harold's bed. Harold waved at her weakly. Constance walked out, heading to the nurse station to ask for more information about Harold.

"Hi," she said to a kind looking nurse with curly brown hair and a nose ring. "Is there anyone I can talk to- to find out more about what's going on with my Uncle Harold? Harold Morgan?"

"Let me check who his doctor is," said the woman, going into some files.

"Oh, right. That's doctor Rosenberg. He just left for the night, but he'll be back in the morning, so you could catch him then. I'm sure he'll be happy to talk to you. We were waiting for the next of kin to come to discuss any directives."

Constance stared at her.

"What do you mean, directives?"

"You know, just in case," said the nurse. "I'm not saying there's any need for that now, but we were hoping that some family would come forward."

"Well, that's me," said Constance. "Let me give you my phone number in case you need it. And I'll be there anytime if he needs me. Otherwise, I'll be here in the morning. What time does Doctor Rosenberg get here?"

"8:00."

"I'll be here at eight," said Constance.

She looked at her watch. It was about 6:00 PM. She was shattered, fatigue digging behind her eyes, making them sore. The idea of going to her soulless apartment and spending the night there alone, after the magical nights with Lorenzo in Italy, felt like nightmare. But she didn't have a choice. She was too tired to try to reach out to any friends. And besides, she didn't think she would be very good company. What did she have to say, other than she was in danger of losing everything that she'd ever cared about, all in one week, just when she finally started feeling that she had a handle on this whole career thing? It was pretty ironic, and pretty pathetic.

She took an Uber across town, asking to be dropped off at the deli on the corner. She picked up a few unappetizing prepared foods. An ugly salad. A soggy sandwich. Some pasta. Canned sauce that made Chiara's dollar store Ragu look gourmet, and some eggs. She lugged her pathetic groceries and her carry on towards her apartment complex.

Turning the key in the lock, she felt a sense of dread, which only increased as she breathed in the stale air of the apartment. This place wasn't for her. Sure, she liked Miami. The party ambience, the ability to be one thing one day, and another the next. But it wasn't just this apartment had never felt like hers. This life had never felt like hers. The only reason she was here was Harold. And now, she realized that Harold understood that. He had sent her to France, knowing damn well what he was doing. He had given her the impossible task of getting the boat featured in a magazine, in order to throw her back into Lorenzo's arms. Well, if she couldn't do this for herself, she should do it for Harold. If she hadn't irretrievably broken the relationship with Lorenzo, she would try to make it right the minute she got back to France, whenever that would be.

Speaking of Lorenzo, he would probably want to know how Harold was. She owed him that, at least.

In Miami. Harold is hanging in there. They took out a mass and are testing in. I'll have more information for you tomorrow.

After a whole minute of hesitation, she added, I miss you. Her finger hovered over it, debating on whether to send it or not. And finally, she decided to stop being an idiot, and just send it. She didn't expect a response, and none came.

She tried to eat, but the salad was wilted and stale tasting. She made herself some spaghetti and added some of the rancid-smelling olive oil on her counter, as well as salt and pepper. Her stomach was too acidic to deal with the sauce she had bought at the deli. Tomorrow morning, she would go see Harold, and figure out when she could get back to France. To finally finish a project. To finally make things right with Lorenzo, hopefully. She closed her eyes, and instantly went to sleep.

Chapter 49

Constance parked her Mini Cooper in the visitor parking of Miami General and hustled over to the nurse's station. She would have gone straight to Harold's room, but she was afraid to find him looking weak or further diminished.

"Hi," she said to a blonde woman at the desk. The brunette she'd spoken to the day before was nowhere to be seen. It was probably not her shift.

"I'm here to see my uncle. Harold Morgan? And I'd like to talk to his doctor. Doctor Rosenberg, please."

"Harold Morgan? The woman looked at the charts in her file. "Oh, I'm sorry he's gone."

Constance's heart dropped.

"What do you mean, gone?" She cried. "You didn't call me! Nobody called me- he's gone? Just like that?"

"Ohh no! I'm sorry," said the woman, quickly. "He's in the cafeteria. I think he's having a chat with Doctor Rosenberg in there."

"Oh," said Constance, feeling dizzy with relief. "Can you direct me to where that is?"

"Sure," said the nurse. "And sorry about my use of words. This of my first days on the job without my mentor. You won't tell my supervisor, will you? I promise I'll remember to not use that kind of vocabulary in the future."

"Yeah, I think that's for the best," said Constance, smiling despite herself, the relief giving her wings.

"Just head down that hall. Go through the section with the elevator banks, hang a right and you'll see signs for the cafeteria."

Constance thanked her and walked down the hall, her shoes squeaking on the hospital tile. As she approached the cafeteria, the smell of old soup, which she had always associated with nursing homes, greeted her nostrils. Poor Harold. She was sure that he was definitely not enjoying whichever meal he was having at this point. She hoped he could get out soon. Maybe she would bring him a meal from one of their favorite spots.

She walked in and looked around the room. Her eyes passed over her uncle at first, and then centered back on the frail old man sitting in a wheelchair, talking to a tall young doctor. That's when you know you're getting old, thought Constance. The doctors start looking young. This one was about her age, maybe less. She suddenly acutely felt her own mortality, as well. Not something she usually dwelled on, but yes, life was short, and she wanted to spend the rest of hers with Lorenzo, if she could.

"Uncle Harold," she said, her voice catching in her throat.

"My sweet girl," said Harold, his voice still a croak. "Stop looking at me like that. I know I look like hammered shit. Did you sleep OK?"

"Who cares about me, are you OK?"

"I'm fine. I'm just waiting to get out of this shithole," said Harold, smiling weakly, as soon as Doctor Rosenberg here says I can go."

The doctor turned around to face Constance.

"Your uncle's quite the fighter," he said.

"Tell me more," said Constance.

"We biopsied the mass. It is cancer," said the doctor.

Constance's heart flew into her throat, a gasp escaping her lips.

"Don't worry," said the doctor, quickly. "It actually was almost completely encapsulated in scar tissue. Your Uncle Harold did so much damage to his lungs that basically, they isolated the cancer on their own. Hard to explain how it works- not because it's too complicated for you, but because it's too complicated for me. I have to say this guy's a little bit of a superhero."

"I knew that," said Constance.

"Now, of course we're going to need to keep watching him and he's going to need to take better care of himself, and I think it's fair to say that smoking is a thing of his past."

"Who told you I smoked?" Harold scowled, glaring at Constance.

"Your lungs," said the doctor.

"Traitors. Next thing you know, my gums are going to start telling my dentist I don't floss."

"Your uncle lives in the right place," said Doctor Rosenberg. "The humidity is good for him. Walks on the beach Don't worry, we'll make sure this cancer doesn't pop up again. But, honestly, it's a bit of a miracle."

"Harold, you scared the crap out of me," said Constance, squeezing him.

He winced.

"Ouch. Don't forget, I just had surgery."

"So, when does he go home?" Asked Constance, a little selfishly.

"I think 2 more days of observation, and he'll be good."

"All right," said Constance. "Well. I guess I'm just going to hang out here until…"

"No, you're not," said Harold. "Why don't you go out and do things? Get yourself some sunshine. Have some fun in Miami."

"About that. I need to talk to you."

"OK, well, when I'm done with the doctor. Come back after lunch."

Constance left the hospital and sat in her car, crying quietly, relief washing over her. It was still cancer. They would still have to do some therapies. He would still have to watch his health like a hawk, but it seemed that Harold had been spared from the worst. He had known all along that there was something wrong with him, hadn't he? He had been running from the truth just as badly as Constance had. Was this a family trait that had jumped from uncle to niece? No matter, she was going to have to be honest with him about her desire to spend more time in Europe. He was going to think her flighty for doing so. But too bad.

She started thinking about putting her apartment on the market. There would be no regrets there. She wondered, not for the first time, if Lorenzo would be willing to be a part of her life, once she was in Europe.

Checked on Harold this morning. It's cancer, but he is something of a miracle, as if I didn't know that. He'll be in the hospital a few more days, and after that, I should be able to come home.

She didn't expect a response to this message to Lorenzo, either, and she probably deserved his ignoring her. She hoped he wouldn't block her.

She killed time before noon by contacting real estate agents, fielding their questions while thinking of her vision boards and her plans for the boat. This was the most complete project she'd ever done, and it felt good. Working with Daphne had been a pleasure. Hopefully, Daphne would still be willing to take on more projects with her in the future, as long as she didn't end up messing everything up. She wondered if Daphne would be traveling the world with Peter, if her plan to get them back together actually worked. But how could she get anyone back together, when she couldn't even communicate with Lorenzo enough to let him know how much she cared about him? When she'd basically thrown away the most beautiful thing she'd ever had?

Just as she was sitting there feeling bad for herself, her phone rang. She was shocked to notice that it was Lorenzo's number, but then again, now that she knew that Lorenzo and her uncle had a whole relationship she didn't know about, it was expected that he would want to know about Harold.

"Hey," she said. "You got my texts, right? Harold's going to be OK."

"I did. Thank you for that and thank God. And I'm sorry. I should have told you that Harold and I kept in touch," said Lorenzo quietly. There was still some residual sadness to his voice, and Constance dared to hope that it was disappointment at the fight they'd had.

"Harold told me," she said. "He told me something else, too," said Constance carefully.

"Oh?"

"Yeah, something about a discussion you two had about me?"

"Yes," said Lorenzo. "But that's ancient history."

"Well, I just want you to know," said Constance, "it mattered to me, to hear it."

"What? Because my word about how I felt wasn't enough for you?" Said Lorenzo bitterly.

"I thought you might say that," said Constance. "And you're right."

She had done the damage and continued to do the damage to their relationship. How could she break the cycle? It was up to her.

"I hope to get the chance to prove to you that I've changed. I've made a few decisions since I left France," said Constance.

"Like what? You're not coming back? Quelle surprise," Lorenzo scoffed.

She flinched, but she deserved that.

"On the contrary. No more running away."

"Right," said Lorenzo. "I'll believe that when I see it."

"I would like the chance to start making you see it when I see you, if you're still speaking to me."

"Well, you're still living in my apartment," said Lorenzo. "So, I guess I don't have a choice."

He hardly sounded delighted, but yes, Constance did have him cornered, in a way, and she was relieved, even though it would be so easy for him to decide to leave town the minute she came back.

"OK, well, it's time for me to head back to the hospital to see Harold again," said Constance. "I'll tell him you said hello."

"Thank you," said Lorenzo.

"I'll let you know when I'm coming home," said Constance.

She didn't know if Lorenzo had caught her use of home, but when she said it, she felt it intensely.

"All right," said Lorenzo. "Well, I'll talk to you soon."

He hung up the phone before she had a chance to say anything further, leaving her disconcerted, and feeling empty and hollowed out. She grabbed her bag and headed back into the hospital.

Harold was back in his room, looking a little bit better, less pale.

"So, what did you want to talk to me about, earlier?" He asked.

"Uncle Harold, I know you're going to think I'm just running away, but…"

"But you want to live in Europe."

A smile played on Harold's lips.

"So, you and Lorenzo, you're getting back together?"

"I wish we were. I just don't think I can fix it that easily. But I promise I'll try. And either way…I do think that Europe is my place and…"

"I know, darling. That's why I sent you there."

"Wait. But did you literally think you were sending me there to fall back into Lorenzo's arms?"

"Maybe. I like to play a little Deus ex machina once in a while," said Harold, a smile playing on his lips.

"Well, that's another family trait," said Constance. "Do you think I'm crazy trying to set up Peter with Daphne?"

"Well, darling, you can always try," said Harold. "But ultimately, it's going to be up to them."

"I know," she said. "But never underestimate the power of Deus ex machina. Hey. Wait a second- Peter never cared about having his boat in the magazine, did he?"

"No," Harold admitted. "But now that you're so close, I think getting it published would be a great way to launch the European branch of Harold Morgan interiors."

"You wouldn't let me head that, would you?" asked Constance.

"No."

Crap. That would have been too perfect, thought Constance.

"I want you to be the global representative for my brand. You have so much potential. You're brilliant. And you know, Penelope will be a great asset for you here in Miami. But you're capable of running so many more projects, in so many more places. My girl, I've always had the utmost faith in you. You just needed to grow up."

"I think I'm doing that," Uncle Harold. "I think I am. I think I'm getting better. But you know, I'm never going to completely change."

"That's your superpower, darling," said Harold. "Now can you do me a favor and just put your apartment on the market already? And go throw yourself at Lorenzo. He never could resist you."

"I know." Constance smiled to herself. How had she told herself the lie that Lorenzo was not as attracted to her as he was to the models that flocked around him, when he had showed her time and time again that that wasn't true? She was so stubborn. But she was learning her lesson.

"They're letting me out tomorrow morning," said Harold. "Why don't you book yourself a flight for the next day?"

"Yes, sounds great," said Constance, beaming.

"OK, now let me rest," said Harold. "Come see me for dinner. Don't get up to too much trouble in the meantime."

Chapter 50

She left the hospital feeling light and hopeful. She wanted to call Lorenzo, but she was afraid that they would just get into another argument. Distance certainly didn't help their understanding. In the past, it had created a chasm between them. But they had both changed, They were learning to talk to each other. She allowed to herself to fantasize about coming home to Lorenzo. Of surprising him cooking in the kitchen and taking him to bed. Feeling his hands on her body. Looking into his eyes as he looked into hers. But she didn't have time to fantasize. She had things to do.

She got back to her apartment and went through all the responses she'd already gotten from the real estate agents she'd contacted, and instead of being hobbled by the number of choices, like she would have been in the past, she decided to just choose one. She would pick the three highest ranked. And whoever she liked best on the phone was going to get her vote.

Fifteen minutes later, she had her lucky winner. Wanda Bloom from Sotheby's Realty, a skinny model looking woman that she never would have hired in the past. But she was going to be the bigger person now, ha, ha, and this woman had a great track record. Wanda let her know that she could come see the apartment that very afternoon.

Constance rushed to the consignment store down the street and picked up a few more pieces to relieve the empty feeling of her casita and give it a tiny bit of personality, but not too much. A few extra pillows for the sofa. A throw. A few modern paintings, and an extra mirror.

Constance got back home and staged the place at top speed. She had barely finished, when there was a knock on the door. She opened it to reveal Wanda, even more gorgeous in real life than in her photos.

The realtor swept in and complimented the space, asking questions about square footage and amenities. When she gave Constance the comps for the property, Constance thought she would pass out. She hadn't realized that real estate had gone up in value so much since she had moved in.

"Yeah, that's the minimum I think I can get for you," said Wanda.

Constance gulped. That sum could buy her a country cottage in Europe, or even an apartment in Saint Tropez. It would open so many doors for her in Europe. And she wasn't going to second guess it.

"Just remember, it's going to be hard to get back into the market once you sell," said Wanda. "You're sure you're not going to want to buy here again?"

"I've never been so sure of anything in my life," said Constance. Except for how badly she wanted things to work out with Lorenzo.

Chapter 51

Constance was still reeling, in a good way, from the figure the real estate had given her, and about to book her return ticket home, when her phone rang. She recognized the number and froze. Fuck. She hesitated, then picked up. The voice sounded oddly tinny, transported as it was across a country and across the ocean. I

"Hi! I didn't think I'd hear from you," said Constance.

"I bet you didn't," said Carlos. "But listen, my ex was using the boat. And apparently, my daughter invited herself for the weekend and asked about that second stateroom. And I realized that you never finished that."

"I didn't?"

Fuckfuckfuck.

"Yeah. You never ordered the sheets, and the platform for the bed is not the way it's supposed to be. There's a gap between the headboard and the wall that shouldn't be there, as far as I can tell."

Constance closed her eyes. No way would Carlos have noticed that on his own. And Sophie had warned her that, if she so much as spoke to her father, she would be telling Lorenzo about them. Silly Constance, stupidly believing that it was just a warning, designed to keep her away, when in reality, it was a trap, which Sophie had lovingly set, and which was about to have spring shut right on Constance's neck.

"I'm so glad you called," Constance lied. "I was just going to let you know that we have someone who's going to come and set all of that up. I was just working through the logistics."

She scrambled through her contacts on her phone, pulling up Penelope's number. This was a desperate situation. It was unfortunate that Penelope would end up looking like she was fixing her problems, and Constance would end up looking unprofessional, yet again.

"I believe I have my colleague Penelope, who is ready to jump on this. Once she arrives, it should be done within the week," Constance ad-libbed.

"You're not going to come and do the work yourself?" Carlos asked, flirtation sneaking into his tone. Evidently, he'd forgotten that Constance had left him and that he'd been quite angry with her at the time.

"No, sadly I am stuck here with another project," said Constance, wincing. Crap. She should have told him that she was stuck with her sick uncle. Carlos didn't like to think he wasn't the only game in town.

"Oh, so are you sleeping with this client too?" Asked Carlos, a bit unkindly, she thought. She hadn't pegged him for the jealous type, but he did have an ego. But she wasn't going to answer this sort of question.

"Why don't I track Penelope down, and I will get right back to you?"

"OK. I'll be standing by," said Carlos.

Constance hung up quickly. Surely Sophie couldn't consider this 'contacting her father,' could she? That would be unjust, to say the least. But knowing Sophie, she couldn't overestimate or underestimate her, depending on how you looked at it.

She thought about what she would text Penelope.

Penelope. You have the opportunity to fix the mess I made, yet again.

Too pathetic.

I hope your project is going great. I know you've got a lot on your plate, but Carlos White's second stateroom just needs a few more things. It's really pretty simple. There's just a headboard that was the wrong size that needs to be reinstalled. The platform the bed is on is janky, and then there are just the bedclothes and a few accessories. I had the references for but then they became unavailable, so if you could just find something that looks about the same, it should work out.

Holy shit. It was a lot. That didn't look good.

How about, If you do this one thing, I will totally owe you?

She didn't want to owe Penelope. Damn it. She was going to have to suck it up and do it herself, wasn't she? That's what adults did.

Her mind racing, she thought about how to optimize what she needed to do. She remembered the installers she'd met in Marina del Rey. They could handle this. She could spend an afternoon planning it, and just get it done. She wouldn't need to talk to Carlos too many times to make that work. And hopefully, Sophie wouldn't catch wind of it.

She would get it done, and she would be back in Saint Tropez before she knew it.

Chapter 52

Constance stepped off the plane and navigated through the throngs of people speeding down the concourse. It felt weird to be back in Los Angeles. LAX had been such a base for her for so long, the jumping-off point for all her comings and goings. Even she and Carlos had flown out of here a few times, when they hadn't gone private.

Carlos. She winced as she thought of him. She dreaded seeing him, wondered how things would go down. He'd been pretty annoyed when she'd left in the first place, without finishing the job, and now, she had no doubt that Sophie had stirred up further resentment against her, just for sport. She didn't know whether Carlos himself or his driver would be picking her up at the airport. Only that someone would be there for her. She hoped it was the driver, to be honest. Nothing more awkward than sitting in the car with Carlos, either rehashing what had gone wrong, or not speaking of it at all.

Thankfully, she recognized Rahul, Carlos's driver, as soon as she stepped into the baggage claim area. Handsome, tall, with curly black hair and a ready smile. Rahul had been with Carlos for years, serving as his driver, his assistant, and his general factotum. It would have driven Constance crazy to work at a position like that, but Rahul was well remunerated, with lots of time off. Whenever Carlos was traveling, when he wasn't in LA or at the Saint Barts house, Rahul could work virtually, and go on surfing trips and humanitarian missions, two things that Constance absolutely did not understand, but that he was passionate about. They'd become good friends over the course of her tenure as Carlos's designer, but she hadn't really kept up the conversation once she had left so precipitously.

"Hey, it's been a while," said Rahul. "You look great, as always."

"Thanks," said Constance. "You don't look so bad yourself. How's it going? Sorry I essentially ghosted you."

"I hear you've been working in France."

"Yeah, the Lombard 4."

"Oh, that's a nice one," said Rahul, who happened to be the consummate yacht expert. He knew the different models and their owners in and out. He had to. Carlos could be competitive about the boats in his fleet, and she happened to know that he'd had his eye on the Lombard 4 at some point. Peter must have outbid him. Well, she certainly wouldn't ask what had happened. She didn't want to add any fuel to the fire.

"So, how's it been over here, since I've been gone?" asked Constance.

"Carlos has been on a rampage," Rahul shrugged.

"What? Surely it doesn't only have something to do with me?"

"Eh." Rahul gave her a look. "And his daughter is up to her old tricks."

"Hmm…"

Either Rahul already knew that Sophie was in fact wreaking havoc on Constance's life in Saint Tropez, or he didn't need to know it. Neither did Carlos, for that matter. There was a good chance that Sophie was wreaking havoc in multiple ways, not just the ones having to do with Constance. Not everything was about her.

"How has business been?" Asked Constance, changing the subject.

"Oh, you know- ups and downs, this and that."

As much as Rahul liked to gossip about some things, he was very protective of his boss, and never shared financial details.

"Got it," said Constance. "OK, so on a scale of 1 to 10- how pissed off is he about the boat?"

"He was fine for a while. But then something stirred him up. So, I would say he's up to an 11 1/2 at this point."

Constance mulled this over. She had seen angry Carlos. The anger had never been directed at her, but she had cringed every time she'd noticed it. If it was to be directed at her now, she did deserve it. She could see that now. She should never have left him high and dry the way she had. An apology was in order.

She and Rahul made more small talk as he expertly navigated them back to Marina del Rey, avoiding all the usual traffic spots.

"You could probably design an app and make a gazillion dollars helping people to stay out of LA traffic," said Constance.

"Yeah, maybe I'll call it Waze?"

"Kind of, but better. An app that doesn't try to kill you by going across four lanes of traffic ... and something that doesn't take you through the iffiest neighborhoods to save a minute."
Rahul laughed.
"Hey, can we make a quick detour? Just five minutes," said Constance.

Chapter 53

They drove down the drive leading to the Marina, and under one of the apartment buildings, and Rahul pulled into a parking spot. Constance felt the dread forming a lead mass in her stomach, which kept expanding, constricting her esophagus. Shit. She wasn't going to have a panic attack, was she? Carlos couldn't possibly be that mad, could he? It was just a few details. She could fix them quickly. She had a good plan in place. The sooner she was done with this, the better. She was committed to doing it right, but she wanted to get back to Europe. Badly. Every day spent here made her look less professional vis-a-vis Peter Holmes. Also, each day kept her away from Lorenzo, away from the conversation she needed to have with him. Now that she knew what she wanted, what would happen?

They walked up to the yacht. Normally, Carlos would have been on the bridge, waiting. But clearly, that ship had sailed.

"He's been in the office all day," said Rahul by means of explanation. "It's not just that he's pissed at you, I promise."

"Right," said Constance, doubt seeping into her voice. It was going to be awkward being on the boat. Having to spend time with Carlos. She stepped onto the yacht, feeling positively nauseous, and made her way over to the office, holding her breath.

"Hey," she said, standing in the office door.

"Hey," said Carlos. He sat behind the wooden desk she'd carefully selected all those months ago, working at his laptop. He got up and went to take her into his arms. Oh, this was worse than she'd feared. She'd hoped he would be cold towards her. Standoffish. This was something she hadn't even considered; that he would hope to pick up where they had left off with their physical relationship.

She attempted to give him a peck on the cheek and otherwise evade his grasp.

"Where are your things?" Asked Carlos.

"My things?" Constance blinked.

"Aren't you staying on the yacht, with me?" He asked.

"No, I got myself a hotel room."

It pained her to do this, and she hadn't asked Harold for a per diem, of course, because this was her mistake to fix and therefore, she would eat the cost. But there was no way she would put herself in the situation of being on the yacht, with Carlos.

"Oh, so it's like that," he said. He repaired to his desk, looking disappointed and defensive.

"So, how've you been?" He said, reverting to business mode. "I'm glad you at least came back to finish what you started, design-wise. I'd thought maybe you might have wanted to continue what we started," he said, looking at her, "but that's not looking good as of now. Maybe you'll warm up to the idea." Constance didn't bother reacting to that.

"I've got a strategy for getting everything done and as fast as possible. I need to get back to Europe."

"Ah. Did you leave another client high and dry? How is it on the Lombard 4? I hear that's your project. You've not embarked on a relationship with Peter, too, have you?"

"Wow. Lovely that you think I automatically have a relationship with each of my clients," Constance huffed, even though she kind of deserved that.

"Whatever you say," said Carlos. "I heard a rumor that you're trying to get that boat into a magazine," he said.

Right. She didn't need to guess where he had heard that so-called rumor. "You didn't even ask about publishing my boat. What, you thought it was somehow inferior?" He asked.

"No, I just thought that you're more private than that, and that Mrs. White wouldn't want the boat plastered all over some magazine."

"Mrs. White doesn't have a say," said Carlos.

Ha. Constance almost laughed out loud at that one. Carlos had always been like this, a bit competitive. Wanting every new thing he saw. That was definitely one of the reasons she hadn't been too upset about things ending between them. He hadn't even thought about getting his yacht in a magazine, until he heard that one of his competitors wanted it.

"Well, I've got some things to do," said Carlos. "Why don't you get cracking on your works since you're in such a hurry, and we can reconvene over dinner. How does that sound?"

Ouch. Dinner. They would have to make a conversation and be in the same place for several hours. But she really had no choice. "Any special place you want to go?" Carlos asked. "I'll make a reservation."

"How about Dear Jane's," said Constance. It was a newer restaurant that she and Carlos both enjoyed with an elegant dive bar atmosphere and phenomenal, fresh seafood. Expensive, for what it was. And dark, but not with a hugely romantic vibe. It would strike the right balance.

"Good choice," said Carlos. "I'll reserve and I'll let you know what time we need to leave."

Constance cringed at how easily he had lapsed into the use of we. Carlos hadn't mentioned where she was to sleep, and Rahul didn't seem to offer any information on this, so she simply left her travel bags in the saloon and headed back to that third cabin, to reacquaint herself with the situation.

As soon as she opened the polished wood door, she blanched, embarrassed. It was far worse than she'd remembered or been willing to remember. A headboard had been slapped up, too small for the bed, creating a visible gap on either side. The mattress floated on a platform that seemed expressly designed to gouge people's legs as they passed by. To make matters worse, it was in an uninspired melamine that would not look out of place at IKEA. There was no attention to detail in any of the accessories or finishes. The whole thing would have to be redone. The only thing she would keep was the mattress that Mrs. White hated so much. Out of spite, and out of convenience. She made a few careful measurements, making sure to check twice before writing them down, and got back to the literal drawing board, repairing to the dining table on the main level and using her iPad to put together a vision board for the space, as the previous vision she'd had for the room no longer excited her, which was rather typical, for her, but warranted, in this situation. The space needed a better headboard, built in, of course. It could be integrated with an upholstered platform that didn't look like it had been assembled by a couple drunk frat boys, and that wouldn't injure anyone else. She researched her options for more luxurious bedclothes, and pictured the art, objects, and soft furnishings that would make the place more homey, channeling Daphne's aesthetic. Of, and it needed a luggage rack. She tracked down a cool Lucite one at a hotel surplus warehouse. She would replace the boring industrial-look straps with something chic. After putting together her initial ideas, she got on the phone, dialing for favors. Trying to find out if anyone had anything pre-constructed or readily available that she could use. After just a tiny bit of begging and promises of glasses of wine, she managed to get her upholstery guy on the bed project. They would do up the headboard and the platform in a light caramel bouclé that would be unique, cozy, chic, and appropriate for all seasons. She checked her watch. She was rocking and rolling. She still had time to visit the Venice collective for decorative objects. They were vastly overpriced, but it was a one stop shop, if she played her cards right.

Forget going back to the drawing board where the lights were concerned. Her thirst for novelty had to be held in check sometime. She decided that, if she only slightly tweaked the design she'd already ordered for the other rooms, it would be different enough, but still cohesive. She called up the architectural lighting place in Culver City, and they confirmed that yes, they could powder coat her fixtures in a jaunty Yves Klein blue that skewed nautical, with a fresh twist.

She put on her jacket, deciding that she should probably Uber. Rahul emerged from the control room, which he used as an office. He didn't live on the boat, having an apartment at the marina.

"Are you going somewhere? Do you need a ride?" He asked.

"Yes, just to Venice. I'm popping in on my upholsterer and then going to the collective. I can Uber…"

"Let me go check with Carlos if he needs me. Otherwise, I can drive you," said Rahul.

Constance nodded and stood in the saloon, waiting for his return. She could hear a little mumbled conversation between the two men in the office and tried not to focus on it.

She looked around the saloon. She'd done a good job here, hadn't she? The whole look was very clean. Modern. But still layered, classic, yet playful. She did have a signature look, if she thought about it. It was collected. A bit quirky, but nevertheless elegant, with an old money spin that the new billionaires appreciated. It gave them some gravitas. This way, they knew that if they invited anyone from a high social echelon, they would at least not be mocked for their nouveau riche tastes.

Rahul returned.

"We're good," he said. "I can drive you. Carlos made a reservation at 7:00. So, you've got plenty of time. Depending on traffic," he smiled.

They started at the upholstery place. The owner, Duke, was an unassuming man who had been in the upholstery business for decades. He'd started off doing car upholstery, and after a stint in prison, a mysterious benefactor had helped him to train to do residential projects. He was now very much in demand but had kept to his fair pricing and classic aesthetic. His stock in trade was hit-end midcentury, and he had always been able to execute Constance's more involved designs without blinking. Also, he happened to have known Constance since she was a child, having outfitted the family yacht all those years ago, and having built a friendship with her father that meant he often joined them on board for dinner.

"How's your dad?" Asked Duke.

"I wouldn't know."

"Still with Evil Stepmother #2, then?"

"That shouldn't make a difference."

"Just remember Constance, it doesn't reflect on you," said Duke. "And it is very much his loss."

She smiled. She was lucky to have these uncle figures in her life. Even though there was still a gaping hole left behind by her mother, and she still dreamed of being part of a perfect, stable family unit sometimes, she still could consider herself blessed. Constance showed Duke her sketches and confirmed that there seemed to be just enough bouclé fabric, left over from another client and forgotten in a corner of the workroom, for this project.

Chapter 54

Back from her errands, Constance looked around the cabin, visualizing how everything was going to fit together. So far, so good. Now, she had time to worry whether Sophie was going to find out that she was there. No doubt she would, because upon seeing that the room had been finished, she would know that Constance had come back to do the job.

Constance shuddered. She'd done enough damage to her reputation, and to her tenuous relationship with Lorenzo, in the past. Now, the thing she wanted most in the world was the chance to start fresh. She dreamed that Lorenzo might take her back, if they were able to move past their issues. She felt a little optimistic about it, especially as she was starting to accept her part of the responsibility in their breakup, but if Sophie informed him that she'd gone back to Carlos, their chances of moving on with the relationship were less than zero. She and Lorenzo might have had chemistry, but he was also jealous, and that would be one affront too many.

On top of that, Constance didn't know whether Carlos would make good on his final payment. That was very much the sort of thing that he would do. Punish her financially. But that was the cost of doing business, and this whole situation was definitely her fault. She would eat the cost if she had to.

Satisfied that she'd put in a good day's work, she returned to her hotel room to get ready. She dressed in a one-piece jumpsuit, the one with a turtleneck and a difficult to manage zipper in the back. It was a garment she usually didn't wear, because it was so hard to get in and out of, but she had decided that armor wouldn't hurt in this situation, and she was glad that she had packed it. She completed the look with some skinny boots, meaning that, even if Carlos tried to reach under the table to stroke her leg, which he tended to do, he would only encounter leather. She put her hair up into a severe ponytail. Nothing seductive about her look. She decided to forgo her normal red lipstick, as she knew he found it sexy. She looked at her reflection in the mirror of the Marina del Rey hotel. She looked positively nunnish. Perfect.

She texted Carlos. See you there?

I can come pick you up, he responded.

I'm literally two hundred yards away. I'll just meet you there in 15 minutes.

She arrived at the restaurant just before Carlos did, and stood at the podium, trying to determine which table would be deemed the least romantic. She finally selected a high top in the middle of the action, knowing that Carlos would probably complain and try to change tables, but also knowing that he wouldn't want to make a scene in public. Carlos arrived just as she sat down.

"You look elegant," he said.

She smiled to herself. In Carlos speak, elegant was the opposite of sexy. It meant she looked unfuckable. And well, that was the goal.

"Why did they give us this table?" He asked. "This one is for peasants."

"This is what they had," Constance shrugged. "I don't mind it. I like that we can people watch all the more easily."

"Fine," he said. "I'm ready for a drink."

"So, tell me about Holmes' job," said Carlos, once they both had a glass of wine in hand. "Are you actually finishing that one?" He asked.

"I hope so," said Constance.

She didn't want to let him provoke her into saying something she might regret. "You're not dating Peter, then?" Asked Carlos.

"No. Why would I?" Constance retorted. "He's not exactly my type."

"Ohh, and I was?" asked Carlos.

"What's that supposed to mean?"

"According to my daughter, your new beau is my complete opposite. So, I'm trying to figure out what you saw in me. Other than maybe what's in my wallet?"

"I'm sorry, but that's never been a big interest of mine," said Constance, truthfully.

"You seem to have dated a lot of billionaires."

"Maybe I just happen to date a lot of guys who have yachts," said Constance.

"What about this Italian guy?" Carlos scoffed. "I doubt he has a yacht."

"He doesn't need one," said Constance.

Oops. That would piss Carlos off. And just admitting her feelings about Lorenzo caused a jab of pain in her heart. She really did miss him so much. She cared about him more than she wanted to admit to herself. More than anything. This was far beyond the addiction to his smell, to his feel. This was her mourning the possible loss, a second time, of a life more beautiful than anything else she could possibly have imagined. Life with Lorenzo wouldn't be about money or about status, even though some people might see it from the outside and think that it was, but it was more about creativity, about leaving a legacy, about doing something real.

"So…what have you been up to?" Asked Constance, changing the subject.

"The usual," said Carlos. "Business deals. I've been renovating the new guesthouse in Saint Barts I bought from… a neighbor." When he said neighbor, he smiled, a little wistfully.

"What's that face?" Asked Constance. "Is there something between you and this neighbor?"

"Maybe," Carlos admitted. "She's not my usual type, I'll tell you that."

"Oh?"

Constance leaned in, pleased to find the tension between them dissipating a bit. "Tell me about her."

"Well, for one, her name is Judy. And this may shock you, but she's what you would call age appropriate," said Carlos. "She's always had a little crush on me," he said, grinning. And somehow, it rang true.

"How could she not?" Said Constance, knowing that flattery was the way to Carlos's heart. "How did she go from neighbor to object of your affection?"

"She and her husband split up, and she was thinking of selling her house, and someone I trust on the island, a fishmonger, of all people, suggested I buy it off-market to make it into a guesthouse. And then, she and I got together to discuss, and, well, now it's more about tweaking my compound so that she feels more comfortable inviting her adult children there."

"Does she know this?" Asked Constance. "No, I was going to surprise her, and…" his expression turned darker. "Well… I guess that our last discussion didn't go so well. She was jealous that you were coming back to fix the yacht, and… I don't know. I guess I just realized how much I care about her."

"Have you told her?"

"No." Realization dawned on Carlos' face. "Listen, do you mind if I make a phone call?"

"Not at all," said Constance, smiling.

He got up and headed outside, leaving her at the table. If someone like Carlos, with an ego as big as his, could get past his pride and contact the person he cared about, and change the pattern, clear up some misunderstandings, couldn't Constance do that, too?

She picked up her phone. Typed out two letters.

Hi.

The response was almost immediate.

Hi. How are you? Where are you?

Marina del Rey.

What?? I thought you were coming back here.

I am. I had a work emergency. I'm hoping I can be back within a week.

Constance, I think we need to talk.

Constance held her breath. She needed to tell Lorenzo the truth. She couldn't just leave things unsaid. How was she supposed to respond to his message? Had Sophie told him something?

But just then, Carlos returned, a smile playing on his lips. Constance hadn't even had a chance to tell Lorenzo not to worry about Carlos, that she was just wrapping up the project- that the new her didn't just cut and run. That she was selling her apartment. But as Carlos started to talk excitedly about his house on St Barth, she decided that she couldn't leave Lorenzo in the dark for another second. She looked up at Carlos.

"Sorry, I need to go to go to the restroom. I'll be right back."

Once in the bathroom stall, she dialed Lorenzo's number. But he didn't pick up.

She took a deep breath, hoping that Lorenzo wasn't silently stewing. She sent him a text.

OK, what do we need to talk about? You know 'we need to talk' is never a good thing in American English, right?

Come on, Lorenzo might be speaking English as a second or third language, but he knew damn well that no one prefaces happy news with those words. She waited for a response until finally, she decided she had been gone for too long.

I just want you to know that I WANT to talk. I want to make everything right between us, she wrote, and reluctantly went back to the table.

She clinked her glass against Carlos'.

"Cheers to having the end of your project in sight. You're going to be delighted."

"I have a feeling I will be," said Carlos. "You seem different, somehow. I'm proud of you, I have to say. You've grown up."

"See, old dogs can learn new tricks. And now, let's drink to Judy."

"To Judy," said Carlos, "I think you'd like her."

"Maybe I can decorate your yacht. The one she'll make you buy. Because she's going to want you to sell this one," Constance smiled.

"True," said Carlos. "But there's no way she would let me hire you, or anyone like you."

"Anyone like me, how?" Asked Constance. She was fully prepared to be offended by whatever Carlos might say.

"Smart, talented, and fucking sexy," Carlos responded.

"Oh behave," said Constance. "We're both different people, now."

"Cheers to that."

Chapter 55

Butterflies fluttered in Constance's belly. Today was the day. she checked her watch. Peter would be here any minute. She and Daphne had been on board all morning, attending to last details and doing the final staging. She surveyed the kitchen, with its gleaming surfaces and its commanding view of the harbor. This would be an amazing place for Peter to entertain friends and host intimate dinners. There was live-edge wood-topped island with bar seating and a resin detail poured to look like the coast of Saint Tropez, with comfortable bar stools with decorative neoprene seats. The adjoining space, the Sky Saloon, as Daphne and Constance called it among themselves, was executed in tones of blue, green, turquoise, and amber, with values ranging from the lightest, palest shade of marine layer to the deep teal of the horizon during a thunderstorm. A massive photograph by Lorenzo held pride of place over a teak wood console. The seating looked and felt like a cloud, complete with cozy throw blankets and pillows. But Constance knew that this was not where Peter would spend most of his alone time, if he in fact had a lot of alone time moving forward.

She headed down the stairs to admire the cozy a library space she had carved out of the previously awkward antechamber that came right after the sliding glass doors. The doors themselves had been treated with a layer of gas between the panes so that Peter could make them opaque at will. The library itself could be made more intimate by pulling heavy floor to ceiling drapes open or closed. Illuminated bookshelves were stacked full of books, including some of the tomes Constance had seen Peter reading, and others that Daphne had suggested for the client that she said she had started to imagine in her head.

"I'm almost scared to meet this client," Daphne had said. "From what you've said, I'm afraid I would be tempted to fall in love with him."

Lucky thing, too, because that was how Constance had managed to keep Peter's identity a surprise.

"I've decided I don't even want to meet him," Daphne had said. "I don't want to ruin my fantasy."

"But Daphne! You did a huge part of the work. I want the client to be able to thank you in person. I want you to get credit for your brilliance."

"No, I've made up my mind," Daphne had said.

So, Constance had lied to her, and had told her the client was arriving first thing the next morning.

She admired her piece de resistance, the special ceiling detail that had been such a headache, but so worth it, rippling overhead. The objects and art that Daphne had helped to select were perfect, as was the small Japanese fisherman's fireplace in the corner, and the custom rugs that Constance had designed, woven to resemble the Persian rugs that Peter had said he so loved, but rendered safe for use on the sea. Tortoiseshell, ivory, and shagreen textures were carried throughout the boat, and created an elegant and cozy space that could be reconfigured for evenings alone, or for entertaining. Constance was beyond proud of how it had all turned out.

The main stateroom, now the only one on the main level, was an ode to a fantasy trip to Egypt. This was a bit of a risk, and Constance had fought with Daphne over it.

"I don't even know if the client has ever been to Egypt. What if it's just not something that would resonate with him?" Constance had argued.

"All men like what you've described have a fantasy of the Grand Tour. It's part of their DNA. And the Egyptian elements aren't super literal. You wouldn't even know it was Egypt if I didn't tell you that was what I had in mind."

"Well, except for that pretty little painting of the pyramids."

"Touché…but it is so damn pretty," Daphne had argued, and she was right. So, Constance had capitulated. That was what being design partners was about.

She had asked Daphne if Daphne would still be open to working with her if the firm was not a new design firm, but the European arm of Harold Morgan Design, and Daphne had tentatively agreed. It was a good start. But for now, Constance had to focus on the matter at hand. Peter was coming in minutes. And she needed to orchestrate this ballet perfectly. She also had to break the disappointing news to Peter that the yacht would not be featured in the magazine. Not that it had even been Peter's idea in the first place, but once Harold had mentioned it, he had been happy enough to go along with it. She hadn't discussed it with Lorenzo; didn't need to. She'd missed the deadline, and she didn't want anything to do with Sophie. Maybe would find another place to have it published.

Constance snapped a few photos of the yacht with her phone and notice that her hands were shaking. She could hardly stand the apprehension. But looking at the photos drove home what an extraordinary job she and Daphne had done. She would bring in a photographer herself to illustrate the project, something to put on the website. She shot off her snapshots to Harold, who quickly responded.

Incredible. I'm so proud of you. You've outdone yourself. I knew you. Could do it.

She smiled; her heart close to bursting. She checked her watch again. Peter was usually quite prompt. He would be here any second. It was showtime.

And then, she saw him, a hundred yards away.

Holding her breath and trying to act natural, she called out to Daphne, who was below deck.

"Hey, Daphne. You're the reigning champion at folding towels photogenically. I did. My best in the main bathroom, but I think I failed spectacularly. Can you go double check on that?"

"Of course," Daphne called back, coming up and heading back to the stateroom.

Constance took a deep breath. Peter was almost at the boat. She lowered the gangplank.

"Welcome home," she said.

"I can't wait to see it- I hope you didn't disappoint me," he said, walking up. But he was smiling. His attempt at humor. Hopefully this gamble had paid off. She was confident of her design, she realized. There was no way that Peter wouldn't adore what she'd done there. Now the other part of the gamble, Daphne. She really, really hoped that worked out, because as much as Peter would adore the boat design, what if he found the fact that she had brought on Daphne unacceptable? It was too late to worry about that now. Because now, she could hear Daphne steps, which set her sweating.

"You actually did a decent job with the…" Daphne's voice quieted as Constance stepped aside. Both Daphne and Peter gasped at the same time, and Constance almost passed out from the tension in the room.

"Peter," said Daphne.

"What are you doing here?" Asked Peter.

"Oh, this is. Daphne. I needed someone to help me with accessories and details, and I found a local person," Constance said. She was saying too much. Breaking the first rule of lying.

"Oh, is that what happened?" Asked Daphne. "What a coincidence. So, this whole time when I was telling you about my failed relationship with my first and only client, you knew exactly who I was talking about?"

"You hired… this woman… knowing that she was the person who broke my heart?" Peter asked. His face was drained of color, save for two red blotches on his cheeks. "I should…. I should…"

"No, I should…" Daphne started to say.

Oh, this was horrible. Constance was an idiot. The only thing these two would bond over was their mutual hatred of Constance, at this rate.

"Just wait, said Constance, her voice quaking as much as her knees. "Peter. Please. Come look at the space. You can get mad at me later."

Peter sighed, rubbing his forehead, as if he was developing a tension headache.

"I should go," said Daphne.

"No!" Constance cried. "You were integral to this design. No matter your personal feelings, you created something awesome, and there is nothing so special as seeing how the client reacts. I wasn't lying that I want to work with you because I think you're talented. It just happened that there was… I don't know… a little side bonus maybe?"

"Bonus?" Asked Peter, incensed. "She broke my heart!"

"Will you stop saying that? You'd absolutely mad! You were the one," said Daphne.

"Enough," said Constance. "Come look."

Now, she was impatient to show the rest of the yacht. She needed to know that she had done the right thing, at least in the design department.

"Let's take the back stair. I want to start at the top," said Constance.

She would keep the main saloon and stateroom as a grand finale. Not that every space wasn't extraordinary in its own way. They walked up the back stair.

"Why do you want to start with the upper deck?" Asked Peter. "There wasn't anything to do there."

"It's not just a deck anymore," Constance smiled.

Peter's mouth fell open when he saw the kitchen and entertaining space.

"You love to cook," said Constance. "Up here, you can enjoy cooking and enjoying the view, and when you're entertaining, you don't have to be away from your guests."

"Even in the morning," Peter agreed. "Making breakfast here will be such a pleasure, compared to being in that little galley. I had never thought of that."

"This wood is beautiful," said Peter, stroking the console in the Sky Saloon. "Daphne found that," said Constance. "She said it was teak, but I've never seen teak like that."

"That chair you had made for me for the other yacht- that was the same treatment, wasn't it? I loved that chair."

"And you've got one just like it. In the lower saloon," said Daphne.

Peter's eyes snapped to her; Constance noticed. Assessing her. Drinking her in.

"Let's go down below deck," said Constance. "I want to show you the bedrooms. Four cabins in all. One the crew, with four cots, and another extra bunk room and more developed staff quarters. Your main stateroom is on the main level, now."

Peter marveled at all the details, many of which Daphne had been integral in choosing.

"Ready to see the main space?"

Peter nodded. When he caught his first glimpse of the saloon, he whistled.

"The ceiling. It's like my book pages."

"It is," Constance smiled. "I wanted to do something for you that had never been done, and well, one day we were talking, and you were folding the book pages and I thought to myself, well, that's something that's very Peter and I wanted you to have something like that."

"It's perfect, he said. "I love this whole library."

"I know how much you love to read, and I wanted this to be a place where you could happy alone, or happy, entertaining. I have three different layouts that can be easily achieved with minimum fuss, just from opening and closing drapes and moving furniture, that can be secured in several configurations."

"Brilliant. How did you even think of something like that?"

"Easy," Daphne laughed. "She can't settle on a single thing, ever. But in this case, it serves her well."

Constance smiled proudly. Yes, sometimes her differences were her superpower.

Peter ran his finger along the bookshelves, admiring all the tomes.

"All my favorites," he said. "How did you know?"

Constance frowned, realization dawning.

"The shelf staging that was Daphne…. wait. I never told you who the client was," said Constance.

Daphne shrugged, innocently. "I designed for my ideal client," she said.

"I get the feeling she means her favorite client," Constance said to Peter, who seemed to still be reeling. But at least he seemed to love the design, so far.

"Let's go look at the dining area," said Constance. She led the way and behind her, she thought she heard Peter whisper to Daphne, "Favorite client? Really?"

"Really," Daphne whispered back.

Constance walked more slowly. This was getting good.

"I've never forgotten you, you know. Even though you left," said Peter.

"I've never forgotten you, even though you left, said Daphne."

"What?" This was said in a tone far louder than a whisper. Constance wheeled around.

"Children! Behave!"

"It seems to me that maybe there is a little guilt on each side-unless one of you is perfect? What was it each one of you were telling me, about how I should forgive and apologize and not make the mistake of losing someone who mattered?"

"You said that?" Peter asked, looking at Daphne.

"Sounds like you did too," said Daphne, which made Peter finally crack a smile.

"I'll admit I made a stupid mistake. If you will," said Peter.

"Alright," said Daphne. "So, who's going to say it first?"

"We can say it at the same time," Peter suggested.

"I'm sorry!" They both said. Followed by, "Chips!" And they burst into laughter.

"Am I the only one who didn't know about this chips thing?" Constance mused.

"Can we try again?" Asked Peter.

"Yes," said Daphne.

"I'm glad that's settled. Now let's go see the dining area," said Constance.

By the time she turned around, Peter and Daphne were holding hands. Her heart swelled. Maybe it was possible, to lose and then love the same again.

When Peter saw the table setting. He simply smiled.

"Beautiful. You always knew me best, Daphne. I know this is your doing. And, Constance, you've outdone yourself. I'm so glad that I fired everyone else. Thank you. Thank you for everything you've done."

"Don't thank me yet," said Constance. "There's still more to see. But Daphne, I don't get it. How did you figure out my client was Peter? Because you figured it out, right?"

"No at first. But, when you first showed me the yacht, I thought I caught a whiff of Peter's scent."

"I still wear the custom cologne you designed for me," Peter shrugged, winking at her.

"After that, once Peter was off the boat, the smell faded, and I started thinking that it had been wishful thinking. But I decided that, even if it wasn't Peter, he was my ideal client. That any man would be lucky to have something I would design with him in mind."

Constance thought she saw her client wipe away a tear.

When Peter stepped into the Egyptian bedroom, he fell silent.

"Do you like it?" Asked Daphne.

"I…I love it," He said. "That trip to Egypt was the happiest time of my life. How did you know?"

"It was the happiest time of my life, too," said Daphne.

"The painting… that's the painting I bought for you," said Peter.

"What if the client wasn't me? You would have given it up?"

"By the time I did the staging for the bedroom, I had gone through the highs and lows of believing the client was you, then convincing myself it wasn't, and having reawakened the emotions, reopened old wounds, I figured that it would only cause me pain to look at it anymore."

Peter just stared at her.

"The colors. They're so beautiful. All of my favorites."

"My favorites, too," said Daphne.

"So… I guess you won't mind spending time here, in that case?" Said Peter.

This was Constance's cue to leave them alone, she decided.

"I'm so glad you're pleased with the design. I'm going to go. You enjoy the boat. Take your time discovering all the little details. I've put a bottle of champagne in the refrigerator and made you a charcuterie board. You two enjoy it."

"How can I ever thank you?" Said Peter, squeezing Daphne to his side.

"You can tell everyone you know that they should hire Harold Morgan Design," Constance smiled. But she felt a little sad. The project was over, and now her brain needed to latch onto something new, and everything was singularly up in the air. She'd left everything she knew behind in Miami. Her uncle. Her Kelly-Green Mini Cooper. Chiara. A perfectly fine apartment that might not have been perfect, but it had been hers. And now? The possibilities were wide open, but it was leaving her feeling unmoored. Where was her anchor?

She picked up her purse and stumbled down the gangplank, wondering where she would go next, what she would do next. And in lieu of an answer, there was Lorenzo.

"How did the big reveal go?" He asked.

"Really well," she said. "My matchmaking went well too. So, in general, he couldn't be more pleased. Even when I broke it to him that I'd missed the editorial deadline. Seems like Harold was the one who had been pushing that agenda, anyway…I can't imagine why."

Lorenzo took her face in his hands and gave her a kiss that left her tingling all over.

"I can't begin to imagine, but I'm glad he did it."

"Me too. But I have to admit, I was actually getting kind of excited about the prospect of having my work published. It would have been useful."

She didn't want to spell out the rest, which was that it would help her as she expanded her business to Europe.

"I spoke to Sophie," said Lorenzo.

"I imagine you did, and I imagine she had loads to say."

"Oh, she definitely did, but now, because of her actions, she's been put on probation. Sophie can't decide what goes into the magazine or not, not until she proves herself to be trustworthy."

"The petty part of me appreciates that, but I don't know if it's fair," said Constance.

Even though she would have loved to see Sophie get fired, on principle, the truth was, she had tried to impact Lorenzo's personal life- nothing she had done had really been tied to the magazine, where she had, against all expectation, been doing a decent job.

"She'll still be allowed to weigh in. But I'm the editor in chief, and I need to be more involved. This was a wake-up call."

"So…do you think there's still time to put the boat in the magazine?" Asked Constance, barely daring to look at him.

"I would say yes. But I've decided not to feature it."

The blood rushed to Constance's cheeks. Was Lorenzo still mad at her? Was her design not as good as she'd thought?

"Constance, before you let your imagination run away with you, I'm not doing it, because I showed the photos to my friend at Elle Decor. They want to cover it. It's the first time they're featuring a yacht. And as much as I would love to be the first to show your amazing work to the world, I knew this would be a better opportunity for you."

"You showed the photos to Elle Decor?" Constance asked. "When?"

"While you were on your way to California," said Lorenzo.

"But at that point, hadn't Sophie just told you that…"

Constance couldn't even say it out loud.

Lorenzo spun Constance around so that she faced him, their breath coming in puffs that mingled in the air between them. He looked deep into her soul, his slate gray eyes like magnets that attracted her gaze, not letting her look away.

"I trust you."

"You trust me?" She asked, looking back at him, eyes wide. "But how could you? You trusted me even before I called you and explained what was going on?"

"Why wouldn't I?" He asked, simply. "Did anything happen with Carlos when you were there? Anything I should know about?"

"No, of course not," said Constance.

"Why, 'of course'? Why did nothing happen with Carlos?" Asked Lorenzo, pressing her.

"Because I'm in…" She stopped herself.

"You're in what?" Lorenzo was smiling at her now, his voice growing deeper. That growl she loved so much making its way heard. "Were you about to say that you're in love with me, Constance?"

Constance started to hang her head down, anticipating a feeling of mortification, or that familiar fear and panic that left her feeling like she needed to run, but instead, she faced him head on. Sure, she had convinced herself that she was just addicted to him, but she had known it for weeks, now. She was in love with him. And he knew it. Which meant he trusted her.

"I am," she admitted.

"You are what?"

"I'm in love with you," she said, adding a defiant tilt of the chin.

"And I'm in love with you," he said, simply.

She wanted to take that at face value, use it to awaken the trust that he clearly had in her, but there was still a shred of doubt.

"How is that different from before? You said you loved me before."

"It's not different."

"But last time, you said you loved me, and you left me for..."

"Constance..." Lorenzo warned. "Look at me. What really happened?"

Constance looked away. Her blood was rushing in her ears. Tears that had come out of nowhere flooded her eyes.

"Well, you were..."

"I was what?"

"Things were getting close... and...I don't know... I feel like... you..."

"I...?"

"OK," said Constance. "Maybe I...I ran away, I pushed you away," she admitted.

"You did. Time and time again. At first, I tried to tell you to stop pushing me away. What did I tell you?"

"You told me you wanted to be with me."

"Yes. And that wasn't enough for you. And who was I to tell you what you needed? So, I let you go."

"If you'd loved me, you'd have..."

Lorenzo's eyes burned, boring into hers, not letting her get away this time.

"I'd have what? Not respected your wishes? Not let you leave, when you so clearly wanted to?"

Constance turned away for a second, ashamed of what she was so tempted to say. But this time, Lorenzo wasn't letting her get away with it. And she wouldn't let herself get away with it, either. He took her face in his hands, forcing her to look at him.

"What are you about to say? That after you left me, I wasn't alone? True, I wasn't alone. The relationship I went into after you didn't matter. I certainly didn't leave you for her. She just happened to step in, to fill the void. It could have been anyone. Just like what you did with the Carloses of this world. And I don't want to hear about any others, because I may have grown and matured, but I am still insanely jealous when it comes to you. But you know what? I trust you. Can you say that to me?"

He seemed upset again, and rightly so. She looked up at him. Everything he'd said and done to this point- Everything had led her to the same conclusion. She could trust him. She could depend on him.

"I trust you."

"Really?"

"Completely," she said. And all of a sudden, it was true. And it felt good.

"In that case," said Lorenzo, taking her in his arms, "I'm going to have to be a little selfish. I know you're finished with the job, and that you probably have a million things to do. But could you stay a little?"

"Sure," said Constance, shrugging.

"Sure? What does that mean?"

"Well, I don't want to leave you high and dry without a roommate," Constance smiled.

"Really?" Asked Lorenzo. "I mean, that's true. You owe me at least a two-week notice. So how long can you stay?"

"How about forever?"

Lorenzo started at her, the expression of his conflicting feelings running across his face like clouds across the Italian hills near his country home. Joy. Disbelief. Puzzlement. Wondering if she was just teasing him.

"I sold my apartment. Tu casa es mi casa, as long as you'll have me."

"Oh, I'll have you," said Lorenzo. "Starting the minute I get you home. And hopefully every day after that. Forever."

Epilogue

ELLE DECOR

A yacht and a love story.

Celebrity yacht decorator Constance Morgan is not just in the business of design- she also knows a thing or two about romance. Morgan is responsible for the stunning redesign of Grace Kelly's yacht, the one received as a wedding gift from Aristotle Onassis, and on which she spent her honeymoon with Prince Rainier. Then, the design she created for billionaire Peter Holmes' yacht, the Lombard 4, was also an excuse to do a little matchmaking. Peter's first yacht was decorated by Daphne Duplessis, now Constance's design partner at Harold Morgan Design, named after Constance's beloved uncle, who just retired, but whose name remains on the company masthead.

"When I decorate a yacht," says Constance, "I get to know the client quite well, and in Peter's case, I realized that there was a love story with a sad ending behind his sale of his previous yacht and, well, I figured I couldn't create a perfect design without recapturing the lost love that had left a hole in his life."

As luck would have it, Constance located Daphne, who owns a shop a mere 45 minutes away from where Peter's yacht was moored in San Tropez. A dash of subterfuge, a sprinkle of magic, and Peter and Daphne are now happily together again, sailing the seas and looking forward to many new adventures. In an example of artful symmetry, Constance also rekindled her relationship with the one who got away, an ex she had never been able to forget, and who, coincidentally or not, so coincidentally, happened to be in Saint Tropez, in the low season, along with her. Was it Harold who acted as something of a fairy godfather for this love affair? Perhaps… Harold will never tell.

The yacht design, in any case, is a labor of love, inspired from the heart, with a mix of original and daring elements such as a folded book page ceiling light detail, but also heartfelt elements such as the Egypt cabin, reminiscent of a trip that Daphne and Peter took, filled with mementos and rendered in a sophisticated color palette. The Lombard 4 happens to have a green hull, a rarity in the yacht world, and both Constance and Daphne felt it was important to go with a unique color scheme, something that an iconoclast like Peter Holmes would surely appreciate. Another unique detail on the boat is the kitchen on the top deck, which allows amateur chef Peter to entertain without being stuck in a dark, cramped galley. This detail has already been requested by other yacht clients, who see the benefit of this design. "It's the modern means of entertaining," says Constance. "Why be stuck below deck or count on a chef to do all the cooking? In reality, there's nothing quite so pleasurable as cooking for one's friends. And I just wanted to highlight that."

The fabrics throughout the yacht were created by a local firm, Yves Bleu, that is revolutionizing yacht textiles. And the rugs are also local, manufactured by Fabrique de Cogolin, a custom design by Constance, who now has her own line of rugs with the company.

When Constance began this project, she was based in Miami, but now finds herself based primarily in Europe, developing the global presence of Harold Morgan Design.

New York Times WEDDINGS

Count Lorenzo di Campofregoso, Miss Constance Morgan.

The bride and groom caught each other's eye over five years ago at a crowded art gallery opening and knew instantly that it was love at first sight. A few obstacles and separations later, the couple found their way back to each other, and are currently enjoying a real-life fairy tale.

The bride was given away by her beloved uncle, Harold Morgan, of Miami, Palm Beach, and Nice. She wore a custom antique lace wedding dress embroidered with feathers from peacocks once belonging to the groom's late mother, Countess Carlotta Buondelmonti. The couple will be honeymooning in the Maldives, before returning to their exciting creative lives. The groom owns a photography studio and is at the helm of Saint Tropez Life magazine. The bride runs Harold Morgan Design, the yacht design firm started by her uncle, which now also takes on hospitality and residential projects. The couple also run a spectacular event venue and high-end hospitality space in Italy, where the wedding took place.

VERANDA

A Palm Beach Thanksgiving

When Harold Morgan extends a coveted invitation to Thanksgiving, one does not refuse. The consummate host had been throwing elegant Thanksgiving fêtes in his Miami home for over a decade, and this was the first such event at his new Palm Beach residence, a classic mansion formerly belonging to grande dame, society doyenne, and legendary decorator C.C. Buttersfield. Harold's beloved niece, Constance, Countess of Campofregoso, shared hosting duties with her uncle, as she always has, despite being heavily pregnant with her first child. Her doting husband, the dashing Count Lorenzo, helped to set a spectacular table complete with the vintage tableware that Harold both collects and sells out of his namesake shop on Worth Avenue.
"I was going to retire once Constance took over my design firm," says Harold, "but I couldn't completely step out of the design world. This is more fun and more manageable. And of course, I have a special selection of yacht appropriate decor."

In attendance were Natasha and Boris Ivanov, of Miami and Saint Barts, restauranteur extraordinaire Sean Willis and his new husband, Ian Slocum, who recently moved to Kent, Connecticut, but who wouldn't have dreamed of missing this event. Art blogger Chiara Norland and her handsome Swedish husband Sven were also there, along with their baby boy, Magnus, Constance's godson. Chiara will be godmother to the new baby. "We've decided not to find out whether it's a boy or a girl," says Constance. "Harold had proposed a gender reveal where we could cut open the Cornish game hens to reveal pink or blue eggs, but we decided that would be a bit crass," she jokes. Thanksgiving at Harold's house began with a cocktail in the spectacular garden, followed by hors d'oeuvres on the veranda. Then, the group adjourned inside. It being a beautiful evening, the windows were thrown open and a fire was lit in the hearth. After having been quite ill in the past two years, Harold has a new lease on life, and a new romance, in the form of his devoted partner, Bob Wilkinson, once a competitor in the design world, and now a willing sidekick for travel throughout the world. Their next trip: to Italy, to visit Constance and family for Christmas at their palazzo. The impressive menu included Cornish game hens, a traditional Chestnut stuffing that is Lorenzo's family recipe, creamed corn, Brussels sprouts, and Constance's Pecan pie. (Recipes on page 124)

Condé Nast Traveler

Passion project

Hunting for your own truffles in the forest. Checking out a vineyard. Enjoying a spa treatment. Taking a tour of a traditional market in a picturesque village and then returning for an inspired cooking lesson, all without leaving the spectacular environs of the Castello Campofregoso, in the beautiful foothills just outside of Rome. This amazing opportunity is all possible thanks to the collective imagination of an amazing creative couple, Count and Countess Campofregoso, who dreamed up this passion project five years ago, when they were first falling in love. The project had to grow and mature, as did their relationship. And now, not only have they developed a number of curated experiences and spaces on the newly renovated property, but they are already also growing a future generation to take over this passion project. Little Charlotte, named after her grandmother Carlotta, is lucky to call this place home, when she isn't in St Tropez or Miami with her parents, And Constance is already pregnant with the 2nd child for the couple. How Constance manages to juggle this unique property as well as her thriving decor business, while supporting Lorenzo in his magazine, boggles the mind.

"I don't know," says Constance with a serene smile. "I guess I'm just a multi passionate creative."

If you enjoyed Low Season in St Tropez, please leave a review here.

Check out Kiki Astor's other books:

Stick and Ball

Ashley Miller finally managed to leave behind her horse farm in Montana to escape her violent, controlling husband, and took a Greyhound bus to paradise: Montecito, California. But Ashley, though she is an experienced horsewoman who proves to be an asset in her new job at the polo club, is a naive country girl when it comes to other things- she's definitely not equipped for the kind of games people play in this wealthy upper-class enclave, and she finds herself very much a fish out of water. Soon, Ashley meets Prince Charming. But, since he's a hot to trot Argentine polo champion who is by all accounts a player- in both senses of the word. Could Ashley be blamed for deciding to play it safe with another guy, one who seems like a real gentleman? Too bad the gentleman is an actual prince. Too bad he's married. Too bad Ashley doesn't realize that- until it's too late.
If you love royals behaving badly, love triangles, billionaires and millionaires galore, romantic suspense, slow burn romances, high society high jinks, equestrian details, hot contemporary romance told from a strong woman's point of view, and immersing yourself in elegant settings, Stick and Ball is the steamy, feel-good romance novel you will read in a single sitting.

 Buy Stick and Ball HERE.

Villa For Rent on St Barts

Brooke's world crumbles when she discovers her unfaithful husband has not only betrayed her but also squandered their fortune. Determined to rebuild her life, she decides to stay behind in their luxurious St. Barts vacation house and rents it out to make ends meet. Little does she know that the battle for her sanctuary has just begun. Amidst the turmoil, Brooke's passion for food becomes her solace. A talented chef, she discovers Antoine, a local fish and meat purveyor, whose charms and fresh, local products capture her heart. As her old life unravels before her very eyes, Brooke discovers the power of love, resilience, and the delicious possibilities that lie ahead.Indulge in this page-turning romance novel that blends passion, suspense, and the mouthwatering allure of St. Barts.

 Buy Villa For Rent on St Barts HERE.

For more about the author and all things Kiki Astor, and to get on the mailing list for the opportunity to be an early reader for Kiki Astor's upcoming books, check out the author website, www.kikiastor.com.